STAR VIKING

THE TRIBES OF YGGDRASIL™

BOOK 3

Hugh B. Long

Praise for The Tribes of Yggdrasil Series:

Dave Farland, NYT Bestselling author of the Runelords, lead judge for one of the world's largest writing contests, and mentor to other NYT Bestsellers such as; Stefenie Meyer and Brandon Sanderson:

"Many authors had written stories about kids going to wizard schools, but none did it as well as Rowling. Similarly, many people have written stories about vampires, but Stephenie Meyer managed to capture a whole generation by making them her own … Last week I came across a writer who has written a few books on Norse history, herbalism, and magic. His name is Hugh B. Long … He's taken the worlds of ancient Norse mythology and reimagined them as military science fiction [in his Tribes of Yggdrasil series], where elves are futuristic explorers who once visited Earth, and now mankind must unite with them to fight a common enemy … he is succeeding in taking a concept and really developing it into something new, making it his own … his works could grow into a hit."

Praise for Star Wolves - Book 1:

"Reminiscent of John Ringo and David Weber…Long

keeps the action flowing in this entertaining space opera.." - Amazon Review

"**Loved it! Classic Sci-fi**....couldn't put it down, the myriad of races are well thought out and diverse. The protagonist is well drawn and engaging. Very nice political subtlety" - Amazon Review

"It has been quite a while since I sat down and read a book in two sittings...[Star Wolves] **kept me up most of the night.**" - Amazon Review

"...a brisk read that grabs your attention and holds it well."- Amazon Review

"...interesting aliens, kickass space battles, and a real spirit of adventure."- Amazon Review

For my good friend and favorite chef, Mike.

Thanks to Paul Perro for his kind permission to use of his children's poem on Vikings. Check out his site at: www.history-for-kids.com

Thanks to Andrew and Janelle Schneider for the amazing cover art! Check out Janelle's work at Heartvisions Studio www.paintbetty.com Watch the silver screen for more of Andrew's work!

Printed in the United States of America

First Printing: Jan 2015

Typeset in Garamond 11pt

> Published by: Asgard Studios
> Ottawa, Canada
> www.asgard-studios.com

> ISBN: 978-1-927646-48-9

Hrymar™, **Illar**™ , **Ysgar**™, and **Tribes of Yggdrasil**™ are Trademarks of Hugh B. Long

Library and Archives Canada Cataloguing in Publication

Pending

Star Viking - Nobility & Military

#	Noble Rank	Title Male	Title Female	Military Rank & Historical Equivalents	Command	Style Male	Style Female	Fief Size	Numbers	Allthing Vote?
1	King, Queen	Konnungr	Drottning	Supreme Commander (Fleet Admiral)	Battle Group	Your Majesty, and thereafter as "Sir/Sire"	Your Majesty, and thereafter as "M'am"	Planet / Group of Planets	0	✓
2	Duke	Hertogi	Hertogaynja	Prime Commander (Admiral)	Carrier / Dreadnought	Your Grace, or Duke	Your Grace, or Duchess	100,000 km sq. up to planetary	0	✓
3	Earl	Jarl	Jarlkona	High Commander (Vice-Admiral)	Battleship	My Lord, Your Lordship	My Lady, Your Ladyship	10,000-100,000 km sq.	1	✓
4	Viscount	Thane / Magister	Thaynja Magister	Commander (Rear-Admiral)	Heavy Cruiser	My Lord, Your Lordship / Magister	My Lady, Your Ladyship / Magister	1,000-10,000 km sq.	12	✓
5	Baron	Hersir	Frihera	Captain	Light Cruiser	My Lord, Your Lordship	My Lady, Your Ladyship	100-1000 km sq.	144	✓
6	Knight	Riddari	Riddara	O-5 (Commander)	Longship	Sir, or Sir Haldor	My Lady, or Lady Gina	10-100 km sq.	1,728	✓
7	Esquire	Athalsmadur	Athalkona	O-4 (Lt. Commander)	Destroyer	Mr.	Ms.	N/A	20,736	
8	N/A	N/A	N/A	O-3 (Lieutenant)	Frigate	Mr.	Ms.	N/A		
9	N/A	N/A	N/A	O-2 (Lt. JG)	Corvette	Mr.	Ms.	N/A		
10	N/A	N/A	N/A	O-1 (Ensign)	N/A	Mr.	Ms.	N/A		
11	N/A	N/A	N/A	NCO	N/A	Mr.	Ms.	N/A		

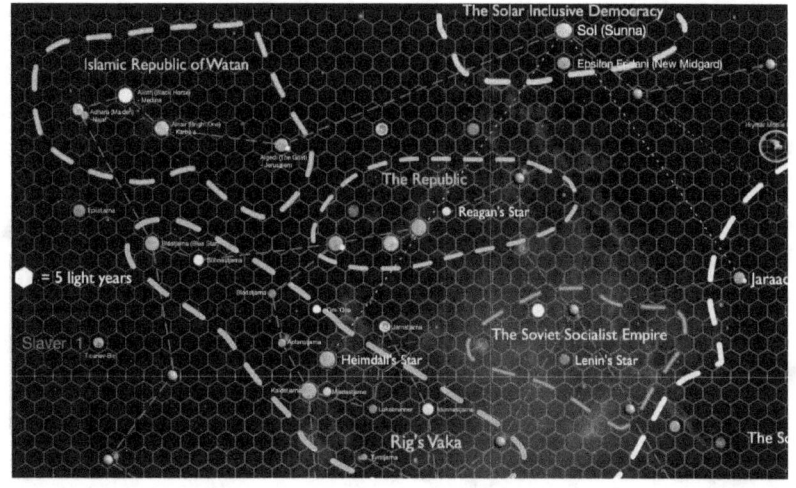

FULL SIZED MAP:

http://hughblong.com/wp-content/uploads/2014/08/TOY3-Star-Viking.jpg

Prologue

SIOBHAN STARTED WITH A GASP when the first explosions shattered the peace. She hurried over to a wall of windows in her third-floor laboratory and looked down to the street. The low buildings surrounding the Ministry of Agriculture burned, dozens of her friends and neighbors scurried around like panicked rats.

The chaotic scene below was in stark contrast with her own tidy appearance reflected in the window; ginger curls framed her pale face and tears welled up in emerald eyes.

Purple flashes drew her gaze—weapons fire. Soldiers, clad head to toe in gruesome black armor, fired into the crowd of unarmed colonists. Each person shot paused in an agonized-rigor before collapsing. New Midgard had no armies or soldiers. She swallowed hard, still in a state of shock and inaction. That ended when monstrous humanoids with limbs as thick as trees and grey, elephantine skin, came shambling behind the soldiers. They piled up the bodies of the colonists onto contragrav-sleds, like limp bags of sand.

Her stomach turned sour as she thought of her son, Ailan; the panic suffused her. He was in school today, and his school was across the street—across the line of soldiers and grey giants.

She sprinted to the elevator, stabbing the down-button five times. "Come

1

on!"

As the elevator doors cracked open, she thrust a hand in and tried to pry them open faster. She hammered the down button inside the elevator car, then remembering to press the close-doors button.

Fingers of ochre light lanced through the windows and into the elevator, as its doors began closing in agonizing slow-motion. Another explosion, she thought.

Siobhan's hands shook as she tried to come to terms with the chaos. She had no weapon, no training. She was a botanist, not a soldier. Where would she go? They'd built no roads beyond her farm, and Norvik was the only city on New Midgard; much of the planet was covered by a dense boreal-wilderness.

The elevator sounded off with an innocent—*ding*—as she arrived on the first floor, as if everything were fine—a normal day at the office. She almost laughed.

With her back pressed against the wall, she sidled along the corridor of elevators towards the lobby. She peered around the corner and through the glassed-in front of the building. The soldiers and their grey giants had moved on. She took a few deep breaths, then moved.

She placed one foot around the corner. A flash of light struck her face. Her hands went up instinctively to save her eyes, but all went dark.

Consciousness returned with a shrill droning in her ears and the odor of burnt hair creeping up her nose. Her head spun when she opened her eyes and her face itched as something oozed down her forehead. She put a hand to her head and tried to stand, but faltered, needing both hands to get up.

She coughed for few moments and finally touched the moisture which now ran into her eyes—blood. Tender gashes painted her forehead and cheeks, and her mouth was sandpaper-dry. Foul tastes of charred plastics and stone dust coated her tongue. She set aside all these strange sensations and discomforts. Her five-year-old son was out there.

Through the dense cloud of dust and smoke, she noticed the glass-wall at the front of the lobby had been obliterated. Nothing remained but twisted wreckage of the metallic-frame. Through the gaping hole she could see all the way through to the next block, right up to Ailan's school. Though she shouldn't have been able to.

A smoking depression marked the former location of Stellar-Joe's, which had faced the MoA building. She sprinted across the rubble and wended her way around the crater, arriving on the other side of the former coffee shop, then crossed the street to Chris Hadfield Elementary School. As she came in view of the cross-street, she froze.

A line of children marched down the sidewalk towards her. One of the soldiers, carrying a large rifle, led them. He was flanked by a pair of the grey-giants.

"Momma!" A red-haired boy screamed. Gods, it was Ailan. He was in the column of children.

A wave of ice crashed down her limbs. She couldn't run. They had Ailan. She stood paralyzed until a soldier in full battle-armor ran up and snatched her by the arm, and dragged her toward the line. She saw a few adults as well—the teachers.

Ailan grabbed Siobhan's legs as she was dragged passed him. Another

3

soldier made to grab the boy, but the first one barked something in a foreign tongue, and they let Ailan stay with her.

Norvik's populace were being rounded up like cattle.

"Momma," Ailan sobbed. "Who are they?"

"Shhh," she said, "I don't know. It'll be ok, sweet-pea."

"Kar shal!" One of the soldiers bellowed in an electronically-augmented voice. Siobhan saw that a teacher had bolted out of line and was sprinting down the street. The first soldier raised his rifle, settled the chin of his helmet onto the stock, aimed, and fired. A purple bolt of energy seared into the teacher's back and seemed to paralyze him before he finally slumped onto the sidewalk.

"D'ar kut albe," the first soldier said, pointing to the still form of the teacher.

One of the grey-giants lumbered past Siobhan. The beast stood at least three-meters tall and reeked like death, its odor a combination of feces, urine, and long-dead meat. Its skin hung like elephant hide, thick, wrinkled, and rough-looking. It was like a troll from the old stories, she thought; and it had to weigh five-hundred kilograms, at least.

As the grey giant ambled to the teachers' body and bent to pick him up, an old woman wearing a pink beret, strode over to the creature, bold as anything, and began pounding at the its back. Siobhan recognized her as Ailan's teacher—Amy Kahn.

"Leave him alone, you bastard!" Mrs. Kahn wailed.

The giant turned with a feral snarl and backhanded Mrs. Kahn, sending her airborne all the way across the street, to slam into the side of a building.

The old woman made no further sounds.

Ailan pressed his face into Siobhan's leg and sobbed. None of the adults made any sudden movements after that.

The first soldier barked a few more orders and they prodded the line of colonists into motion. They marched. To where, and to what end, Siobhan didn't know. As they moved forward, she glanced down at the still form of Mrs. Kahn, her pink beret lying a few meters away.

Siobhan gasped as Ailan darted out of line and stooped on the street. She went to grab him but stopped. He'd picked up Mrs. Kahn's pink beret and tenderly placed it on his teacher's head. He returned to Siobhan's side and said nothing as they continued the forced march.

They walked for several long minutes until they arrived at Colonial Park, outside of town. The park was a haven for species of flora from Earth—a little piece of home to remind the colonists of how far they'd come. White and scots pines, birch, and a variety of other northern european species of trees surrounded the field of hardy fescue grasses.

Scores of the grey giants encircled the park, hemming in hundreds—perhaps thousands—of colonists, while soldiers ushered them into several drop-ships. *My gods, where were they taking them?*

She did a double take as she saw one of the soldiers without a helmet; blue skinned with humanoid features, but not quite human. *Who? Not Alfar, no. They were pale, white-skinned creatures. But these had a similar, if more brutish, appearance.* One of the soldiers shoved her forward, ending her rumination. Ailan whimpered, and she shushed him again.

The columns of captives were directed at a row of soldiers, who, aided by their giant helpers, sorted the people by sex and then by age. The giants shoved men into one column, women into another, and children ... into a third.

The realization struck her like a hammer blow. No! Like a wild animal, Siobhan shot a look left and right. She was completely hemmed in.

Mothers and fathers screamed as their children were torn from them and marched off to a different drop-ship. She and Ailan were still four rows behind the split.

Like an elastic stretched to breaking, Siobhan snapped. She swept Ailan off his feet and tried to run, but was immediately frustrated by the dense mob of her own people. Every step she took, blocked or slowed by another colonist. Until finally she spied a break in the mob. As fast as she could, she ran. With Ailan in her arms, she managed only an awkward loping, but she pushed and pushed. Every ounce of her determination spent on this last and desperate gamble. She headed to the evergreen forest on the edge of town. The dense trees should provide good cover. She might elude capture in there —for a while at least.

Ten meters from the tree-line, searing agony suffused her body. Her limbs went into uncontrolled spasms and Ailan fell from her arms. She was paralyzed. She couldn't even maintain her balance now and fell forward into the damp grass.

She heard Ailan crying out her name but she couldn't feel anything.

"Momma! Momma, please! Get up!" Ailan cried.

He must have been lying across her back, because she heard his voice like he was yelling in her ear.

Next she felt a rumbling under her belly coming from the grass beneath her. A baritone voice snarled, but she understood none of what the giant said. Ailan was still sqawking. Suddenly she was spun onto her back, and saw one of the grey giants grabbing Ailan, but Ailan still held onto her arm. Her son kicked and slapped—like a fly swatting an elephant.

She couldn't move her head and lost sight of the grey giant taking Ailan away.

Hal bolted up, his heart pounding, his breath ragged. He wiped the back of a hand across his forehead. Gods in Asgard, he was soaked in sweat. It had been a nightmare about Siobhan and Ailan, again. One of several versions that haunted him, though less frequently in the last few years.

He hadn't actually been there when his wife and son were taken and killed by the Hrymar slavers. He was supposed to have take Ailan to school, but instead, had left the previous day, eager to fly off to some new discovery.

These horrific movies played for him at night showing him what might have happened. They were both long dead, which was a small mercy perhaps. The thought of them in the hands of a slaver would have been too much to bear.

His mind wandered back to the last time he'd seen Siobhan. He'd left the morning prior to the attack. She'd kissed him goodbye, and he'd said ... What had he said? For that matter, what do you say to the one you love when they'll be the last words you ever share? See you soon? He would have chosen differently had he known Siobhan and Ailan would both die that day.

Chapter 1

YEAR: 2137 CE / LOCATION: PATROLLING in hyperspace

As his starship careened through hyperspace, Haldor Olsen stood in his bathroom, leaning in toward the mirror, one hand on the edge of the sink, the other pulling the pale skin taut under his chin so that he could shave around the three-inch scar. He remembered getting that one. It'd been a boarding operation, and some bastard had a small knife hidden, literally, up his sleeve. Haldor paused and stepped back from the mirror to get a view of his entire upper body and the myriad scars and marks. Here was his resume, rendered in lumps of healed flesh. He imagined the date tattooed on each one.

Today was his forty-third birthday. But the body in the mirror didn't seem forty-three. He'd always looked very young for his age. Good genes maybe? He leaned in again, scrutinizing one of his downturned, hazel eyes. They didn't match the rest of him—that's what always made him feel like he was joyriding in someone else's body. It was the eyes. They were forty-three, sixty-three even. The body, maybe thirty. He was like a new car, without the new-car smell. There was just something off.

He supposed he shouldn't question looking young. A blessing, right? But he'd rather have looked old and still had his wife and son alive. That would have been a true blessing. No, no time for a pity-party today, he chided. I was shaving. Right.

He ran a hand over his cheek and chin. Just like granddad's, he thought. Good square jaw-line tapering into a shallow v at the chin. Proper Viking stock. Except for the pine-bark-brown hair; some ancestor from southern lands had snuck into the chicken-coup one night. Maybe two.

As he finished shaving, he did the two-finger test for his side-burns. There he stood, one finger poking horizontally at the bottom of each sideburn. Gods damnit, crooked again. But it wasn't the side burns, it was his ears. Why hadn't they come level at birth? Maybe his internal scales were imbalanced. Could he add some ballast to one ear? He smiled at that thought. That felt better. He had a great smile, didn't he? But then he relaxed his face. *Smiling invited the crow to dance*, his grandmother used to say, referring to the crows-feet by her eyes. That had been her excuse for being a cranky old horse.

Morning routine complete, he began work in the office just off his state-room. He began pouring over a star map projected by the surface of his desk. He glanced at each of the red and blue dots; the red dots represented the network of runestone-portals, the blue, the interstellar-bridge-nodes. Constructed by some ancient race, or perhaps the gods themselves as many believed, these networks enabled instantaneous travel across the stars.

How they worked was still a matter of debate and scientific inquiry. The working theory posited that the networks took advantage of the lines and clusters of dark matter. The man-sized portals, or ship-sized nodes, were activated by a complex signal which mimicked human brain waves, and was known as a thalamo-cortical-resonance-pulse. Each of the portals and nodes had a finite number of destinations, and each destination required a unique

TCRP. Only a handful were currently known; one of the Solar Inclusive Democracy's highest priorities was to find the keys to additional destinations.

With an expanded network mankind could travel across the galaxy with greater ease, and colonize or trade with other species and polities. The networks were the new frontier. But all this was a distraction at the moment. What Haldor needed to do was review the crew roster for his new ship, the *Drekkar*.

He waved a hand across the desk, closing the stellar-cartography application, then picked up his half-drunk mug of coffee and took a swallow. He heard a groan and glanced down at the carpeted deck where a two-hundred kilogram direwolf lay, her eyes questioning him.

"What?" he asked her.

His long-time companion, Venn, groaned again in response. But she was sending him a feeling of danger through their shared telepathic-bond, or at least that's how he thought of it. She was the only one of her kind known to man, as Hal had rescued her from a slaver camp nine years ago.

He hefted the mug and examined the brown liquid, then looked back at the wolf. "It's only my second cup today. Quit being such a mother-hen."

Venn rose and padded over close to Hal's chair, then lay back down with her warm, grey body in contact with his legs. He smiled as she licked his arm.

"Is that what you're complaining about?" When she didn't answer, he said, "All right, this'll be my last mug."

She begged him with her massive black eyes.

"I promise!" he said, laughing at her.

An alert chirped from his wristcom, startling him. "Yes?"

"My Lord, we've made contact with several Hrymar slave-ships," said his comms officer.

"Be right there, Kappa" he said. He looked down to Venn. "Time to get to work. You ready?"

Venn stood, her tail wagging.

Beside the door to his state-room hung an antique Viking sword. As was his tradition, he touched the handle as he left, a reminder to keep his weapons close.

The bridge's forward view-screen tracked five Hrymar slave-ships in normal space, which the combatives officer had designated: H1 through H5.

Most of the enemy's ships were converted freighters—better to haul their sentient cargo—with armor and weapons cobbled on to enable them to reap the harvest of less defended worlds. The ships themselves were no match for the Longship-class, which had been purpose-built for raiding and the destruction of other ships. The problem came in preserving the slaver's cargo; their cruel ships held sentient beings. Without that innocent cargo, he would have attacked them without mercy or regard for Hrymar lives. The blue-skinned bastards were parasites and deserved no less.

"Can you give me a life-sign count across the five ships, Meiriona?" he asked.

Currently on sensor duty, Meiriona had been a rising star in the Alfar physics community, recently abandoning academia to join the Tyrmundr. "Yes, my Lord." The young woman glanced at her console. "I'm detecting 4,212 life-signs. That includes any Hrymar crew. Accounting for approximately thirty Hrymar per ship, that leaves- "

"That's close enough, thank you," he said.

Meiriona blushed, tucking long strands of brown hair behind an ear.

She was eager, he had to give her that. There were so many young people on his bridge now. They were another of his anchors to this life, more threads the Wyrd Sisters wove to bind him to his duty. He reckoned that was a good thing.

"Shizari, any chance we can take them out all at once with EMP torpedoes?"

"No, Captain. They're spread too far. We *might* disable two before the others could react," the combative-systems officer replied. Shizari was a promising young officer of Arab extraction with a serious demeanor and hawk-like features.

It was always risky engaging the enemy and Hal didn't want to put his people in any more danger than was absolutely necessary; the Hrymar had taken too many lives already. He peered up at a tiny red light on the ceiling of the bridge and asked, "Skallgrim, recommendations?"

The disembodied voice of the ships's Level-6 Emergent Intelligence replied, *"Based on the current sensor data, we have a 95% chance of disabling two of the five Hrymar vessels with EMP torpedoes, as your combatives officer advised. I suggest that we deploy the Atgeir to the third vessel, as we pursue the fourth. There is a 75% chance that the fifth vessel will escape."*

The Alfar made extensive use of artificial intelligence, and this new breed of Emergent Intelligences, could evolve and learn, much like any crew.

"All-righty then, two birds with one stone it is." He tapped his wristcom. "Gina, are the Atgeir ready to go?"

"Damn straight, Captain. We're in the tubes and ready for a kick in the ass," Gina Russo replied.

Hal nodded to himself. "On my mark, drop out of Hyperspace, then fire EMP torpedoes at H1 and H2, launch the Atgeir at H3. Combatives, prepare to close on H4 immediately after and target its engines. Ready … mark!"

The sleek, muscular form of the *Drekkar* translated down into normal space; nine-thousand tons of advanced composites and organic armor, suddenly materialized a mere 10,000 km behind the slavers—spitting distance in space.

Through the arms of his command-chair he'd felt a slight shudder as the black of hyperspace was replaced by a flash of soft light, suffusing the bridge momentarily. Then, the familiar tableau of stars and galaxies met his eyes via the main view-screen.

The *Drekkar* had appeared directly behind the five Hrymar slave-ships; simultaneously, two flickering-blue fireflies—EMP torpedoes—leapt from the Longship. A second later, fifty smaller projectiles exploded from the starboard launch-tubes.

He watched anxiously as his Atgeir—veterans specialized in breaching and boarding—were launched into space, wearing only their Extravehicular Combat Armor. Each ECA suit was a tiny spacecraft, armored, but vulnerable to a ship's Point Defense Batteries. Specially designed launch tubes catapulted them into space at unholy speeds. The suits looked like metallic lobsters; the claws being external thrusters that could rotate to vector thrust where needed.

He followed the two EMP torpedoes as they arrived on target. Bright, azure ball-lightning engulfed the ships as the EMP current penetrated the vessels, conducted through any metallic wire, conduit, or surface, and frying any circuits in the process. Each of the ships began to list and float away under their current momentum.

His eyes bored into the view-screen as Gina and her team approached the third enemy ship. He relaxed his hands as he realized he'd been squeezing the arms of his command-chair, his knuckles now bloodless and aching; he might have seen them go white if not for the bridge's red battle-lighting.

Fifty dots on the view-screen converged with a representation of the enemy vessel H3, now appearing as one entity on the targeting-sensors.

"We're on the hull. Cutting through now," Gina said.

Hal inhaled sharply and switched his focus to the next target. He had to trust Gina—and he did, but the team she'd designed to go EVA and attack ships—well—he knew it worked, but it was damned risky. That was Gina though.

"Fire on H4's engines," he ordered.

The Drekkar's particle-beam cannons belched out a dozen, short bolts of highly-charged particles designed to disrupt the structure of its targets. The ethereal purple-bolts slammed into the aft section of the Slavers' ship, causing it to lurch several degrees as sections of its hull de-stabilized; its thrusters sputtered, then went out.

Suddenly the Drekkar shuddered and lights flickered on the bridge.

"Meiriona, what happened?" He shouted.

"Not sure, Captain. It appears we've *also* been hit by an EM pulse of some kind." Meiriona glanced back over her shoulder at him. "Engineering reports several impact zones. It appears we may be in an EMP mine-field."

"Engineering, damage report?"

"Edvit here, Captain. The hyperdrive has been damaged. All other systems are operational. I will provide an ETA for repairs as soon as I can."

Hal thanked the gods that their new ships made extensive use of Alfar organic technology, which was much less susceptible to EMP. Certainly, even organic circuits conducted electrical impulses—as the human body did—and these could be disrupted by EMP, but they wouldn't burn out like normal conductive circuits; they had the innate capacity to suppress excess current and could regenerate most damage.

Magnetically clamped to the enemy ship's hull, Gina watched as one of her Atgeir, the elite of the Tyrmundr, burned through the outer-hull. The plasma cutting-torch made quick work of the thin alloy. The Hrymar's reuse of old freighters as their main ships, was a chink in their armor, she thought. If they'd bothered to invest in real warships it would make her job much more interesting.

"We're through," the soldier on the torch said.

Five teams-of-ten were simultaneously breaching the ship at a variety of critical locations. Gina's squad had taken on the most sensitive objective—that of safeguarding any sentient cargo.

"Go!" Gina ordered, and waited for the nine Atgeir in front of her to enter. She turned back toward the *Drekkar* before she slid through the breach —and gasped. Through the screen on her HUD, she witnessed tiny electrical-explosions pelting the bow of the *Drekkar* as it closed on the fourth Hrymar ship. It was like a gods-damned hailstorm. Bastards, she fumed, it *was* a trap. But it didn't matter, she had a mission to complete.

"Eyes open! These blue fuckers are getting crafty. We're likely heading into trouble," she barked.

Several of the Atgeir cheered, relishing the challenge. They *needed* a fight. Most of the soldiers had family who'd been killed or captured by the Hrymar —this was payback.

Despite their bulky ECA suits, they flowed through the corridors like liquid mercury, killing any Hrymar on sight. Most of the enemy were innately cowards, and tried to ambush their foes. But Gina knew and expected this. She'd boarded dozens of Hrymar slave-ships now, and killed hundreds of these subterranean dwellers—some with her bare hands; those were the best, she mused.

She glanced at the map now displayed on her HUD. It indicated a series of cryo-berths ahead. The Hrymar used these to freeze their slaves, as it saved money they'd otherwise spend taking care of them on the journey to market.

"Around the corner. Ready?" She asked.

Nods all around, and they rushed the chamber, weapons ready. And … it was empty.

Gina cursed silently. "Teams two through ten, report. Have you seen cryo-berths? Or live cargo?"

None had.

"What in Hades?" Then Gina saw some kind of glinting machine in the corner. As she walked close to the device, she could see it was the size of a small ground-car, and judging by the pulsating orange-glow of the core, appeared to be powered by a fusion reactor. "Somebody please tell me what this is?"

One of her soldiers began a scan of the device. "Gina, this is where the life signs are coming from."

A Decoy. Another trap. Fuck.

"Captain, I'm detecting an energy build-up on the ship the Atgeir are currently assaulting. Reactor overload, probably?" Meiriona said. "Looks deliberate, sir."

"How much time do they have?"

"Two-minutes—maybe a few more seconds."

Hal took in a sharp breath. "Comms, do you have them?"

Anouk Kappa nodded. "Aye, Captain, lots of interference from the reactor build up though. Patching through … now."

"Gina, do you read me?" He asked.

Static, heavy with popping and hissing, came through the comm system.

"Cap…w….an…arely…era…ou. Device he…fak…ife..sig."

"Gina, get out. Get out now.

"Rog…ving..n. Ou."

Hal spun to Meiriona. "Is there anything we can do to stop this?

The *Drekkar* rocked as weapons fire raked her hull.

"Sir! Incoming torpedoes. Two bogies, eta sixty-seconds," Shizari shouted.

Hal ignored combatives, and kept his eyes locked with Meiriona's. "Well? I asked you a question."

"Captain, it'll take them four to five minutes to get out of there," Kappa interjected.

Meiriona shook her pained face. "Nothing I can do from here, sir."

"Fifty-seconds to impact, Captain," Shizari reported.

Hal stared down at his feet, ignoring the update, and flipped through the course of actions open to him. He jerked his chin up at Meiriona. "Where's the buildup?"

"Aft section—in the engine room."

"Is there a team in that area?"

She nodded. "Yes, sir, but they're moving out of the area now."

The bridge shook as more energy weapons seared the *Drekkar's* hull.

"Ok, as soon as they're clear, let me know. Shizari, when they *are* clear, fire the Dark-Matter-Lance. I want to cut the aft section off that ship." He peered upward, as one might when begging favor of the gods. "If you have any other suggestions tin-man, I'm all ears," he said.

"Not at present, sir," Skallgrim said.

"Forty-seconds remaining. And … they're … clear!" Meiriona shouted.

"Firing." As Shizari engaged the dark-matter-lance, a humming vibration suffused the entire ship. From stern to bow, the dark-energy cannon ran the entire length of the Drekkar-class starship. The hum raced to a whine, then exploded in a magnificent crescendo, releasing its deadly energy.

Hal watched as a black finger reached out to the Hrymar vessel. In point of fact, there was no color to a dark-matter-lance. The path, from weapon-to-target, was a window into an alternate reality—D-space—where dark matter and dark energy resided.

As the dark-matter-lance pierced the Hrymar ship, the *Drekkar's* nose pitched up, so that the lance cut through the enemy vessel like a laser-torch through butter. Anything in the path of the lance was transported from this reality to D-space. It didn't destroy matter per se, it simply moved it elsewhere.

The effect was awesome. The aft end of the Hrymar vessel was severed cleanly, except for the atmosphere and debris raining from the pressurized hull.

Meiriona projected the event-timer on the view-screen. "Thirty-seconds."

"Combatives," Hal said, "disarm the warheads on two anti-matter torpedoes and fire them at the aft section of that ship. Now. Let's see if we can give it a push."

"Twenty-five seconds."

"Is Gina's team out yet?" Hal asked.

Meiriona shook her head. While they watched, the timer continued to race. "Fifteen seconds."

"Shizari, where in Niflheim are my torpedoes?"

"Firing … now."

Hal watched as two points of red light on the view-screen raced toward the aft section of the Slavers' vessel.

"Ten seconds," Meiriona reported.

"Time for torpedo impact?" Hal asked.

"Twelve-seconds to target," Shizari said.

"Gods damn it, Gina, move!" He shouted impotently.

"Five."

"Four."

"Three."

"Are they out yet?" Hal asked.

Meiriona shook her head somberly.

"Two."

"See you in the next life, old friend," Hal whispered.

"One."

The aft section of the Hrymar ship nova'd in utter silence, concentric spheres of light and debris moving outward in all directions. This wreckage struck the forward section of the Hrymar ship and shattered the remaining segment of hull.

Venn whined as she studied at Hal from her place beside his command-chair.

He looked down and nodded, eyes closed. In a quiet voice, he said, "Meiriona, scan for survivors."

"Are you planning my funeral already?" Gina asked through comms.

He smiled, eyes still closed, and shook his head. That is one hard bitch to kill, he thought. "In fact, I was writing your eulogy in my head."

Gina laughed. *"I hope it was epic. Lots of good stuff for you to say about me, right?. Saved these people, killed those bad guys, etc, etc. Ad-nauseum?"*

"Something like that."

The *Drekkar* lurched and rumbled.

"We've taken two torpedo hits, sir," Meiriona reported.

"Damn it. Gina, we still have a target to deal with here."

"Roger that. Pick us up when you can. I'll pop my beacon once your friend has been put to bed."

"Olsen out. Alright folks, lets kick some Hrymar ass. How long for the dark-matter-lance to re-charge?"

"Two minutes, Captain."

Hal nodded. "All energy weapons batteries, fire at will. Shizari, ready a spread of six anti-matter-torpedoes. Helm, bring us around. I'm sick of getting shot in the ass today."

Gina flopped into one of Hal's leather chairs in his stateroom. Hal loved the smell of real leather. Synthetics could self regulate temperature, and lasted for decades, but he'd held on to a few anachronisms. Gina let out a long sigh. "Well, that was interesting. Who knew the Hrymar could be so crafty?"

He nodded knowingly. "Indeed. I feel a shift in the weather."

She peered at him, her eyes narrowing. "Why now, I wonder? What's changed? They've been on the defensive for seven years."

"We need to find out. That little mouse-trap might have snared one of our less experienced Captains."

"Might have," she agreed. "Um, by the way, happy birthday?" She offered tentatively.

"Thanks, I guess." Birthdays were another of the ghosts that continued to haunt him. They'd been such contented times with Siobhan and Ailan. He could even remember the last birthday gift Ailan had proudly presented him— a captain's hat made of stiff paper. Ailan's kindergarten teacher had help him put it together for Hal's birthday. Every year since their deaths he'd declined to celebrate.

"Hey, aren't you going to offer a girl a drink?"

He chuckled.

"What are you snickering about?"

"I have a hard time thinking of you as a *girl*, Gina."

Gina leapt up with mock indignation. "Excuse me? I might prefer guns to dolls, but I'm all girl, old man." She returned to the chair shaking her head with a playful smile.

"Consider me re-educated." He stood and walked over to a small bar and poured some whiskey. He looked over his shoulder at her. "It's really great to be together on a ship again, Gina. I miss these little lessons in humility." He chuckled.

"Ditto, boss. Nice to get off planet for a while. Training our new crop is rewarding, but sometimes …" she made a fist. "I just wanna smack the shit out of those recruits."

"I believe you have occasionally *'smacked the shit'* out of some of the recruits."

She shook her head innocently. "Never been a report filed. Vicious gossip, I say," Gina finished with a faux-pout.

"So, how'd you like the new ECA suits?" He handed her a crystal glass with three-fingers of Myken whiskey.

"Seemed to work. I'd like to see a portable shield generator added though. I got a bit *fidgety* when we got in range of their point defense batteries. One shot—*dead*."

"We're working on that. Need to get the form-factor shrunk first. Otherwise boarding operations could be awkward." He took a sip of his drink and closed his eyes. "Damn that's good. And people think only the Scots can make good whiskey."

"Your people make this stuff?" She asked,

"Indeed. The first whiskey ripened under the midnight sun and northern lights." He raised his glass. "To Norway."

Gina returned the toast, and they drank in silence for a few moments, decompressing from the stress of battle.

"So, sensors detected a planet close-by. Might be the Hrymar were protecting it with their little mouse-trap. We'll head over and do some recon."

Gina took another drink. "Sounds good."

The door to Hal's stateroom whisked open and Venn padded into the room.

"Hey there, you big furry thing!" Gina beamed.

Venn trotted over to Gina, nearly knocking her off her chair when she nuzzled into Gina's shoulder.

"Easy, Venn," he said.

Venn just grumbled, and plopped down beside Gina—close enough to have her ears rubbed.

"I like dogs and all, but I always wanted a cat," Gina commented.

Venn cocked her head and whined in protest.

"Kidding, buddy." Gina chuckled, rubbing Venn's fur more vigorously. The *Drekkar's* main view-screen filled with starlight as the Longship translated down from hyperspace.

"Entering the Kusi System, Captain," helmsman Eino Timonen said.

"Sensors," Hal asked, "what have we got?"

"Scanning now," Meiriona said. "Hmm, it's a busy system. There's a G5V Yellow Main Sequence star with a companion M8V Red Dwarf. Eight planets around the G5V. Two are terrestrial: Our database says Veni J'otopp, and an unnamed terrestrial, designated Kusi II. Kusi II has four moons. It's actually quite pretty. All data now on the view-screen. You'll note a small colony on Veni J'otopp."

Hal scanned through the planetary and stellar data on screen. "Run a detailed scan on the colony. Give me lifeforms and any energy emissions."

"Aye, sir."

Gina strode onto the bridge sporting her red, form-fitting bionan-suit. She stopped beside Hal, inspecting the data and images scrolling across the ship's massive view-screen.

"Captain," Meiriona said, "neural sensors detect life-signs down there ... in the order of fifty-thousand or so."

"Any human?" He asked.

Meiriona gasped.

"What is it?" Hal and Gina said in unison.

Meiriona turned back to them, her face slack. "Children ... thousands of them."

Chapter 2

PLANET: ORBITING VENI J'OTOPP / STAR: Kusi

Hal placed his palm on the door's DNA-sensor. A horizontal beam of blue-light scanned his hand.

'Identity confirmed, Jarl Haldor Olsen, High Commander of Rigsvaka Armed Forces, Captain of the Drekkar. Access granted,' the system informed him.

The massive armored-door slid sideways, like a predator opening its jaws, revealing the ship's armory. Six Berserkers—heavy shock-troops, and his most elite force—were donning their Ursa-class Powered Battle Armor. Each suit was like a small tank: weighing in at nearly 1,000 kilograms, standing three-meters tall, heavily armored, and sporting a fearsome array of weaponry.

The defining feature of each suit though, were three-foot claws, projecting menacingly from each finger of their massive gauntlets; not only were they made from nearly unbreakable alloys, they conducted a matter-disruption field, giving them the nick-name MAD-Claws; anything they touched would have its sub-atomic bonds disrupted, allowing them to rend a vehicle's armor, penetrate fortified walls, and what they did to men … well, that was a gruesome sight.

"Captain," Gina said, as she stood. "Come to wish us well?"

Venn padded in behind Hal.

"And to suit up."

Gina cocked her head. "You're coming with us? Is that wise?"

His basilisk-stare could have frozen her in place. "There are children down there."

"Sir, I understand, but we don't know what else might be there. Could be another Hrymar trap. They surprised us during this engagement. I don't like that."

He nodded. "I want to get my own eyeballs on the ground. I'm not taking any chances with children in the picture, Gina."

"Captain, it's too risky. You're the leader of Rigsvaka. It's just too- "

"Don't ever tell me it's too risky!" He snapped. "Not until you've lost your wife and son." He took a breath.

The Berserkers, with all their lethal kit, turned away meekly.

"I appreciate your concern," he said in a more even tone.

"That *is* my job, boss."

"I'll have Venn with me. She's more than a match for any Hrymar."

"You are the boss, boss. Just don't make me sorry I didn't put up more of a fight, yeah?"

He just shot her a smile that didn't quite make it to his eyes.

The *Drekkar* pierced the planet's atmosphere, buffeting under the variations in wind speed and air density.

Hal leaned forward in his command-chair. "Still no planetary defenses?"

Kappa shook her head. "No, sir, which is peculiar. At almost every Hrymar installation we've encountered *some* resistance while landing."

"Agreed," he said. "Another trap, maybe."

"I'm not detecting any major energy sources—other than what you'd expect at any colony. There was a gravitic fluctuation on the planet, maybe an ERBT?"

He cocked his head. "A stellar-comm, here? Unlikely. That would be another anomaly for the Hrymar."

"Captain, the majority of the life-signs are located in one building. The data's on your HUD now," Meiriona said.

"Thanks." He looked to the Helmsman. "Timonen, did you find us a nice spot to touch down?"

"Aye, Captain. There's an open field one-click south of the colony. There's a landing pad north, but that could be guarded. Touch down in two-minutes."

"Gina, you hear that?" Hal asked.

"Sure did. We've kept the comms to the bridge open. We're lined up and ready to hit the ground."

After completing a final systems check of his Ursa suit, he considered Venn, now encased in a custom-tailored suit of armor purchased from the Dvergar. She was ready.

He was mulling over Gina's admonishment. But he wanted to get in on the action—no, he *needed* to get in on the action—especially this time. And it was good to get his own eyes-on-the-ground to really get a sense of things. Where children were involved, he'd take no chances. But could this be another Hrymar trap? There had been a shift of late. The tide of Hrymar were flowing again, where they had been ebbing for years. What had changed, he wondered? Was Devrim still their Over-Chieftain? Perhaps he'd been supplanted? All questions for another day, he supposed.

"Chandra, you have the bridge," he said to his first officer.

"I have the bridge, aye Captain," Chandragupta Maurya confirmed.
The *Drekkar's* over-sized ramp began to lower. It seemed as though the ship
was being cut open and bleeding, as blood-stained light seeped through the
widening gap. They were under a yellow sun, but had landed during the local
dawn, and the red light fit his mood, and his intentions for the battle.

The ramp struck the ground with a shudder, and over two-hundred
heavily armed soldiers crashed down the ramp like wave. It was a sight
designed to strike fear and awe into the Tyrmundr's enemies. And it had done
so, time and time again.

Six Berserkers, in their Ursa suits, led the vanguard. The sheer weight of
their footfalls caused the ground to tremble, as if in fear of these metal
demons and their wrath.

Hal flexed his powered-gauntlets around the haft of a three-meter long
hammer—Ice Breaker. His was the only Ursa suit without claws. Venn loped
along beside him.

"Move out!" He ordered

At 50 kph, the Berserkers hit the compound gates in two-minutes flat. A
couple-dozen Hrymar began firing on them from a fortified-position inside
compound's wall.

The first Berserker to arrive sent the metallic gate flying with a single kick,
his armor deflecting and absorbing most of the laser and plasma hits.

Hal sprinted past his first soldier, heading straight for the defended
position. When he was within twenty-meters, he stopped, raised his hammer,

and slammed Ice Breaker into the ground. A three-meter wide shockwave of rippling-earth undulated toward the enemy. When it struck, they toppled like bowling pins, the ground beneath them yanked and heaved. The standing-wave Ice Breaker created, affected most materials. It was designed to take down fortified walls and disrupt entire troop formations, by undermining the *solid* ground on which they stood.

The other Berserkers shot past him now, arms wide, claws gleaming, ready to butcher the slavers. It was ghoulish business, but he'd decided that they needed to strike fear into the enemy, and so, these Berserker claws were designed to dismember bodies with a single stroke. In short order the soldiers were knee-deep in a sea of gore. The only sounds on the field were the Ursa suit's systems, humming and whirring, cooling the units after their grim exertion.

A dozen soldiers shimmered into existence as they dropped out of the shadows, the stealth fields of their Recon Combat Armor switched off. The E-5 that commanded the recon-squad approached Hal.

"My Lord, orders?"

He didn't make eye contact with the soldier. He was still focused on something, a thought yet unfinished. "Spread out and give me a full report on any defenses we didn't see from orbit. We'll hold here until I hear from you."

The E-5 bowed slightly and barked orders to his squad. After which, they dispersed across the front of the compound, disappearing back into the shadows.

He'd just noticed that Gina was standing beside him, also in a Recon suit; she'd once said she preferred a scalpel to cleaver.

29

"Does this seem a little too easy for you?" he asked Gina.

"I'm not sure yet. This doesn't *feel* like a Hrymar facility."

"One they commandeered, maybe?"

Gina shrugged. "Probably. I have a few thoughts, but let's wait to get a report back from the recon squad first." She walked back to the wall and knelt, picking up a handful of dirt. "Boss, come look at this."

He obliged. "What am I looking at?"

"The dirt—it's fresh. This wall hasn't been here long."

The recon squad returned inside of five-minutes. "My Lord, it appears this was, or perhaps still is, a mining-operation of sorts. Our Neural Activity Detectors indicated that the children are underground. There are four elevator shafts," the E-5 pointed to a map on his tablet, "here, here, here, and here."

"Defenses?" Hal asked.

"None on the surface. All the life-signs are crowded together. I would hazard a guess that the Hrymar are using the kids as human-shields below the surface."

Hal exhaled sharply. "Damn it. That does complicate things. Alright. Gladden!" He shouted to an O-3. Hal had introduced the SID and Alfar numeric ranking-structure into the Rigsvaka forces. He was not overly fond of hierarchy, but structure and organization were crucial beyond a single ship or platoon.

"My Lord." Gladden dipped his head.

"I want you to deploy a squad to each of the elevator shafts. Nobody goes up or down. Got it?"

Gladden nodded curtly.

Hal returned the nod and Gladden spun, mobilizing his troops.

Now, he wondered, how to get down there and keep the children safe? If they used an elevator shaft, surely the Hrymar would open fire as soon as they reached the bottom. Hal wasn't worried for themselves as much as he was for their return-fire, which might hit a child. No, he couldn't do that. "E-5, is there any other way down?"

The E-5 shook his head. "I'm afraid not, my Lord." Then cocked his head.

Hal noticed the thoughtful look. "You think of something?"

"I'm not sure if it's imortant, but there is a tiny shaft. Might be big enough for a kid to climb down. I believe it's an ore escalator. None of us would be able to get in though."

Hal smiled. "That will do nicely."

"It will?" The E-5 looked perplexed.

"Gina!" Hal bellowed.

Six Tyrmundr descended the first elevator shaft, weapons ready. They expected stiff resistance.

The elevator clanged as it reached the bottom. The soldiers tensed, glancing at each other briefly. Three of them kneeled, giving the trio behind them a clear shot over their heads.

The door rattled open, revealing an empty corridor.

"Report," Gina ordered through the comm system.

"No contact yet, m'am. The corridor seems clear. We're proceeding now."

The front row of soldiers stood, the barrels of their plasma-rifles tracking back and forth as they swept down the corridor.

A clanking sound alerted the soldiers to a small object skittering across the hall.

"Shield-wall!" A soldier shouted.

The first three soldiers whipped their cloaks in front of them, lowering their heads. The overlapping red and white, striped-fabric went rigid, forming a defensive shield-wall across the corridor in front of them.

The soldiers leaned in as an explosion crashed upon their defensive barrier. The rearmost soldiers began firing over the shield-wall toward the enemy; bolts of blue lightning arced down the corridor, scorching the far wall. They stopped firing, but saw no bodies.

"Gods damned bend in the corridor!" One of them said. "Move forward, slowly!"

The Berserker suits were never designed for civil-engineering, but, Hal had to admit, they performed admirably. The Berserker in front of him used his suit's claws, and their matter-disruption-field, to dig, widening the narrow ore-escalator-shaft.

He heard Gina laughing, and turned back toward her. "What?"

"A badger!" She said. "He looks like a rabid badger! Oh, I pray to Zeus the suit designers never hear about this."

"It does seem to be working rather well," he said. "I wish I had one of these during my military training. We had to dig holes with an entrenching tool."

"I remember them well," Gina said.

The Berserker broke through the final section of the shaft and dropped to the floor.

"Breaching teams one through four, press your assault, now!" Gina ordered through the comm system. The four teams assaulting the elevator shafts would now distract the Hrymar while the Berserkers secured the children.

As he followed the other Berserkers down through the widened-shaft, he felt a wave of fear punch him like fist to the temple. He buckled at the knees momentarily, which was barely noticeable inside his Berserker suit. What in Odin's name was that? He probed his own mind, trying to suss out the source of the intense emotion. There was no rational reason for any fear. No enemy lay before them, as far as he knew. But wait, it was not *his* fear. It belonged to someone else.

"Gina, go slow. The children are close."

"How in Hades do you know that?"

"Trust me."

The Berserkers were all through the widened shaft, accompanied by several of the Valkyrie medics, ready to tend to the children if needed. While marching down one of the subterranean corridors, a door abruptly opened. A wrinkled, grey creature, as big as a Berserker, stormed out—a Graal. He'd seen them before. Troll-sized creatures the Hrymar and Dvergar employed as guards and shock-troops. They were fearless, and as he expected, this one charged!

Like a rhinoceros, the beast barreled toward the front line of the Berserkers. It held a long staff-like object, which it thrust into the first Berserker. An explosion of white-light arced over the Berserker's armor, and the Graal switched to its next target.

Gods damned EMP, he thought.

One of the Valkyries, clad in black armor, and wielding her own staff, leapt forward, slamming the butt of her weapon into the ground, sending a kinetic stun-wave forward. The Graal was swept off its feet. It lay on its back, shaking its thick leathery-head as one of the Berserkers tackled, then disarmed it.

A second Graal exploded from a door opposite the first. The same Valkyrie spun around, her back to it, extending a set of black wings. They went rigid as the Graal crashed on them like wave, and bounced back. She spun again, firing another kinetic-stun-wave, toppling the second beast.

The Berserkers poured into the two auditorium-sized rooms where the Graal had emerged. As Hal entered, his heart wept at the sight. Thousands of children, milling about in squalid conditions. They were sorted, it seemed, by race and size, separated by flimsy pens. A pair of Hrymar in each room surrendered without a struggle.

"Teams one through four, children secure," Gina said.

He felt a wave of relief wash over him. Then, once again, he was struck by another's emotions. He tried to focus on the source and subtleties of the feeling. His eyes and mind sweeping across the sea of pitiful children. There was so much mental-noise in the room. He walked down the aisles of the Hrymar's *livestock*. He wanted to scream as he witnessed each of their helpless, little faces. Visions of Ailan, and Siobhan, coming unbidden to rip into his soul.

There. A little girl. Human. She was in a wretched state; her face and fingers filthy, her brown hair matted and tangled. Then he felt a wave of horror hit him as she saw his terrifying Berserker suit. He raised his helmet visor immediately, then smiled at her, his face now visible. She might have been eight or nine, if that. Just a little older than Ailan, when he was murdered —by these—bastards.

He tried to dampen his rage, and bring out the soothing paternal warmth he knew lay buried deep inside him.

'You can hear me?' He thought to her.

Her green eyes went wide, but she remained silent. She finally nodded. *"Yes,"* she thought to him.

Venn padded up beside Hal, and for a moment, he panicked, thinking the beast would terrify the girl. But she lit up with joy. Venn padded right up to the little girl and licked her face. She giggled.

Hal slid down his visor to hide the tears he could no longer contain. Hal, now free of his Berserker suit, sat in the cavernous room at a table, talking with the little girl—without actually talking. He'd suspected for years that the connection he shared with Venn was more than just Venn's ability to empathize. *He* had some kind of gift. So did Venn, and so did this girl. But what? And how? The communication he and the little girl shared went so far beyond words, that Hal knew this girl's life as if he'd lived it; and she, his. She shared his sorrow for the loss of his family, but equally, shared the joy of their lives. The little girl had instantly bonded with Venn, as Hal had.

Later that day, she was riding on Venn's back, brimming with delight. The sight played his soul like a master pianist, the melody so joyful, he could barely stand it.

The poor child had no name. She'd been born in captivity, taken from her mother at birth. Many of the children had been similarly ripped from their parents, and were *broken*; their little hearts shriveled without the love and nurturing a parent should have provided. They'd been cared for by older Humans, which was *something* at least. Even the older humans had been born, and lived, like cattle.

As the girl was playing with Venn, Gina sat at the table with him. "How you doing, boss?"

He exhaled and gave her a nascent smile. "I guess I'm ok." He dared not say more; he was at a tipping point right now.

"Listen," she said, "we can handle wrapping up down here. The kids are ok, and we have the facility secured."

"I know. You did a great job today. Let the troops know how proud I am of them. I'd tell them myself … but, just … not today."

"You got it. They did mop up those bastards good, didn't they? And I will *never* get the image of the burrowing-Berserker out of my head. I wish someone had recorded that."

"Oh, you can bet someone did."

"So, if I'm not out of line, what's your interest in the kid?"

"She's a very *special* girl."

Gina seemed ambivalent. "A great smile, I'll give her that."

He shook his head. "There's much more going on here, Gina."

One of the Valkyries approached their table. "My Lord." She inclined her head. "The children are doing as well as can be expected. Physically, there are no emergencies. Psychologically and emotionally, well, time will tell I suppose. We can safely evacuate them now."

"Thank you." He turned to Gina. "I want the corpses of these *things* hung up for their masters to see, should they come back. And let's raze the buildings. I want nothing for them to return to." He tapped his wristcom, opening a channel to the *Drekkar*. "Kappa?"

"Here, Commander," Kappa said.

"I want you to schedule a message as soon as we're in range of a stellar-comm. Addressed to Jin Wudai, he's an applicant for our intelligence service. I want him to start investigating any connections between the Hrymar and all these children. I want to know what in Niflheim they're doing with them here. Oh, and tell him he's got the job. Olsen out."

"Aye, sir. Message queued. Kappa out."

Chapter 3

Gwynahra felt decidedly anxious as she approached her mother's house. She tried to concentrate on the cool moss beneath her bare feet; that sensation had always soothed her. She was glad of the shade the leafy, ywen branches provided; that way passers-by couldn't read her anxiety. She was ninety-three—seven years shy of adulthood, and the decision which would shape the rest of her life. She already knew which of the nine-classes she'd choose—Wydonwyr. They were the keepers of all things scientific, including medicine.

The last seventeen years, she'd studied the healing arts, specializing in trauma surgery, and was more or less finished with her studies. As far as she was concerned, there was no need to wait seven more years before committing to the Wydonwyr. She wanted to get off the planet and out into the stars. There was so much to see, and do. Her concern, was her mother's reaction; she had to get Ambassador's Saeran's permission to commit to her class before she was of age. Would her mother give it?

Certainly, it would be mildly scandalous—especially for a former Ambassador's daughter—but she had not been grown from the same seed as her friends and classmates. Where they were cautious and slow, she was daring and impulsive. Maybe she was adopted? Maybe she wasn't even Alfar? A refugee maybe? No, she quite resembled her mother—except for hair color. She shook her head. Don't be silly, she chided herself.

She placed her hand on the white bark of her mother's door. A smooth section slid sideways, revealing a spiral staircase at the far end of the confines of the ywen's titanic trunk. She strode the ten-meters with poise, trying to bolster her confidence as she crossed the indoor fungal-garden. Her lithe form made swift work of the twenty-meter ascent to the first floor.

She performed a cursory scan of the kitchen and dining room, but found no one. Another few meters up the staircase, and *there* she found her mother, book-in-hand, reclining in a chair on the balcony. Gwynahra took a deep breath, trying to slow her heart rate. Confidence. I have to be confident and certain. I can do this, she thought—not so certainly.

"Hello, mother," she said.

Former Ambassador Saeran set her book on her lap and smiled at her daughter. "Gwyn, what are you doing home?"

"Mother, I'd *hoped* for a warmer welcome?" she said with a pout.

Saeran shook her head and stood, her face beaming. "Come here, darling. Give your mother a hug."

She danced to Saeran, her jet-black hair bouncing as she did. Mother and daughter embraced. Saeran pulled back a bit, brushing some of the hair out of Gwynahra's face. The warm afternoon sun bathed her mother's face in a radiant gold.

"It does me good to see you. How's school?"

"It's going well. Almost finished, in fact."

"How so? You have seven more years, unless my faculty for mathematics is fading like my youth."

She lowered her gaze. "That's why I came home. I need to speak with you."

"Oh?" Saeran said. "So you've decided then."

Gwynahra cracked a half-smile and raised her eyebrows. "Does that mean you approve?"

"I approve of *you*, my dear. Whatever you do, whatever you are, you are mine. And how can anything of mine be wrong?"

They both smiled. Saeran gestured to a mossy sofa back inside the tree.

"Where will you practice your healing skills?" her mother asked.

"I want to work on Rigsvaka."

Saeran's smile evaporated.

"Mother?"

"Daughter, that is a war-zone," she said evenly.

"Yes, mother. I know very well *what* it is. Where better to be a healer?"

Saeran remained silent long enough that Gwynahra felt compelled to continue.

"Mother, is that not a noble place to offer my gifts? They fight to defend us from the Hrymar."

"We are in no danger from the Hrymar here!" Saeran said, voice raised.

Gwynahra was taken back by her mother's reaction. She'd not expected this; resistance that she was choosing seven years early, certainly. But this? Gwynahra felt a mélange of intense emotions brewing inside her mother; equal parts grief, fear, anxiety and anger. She'd never seen her mother angry. Not through all her time Saeran had been the Earth's Ambassador, or member of the White Council.

Saeran finally spoke. "I lost your father, Gwynahra. And I miss him terribly. I cannot lose you as well."

"Mother, you won't."

Saeran wore a sad smile now. "Your father said the same thing when he went off to battle the Ysgar." A heavy tear trickled down her face. "And he never came back to me."

What could she say? Her mother was right, of course. Working in a war-zone, though she'd be a non-combatant, was still a perilous occupation. But that was the key, wasn't it? Peril, adventure. Gwynahra craved some kind of stimulation to feel alive. What was life without risk? But what would it do to her mother if she *did* die? Her father had died young and her mother had never loved again. Alfar lived long lives and that meant, for Saeran at least, centuries of loneliness.

"I feel as though the Norns have woven this path for me. It's as if I'm being pulled."

Saeran said nothing.

"I suppose I can't promise nothing *could* happen, but I *can* promise you I'll not take unnecessary risks, and be as safe as possible."

Saeran stroked Gwynahra's cheek and tried to smile at her daughter. "Every parent dreads this day, my love. When the seed is blown from the tree, carried on the winds of Wyrd to find her own fertile ground, and there, to grow in her own way. It's a part of life, but one we deep-rooted, old trees still find hard to bear.

Planet: Entering Rigsvaka orbit / Star: Heimdall's Star

Gwynahra squeezed her eyes shut and clenched her hands on the straps of her acceleration-chair harness, as the shuttle ferrying the recruits to their new homes broke atmosphere. The shuttle shook and rattled and lurched as it was buffeted by gale force winds. She clenched her belly to prevent the sour contents of her stomach rising into her throat.

She remembered her mother's words about being a seed blown on the wind; she'd imagined a gentle summer breeze, not brutal, hurricane-force winds. The dark interior of the shuttle was broken only by the flashing red light, indicating that it was not safe to leave your harness. She was a seed, she reminded herself, floating on the wind. Lord and Lady help her.

For the next two months, she would eat, sleep, and breathe under the watchful eye of Tyrmundr instructors. The Tyrmundr were the *'Hands of Tyr'*, an elite, military organization formed with one purpose: to meter-out justice in an increasingly chaotic region of space. Their mission was, firstly, to defend against further Hrymar incursions into human and allied territory, and, secondly, to take the battle to the enemy. They raided Hrymar outposts and struck at the heart of the enemies seats of power.

Gwynahra's heart pounded as she imagined what lay ahead. Part of her anxiety was anticipating the high-gravity. Alfheim was a 0.9g planet. Rigsvaka boasted a torturous 1.58g. It was chosen to be brutal and to turn the Tyrmundr into iron-clad warriors. This would be a cruel test, she had but to endure.

She had specialized in trauma-surgery, specifically to deal with any battlefield wounds, ranging from laser and plasma burns, to projectile trauma. What better place to practice her craft and be of service to her deities, Freyr and Freya? Her skills would do the most good where there was conflict, not at home on peaceful Alfheim. At first she'd resented her mother's negative reaction to the choice. She understood a parent's concern, but not to risk everything in pursuit of your passions … well, it seemed a hollow attempt, a shadow of a life.

From the short-lived humans, she'd learned the concept of sacrifice. The Alfar were normally conservative, cautious. But that made their lives so predictable, so banal. She was clearly grown from a different seed.

She'd been so preoccupied with her own thoughts that she hadn't even noticed the girl beside her—also Alfar. The woman shared a nervous smile when Gwynahra glanced over at her.

The flaxen-haired Alfar proffered a hand to Gwyn. "Greetings, sister. I'm Lythrael."

Gwyn tried to appear happy to meet her, but failed. "I'm Gwynahra. My friends call me Gwyn."

"It's a pleasure to meet you Gwyn. It comforts me to see another Alfar on the shuttle. I thought perhaps I'd be alone among our people."

She shook her head. "Many Alfar are counted amongst the ranks of the Tyrmundr now."

Lythrael beamed. "That's welcome news. What's your chosen class?"

She tried to mask her feeling of discomfort, but squirmed at the question. "I … have yet to *officially* pledge," she said tentatively, but followed up in a more confident tone. "Though in my heart, I have. I *will be* Wydonwyr, specializing in battlefield surgery. My training is almost complete, and I was given special dispensation to join the Tyrmundr prior to my one-hundredth birthday."

Lythrael's face betrayed a mild hint of scandal, for Gwyn's actions were virtually unheard of. "I'm certain our Lord and Lady must be guiding you."

"And what of you?" Gwynahra asked.

"I chose the Rhyfelwyr. Though I'll be a warrior, in some ways we'll be performing similar functions."

Gwynahra was curious. "How so?"

"The Tyrmundr cross-train warriors as their battlefield medics—the Valkyries."

She'd heard of this order; composed of all woman, which harkened back to the ancient myths. "That's a noble and brave path you've undertaken."

"No more so than the years of study and dedication to which you're devoted. I simply enjoy the use of a weapon from time to time." Lythrael grinned.

The shuttle dropped abruptly and Gwynahra's stomach flipped. She squeezed the arms of her seat as she looked over to Lythrael, who appeared completely unfazed. Finally the shuttle landed, slamming onto the ground and jarring its passengers. Almost at once, the shuttle's ramp dropped and a grizzled, old man burst in shouting.

"On your feet! You're here to train not sit on your arses! Move! Move! Move!" He motioned out the door.

Like a startled herd of grazing animals, the recruits stampeded through the shuttle and onto the bleak, sub-arctic landscape. Another instructor began prodding them into lines and columns. Several other instructors screamed orders and dressed the lines.

Sitting in the oppressive gravity had been a strain; walking had been an exercise in lunacy. Gwynahra had stumbled and tripped several times just getting off the transport. Now, as she stood, she felt fingers-of-cold probing into her flight-suit.

The land about her was mountainous and frozen; a collage of greys, blues, and white, speckled by dark evergreens. Though the *trees* were more like shrubs, to her mind. On Alfheim they grew a hundred times taller. But then the gravity here was burdensome.

The recruits now formed near-perfect lines and rows, standing tall—as far as was possible under the relentless pull of the planet. A man with long, golden tresses, hands clasped behind his back, approached slowly. His eyes wandered to the ground, as if lost in thought. Another Alfar, she noted, though older, and sporting a battle-scarred face.

He stopped when he was in front of the center rank and glared at them. "I'm Hersir Cadfael, in the service of our Jarl. I am Alfar, of the Rhyfelwyr class. I've lived as a warrior for almost a hundred years. Far longer than any of you have lived. So if you begin to think you know more about battle and war than I do... you are in error.

I fought along side Lord Haldor in the first Hrymar War. Before that, with my people against the Ysgar. I've taken many lives. Though I regret each. I am a warrior because our peoples need warriors. The Hrymar kill, other races kill. But what makes us different, and the Tyrmundr in particular, is that we kill for a noble cause; that of justice. We kill to hold back a dark tide that threatens to wash away our civilizations.

The recruits listened wordlessly, many with trembling legs as they fought against Rigsvaka's heavy hands, pulling them to her core.

"What lies before you," Cadfael continued, "is pain. Misery. Torment. This may well be the most unpleasant two months of your lives. But don't hold too tightly to that thought. As we battle the Hrymar you may well see misery beyond anything we dole out here. You may be captured. Sold into slavery. Sent beyond the reach of the Tyrmundr to rescue you. You may die a horrible death—short, or protracted. I don't say these things to frighten you, only to prepare you. You must set your mind to these possibilities, and accept your coming death. Only then will you be able to drive our foes back to their dark homes. You'll see me often in the coming weeks, and I wish you well and much luck in your training. Your act of simply coming here does great honor to your people and your families." Cadfael bowed deeply to them, then left. The first two months of training at the academy had been almost entirely strength conditioning; now they were building endurance.

The 20 km course wound up a frozen mountainside. It was a day when any recruit would have preferred a crackling fire, but instead they had a frigid wind cursing at them; its shrill bursts and icy threats, blowing and gusting.

This was the recruit's first time running the course, and since they were allowed no timers or other electronics, Gwynahra had no sense of how far she'd come, or how much lay in front of her. On such a long and treacherous run, time seemed to have no meaning. She was forced to push her body and mind to extremes she'd not thought possible. The Alfar weren't known to be sedentary, but this was beyond anything she'd experienced. And that's exactly why I'm here, she reminded herself.

Given the ice and snow surrounding her, she'd expected to freeze on this course. Owing to the arduous incline, quite the opposite was happening; her legs were on fire. With each step, a searing bolt of agony thundered up her lower extremities. Then there was the vicious gravity, chasing and hounding her; there was no escaping it.

Lythrael was in far better physical condition, but she too, was struggling. The small handful of stout Dvergar were much more at ease, contending with a mere 30% increase in gravity, as opposed to an extra 75%, as the Alfar did.

Gwynahra tripped on a stone jutting up from the slick trail. "Rot!," she yelled, as one leg flew backward and she lost traction. Lythrael caught her arm and pulled her up.

"Thank you!" Gwynahra said loudly, trying to be heard above the screaming winds.

Lythrael simply nodded, mouth open, panting.

Nearly one-hundred recruits snaked ever higher around the mountain. The trail began to narrow to perhaps two-meters across, which would have been wide enough, if not for the icy conditions and the abyss that bordered the trail. Recruits had been slipping and sliding on the even-ground approaching the mountain: now on this wicked gradient, they were in danger of falling thousands of meters to a rather gruesome death.

A Gwynahra labored, she kept her body as close as possible to the left side of the trail, and the relative safety of the mountainside. Occasionally glancing down into the precipice between peaks, it occurred to her that this was a perilous method for endurance conditioning. Wouldn't an indoor machine have been more efficient? And safer?

Just then a sudden gust slammed her into the rock face. She thanked

47

Freya and Freyr that it had not pushed her toward the chasm on her right. With both palms and her left cheek pressed hard against the rock-face, she felt the chill of the mountain creeping into her skin. She pulled her face away tentatively and regained her footing.

Above the near-deafening winds, Gwynahra heard a piercing scream and trudged ahead to investigate. One of the human's had simply fallen on the trail, but he'd shattered his leg on the toothy-surface. Bits of bone and gore protruded from a foot-long tear in his bionan suit. Instinctively, she bent down to help the man, but one of the instructors shouted at her to *move on*. She shook her head and pushed forward, now well behind Lythrael. The incident had diverted her from her own misery, to someone else's. That short respite was a small blessing, her mind reset, if only for a moment.

Her lower legs began to itch. A quick look down, and she realized she'd torn her bionan suit on the shin, compromising its ability to maintain her temperature. Now she risked frostbite, or at least frostnip. The suit would repair itself, but not before she finished. One more hardship, she thought.

She rounded a tight corner and found Lythrael on her knees. "Are you all right?"

Lythrael nodded, lifting a hand. "Just- slipped." She began to rise, steadying herself, but her foot hit a tiny patch of mirror-like ice, her balance destroyed. Once again she fell, this time, on her stomach. But her body didn't stop there. Her legs, pointed toward the abyss, rocketed down, the cruel gravity pulling. Lythrael's hands reached out impotently, her face a mask of terror.

There was no thought to what Gwynahra did next. Her body and mind acted on instinct. With her left hand she withdrew a small dagger—the only piece of gear they were issued on the run—and in one fluid motion, leapt forward onto her stomach, stabbing the dagger into the ice, stretching out with her right hand to grab Lythrael. The dagger acted like pivot-point, and Gwyn's legs arced toward the ledge like a pendulum.

Now both women careened over the edge of the cliff. Gwynahra's dagger in the ice was all that kept them from plummeting to their deaths. Her left arm holding the dagger, still crested the lip of the cliff, but her right arm and leg dangled over the hungry chasm. Lythrael's entire bodyweight hung on Gwynahra's right arm. Lord and Lady, help me, she prayed. She felt the dagger begin to move, to lose traction as the combined weight of the women, and Rigsvaka's ravenous gravity, conspired to devour them.

A quick-thinking recruit jumped on Gwynahra's arm, keeping the dagger firmly embedded, and the women alive. In short order they were dragged to safety, both trembling.

Their head instructor Lord Cadfael, arrived on scene—apparently he was bringing up the rear column of recruits. "You're both uninjured?"

Neither answered, instead, each performed a cursory exam of their bodies.

"They seem to be, sir," another recruit said. "We checked them over. Damn close call though!"

"Gwynahra, Lythrael, if you're not seriously hurt, then I expect you to get up and move. Motion is life. If you standstill in hostile territory, you'll soon dine with the Lord and Lady." Cadfael glanced around at the dozen or so recruits milling around. "Everyone, move!"

Lythrael got up first and proffered a hand to her. "I owe you my life, sister. I'll not soon forget that debt."

Gwyn took her arm and stood, and they both ran.

Location: Lyfjaberg / Planet: Rigsvaka

Thousands of Rigsvaka Military Academy recruits and instructors crowded the training grounds at Lyfjaberg—the Hill of Healing. It was the RMA's version of a medical school. It catered to the needs of future ship's surgeons, as well as Tyrmundr combat medics—the Valkyrie.

Gwynahra sat in the top tier of raised-benches, overlooking the simulated battlefield. A platoon of soldiers in Powered Battle Armor was closing on an enemy-held position. Their red and white-striped amdifynn-cloaks fluttered in a biting-breeze that tore across the field. They marched at a deliberate pace, neither too fast, nor too slow; relentlessly closing on the enemy.

The shrill bark of energy weapons warred with the howling wind. Red beams of low-energy laser-fire speckled the advancing Tyrmundr. None would be permanently injured—as this was only a demonstration, but their intelligent armor would inject the site of a hit with a powerful neural stimulator, causing pain far beyond what they might expect at the hands of the enemy. It ensured they did *everything* possible *not* to get shot.

The Tyrmundr re-deployed their amdifynn-cloaks in front of themselves; they went rigid like shields—which was exactly what they were designed to do. The barrage of weapons fire was deflected by their shield-wall.

As the fire on their frontal position began to die down, another assault came from their flanks. This time, area-of-effect munitions, such as stun-grenades, rained down on them. Like a hard-backed millipede, the Tyrmundr curled around each other, their shields facing outward. As they bent their ranks, the shields curled above them as well, forming a near dome-like structure. The maneuver complete, they charged.

Several soldiers dropped from the defensive bubble, which ancient humans—the Romans—called the *testudo*—the tortoise. The wounded were abandoned by necessity as the testudo continued moving. But were they really abandoned? Of course not, she thought. Gwynahra looked for Lythrael in the sky above the fallen, but couldn't yet pick her out. Then she saw her. Under great, black wings, the Valkyrie glided down to her charge.

An enemy began firing at Lythrael as she bent to tend to the wounded soldier. With augmented-speed, Lythrael rolled, got up on one knee, and fired back, taking out the threat. Without a breath she was back over to her patient. Her black wings spread above him and around him, completely encircling him. Under this defensive structure, she could administer whatever healing he needed. If he was gravely wounded, she would evacuate him from the battlefield.

It seemed that this recruit was lucky, his wounds only minor. Her charge healed, Lythrael straightened her black wings, crouched, then leapt up; the contragrav in her Eir-class Medic's Armor pulling her skyward. Then she vanished, stealth engaged, hovering invisibly above the battlefield. The Valkyrie would wait until she was needed again.

Chapter 4

PLANET: NIFLHEIM / STAR: ALNITAK AB

In one of Niflheim's caves, under the pale glow of fungal-lighting, Kadir circled his opponent, eyes wide and focused on Bora's feet. At fourteen, Kadir was taller than any of the blue-skinned Hrymar. Being human-born had its advantages. Though Bora's Hrymar eyesight was better suited to the dim subterranean conditions.

Bora thrust the dagger held in his left hand, then slashed backhand with his right. Kadir blocked both and left Bora with a bright, red slash across his left cheek. Bora put a hand to his cheek and inspected the blood.

"Lucky," Bora said, and spat on the black sand of the training-hall.

"No such thing as luck. Only skill, which you seem to lack," Kadir said with a smirk.

"We shall see."

"Judging by your face, we have already *seen*."

Bora's blue skin darkened as the fury from Kadir's insult percolated to the surface. Bora crouched lower and flipped the left dagger from a forward grip to an ice-pick grip; better for stabbing. Bora shot a lighting-fast right thrust at

Kadir's belly, then sidestepped around Kadir, and slammed his left dagger into Kadir's side as he pivoted.

Bora smiled as he disengaged and watched Kadir wipe blood off his ribs. "Perhaps you were right, human. My skill will win the day, you flame-haired bastard."

Kadir didn't respond, though he did grimace at the pain.

Bora wore a hungry smile now; one of confidence and certainty; one of a hunter in sight of his prey. This time Kadir attacked, thrusting in toward Bora's groin. Bora parried it easily and slashed Kadir's cheek in return. Now Kadir put a hand to his cheek and saw blood.

Bora shook his head and laughed. "A human has no place in the kimlik-sorma."

Kadir could feel Bora's rising confidence, while he limped heavily now, and winced at the pain in his side.

Bora arced his right dagger at Kadir's temple. He straightened up with a broad grin and slammed his foot into Bora's stomach, then lunged after him and followed up with an elbow to Bora's ear. Bora fell to the sand like a bag of rocks.

Kadir kneeled over his back and turned him over roughly by one shoulder. He placed both daggers across Bora's exposed throat in a scissor-like fashion.

"Did you say I had no place in the combat-ring? Do you yield?" He pressed the daggers harder, drawing two lines of blood from Bora's neck. "Perhaps you didn't hear me?" Kadir slammed his knee into Bora's groin. "I said, do you yield?"

Bora choked under the pressure from Kadir's daggers, but managed a nod.

Kadir sprang up like cat and wiped the blood off his side. There was no wound.

Bora clutched his throat as he sat up. "B- but I stabbed you?"

"I allowed you to *think* you stabbed me. I wiped some of your blood from my dagger, onto my side. Where you *would have* stabbed me. Then I behaved as if wounded, bolstering your confidence and tearing down your caution. Your own arrogance defeated you, Bora."

He offered Bora a hand. Bora took it, and Kadir yanked him to his feet.

"How have learned so much already, Kadir? You are but a human?"

"Had I not learned quickly and well, I would have been dead long ago. There is no place for the weak, especially a human. My years at the Egil Arkek boys-camp taught me that much."

Despite the mocking, Kadir was inches taller than any Hrymar, and heavier set. He had the genetics of human parents and nine years growing up on a heavy gravity planet. Combined, they made him one of the best warriors on Niflheim. Though not respected, he was feared.

He caught a glimpse of an older Hrymar, a grizzled veteran and his mentor, Serkan. As Serkan strode out onto the black sand all the trainees bowed before him. Serkan was the right-hand man of the Over-Chieftain, Devrim, and one of the most powerful men among the Hrymar tribes.

Serkan stood before Kadir, and although a couple of inches shorter, was a more imposing figure by far. It may have been the breadth of his shoulders, or the many scars that decorated his body—a legacy of his many victories.

"Youngling, it is time for the next phase of your training."

Kadir inclined his head. "Master. Where are we going?"

Serkan pointed a finger above him. "To space. Time for you to cut a path through our enemies."

He slammed his clenched fist across his heart in salute. He'd longed for this. Longed for the moment when he could bathe in the blood of humanity. Ached for the moment when he could plunge a dagger into Haldor Olsen's heart. His father's heart.

Location: Undisclosed Military Shipyard / Planet: Niflheim

Kadir stepped off the high-speed tram and walked up to a fortified entryway. Dozens of guards stood there, alert for anything unfamiliar. When Serkan stepped off the tram behind him, the guards bowed, quick to show respect and fearful of Serkan's wrath.

They were ushered through several security checkpoints, and finally, into what appeared to be a shipyard. He'd not been to any manufacturing facilities in his ten years on Niflheim.

He'd spent the first few years enduring the Egil-Arkek boys camp. Hrymar males were not raised by their biological parents. Instead, they were thrown into an all-boys, militarized boarding-school. Given the lax supervision, the stronger boys harassed the weaker, and even killed them on occasion. Life there was brutal, but it was meant to teach Hrymar their lot in the grand scheme; which was to be brutish, savage, unrelenting, and merciless. The strong ruled and the weak served.

As they continued deep into the cavernous shipyard, he saw a massive starship. It was unlike any Hrymar ships he'd ever seen; and larger beyond his imagination.

Serkan, clearly noting the boy's awe, said, "We are tearing down the old, and building the new, Kadir."

He followed his master silently, his eyes locked in wonder at the deadly machine being birthed in front of him.

"Your foster-sire is a man of great vision. Our place in the galaxy has been but a small speck in the vast interstellar sea. Now we shall cast shadows over whole sections of the galaxy and strike doom into the hearts of our enemies. Even the Ljossalfar and Dvergar will not be able to withstand the coming onslaught."

He caught sight of his foster-sire, Devrim, sporting an unusual smile.

He bowed low as he approached the Over-Chieftain. The man who held sway over billions of Hrymar across known space. "Sire, it's an honor to stand before you once again," he said.

"Rise, fosterling. Serkan tells me you have crushed all men who stood before you in the kimlik-sorma."

He simply inclined his head.

"Good," Devrim continued, "soon you will strike fear into the souls of our enemies all across the galaxy ... and, Ymir willing, perhaps beyond."

He cocked his head. "Beyond?"

"Indeed. There is much you now shall be privy to. First, let us look upon our new instruments of triumph." Devrim motioned for Kadir to follow him.

They approached the gargantuan starship. It lay like a great metallic-whale, beached. It had to be one-hundred-times the size of the standard Hrymar slave ship. He guessed at least one-hundred-thousand tons. It eschewed a boxy form—optimal for cargo—for a triangular, wedge-shape, which looked like an arrow-head. Serkan spent a few minutes detailing the array of weapons and armor.

Devrim motioned to the vessel. "This is the new Korku-class."

"Horror-class?" Kadir asked.

"Just so. Fitting, is it not? That is what they are designed to inspire—horror. We carved our territory from the nearby stars, raiding the weak. But our sphere of influence has not expanded for a century or more. Our new prey on distant borders are *not* weak. The humans on their blue planet, the Dvergar in their dark caves, and the Ljossalfar in their leafy forests—all shall be ours for the taking. This first ship is called *Isik Azap—Light's Doom*."

"Sire, I mean no disrespect," he said, "but one ship? The Dvergar and their Sons of Ivaldi Corporation own hundreds of advanced vessels. And I've heard tell of the marvels of the Alfar's living vessels, able to heal themselves during battle."

Devrim smiled and motioned for Kadir to follow him. They walked through a doorway and into the largest cavern Kadir had yet seen on Niflheim. They stood on a balcony, and below them … Kadir gasped. Stretching several kilometers in all directions lay a herd of sleeping *dragons*: dozens, and dozens of the new Korku-class in various states of construction. This was a fleet meant to subjugate the stars.

Location: Throne Room / Planet: Niflheim

"You leave tonight then?" Devrim asked.

"Indeed, my Lord," Serkan said.

Their voices echoed throughout the lengthy, stone throne-room. Today, it stood unusually empty of petitioners and courtiers; such as there were in Hrymar tribal society.

Devrim bored into Serkan's mind with his sharp gaze. "Are you confident that my fosterling will be up to the task?"

"I will not leave that to chance. I've taken certain *steps* to ensure completion of this most sensitive mission."

"Very well. You understand what is at stake. We are hemorrhaging profits at an unsustainable rate. Our losses at the processing and holding facilities on our borders have been crippling. I underestimated this human, Haldor Olsen. Had I an inkling of what was to come, he would have never left this planet alive all those years ago." Devrim shook his head in a rare moment of vulnerability. "We must not look back. Ever. We have a well formed plan and are moving forward."

"I agree, my Lord. One way or another, the human *will* die."

"Of that I entertain no doubts, loyal Serkan. This is but one of many contingencies in play. Though this is the plan I most desire to see *executed*."

Serkan laughed, which was a rare sight.

"You are confident! That is good." Devrim pushed a button on the arm of his throne. A pale, stout creature trundled into the throne-room from a side door.

"My Lord?" The Dvergar asked.

"Zekil, Serkan and the boy will need some entertainment this afternoon before they leave. Bring some in."

Zekil bowed. "Immediately, my Lord." The four-foot tall Dvergar shuffled off at an astounding pace. Zekil acted as the Over-Chieftain's whore-master, among other more strategic roles.

In seconds he was back with six of the loveliest slaves in his stable. A pair were Hrymar—possibly the wives or daughters of men who'd fallen out of favor. The rest were human; two women and two men.

"My Lord," said Zekil. "I am quite familiar with Serkan's preferences. I have two which I'm certain will please him. I am however, *not* familiar with Kadir's ... *inclinations*? I hope one, or all, of these four will please. They are the most attractive of the humans we currently own. So I am told." The little man shrugged.

Devrim nodded once. "Go, Serkan. Enjoy some distraction before your trip. And make sure Kadir does as well?"

"I will, my Lord."

Zekil handed Serkan a couple of the small devices that operated the slave's neural-control-collars. With it, they could administer pain, or pleasure, in crippling doses.

Serkan bowed deeply and left the room, his *entertainment* in tow.

Location: Kadir's state-room on Light's Doom / Planet: Orbiting Niflheim

----

Devrim was told, in no uncertain terms, that he was to take one of the slaves this afternoon, and *enjoy* himself. He was not quite sure what that meant. He was just turning fifteen Earth-years old, and he'd not even seen a human female since they took his mother away all those years ago. He could hardly remember her. Of course he had developed feelings for a couple of pretty Hrymar girls he'd met at court, but their fathers had seen to it they were never alone with him again. So many days he wondered why Devrim wanted him as a fosterling. Clearly the Hrymar at court considered him an abomination.

He had no clue why Serkan showed him the two men, so he simply ignored them and examined the two human girls. He swallowed hard. They were beautiful—both of them—and naked. He began to feel fidgety, and so, to end his torment, pointed to the girl with red hair. She reminded him of his mother.

"Her?" Serkan asked, clamping an iron-grip on her shoulder. The girl cringed.

"Yes, Master."

"Just the one? Are you certain? You may take any or all of them if you wish."

"Just her, Master. Thank you."

"Very well." Serkan shoved the girl toward Devrim. "Call the steward when you are finished with her. He will take her away. We leave orbit in six hours, so make the best of your time, boy!" Serkan grabbed both of his companions and strode off to his room.

Kadir held out a hand to the girl with the long, red curls as the steward finished slapping a translucent-white robe on her.

She took his hand without looking up at him. Her skin was so pleasant to touch. It made him shiver. His heart was pounded so hard that he thought his chest might explode. He led her down the length of the ship, then up an elevator a few decks to his small state-room. He gestured for her to sit on the edge of his bed. She complied.

Kadir sat beside her, not quite sure what to say. His breathing was leveling out, and his pounding heart slowed to a mere flutter. "My name is Kadir. Well —it used to be Ailan—when I first came here, that is."

She said nothing.

"I like your hair. It looks like mine, and my mother's." He could smell her hair from here. It had the fragrant scent of some exotic moss. A faded memory shimmered in his mind; of his time as a child on New Midgard. She smelled like Springtime on the farm, he thought. Familiar.

"Do you wish me to take off my clothing now?" She asked in a tiny voice, still not making eye contact.

"No!" He blurted. He sort of did, but that was not what came out of his mouth. "I mean, you're lovely. Really. I just mean … well, I didn't bring you here for *that*."

She finally looked into his eyes. They were green. Again he thought of moss. Caves, moss, and fungus, had been his only frames of reference for the last ten years. Grass, he thought. Yes, they were green, like grass. He remembered that from his mother's farm. He would never call it his father's farm; as far as he was concerned he had no father. If he had, one surely would have rescued him by now. No, he had no father.

"Is there something else you want me to *do*?" The girl asked tentatively.

Kadir shrugged. He felt helpless. Just like when he'd first arrived. It was a foreign feeling now, though. He was a lethal warrior, and Hrymar trembled when they stood in the combat-ring before him. But this ginger-haired wisp-of-a-girl had his courage in her hands. "Talk, I suppose. Your name. What's your name?"

"I am called Hayal."

Kadir looked surprised. That was a Hrymar name. He'd heard it before, attached to another. "Do you have a human name?"

Hayal looked pensive for a long moment. "Nee- Nee- vh. I ... was called Neve. It has been very long since I heard that name. Even from my own lips. Neve Madigan."

Kadir smiled. It was the most beautiful name he'd ever heard. No single word would ever again bring him as much joy, as Neve. He reached for a lock of her hair to smell. She closed her eyes suddenly and remained perfectly still.

"I'm sorry. I just ... well your hair, it's just so ... beautiful. I wanted to smell it. I've never been around girls ... I don't know what to say, or do. I'm sorry." He faced away from, ashamed by his lack of confidence.

As if sensing his discomfort, she moved closer to him. Her legs touched his. Then she lay her head on his shoulder, and now her hair brushed against his cheek. "I don't mind."

Chapter 5

LOCATION: TYRMUNDR PARADE GROUND / PLANET: Rigsvaka

Haldor Olsen considered the semester's graduates of Rigsvaka Military
Academy. He felt proud of them. All the men, women, and other sentient
beings that stood here, had committed their lives to the pursuit of justice,
loyalty, and honor. And that was no small thing; mankind had long ago
trivialized such simple, yet powerful virtues.

Lives were filled with distractions such that men and women were too
busy to worry about trivialities like strength of character. Life became
transient, meaningless. In that hollow existence an ancient ember had gone
cold. An ember bestowed by the gods themselves. A gift. A precious gift. And
yet, it was not quite out of reach. That gift could be re-kindled here, and
Haldor could be the spark.

"As I look upon all of you here today I can't help but remember stories
that my grandfather told me as a boy. They were fanciful and exotic. Tales of
gods and men, good and evil. The battlefields changed, heroes died, others
were born. There was one thing that every story had in common—honor."

Haldor took a breath and swept his gaze across the sea of recruits. Every one, silent, still, and majestic. They were truly breathtaking. Dozens of graduating classes had stood here, though each one kindled more pride in Haldor than the last.

"Honor," he repeated, "the good had it, the evil did not. Many will tell you that honor is a vague and abstract term. Perhaps it is … to those who don't have it. For those like you, who stand before me, it's much more real. Honor is a being's quality of worthiness and respectability. It defines an individual … or should. Some may ask how you define worthiness or respectability? Is there a standard, or set of measures by which one defines honor? I believe there is. My human ancestors codified such things in myth and story, and in the sagas. By the deeds of noble heroes we witness those standards being demonstrated. Why are those standards best, you ask?

For the simplest reason of all. Survival. For my ancestors to survive in a harsh and unforgiving landscape, they had to be worthy, respected. Worth and respect implied that they had something to contribute to the survival of the group; perhaps knowledge and wisdom, a strong arm with a spear, a keen eye for game, or nimble fingers for weaving. The lore tells us that even a blind man can tend cattle. Any contribution, however small, was respected, and imbued worth to that person. The ones who refused to share their gifts were not honored.

There's another component of honor—that of doing what is excepted—within the mores of your culture. To my ancestors, that meant avenging the death of a relative, marrying a woman you got with child, feeding a widow and her children—if her husband died nobly in battle, and it was in your power to help. It meant doing what was right; even when nobody was watching."

Just short of ten-thousand graduates of RMA heard Hal's speech. The number of graduates had grown steadily for seven years, as recruits from as far as a thousand light-years away, offered their service to the Tyrmundr's cause.

The head of the RMA, Sandy Pearson, an Australian by birth, had scheduled some of Hal's time to meet with a select group of graduates. The fifty-something ex-General introduced Hal to several Dvergar candidates. He'd initially opposed the Svartalfar's inclusion into the Tyrmundr. He remained unconvinced of their neutrality. They were analogous to Switzerland, by some measures; they professed neutrality, and usually participated in no conflicts with any of the neighboring sentients. But there was also the possibility that they would sell their advanced technologies to the enemy—they were famous for engineering—that, and making fat profits.

At Hal's urging, the Dvergar signed a binding-neutrality-pact, specifically excluding sale of weapons or defensive technologies to Humanity's enemies. He had no real faith in the document; the Dvergar had the largest fleet of warships in local space. If they wanted to break the pact, there was nothing Rigsvaka or Earth's government could do to censure them; stop purchasing their technology, certainly. But the allies were a fraction of the overall Dvergar market. Hal knew that the Dvergar profited more from the Hrymar slave-trade.

And yet, here they were. Four stalky, subterranean engineers par-excellence.

"It's a pleasure to meet with you," he said, dutifully shaking their pale stubby-hands.

"And ours, Lord Haldor!" beamed one of the Dwarves—which was how Hal thought of them, and in truth, what they were. Their species, the Svartalfar, meant 'Dark Elves' in Old Norse, and Yggdrasi, and referred to the short under-ground dwellers that modern man knew as the Dvergar, or Dwarves of fantasy literature. The Ljossalfar, or Light Elves—most commonly called Alfar, were the Elves of legend. Tall, and sylvan, graceful and long-lived. There was no historical analog for the Hrymar, but in Hal's mind, they were like J.R.R. Tolkien's Orcs; made famous in his 20th century novels about some evil Lord and a magic ring.

"Lord Haldor," Pearson said, gesturing to a raven-haired Alfar girl, "may I present, Gwynahra."

He gaped as he drank in her cornflower-blue eyes. She was absolutely hypnotic. Gods in Asgard, she was the most beautiful creature he had ever set eyes on. Her skin, milky porcelain, her features fine yet bold. Then it hit him like a bucket of ice-water—he knew her. Where had he seen her before? The dream. Yes! Seven years ago he'd dreamed of an Alfar beauty with space-black hair and eyes like sapphires. Here she stood. But how?

"Hal?" Pearson patted him on the shoulder.

"Oh, yes, sorry. It's been a long day." He smiled awkwardly at Gwynahra. "It's a pleasure to meet you, Gwynahra." He shook her delicate hand, reveling in its warmth and her drowsy scent. "What's your chosen class?" He finally managed. He knew of the Alfar classes and had studied the Atebol, their book of holy virtues.

He saw Gwynahra blush and hoped desperately his lascivious glances and bumbling hadn't upset her.

"I am *hoping* the Tyrmundr will employ me as a trauma-surgeon and part-time councilor, my Lord." Gwynahra inclined her head slightly. "I received dispensation prior to declaring my chosen class. I have seven more years until my hundredth birthday."

"Oh," he said. Thanking the Gods that was the likely explanation for her discomfort. "I'm sure you're well qualified in any case," he continued, with absolutely no basis in fact. His mouth grew dry and speaking became a chore.

Gwynahra waved a delicate arm in the direction of another young Alfar woman with flaxen hair. "May I introduce my classmate?"

"Certainly," He said.

"This is Lythrael. She is to be a Valkyrie in the Tyrmundr."

Lythrael gave Hal's hand a firm hand-shake. Enough to make his hand tingle.

"Well, that is quite a grip young woman."

"Better to hold a shield and defend my brothers and sisters, my Lord."

Hal smiled. "Indeed." He stole more glances at Gwynahra as Lythrael prattled on about her plans.

"We'd better let the Jarl get back to making his rounds, ladies," Pearson said. As the women turned, Sandy shot Hal a mischievous sidelong glance.

Had he been that obvious? Sandy had certainly picked up on it. Hal felt guilty for the less-than-pure thoughts he was having about Gwynahra—she was an RMA graduate, and a soldier under his command. He'd no business thinking about that young woman. Those days were long behind him anyway —at least he'd *thought* they were.

"Well, sister," Lythrael said, "Lord Haldor was most smitten with you!"

Gwynahra blushed. "Lythrael, please! He's the Jarl of Rigsvaka, and besides, I'm certain he knows more interesting women. What would he want with some girl who hasn't even reached her hundredth birthday. I'm unremarkable, truly." She shrugged and tried to swallow her own self-deprecation. But she concealed the truth. She'd felt instantly connected to this extraordinary man. And she remembered him. Had they met? Perhaps on Earth when her mother served as Ambassador? No. It had been a dream, a vision of sorts. And that was years ago. How peculiar. And wonderful. She smiled.

"Sister, I know the look in men's eyes when they desire something. I am not without *experience* in this matter."

She blushed. She knew it to be true. She'd felt his desire intensely. It wasn't just physical cues that betrayed his desire, but rather, something much more subtle, and yet stronger. She *knew* he wanted her; desperately. He'd always wanted her. And she … well … her heart still reeled from the meeting. These were odd sensations. She'd always been a focused and certain young woman. These intense feelings were … *unsettling*.

"I have no experience with men, Lythrael. I've always focused on my studies, or spent time alone in the wild groves. My mother served as Ambassador to Earth for several years. There I spent all my hours studying its history and culture. What time did I have for romance?"

"Well, perhaps now is the time. Or, if you aren't interested in him, maybe he'll find me suitable consolation?" Lythrael giggled.

"Lythrael! Are all Valkyrie so bold?"

"Confident, sister. We see an objective, and we take it!" They both laughed this time.

"You're sure this is a good idea?" Andrew Zelinski asked.

Hal continued placing items of clothing into a travel-case. "It's long overdue. You know I've had these *issues* for years, Drew. I'm just finally convinced I need to do something about it."

Gina sat silently, arms crossed.

"But we have another class coming in a week," Drew said.

Hal threw his hands wide, palms out. "C'mon old friend. You'll need to get a bit more inventive with your appeals. You don't need me here to babysit recruits."

"How long do you expect you'll be gone?" Gina said in a low voice.

"Give me a week. I'm sure I can get some answers by then."

"You taking the girl?" Drew asked.

He nodded. "And Venn."

"Been a while since you've taken care of a kid," Gina said.

"Yep." Hal turned to Gina. "And you know what?"

She jerked her chin at him.

"I'm kinda looking forward to that. She's a special kid, Gina. I want to make sure she doesn't need to worry about these—whatever in Niflheim they are—skills, abilities, whatever. That child has had a lifetime of worry and neglect. I intend to make sure it's at an end."

Drew sat in a chair opposite Gina, while Hal continued to pack. "I guess you could use a vacation," Drew muttered.

Gina chuckled. "What is this *vacation* you speak of?"

Drew shook his head with a smile. "Hal said it was part of the benefits package when I signed on. Seven years later, and I'm still waiting."

Hal studied at the travel-case thoughtfully, nodded, and closed the lid. He sat on the end of his bed and considered his two long-time friends. He took a breath and peered into their minds—a new skill. He'd previously been limited to sensing powerful emotions, such as lust, love, hate, and the like. Now, he could probe deeper, and at will. He felt their worry for him, about his drinking, and about his state of mind. They thought the children they'd recently rescued had sent him over some kind of precipice.

"I'm ok," he assured them. "Better than ok, actually. I know we've done a lot of good over the last seven years, but- I don't know. It's been all at arms length for me. I feel like by helping this child, and helping myself, I'm actually doing *something*. You know? It's tangible. And in any case, this is long over due. What Venn and I share needs to be understood. This could be very important for us. The SID has been studying the Illar we captured, but since they were dead, we're no closer to understanding how their minds work. All they know is that they're all telepaths. That kind of scares the shit out of me. You know?" He stood, holding his travel-case.

Gina and Drew stood as well, and he smiled warmly at them. They were the closest thing he had to family these days.

Gina shocked him with a crushing hug.

He grunted. "Easy!"

As she released him, his smile turned to ponderous grin, one eyebrow cocked.

"What?" She asked.

"I've known you almost a decade, and you've never hugged me before."

"Don't get used to it. I had a moment of weakness." She stood sharply, and saluted. "Sir. It will not happen again."

They all laughed as they led him out to the runestone-portal

Location: Long Range Patrol - Light's Doom / Sector: Unknown

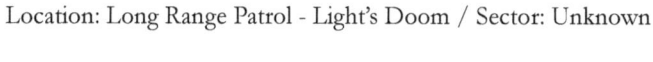

Weeks passed aboard *Isik Azap*, which Kadir found eminently more bearable with Neve along. For the first time in a decade, he'd rebelled against Hrymar authority, actually challenging Serkan to a duel to win the right to keep Neve. Serkan declined, and a protracted and bitter verbal battle ensued. But Kadir had won, and Serkan allowed to Kadir to keep Neve aboard during their patrol; with the express condition that she not leave his stateroom for any reason. That suited him just fine. All Neve's needs were met there. He had a shower, food dispenser, a room where she could relax. This way he didn't have to worry about other crew competing for her attention.

Secretly, he yearned for the love of a woman, like his mother, who'd been ripped from him. The images in his mind were thread-bare, but he fought to keep them. He felt like Neve was helping to anchor some of those memories. Or was she?

He woke early one morning and lay quietly watching Neve sleep. He hadn't slept deeply in years; a relic of his days at the boys-camp. One never knew who, or what, would come in the night. Just as he had come in the night for his friend, Halil, and culled him from the herd. The strong rule and the

71

weak serve — that was the Hrymar way. He knew no other. He felt such peace watching Neve breath; in and out, the rising and falling of her breasts beneath a green lace-fabric. Did he love her? He wondered.

"Good morning, my Lord," she whispered, eyes still closed.

"Did you sleep well?" He asked.

"I sleep too much. It's all I can do here. Do you think your sire will allow me to come back to Niflheim with you?"

"I don't know. I'll ask him, if that's what you wish."

Her eyes were open a little now, and she rubbed the sleep from them with the backs of her delicate hands; a wan smile growing ever brighter.

"Do you remember your mother?" He asked.

"Some."

"What was she like?"

"Beautiful. Like me, of course," she said, tossing her hair back playfully.

He nodded. "I have no doubt." He ran a hand down her red curls, watching them bounce back as he tugged them. "Do you love me?" He asked.

Her face went slack. "Love? I- I'm not certain I know what that feels like."

"The way you feel for me, of course. Happy, safe. The way you smile at me. Is that not love?"

"Perhaps. No Hrymar has ever said such things to me. Nor ever been kind. They used me, and … well, that's all."

He wanted her to say it. He wanted to be reassured that she loved him. He *needed* for her to love him. His heart sped up, his mind revving. "I love you." Was all he could say. He hadn't taken her body; he wanted to, but wanted her to offer it even more. They slept together every night, mostly just talking until early morning. But that was all.

"That makes me very happy, Kadir. But, I'm not sure what love is. Perhaps … we can learn together?" She stroked his arm.

He could feel his face growing hot, flushed. The strong know what they feel, he thought. They do not equivocate or prevaricate, as she seemed to be doing. Was she not grateful for his kindness—no, his love? She didn't *know* of love? Or what it felt like? It *was* what he felt now. No. Now he felt was rage. Hate. Abandonment. Fucking whore, he thought.

Her face grew stiff and her eyes wide. She pulled back. "I'm sorry, Kadir. I think- yes, I must love you." She nodded rapidly. "Yes. It was simply that you surprised me." She forced a smile and shuffled closer to him, but he pulled back.

She was lying. He knew what that looked like. He could read her face like the body of an opponent in the kimlik-sorma. He knew when they would feint, and when they meant to commit to an attack. This was a feint. A weak attempt at that. Fucking whore.

He watched as the red line began to form across her throat. She clutched at it. It was no use. Kadir's dagger had bit into her pale-white throat. Its beauty marred by the familiar sight of blood, oozing, trickling, but not gushing. His cut had been deliberately shallow. He wanted her horror to be drawn out.

No, he'd never loved her. He'd been deceived. Thankfully he saw through the ruse before it was too late. Cull the weak. It was the Hrymar way.

He stood and walked to the door, then pressed the button which called the ship's steward.

"Yes, m'Lord?"

"I am done with the girl now. You may come and get her."

Chapter 6

LOCATION: RUNESTONE ARRIVAL AREA, LLANGERNYW / Planet: Alfheim

----

Hal and the little girl stood before the black, three-meter tall, neutronium runestone-portal. Etched with glowing blue runes, the portals opened a gateway across the stars, piggybacking over lines of dark-matter. Scientists had yet to fully understand how they worked, or whether the larger, inter-stellar-bridge-nodes operated on the same principles. What was known, was that these artifacts were created nearly 200,000 years ago, by an unknown race of men; some said the gods themselves had built them for mankind.

The little girl squeezed his hand as they stepped through the shimmering pane of energy created by the portal. There was no strange transition, no peculiar sensations; it was simply like walking through a door. The only notable difference was the exchange of air and scents between worlds.

They stepped onto Alfheim soil beneath a canopy of titanic trees.

'It'll be ok. I promise,' he thought, looking at the nameless girl. She didn't return his thought, but simply held tight, and kept her eyes focused forward.

He stopped and took a deep breath of Alfheim air. It was one of the wonders in life. He'd often marveled at the scents in the northern woodlands of his boyhood home in Norway, back on Earth. Alfheim had a symphony of scents far stronger, and more intricate. Like french lace composed of complimentary odors. Magnificent.

He slid his portal-key into a pocket as he looked back at the runestone-portal. These standing-stones were far fewer in number than the much-larger Interstellar-Bridge-Network Nodes. The runestones were only big enough for one large humanoid-sized object to pass through, one-at-a-time, whereas the Bridges, were moon or asteroid-sized objects in space, that could accommodate a massive starship. Rigsvaka had been chosen specifically for the presence of a runestone-portal which lead to Alfheim and Earth. This of course made their presence a great security risk, but at the same time an incalculable advantage.

"Take a breath," he said aloud. He raised his eyebrows. "You won't be sorry."

She took a small breath and held it. Then in a moment she gave a grudging smile.

"Would I lie to you?" *Could* I even lie to you, he thought to himself.

'No.' She thought to him, and giggled.

"Hey now!" He admonished playfully. *'Don't go peering into people's minds uninvited.'*

She rolled her eyes, as little girls were wont to do.

A rumbling groan erupted from behind the pair. They both looked back to find Venn rolling on her back, luxuriating in the tough moss.

"I can never tell if she's scratching her back, or trying to camouflage her pungent scent," he said.

Venn flipped onto her feet and padded over to the girl, who promptly grabbed a tuft of fur, and pulled herself onto the wolf's back. She enjoyed riding Venn whenever she was off-ship. Venn didn't seem to mind. It reminded Hal of the pony he wanted and never got. He muffled a little chuckle.

Two Alfar sentinels flanked the runestone. They looked more tree-like than humanoid. Their heavy armor, bark. And that wasn't far off, he realized. They wore organic armor, which was every bit as protective as the Powered Combat Armor worn by the Tyrmundr. They inclined their heads when he made eye contact, but otherwise, these unmoving soldiers stood silent.

"How far to Searan's house?" she asked.

"About an hour's walk from here—or *ride* in your case. I wanted to give you a tour of Llangernyw since we're here. It's the most beautiful place you're likely to visit any time soon. It's also the largest grove on Alfheim."

"What's a grove?"

"It's like a city, only much nicer."

"What's a city?"

He inhaled sharply. "Well, a city is where a lot of people live. And usually they're noisy and crowded."

"I prefer groves," she declared.

The made their way along the branching mossy-paths. He watched as the girl marveled at the sheer mass of the white-barked ywen trees, which were not simply trees, but Alfar sky-scrapers. Balconies protruded gracefully, handrails decorated the thick upper limbs, and flowers grew with artful proliferation.

"They practice something called arbortecture," he told her. "Each of their homes and buildings is grown. The pathways you see above us are enticed to grow this way and that, as the Alfar have need. In fact, most of their machines are alive. Why bother creating a mechanical device that wears out over time? The Alfar's organic machinery heals itself, and makes more of themselves where needed."

Not listening to his tutorial at all, the little girl stopped as they crossed a babbling brook. She skittered down from Venn's back and knelt on the soft blue moss, peering into the water. *'Fish!'* She thought to him.

"Let's practice speaking in public, all right?"

"I see fish. Lots of them!" She turned back to him, her face brimming with childlike wonder.

He choked when he tried to respond. Instead, he just nodded. He watched as her eyes followed the rainbow-hued fish. She placed a finger on top of the water as a fish came closer to the surface. It popped a bubble of air into her face, causing her to sputter and laugh.

They arrived at Saeran's home a little later than he intended—the girl demanded to stop and touch, smell, and even taste, everything she could. He didn't mind. This was the most relaxing day he'd enjoyed in years.

He placed a hand on the door, which was a section of bark at the base of the ywen's enormous trunk.

"Touch the bark," he told her.

The girl reached out a hand and smiled. "It's warm."

He nodded.

The door slid sideways and they entered, approaching the stairway at the far end of the trunk.

"Haldor!" Saeran said, as she placed her arms around him. "It does me good to see you." She stepped back and held his shoulders, inspecting his face. You haven't aged a day since I met you."

Hal chuckled. "Must be the clean living, and a daily gallon of mead."

She looked down to the little girl beside him. "And who is this little beauty escorting you?"

He hesitated, then cleared his throat. "She doesn't have a name, yet."

"Oh?"

"She's the girl we rescued from Veni J'otopp. She's been with the Hrymar since birth, and those bastards—pardon my language—didn't feel she needed a name."

He saw the girl dip her head, as if in shame. He felt her sadness eclipse the joy she'd experienced earlier.

"That's an easy thing to fix," Saeran said. "Just pick one. Are there names you like?"

The girl looked up bashfully and shrugged her tiny shoulders.

He looked to Saeran. "Maybe we can show her a list of names and let her have some time to pick one later."

The girl looked up at Hal. *What was the name of your wife?"* she thought to him.

"Siobhan Chloe." He returned

"I would like to be called Chloe. In honor of Lord Haldor's late wife," the girl said with eloquence beyond her years.

Hal couldn't speak.

"That is a beautiful name. And I'm certain Lord Haldor's wife would be pleased that you choose to honor her this way. Welcome to my home, Chloe." Saeran inclined her head.

Chloe clutched Hal's leg, and he put his arm around her shoulders, squeezing her to his side.

A dark-haired girl descended a staircase and locked eyes with him. He would know those cornflower-blue eyes anywhere—Gwynahra!

Gwynahra stood, mouth agape, staring at him, and he, equally stunned, stared back.

"Gwynahra," Saeran said, "allow me to introduced Haldor Olsen, Jarl of Rigsvaka. And this is his companion, Chloe."

He saw Gwynahra nod slightly and take a few tentative steps toward them, her mouth still agape. He felt the fluttering of her stomach—or was that his? Or both?

Saeran gave them a curious glance. "Have you met?"

He could barely hear Saeran over the sound of his pounding heart and the blood churning through his veins. You are magnificent, he thought.

Gwynahra blushed.

"This is my daughter, Gwynahra."

Daughter? Sweet Freya. "I- uh- we- yes. We've met." He cleared his throat again. "At the graduation ceremony."

Gwynahra nodded. "That's correct. Lord Haldor was kind enough to welcome my friend Lythrael and myself to the ranks of the Tyrmundr."

"It's a pleasure to see you again, Gwynahra."

She inclined her head. "It is my honor, my Lord."

"Please, no *my Lord* here. On Alfheim, I'm just Hal."

"Haldor," she said.

The sound of his name sliding of her tongue was lyrical. The way she rolled the R, in the old way. He'd rarely heard his name sound so sweet. He wanted her to say it again. He desperately wanted to stroke her long black hair, and that alabaster skin. She was a goddess. He could not imagine Freya herself matching Gwynahra's beauty.

He saw her blush again, and felt his own face grow hot with embarrassment. Could she hear his thoughts? Gods, please no. He felt like a schoolboy just now.

She wore a mischievous smile now. "It was a pleasure to meet you again … Haldor."

He stood speechless, and just nodded. He watched as she left the room and moved off to another area of the house.

"Please," Saeran said gesturing, "follow me to the balcony. We can sit and talk."

She led them to an open-air balcony, fenced with finger-thin branches, intertwined in the shapes of animals. Chloe ran her fingers gently across the top rail, itself a larger branch, inscribed with runes.

Saeran took a seat in a moss-covered depression at the edge of the balcony. It formed a chair, and was surrounded by several others. In the center of the chairs, a flat knot of wood grew up to form a small table. On it was a glass-pitcher of liquid, drops of water condensing on its sides, and an array of cups beside it. Several Alfar delicacies adorned the table—a light lunch, he mused.

"Please help yourselves," Saeran said. "There is unfermented mead, as well as some food. I have a special dish prepared for Venn as well." She gestured to a large set of bowls placed on shorter table. One had cuts of fresh meat, and the other, water. Venn wasted no time, and trotted over to sample the food.

As they drank and nibbled, Hal explained his long-time connection with Venn, and the recent discovery of his connection with the girl.

"I am surprised you never mentioned the bond between yourself and Venn before, Haldor."

"Honestly, Saeran, there were times over the least few years that I thought I might be losing my mind. I didn't know if I was imagining all this. But recently, I started getting feelings from others—not just Venn. I could *feel* strong emotions and powerful thoughts. I knew when Gina was pissed-" then he censored himself, as he remembered Chloe was present, "sorry—upset. I could get a feel for the morale and mood of the crew. I guess it's been helpful, but it also made me uneasy. My connection with Venn has also grown more intense. I know what she's thinking, and she, me. In a real sense, we can speak with each other now."

Saeran's visage remained neutral throughout the whole of his confession.

"Then, when we assaulted the slaver's outpost on Veni J'otopp, I heard Chloe. I felt her fear, and knew where she and the other children were being held. Then, we just started talking—mind to mind. That convinced me that something kind of profound was happening. As far as I know, there's nobody on Earth, or the sovereign colonies, that can help me. And so, here we are."

Saeran began a slow nodding and a smile began to grow across her face. "There is so much I need to tell you, Haldor. And you too, Chloe."

Venn groaned.

Saeran looked over to the pony-sized wolf. "And you, noble Venn." She turned back to Hal.

"First, I must ask that what I am about to tell you, never leave this room —at least for now. I shall have to discuss it with the White Council before this information goes beyond us. Are we agreed?"

They nodded.

"Good. I have much to share," Saeran thought to them, without speaking.

He nearly fell out of his seat.

Location: Novaya Leningrad / Planet: Vilga I / Star: Vilga

Colonial life was one of routine. Irina Cherenkov embraced it. These routines gave her comfort and familiarity in an utterly unfamiliar place. The colony of Novaya Leningrad, a part of the Soviet Socialist Star-Empire, was a new appendage on an already awkward political-child, and only six-years old.

The SSSE was growing too quickly for most of its citizens's tastes, but it was a Socialist Dictatorship. They chose this form of government as the most efficient, yet egalitarian, mechanism to build a presence off Earth and beyond the population controls of the Solar Inclusive Democracy. Many days Irina wondered whether this choice would be their undoing. But not tonight.

Tonight, she was preoccupied with getting her five-year-old twins to sleep. Her golden haired girls, Galina and Veronika, were particularly restless this evening; they told their mother they sensed monsters coming, and that they needed to hide. Irina had heard this ploy before. Monsters coming would necessitate another story, which she was simply too tired to read tonight.

"Not now, girls. Momma is too tired. It's been a long day in the fields."

"But, Momma!" they both cried in unison.

"Enough! You want to go the fair next week?"

That stopped their whining in its tracks. Two small heads nodded vigorously and in unison.

"I thought so. I shall let you choose. A story tonight, or the fair next week?"

Both pulled the sheets up to their necks and beamed warm smiles at their mother. "The fair."

She kissed each girl on the forehead and closed their bedroom door. She trudged alone to her bedroom. She longed for the comfort of her husband's arms, but Maxim was working an overnight shift at the local factory. There was much to do on a nascent colony. She understood that in her head, but her heart wondered at the fairness of it sometime. She crawled into the chilly bed alone, and in moments, the strains of the day urged her to sleep.

Irina was awakened by sharp sounds and a rumbling vibration. She rolled over to her bedside table. The chronometer read 4:26 am local time. Middle of the damned night! What the Hell were her neighbors up to? Not more death-metal music? The boy next door had done that before—with his parents both on a night shift, he would invite friends over. Such gatherings got quickly out of control. Damn his toes, she thought.

She pulled on her night-gown and slippers, and marched with deliberately heavy footfalls to the front door.

"I'm going to slap them silly. Stupid Yuri and his damned death-metal," she seethed. "Why can't he listen to some nice Russian folk-music? And quietly." She would have reported him to the authorities, but he was not always so bad. And she worried they might send him to work in the mines full-time as punishment. The boy was still in school, and his mother said he was doing well. Irina's complaints might seal his fate, and so, she kept them them to herself. But she was not above solving the problem herself.

She yanked at the door and was about to move her right foot across the sill, when she saw the sky. Fire! Buildings burning. Men and woman running. Hrymar! The slavers were here! In Lenin's name, how did they find the colony?

She heard the whine of Hrymar stun rifles, and chaotic screams of people being rounded up. She slammed the door shut as her body grew cold. She stepped to the curtain over the window and peeled it back, just enough for her eye to catch the horrific scene unfolding. Dozens of small ships screamed across the sky, guns blazing. She gasped as one ship landed two-blocks from her home. It belched forth ten Hrymar in powered-armor and carrying their infamous stun-rifles; some kind of neural disruptor, she'd heard. Extremely painful, but not lethal—usually. They wanted to herd their cattle, not slaughter them … at least not yet.

The girls! Marx and Lenin save them. She had to get them to safety. A weapon, yes, she needed a weapon. She rummaged through her bedroom closet, tossing items behind her like a burrowing animal. There it was. It was an older plasma pistol, but it was loaded, and she knew Maxim kept it in working order. Colonists were forbidden from possessing firearms, but he kept it nonetheless.

She pulled on a set of rugged work-wear, tucked the pistol under a belt, and strapped a knife strapped to her right thigh; it had been years since she had occasion to use it, but she still knew which way to point the tip. Voices! She heard voices getting louder. She sprinted to her daughters's room, tossing the idea of getting them dressed. There was no time.

"Up, up, up! It's an emergency, girls!" she shook them both. Their little hands wiped at eyes still mostly closed.

"Momma? What is it?"

"No time." She dragged them out of bed by one-hand each, ushering them to the back door. Something slammed at her front door, and she looked over her shoulder in panic.

"Please, God almighty, please," she implored the heavens.

She inched open the back door and peered through the crack. Seeing no Hrymar, she opened it all the way and pushed the girls outside.

It was still dark, but she could see the way ahead, backlit by the fires of her neighbor's homes. The colony was burning. She ran with the girls, as fast as their tiny feet could move them; which was not fast enough, she judged. The smell of burning wood and plastic was terrifying, and stung her eyes. She heard the twins coughing.

"Psst! Hey!" Came a voice in the darkness beyond the light of the fires.

She stopped suddenly, yanking back on each girl's arm. She couldn't see a face — she was still night-blind from the light of the fires.

"Who is it?" She whispered.

"A friend. Come. This way."

He was Human, so she moved closer. She could make out his red hair. Definitely human. Thank Lenin. But not Russian, she noticed. No accent, nor were the features quite right. Western European, perhaps, but not Russian. English or Irish maybe?

"What is happening?" She asked him.

"The Hrymar. They're attacking the colony. I ran."

"Yes, I gathered. Do you know if they are south? Can we go that way?"

The man—no, boy—nodded. "Do you have any means to protect us? A weapon perhaps?" He asked.

She nodded, pulling the pistol from her belt. "Just this."

The boy lunged forward, his palm hitting her square on the nose. At the same time, he grabbed her pistol.

She fell to the ground, barely conscious. She heard her girls screaming. He had the gun pointed at her now.

"Tell these little bitches to shut up or I'll shoot this one." He pointed the pistol at Galina's tiny head.

Irina could taste a warm coppery-liquid in her mouth. "Gir- " she coughed and spat blood. "Girls. Quiet, please!"

They dropped to the ground and clutched their mother protectively, and seeking sanctuary themselves. She watched, helpless as the boy tapped a device on his wrist and spoke.

"I have three here. A women, and two young girls. Pretty too. They should fetch a good price."

What had he just said? But, he was human? "Why?" She asked.

The boy laughed.

Several Hrymar arrived, clad in their brutish armor, and carrying their wicked rifles.

"But, you are human. Why do you help them?"

One of the brutes grabbed her by the shoulders and hoisted her up on her feet. The other two grabbed one of the girls each. There was *nothing* she could do. She was utterly helpless and at the mercy of slavers; betrayed by her own kind. She remembered her girls warning her about the monsters tonight. They had tried to warn her. *Somehow* they had known.

The boy spoke as they dragged her and the girls away. "I'm no longer human. I may have been born of human parents, but I'm Hrymar now." He shrugged. "Cull the weak. It's what we do."

Chapter 7

LOCATION: MAGISTERIUM OF ATHRYLLITH / PLANET: Alfheim

An entire ywen tree—the size of an Earth-bound skyscraper—was dedicated to housing the Magisterium of Athryllith. For the most part, the interior of the structure had been abortected to feel like any eco-office building; in that, it had ample natural lighting, native plants species to enhance air quality, and highly distributed, in-situ herb, vegetable, and flower gardens. Humanity had been trying to go-Green for two centuries; the Alfar were born, lived, and died Green. This building, like all in Llangernyw, was the Green-Standard for eco-engineering.

In contrast to the highly ordered, airy feeling of the rest of the Magisterium, the office, or maybe *laboratory,* Hal now found himself in, was dark, disorganized, and smelled entirely *unnatural.*

A hunched and wizened Alfar removed wispy-tendrils which had been attached to Hal's head. "Wow," he said. "How many of your people have these *abilities?*"

"More than most races," Magister Faelar said evasively.

Hal glanced over to Chloe, who sat on a bench at the edge of laboratory, absently stroking Venn while she gazed around at all the strange living things in the Magister's lair. The Alfar's extensive use of living machines created a dream-like environment for curious minds.

"But it's rare in humans?" He asked.

"Not as rare as your governments would have you believe."

"Why would they hide something like this?"

The old Alfar threw up his hands, palms up. "Fear, I suppose. The more of your people who knew, the more real it would become, and the less control your officials would have. Many consider the gifts you possess to be very dangerous, Haldor. I, of course, do not agree with this. Long ago we Alfar formed the Magisterium of Athryllith to study and harness these powers. These are truly gifts from the gods. We believe that if Freyr, or Odin, did not want us to have such power they would not have been granted to us. And so, with thankful hearts, we master these skills and cherish them. But know this, Jarl Haldor, the gods foretold that there would always be a gift for a gift."

"I'm familiar with the concept. It's why we sacrifice to our Northern gods and goddesses."

"Indeed," the old man said. "So you understand that there is a price to using these gifts?"

"What kind of price?"

"The way most use the Athryllith, such as to communicate, to share emotions and such, there is no harm at all. But should you abuse it, or use the Athryllith for less than noble purposes, the gods will demand payment. And for such a gift, there is but one currency."

"I'd die?"

Faelar shook his head. "Not straight away, no. But each time you use the Athryllith in a way the gods find displeasing, you will trade some of your life-force; you will age."

Hal was disturbed. He'd just been handed a miracle, then told it was essentially a curse. He exhaled and sat up, then scratched his head with both hands. "So how do I get better at controlling these powers?"

"Had you been born of Alfheim, your abilities would have been identified early and you would have been be paired with a mentor. I will recommend that we do the same in your case, if you agree. The White Council would assign a mentor to accompany you back to Rigsvaka."

He nodded. "I'd like that. I would also like us to start screening other races on Rigsvaka for these abilities."

The old man nodded. "I believe you may be surprised to learn how many people have some measure of these powers we call the Athryllith. Do be sure to let your folk know that this is a blessing, when used prudently. Some may fear being ostracized. Remember your Salem Witch Trials?"

"Surely we're beyond such fears now?" He said.

"Dear Haldor, we sons and daughters of Yggdrasil are always afraid of the unknown. It matters not whether you are Alfar, Dvergar, Hrymar, or human. The unknown is not always welcomed. It is a universal condition that transcends race and time." The old Alfar bent over a table and hefted a jar of steaming liquid."

"Another test?" Hal asked.

"No test," Magister Faelar said, "tea." He smiled.

Hal was getting much better at speaking with Chloe mind-to-mind. He tucked her in and gave Venn a pat on the head.

"Goodnight, little-one. Venn will keep you safe," he thought to her.

"Nighty night," she thought, then placed an arm on Venn's back. The dire-wolf was lying on the floor beside the bed, but still came up past the top of the mattress due to her girth.

Venn loved her new companion, and the girl adored the beast. Every time he saw them together he smiled. He tried to keep these simple feelings vivid in his mind. He just realized that he'd been drinking less lately. Seeing these normal acts of kindness and love was good therapy, he had to admit.

"Dinner is on the table." Saeran said, sweeping an arm across the myriad Alfar delicacies.

He noted there were three places, and Saeran noted him noting that, for she said, "Gwynahra will be joining us."

He smiled to hide his anxiety. Why was he anxious? She was a lovely girl. It would be nice to have a quiet dinner with an old friend and her daughter.

"That's great. How's she enjoying her break from training?"

"Quite well, I believe. Hal, before she arrives there is something very important I need to speak with you about. It concerns Gwynahra and yourself."

Oh shit! He thought. Here it comes—stop ogling my daughter, you lecherous human bastard. He braced himself for an earful, which he reckoned he deserved.

"Please, sit," she said.

He tried to maintain the facade of calm, but it was crumbling.

"I am concerned about Gwynahra, Haldor. She's young, and impulsive."

He sighed and closed his eyes, just nodding slowly.

"I need someone in a position of authority to set a good example for her. Someone other than myself and her father."

Shoot me already, he thought.

"I was against her joining the Tyrmundr. For selfish reasons of course. I believe in what you're doing out on the borderlands—whole heartedly. But … she's my only child, Haldor."

And I'm not good enough for her—damaged goods, he thought.

"I want to keep her safe. It's what mothers do, is it not?"

"Completely natural," he finally managed. Saeran smiled. Gods, why did she have to be nice about this?

"Can you find her a safe posting? Perhaps on your flagship?"

What? He thought. Safe posting? My Flagship? "You want her *with* me?" He stammered.

"If it's not a great inconvenience?" Her face pleaded.

His entire body relaxed. He'd not realized how tense he was—coiled like a spring.

"Of course, Saeran. I'd be happy to."

Saeran let out a sigh, and covered his hands with hers. "Thank you, Haldor. I knew I could rely on you to keep my daughter safe."

But is she safe from me? He thought.

He heard light, but rapid-footsteps ascending the staircase behind them.

"I am sorry for my tardiness mother. It's been months since my friends had an opportunity to share gossip with me. We had lot's to catch up on." Gwynahra was flushed, but not breathing hard.

He averted her gaze and stared at a painting on the living room wall.

"Not to worry, daughter. We were just about to sit down."

"Haldor," Gwynahra said, inclining her head in greeting.

Hearing his name he turned back to Gwynahra. He tried to truncate his smile. He wanted to beam and gush at the very sight of her, but that would be undignified, and entirely inappropriate. He swallowed hard and picked up a glass of mead to hide his face.

As dinner progressed, Gwynahra's attempts at hiding her fascination for Haldor were becoming less successful.

Then, disaster struck—her mother was called away to an emergency meeting in the middle of dinner. She would be *alone* with *him*.

"Mother, can't you postpone this until tomorrow? We have Lord Haldor in our home."

"I regret that I cannot, daughter. And Lord Haldor knows of duty all to well I suspect."

"Um, of course. I understand. Please don't worry. I need to … " Haldor stammered.

Was he about to say he had to leave, she wondered? Perhaps, but he was staying with them. Chloe and Venn were already asleep in another room. No, he wasn't going anywhere.

"Please, enjoy dinner. I should see you later this evening," Saeran said, as she left.

Gwynahra swallowed hard, and she noticed Haldor doing the same. They were alone. She could feel his unease as clearly as if he were explaining it.

"So, Gwynahra," Hal said, "how did you enjoy training at the RMA?"

"Enjoy would not be my choice of words, respectfully, of course. Though

I am pleased to have completed it. But it was an arduous period."

He smiled at her. "As it's meant to be. Lord Cadfael says you did very well."

He'd asked her instructor about her performance? Well, that *was* flattering. "Did he? How gracious. I was less than confident on the long distance course. The ice was treacherous, and my classmate, Lythrael, nearly fell to her death."

Haldor nodded. "I heard about that." Then he smiled.

She scowled. Why was he smiling? My friend nearly fell to her death and he found that amusing?

His smiled faded. *"I'm sorry, I didn't mean that it was amusing…"*

He'd not spoken those words. "What did you say?" She asked.

"I said that I had heard about your friends accident."

"You said something after that."

Hal shook his head slowly. "No … that was all I said."

"I heard you," she thought to him.

His mouth opened and he stared at her in utter shock.

Her eyes narrowed and she probed deeper. "So you went to the Magisterium of Athryllith today. Fascinating."

"How?" Haldor said. *"Can you hear my thoughts?" He thought to her.*

She nodded once, eyes narrowed, and very curious.

"Should you be doing that?" He thought to her.

"You read my thoughts first, which you shouldn't have done. But when you did, it gave me implicit permission to do likewise." "These are things you need to learn, Lord Haldor," she said aloud grinning mischievously.

"Please, accept my sincerest apologies. This is all so new to me. I didn't mean to invade your privacy. It sometimes feels like people are shouting at me —and yet not speaking. I can't *help* but hear them."

"You'll learn to block them out." She relaxed. Knowing that he just learned of his abilities, she accepted his apology as genuine.

"Have you been able to read people's thoughts all your life?" Haldor asked.

"No, not nearly. It manifested perhaps twenty years ago."

"Well, then you've had a lot of opportunity to practice. Does it take long to learn? I mean, to block all the noise?"

"You just need a teacher, a mentor. That person will help you master these abilities in short order. The real effort is in the practicing." She could feel his previous attraction to her outward beauty now shift inward to her mind. How curious. She stood and approached his chair, proffering a hand. His face grew flushed again, and the fear of his physical attraction for her returned; so much so, it made *her* blush.

"If you give me your hand, I'll teach you something. I need to make contact with you."

She pulled out the chair beside his and sat down. Hal gave her his hand. It was strong, warm. She shook off those thoughts and spoke to him, mind-to-mind. *"Picture yourself in a crowded room, full of noisy people. Hear the voices."* They both heard them. They were on the bridge of his ship, the *Drekkar*. She could see the faces of the crew, could hear the tumult of minds that Haldor felt when on the bridge. It was amazing that he could function like that. *"Now, imagine a bubble forming around you. Just like a soap bubble. Growing larger, but transparent. It blocks only their minds, but not their voices or faces."*

He did. And suddenly there was silence on the bridge. She smiled at him. "That's all you need do. Now you can practice that simple exercise every day, any chance you get. If you're trying to block another person with the Athryllith, you're better off trying to build a stone wall on front of them. But we'll try that another day."

"That was amazing!" He said. "I thought I'd been going mad. If not for Venn ... I would have."

"It's likely she has some ability as well. I saw in your mind that you visited Magister Faelar today. He said she is also gifted with the Athryllith."

He nodded. "So he told me. As is Chloe. That's why I was able to find the children she was with. Her mind was screaming. It was like a stellar-beacon. So powerful."

She realized she was still holding his hand, and was very close to him. He smelled wonderful, masculine. She shivered and pulled away suddenly, then stood. "Well, as I said. Practice that technique, and in no time you will have much more control of these gifts. There are many who go mad because they don't know what's happening to them."

"Thank you, Gwynahra." Hal thought to her.

"It's nothing. I'm simply trying to ingratiate myself with my commander." She said shyly.

Hal survived his dinner with Gwynahra, barely. Chloe was in good humor when she arrived to the outdoor-dining-room for breakfast and regaled him with fantastical dreams she had during the night. Mind-to-mind he was able to see what she saw. This gift was intriguing. The outdoor-dining-room was perched on a massive branch, one-hundred-meters up the ywen tree that was

Saeran's home. The view of the forest below was breathtaking.

"Good morning all," Saeran said as she entered. Her green gossamer-like gown rippled in the gentle morning breeze.

"Morning, Ambassador," he said.

"Hi, Saeran," Chloe said, with wave of her tiny hand.

"Good morning, little one." Saeran stroked Chloe hair and looked to him. "My regrets for not being able to finish dinner with you last night."

"No worries. Gwynahra kept me entertained."

Saeran smiled. "That is nice to hear. I am warmed that you finally get to spend some time in my home. We've known each other through many trials over the last decade."

"Indeed we have."

"Speaking of Gwynahra, I believe I may have a solution to your problem and mine."

He was curious now. Which of *his* problems was she referring to? He had a bunch. "Oh?"

"I was called to the White Council last night on other business, but one of the topics discussed while I was there, was your need for a mentor in the Athryllith."

"Ah, right. And? What's the verdict?"

"As I hoped to have you keep Gwynahra close to you, and you need a mentor, why not 'kill two birds with one stone' I believe you say?"

Oh shit! Was she going to recommend what he thought she was? Damned sure sounded like it, he thought.

"My daughter is gifted in the Athryllith, and, could be in a position to assist you in developing your skill. Given she's your subordinate, I dare not call her your mentor, but assistant, perhaps?"

"That would be wonderful!" Chloe exclaimed.

He realized he was nodding, and intended to say something, but his lips weren't moving.

"Haldor?" Saeran asked.

"Right. That … makes sense." That was all he could think to say. Having Gwynahra on his flagship was one thing, having her tutor him in these rather *intimate* abilities … gods help him. He could *not* have a relationship with Saeran's daughter, or any involvement with here for that matter. But saying no to this eminently logical proposal would be ridiculous, and may insult one of his most powerful allies. Oh crap, he just realized that Saeran could probably hear these doubts, given how loudly they were echoing in his mind. Maybe not. She was certainly trained to block unwanted thoughts.

She looked at him askance. "Are you all right?"

"Yeah. This whole Athryllith business just caught me off guard. I suppose I'm still adjusting to the whole concept. If Gwynahra is willing to help, then I'd be foolish not to take advantage of her-" Oh sweet Frigga! Did he just say that? "- of her assistance. Yes, that would be great." Where was that bottle of single malt?

Irina and the girls were shoved off the transport into a long airlock-passageway. With heads bowed, they trudged across the airlock seal and into another ship; its darkened passageways and deck were rusted and filthy. She heard the sounds of dripping fluids, and smelled the sour odor of nameless horrors. This was a ship of death.

The brutish handler slammed her into the wall and barked an order for her to stand, and not move on pain of death; she had no will to move.

Through the edges of her vision she could see dozens of other captives —her fellow colonists. The hard working folk of Novaya-Leningrad. They had not asked for this conflict, and wanted no part in it. They simply wanted a life with enough food and small comforts to be happy. Austere, but peaceful; such were the stuff of Russian dreams.

She gasped as she saw giants! There was no other word to describe them. Maybe Trolls? Their heads scraped the mottled ceiling as their footfalls shook the deck. Clad in grey leathery-skin, they looked to be closer cousins to elephants than mankind. Aside from the Hrymar which she had just met, this was her first alien encounter. She knew of the Hrymar from books and safety vids. But these beasts — no, she had never heard of these.

Then a terrifying memory burst from the depths of her memory— Chuhaister. The forest-giants of her Russian homeland. Her great-grandfather had told her of these beasts—or ones that looked just like them.

One of the gray giants began separating men from women, occasionally pulling out a female mistakenly, only to be struck with a stun-stick by a Hrymar guard. It appeared they were prisoners, or slaves, as well.

As the giants dressed the lines and marched the men away, she saw the Human boy again,, walking along with an older Hrymar. They spoke in a language unfamiliar to her. Not Yggdrasi, that was certain. She was not fluent, but spoke it well enough. And it sounded like no Earth language she had ever heard.

"Master," Kadir asked of Serkan, "why do we not separate the children as well? I see you have the Graal separating men from women, but why leave the children with their women?"

Serkan looked at him askance. "Do you want to clean up their piss and shit, or keep them quiet? No, we keep them together until they get to market. Their mothers can keep them healthy until they are sold."

He nodded in understanding. Very clever, he might not have thought of that.

"Why do so many of them have golden hair?" He asked.

"These cattle are mostly from a region called Russia, back on Earth. Lots of golden haired slaves. When we conquer Earth, we shall have many more of these."

Kadir wondered why his mother had red hair, as he had, then remembered she was from a place called Ireland. Did they all have red hair there as well? He dared not ask Serkan too many useless questions. His patience was short.

The woman he helped capture looked at him and spoke in a strange tongue. Serkan shoved Kadir aside and back-handed the woman, so hard, she was lifted off her feet and fell to the ground in a loose heap.

"Never utter a word in that barbarian tongue again! When you speak, you speak in Yggdrasi, or not at all. And only speak when spoken to. Do you understand?" Serkan bellowed.

The woman was barely conscious, he could see that plainly. Serkan must have taken her lack of response as defiance, and his face grew dark.

"Let me demonstrate the consequences of disobedience," Serkan said. He pulled out his dagger and walked to the woman's daughters. He smiled wickedly and kneeled.

She tried to rise, but could not manage it. Serkan laughed and shook his head.

"No, I shall not waste these ones. They will bring much in trade, and have many *uses*." Without warning, Serkan slashed the throat of a Human male standing near him. The man clutched his throat, mouth gasping like a fish. The man fell to his knees spitting blood on his neighbors.

"When you disobey," Serkan said in a measured tone, "I will not kill *you*. I *will* kill someone else, so that you learn a lesson. Killing you would be too easy. The second time you disobey, I will kill two, and so on. Understand me now, bitch?"

The woman's eyes were filled with tears, she squeezed her girls tight while she nodded.

Kadir felt nothing for her. She was weak. Cull the weak. It was the Hrymar way.

Chapter 8

LOCATION: RMA - BARRACKS / PLANET: RIGSVAKA

Gwynahra sat on the edge of her bunk as she sorted through some of her personal items, and saw Lythrael sprinting toward her, gripping a piece of paper with both hands.

"My assignment!" Lythrael squealed, proffering the paper.

She extended a hand to take it, but Lythrael pulled it back to her bosom.

"Guess," Lythrael demanded with mock seriousness.

"I'm not a mind reader, Lythrael." Or at least I choose not to read yours, she thought.

"Humor me, sister."

"I didn't make you guess when I told you about my assignment to the flagship."

Lythrael nodded encouragingly.

Sudden realization made her grin. "Rot! You're on the *Mjolnir* as well?"

Lythrael bowed in mock formality. At your service, dear Gwynahra."

Lythrael plopped down onto the end of Gwynahra's bed. "I wonder if they might let us share a cabin?"

"I don't think we get to influence such trivial things. Besides, you'll be quartered with other Valkyrie, I would expect."

Lythrael looked suddenly glum. "Of course. I hadn't thought that far."

"Don't despair, as long as we're on the same ship, I'm delighted."

"True. It's just that we've endured so much together, Gwyn. It would sadden me to be parted after our friendship has grown so."

She threw her arms around Lythrael. "I feel the same. I'd often wished for a sister when I was younger. Now I have one."

Lythrael stood suddenly and paced around. "I'm eager to sink my sword into a Hrymar!" Lythrael rolled-up her orders and flourished them like a sword.

"Isn't your duty not more focused on healing our wounded combatants?"

"Of course. But when I get a chance—watch out sons of Jotuns!" Lythrael said, finishing with a thrust of her make-shift weapon.

"I'm glad you're so eager. Thinking of a battlefield makes my heart ache. I want to see men and women healed, not be wounded. I abhor violence."

"I would as well ... if not for the Hrymar. But since the enemy lives, my sword arm will be ready."

She noticed the solemnity in Lythrael's tone. What caused her to hate the Hrymar so? Of course she despised what they did, but she didn't hate *them*, simply their actions. She was tempted to peer into Lythrael's mind, but that went against everything she'd been taught.

She removed a few more personal items from her locker, placing them into the travel-case on her bed and closed it up.

"Is that it?" Lythrael asked.

She nodded. "I will *not* miss this place. Only the friends I've made here." She hefted her case and the girls left the barracks.

School was out.

Planet: Orbiting Wei Su II / Star: Wei Su

Kadir knew that historically, the Hrymar had re-used stolen starships. *Light's Doom* had been the first starship the Hrymar had designed and built. *Light's Doom* would never be accused of being graceful, and seemed much like their subterranean homes on Niflheim; twisted, dark and cold. This inspired design reflected the spirit of Hrymar creativity; which was to say, there wasn't any.

Per Serkan's command, Kadir was reviewing and analyzing the planetary data as fast as the sensors put it on-screen.

"What do you see?" Serkan asked, from his seat beside the Captain.

He squinted as he tried to deliver the answer that would best please his Master. "No planetary defenses ... two colonies ... I see no major impediments, Master. I would land the ship without any initial bombardment. A pity to ruin any of our harvest."

Serkan was not nodding, nor did he acknowledge Kadir's guidance. "Master?"

He felt a wave of disappointment hit him.

"Look- there," Serkan said, pointing a finger on the image of the planet that was overlaid with data.

He looked again. What had he missed? He glanced at the tectonic data, mineral distribution, hydrographic charts. But he saw nothing to be concerned about. He shook his head. The usual indicator was an intense energy reading, but the electro-magnetic sensors showed current draw and EM emissions typical for a city of civilians. There were no hotspots like Plasma Cannon batteries, or Ion Cannons. "Master, I am sorry. I see nothing unusual."

Serkan shook his head in disgust. "For Jotnar's sake, boy. There!" He stabbed a finger at the display and caused it to zoom in.

It was the size of a speck of dust. Had Serkan not been pointing to it, he would never have spotted it. It was not a thing, as much as an absence of something.

"Do you see it now?"

"Yes, Master. A discontinuity in the surrounding rock."

"Exactly. And what would you expect to find there?"

Perhaps a concealed or shielded missile battery, or a command post?"

"Finally. And?"

"We should order a kinetic bombardment of that, and any similar discontinuities."

Serkan nodded. "Then see it done."

He re-examined the display and noticed more than a dozen such specks. He highlighted them on his console. "Fists, fire on the targets I have marked."

The weapons captain nodded, but did not verbally acknowledge the order. He'd yet to earn their respect, and until then, he was just the ex-thrall and Human-pet of their Over-Chieftain. Nothing more.

The ship shuddered as six kinetic-rounds per salvo were hurled toward their targets planet-side.

He watched with a fascination. This was his first time ordering a planetary bombardment. It was intoxicating power. Thousands might die with a single word from his mouth. The metallic-slugs began burning as they entered the atmosphere, appearing like small meteorites as they grew closer to the surface. Each was nothing more than a chunk of mass, shaped for better aerodynamic performance, but otherwise, it was like throwing rocks from space. But, accelerated to a significant fraction of light speed, these rocks were devastating, wreaking havoc orders of magnitude beyond any ship's energy weapons. If only other ships would stand still, they would make short work of any naval engagement.

As the first salvo struck their targets he watched the silent shockwave spread out from the point of impact. It was an awesome sight!

"Alarm!" Yelled the man at the defensive station.

"What is it?" Serkan barked.

"Incoming missile, my Lord. *We* seem to have missed one of their defensive batteries." The man said, clearly pointing the finger at Kadir.

That ignorant bastard implied that *he* had missed one. And *he* had. He would pay for it later. But then so would the observant asshole. He would find a way to make him sorry for his insult.

He watched as the missile left the atmosphere and grew larger on the view screen.

"Kadir, are you planning to do something about that missile? Or shall I get out and challenge it to a duel?" Serkan said impatiently.

"Yes, Master! Fists, target the incoming missile. Fire now!"

In a heartbeat the missile exploded. It was no threat, really, but Serkan wanted to make a point.

Serkan took his eyes off him and barked orders to the bridge crew. "Take us down. Our harvest awaits."

Location: Battleship RSS Mjolnir / Planet: Orbiting Rigsvaka

JARL'S PERSONAL LOG:

DATE STAMP: 2:20pm TST, Friggasday, 22'nd day of Shedding, 2137 CE

USER: Olsen, Haldor

Today I took command of the Rigsvaka Star Ship *Mjolnir*; first of the new Mjolnir-class Battleships. She's stunning! She's 200,000 displacement-tons of advanced composites and the latest Alfar organic-armor. Hard to believe, but her outer skin is actually alive.

She's tuff, and she's got teeth; bristling with point-defense laser-batteries and several plasma-cannon turrets. But her main weapon is a spinal-mounted Dark-Matter-Lance. I can't wait to use that on the enemy again—the DML can cut smaller ships in half. We have to get in close and personal to do it—within 10,000 km, but that's half the fun.

The crew all seem so young, or maybe it's just that I'm getting old? Yeah, 43—no spring chicken. They seem a good bunch though. We've got almost four-thousand of the top recruits across several Human colonies—and three different species—serving as my officers, non-comms, and marines. Gina

Russo, who head my marine contingent, is the only familiar face though. But I did poach some officers that served with on the *Drekkar* these last few months.

The *Mjolnir's* bridge is far better protected than most. Instead of being mounted on the outside of the hull, for an ostensibly scenic view—making it susceptible to being targeted by enemy fire—*Mjolnir's* is deep at center of the ship. Three of the bridge's walls are covered by what look like four-meter tall windows, but they're actually view-screens.

I like my chair this time. Seems silly, but a decent captain's chair is hard to come by. And if I'm expected to sit in the thing for 12+ hours at a stretch, I want my backside well cared for. An interesting development was the installation of escape-pods beneath each chair on the bridge, including mine. Hit the button—*bang!*—you're shot down through the floor and off into the black.

For all her martial prowess, the most pleasant surprise was the woodsy smell. Our air re-circulators flow through hydroponics and there must be something pine-like growing in there; a few times I could have sworn I was in a forest, not on a starship. I'm definitely a fan of the Alfar's organic-integration philosophy. Mjolnir's organic systems, including the armor, are also self-repairing. That should minimize downtime between raids; which is what I need to get back to; we're currently patrolling hyperspace bridges that form along lines of dark-matter. It doesn't provide a fully-meshed network of FTL-paths between our colonies, but where they do exist, we save a lot of travel-time. Trudging through normal-space at a fraction of light-speed sucks.

Now that we're out here with more than one ship the crew are obliged to

call me High Commander instead of just Captain. I suppose I'll get used to it
—eventually.

Olsen out.

- Jarl Haldor Olsen, High Commander of the Rigsvaka Armed Forces,
commanding officer, *Mjolnir*

<<< END OF ENTRY >>>

KEY:

-----

* TST - Tyrbjorg Standard Time (a timezone on Rigsvaka)

* Friggasday - Old Earth Friday

* Shedding - Old Earth month of September

* CE - Common Era

As Hal tried to adjust to his new place on the *Mjolnir's* command-dais, he
looked at the crew roster again. It was the [crew total] field in the report that
had him astonished: 3,943 souls; half sailors, half marines. He never imagined
he would be in direct command of so many people. Of course there were
many times that number on Rigsvaka, but he had others to help manage the
burden. And he supposed that the same was true here. He had department
heads for everything. Good heavens, he thought, even the number of officers
and department heads was daunting—nearly two-hundred. He imagined some
very long meetings in store. That would serve him right for trying to save the
Galaxy.

He had to admit that he enjoyed commanding different starships. *Mjolnir* was now his flagship, but when the first Skaldbjorg-class dreadnought was complete, it would become his new flagship.

The view-screen on *Mjolnir* was nothing short of epic. It was shaped like half of a hemisphere, and wrapped around the entire bridge—except for the rear wall. It continued up the ceiling, giving viewers the sense they could see all around them. It provided an almost planetarium-like view of space.

The bridge layout reminded him of a trendy nightclub; it had a ceiling two stories high, and he sat on the raised command dais, imagining groups of people roaming around the would-be dance-floor, talking, flirting, whatever. Only the groups of people here were all sailors and soldiers; all working to a grim purpose. Still, this was one helluva bridge. Where was a waiter when you needed a drink?

Hal waited until the last of his senior officers were seated at the conference table, then spoke. "We have a report of another Hrymar attack. I'll let our new intelligence officer brief you on the details." Hal gestured to Jin Wudai.

Wudai nodded to him as he stood. "I received a private message from one of my relatives on the Wei Su colony. The Hrymar attacked two days ago and captured over half the colonists. Including several of my extended family," Wudai said with no hint of emotion. "They then proceeded to burn down the major buildings and industrial facilities. Wei Su is within Mang's Republic of China territory. Of course you know that the MRC is the closest new stellar power to SID space. That means that the Hrymar are raiding on our borders again, and have moved past our patrols in Rigsvaka space. And on top of that there seems to be a trend with the Hrymar gathering up children. To what end, we don't yet know. But there has to be an end customer for them."

Engineering-Head Magister Edvit Jerresson, shook his orange beard. "Those blue-skinned bastards."

"Needless to say," Wudai continued, "this is chilling news. We believed we were driving the Hrymar back, and now they seem to have surged forward. I have no intel on how they managed this. There are no reports from any of our listening-posts, nor anything from our allies."

"Are they employing stealth-ships perhaps?" Senior science officer, Meiriona asked.

Edvit shook his head again. "I have a hard time believing they developed the capability on their own. And I can guarantee you, my people did not sell it to them. We Dvergar do not trust those icy shits. Not one quark."

Captain Chandragupta Maurya, Hal's new first officer, said, "I shudder to think, but is it in the realm of possibility that they have access to an inter-stellar-bridge node?"

Hal nodded. "It is. We know that Gridrmann sold secrets to the Hrymar, seven years back. What all he sold, we don't know. But he certainly had access to that knowledge. His daughter Nila, my ex-navigator, helped map the first nodes—she's still in prison on Earth, by the way. She was also present when we tested the key. Of course we've learned lots since then, but what she knew could be very dangerous. If the Hrymar haven't used them till now, that's surprising. We *knew* this was coming. If they have access to the bridge network, then they have the keys to our backdoor."

The other officers at the conference table whispered amongst themselves.

"Meiriona, I want you to contact your counterparts in the SID Ministry of Science and find out if there have been any anomalous energy readings near that sector—anything out of the ordinary. Jin, same goes for you. Look for anything. Even seemingly natural events that might be rare."

Both nodded.

He looked to his combatives officer, Ali ibn al-Hassan Shizari. "Make sure the gunners and missile battery crews are at full readiness. Hopefully we'll get a chance to see what kind of pounding *Mjolnir* can give the Hrymar."

Shizari nodded. "Aye aye, High Commander."

"Cabrillo, plot us a course for the Wei Su colony. We'll need to make a stop at the MRC border and get permission. But I don't expect any push back on our offer to help. Let's get to work people."

"Comms, are we ready?" Hal asked.

"Ready, my Lord."

"May I have your attention please. It's High Commander Olsen speaking. I wanted to take a minute to share my thoughts on our mission, and the days ahead. I know all of you are proud to be serving on the *Mjolnir*. I certainly am. None of us are here by accident. We are here, because we dreamed of something better. We weren't satisfied with the status quo. We couldn't abide evil living next door. What they did to us, and to others could *not* go unanswered. We don't head out seeking revenge. We seek justice. We are not an angry mob, bloodthirsty and blind. We are thinking and feeling individuals, governed by common sense, and by the strongest virtue of all—honor. Tyrmundr literally means Tyr's Hands—the hands of justice. That is what each of you are, and collectively. Hands of justice. Don't ever forget that. Don't let battle-lust cloud your hearts. We kill the enemy because we must. Not because we want to. That is duty. That is honor. Doing what we must, even when it's distasteful.

We've just learned that the Hrymar have struck again. They decimated the Wei Su colony in the MRC. We are taking *Mjolnir* to investigate. Once we complete that mission, we'll be taking *a* deep into enemy territory. We'll skip their small processing centers and distribution rings for now. We're going to attack the heart of the beast. There are twelve Hrymar Chieftains. Each governs his own territory. Some are fixed, others are mobile. These are the major centers that we'll be attacking. It's going to be dangerous. Not all of us will make it back to Rigsvaka, or our homes on other worlds. But we will ensure that the enemy knows his days are numbered. I'm proud of all of you. That is all, Olsen out."

Even with the comm off, he could feel the cheering voices and clapping suffusing the ship. They were ready.

Planet: Wei Su II / Star: Wei Su (M8 V Red Dwarf)

Timonen opened the hatch and Hal stepped out of the assault-shuttle, laser-carbine in hand; he wasn't taking any chances—there could be Hrymar still skulking around.

He was met with the acrid scent of burnt polymers and the bitter taste of smoke that still hung in the air. As he surveyed the destruction, husks of a nascent colony stood like grave-markers. Souvenirs of a shattered dream.

Gina and a platoon of her marines followed Hal.

"O-2," Gina said, "take the platoon to the Facility Manager—he's the man in the blue jacket over there," she pointed. "See how we can help."

The young officer saluted crisply, and ushered his troops off to assist the colonists.

Gina shook her head. "Quite a fucking mess, boss."

"Uh huh. That it is."

Gwynahra had accompanied them, as part of her Battlefield Medicine training included providing PTSD and grief counseling. She was now Mjolnir's de facto Counselor / Psychologist.

"My Lord, I would like to see if I can help them as well," Gwynahra said.

"I'm sure they could use a shoulder. Thank you, Gwynahra," he said.

Accompanied by an older man, Jin Wudai was walking toward Hal and Gina. Wudai had come down on an earlier shuttle to take the measure of the situation and to speak with his surviving relatives.

"Lord Haldor, may I present Qin Shi Huang. He is the Elder of the colony, and is also my Great Uncle on my mother's side."

Hal bowed. "Elder Qin, it is an honor to meet you. Please accept my sincerest regrets at this vile attack."

Qin returned the bow. "I thank you for coming Lord Haldor. It is sad day."

"When Jin told us of the attack, I wanted to come and put our resources at your disposal. With your permission, I would like to investigate the attack and try to track down these fiends. While our marines are helping your citizens with the cleanup, I'd like to have Jin lead a team to search for clues."

Qin bowed again. "We are fortunate Jin Wudai has such associates. I thank you, and graciously accept your assistance." Qin trundled off, looking as if he had aged a hundred years in the few days since the attack.

Hal began walking through the decimated streets. He noted the garden plots behind every home — now just blackened-furrows. This would have been a beautiful place, he mused. This destruction hit close to home. It was only nine years since the Hrymar had attacked the Colony of Norvik, on New Midgard; his colony. The colonists here were lucky. Wei Su had been attacked, buildings burned, people taken. Norvik had been nuked; its existence completely erased, leaving nothing but a crater of green trinitite. Wei Su could be rebuilt. He knew that the colony on New Midgard *had* been re-established, and now was home to the myriad refugees from the Hrymar. The site of their first attack in Human space had become a haven for their victims—fitting. He didn't have the stomach to see it, though.

Hal's wristcom chirped. *"High Commander?"*

It was Captain Chandragupta Maurya, his first officer. "Olsen here, go."

"Sir, we've detected a scout ship entering the system — affiliation unknown. They've yet to broadcast any IFF signal. They're weighing in at between 75 to 150 tons."

"Go to battle stations and intercept. Update me when you've made contact."

Chapter 9

PLANET: ORBITING WEI SU II

"Helm, intercept the contact if you will," Chandragupta Maurya said.

"Aya, sir," said helmsman Braylan Jones.

"Combatives, power weapons and raise shields. Sensors, can we get a better reading on the size of the contact?"

Meiriona's deft fingers rattled over the keyboard on her sensors-console. "Sir, I'm afraid that's not possible. In fact, the mass is continuing to fluctuate between 75 and 150 tons. It's almost as if they had a gravitic oscillator. Yet even ours don't create such a large fluctuation."

"Very well. Continue to scan as we close with it. Maybe getting closer will give us a more accurate reading."

Anouk Kappa peered up from the comms-console with a smirk. "Sir, I believe we have their attention now. They're hailing us."

He nodded.

An American accent erupted from the bridge comm system when Kappa connected the hail. *"Why the Hell do you have weapons trained on me? Holy shit! I'm an unarmed trader. For God's sake people, relax!"*

"This is Captain Chandragupta Maurya, first officer of the *RSS-Mjolnir.* Identify yourself."

"Only if you promise to power down weapons!"

Maurya gave a single nod to Shizari.

The image of a stout middle-aged man appeared on the *Mjolnir's* view-screen. *"Well, that's better. I'm Captain Chuck Bodey. My ship's the African Queen."*

"Please explain your presence in the Wei Su system, Captain Bodey."

"I'm a free-trader. Come to trade."

"Captain Bodey, I can assure you, this is not the time to be looking for trading opportunities. We presently have authority granted by the MRC to investigate an incident. Please prepare to be boarded. We will pull along beside you and search your ship. I suggest you cooperate."

Bodey went red in the face and stabbed a finger at his console. His image evaporated from the view-screen.

"A rather nasty fellow, isn't he?" Chandragupta said to Kappa.

She just shrugged.

Maurya watched a video feed of the marines boarding the *African Queen*; it was like a movie unfolding.

The hatch opened with no trouble, and they were now in the airlock. The ship turned out to be a 200 ton Light Scout. It had been equipped with jamming systems which had caused *Mjolnir's* gravitic sensors to be confused.

"Airlock door opening, entering the ship," the E-6 said.

There wasn't much to this tiny vessel, at only seven-meters feet across. The Marine looked right then left. The Marine's camera showed three staterooms. As they moved forward they came to the ship's bridge. There sat the portly Captain Chuck Bodey, looking none too pleased at this intrusion into his sanctuary — humble as it was.

"Here to arrest me?" Bodey said, a look of scorn on his face.

The E-6 shook his head. *"No, sir. We're just here to search the ship. We'll be as respectful as possible."*

Maurya admired that about the marines. They could stand toe-to-toe with a belligerent ass, and not lose their cool. He would just as soon stun the fool and be done with it. That's why he'd joined the fleet, and not the marines.

He watched as the other four marines began a thorough search of the ship, scouring every corner. One Marine descended to the second deck and found an empty cargo bay.

"Sir, the ship is clean. There are eight cryo-chambers and a cargo hold, but they're all empty. And no contraband, we've turned her upside down." the E-6 said.

In the newly-settled human star-systems, contraband, in this case, just meant anything hidden. There were very few restrictions at present, and smuggling was virtually dead. But something hidden would be seen as suspicious, and more closely scrutinized.

"Thank you, E-6. I'd like to see the ship's astrogation logs—let's see where she's been recently."

The E-6 nodded and walked forward to the bridge again. After a few minutes on the controls he stood. *"Sir, the logs are encrypted"*

"Captain Bodey, would you be so kind as to decrypt the logs?" he asked.

"No. I will not. You can see I've got nothing to hide. You've got no damned business digging into my logs. Now get the fuck off my ship!"

Meiriona tapped Maurya's shoulder and whispered to him. "Sir, I can decrypt them. Just have the E-6 place his hand-scanner on the instrument panel. I should be able to hack in and decrypt them."

He relayed the order, and in seconds, Meiriona was analyzing the data on her science-console.

"Cabrillo?" Maurya comm'd the astrogation officer.

"Cabrillo here, sir."

"Please come to the bridge. We may have some astrogation data that needs your attention."

"On my way, sir."

By the time Juan Rodriguez Cabrillo arrived on the bridge, Meiriona had the files decrypted and sent them to the astrogation-console.

The tall Spaniard cracked his knuckles and beamed a smile at his crew-mates before sinking his head into the data. He was the most enthusiastic member of *Mjolnir's* crew, and nephew to Antonio Cadena, Lord Haldor's oldest friend, and now Thane.

"Oh, now that is extremely interesting," Cabrillo muttered.

"What is it?" Kappa asked.

Cabrillo just raised a finger to silence her, his eyes still focused on the data.

"Well. Fascinating," he said.

Kappa looked at Meiriona and rolled her eyes.

Cabrillo like to dramatize his work, and was infamous among the women.

"Ah! Ooh," he continued.

"Mr. Cabrillo, if you please?" Maurya asked.

"My sincerest apologies, sir. I am simply passionate about my work," he said, hands wide and an innocent smile adorning his face.

Maurya wanted to slap him, but that the same time he had to work to keep a smile off his own face.

"Here we are," Cabrillo said, and a field of stars appeared on the main view-screen, followed by a red line connecting the dots. "Our friend has indeed been in the Wei Su system already. Four days ago, in point of fact. Then, he went here." Cabrillo zoomed in on a planet several light years away from Wei Su, and north-east of the Galactic Core.

"What's there, Mr. Cabrillo?" Maurya asked.

"There is no information on the charts, sir. It happens to be a class M star, M0 V to be precise, but we have never surveyed it. Captain Bodey, or at least this ship, was there for one day, then returned here to Wei Su."

"Thank you Mr. Cabrillo." Maurya keyed his comm to the marine boarding team "E-6, please take Captain Bodey into custody. We'll be seizing his ship and taking her into the cargo bay."

"Aye aye, sir."

"What has this Captain Bodey been up to?"

Hal and Gina watched through a vid-screen as the Captain of the *African Queen* fidgeted in the *Mjolnir's* interrogation room on the other side of the bulkhead.

"What do you think he was up to?" Gina asked.

"We'll know soon. Jin's going in. You know, I thought *you* were scary … till I meant Jin. I would *not* want to be on the other side of the table from him. Especially where his family are involved."

"Isn't that a conflict of interest? Having Jin interrogate Captain Dipshit?"

"Only if Jin had something to gain. Which I'm certain he does not. Jin's a pretty cool customer. You watch. He won't lose it. I hand picked this guy,

Gina. There were lots of people vying for intel positions in our fleet. Jin really impressed me."

The door to the interrogation room opened and they watched Jin Wudai enter while Captain Bodey got visibly more anxious. Jin began with some basic questions to establish a baseline of reactions - much like they used to do with ancient lie-detector machines. In the case, Jin was the lie-detector.

Hal felt the door behind him open and saw Gwynahra enter.

"Commander, I hope I'm not interrupting. I thought I might be of some use here," Gwynahra said.

Gina smiled. "Right, the Athralad?"

"*Athryllith*," Gwynahra corrected.

"Got it. So how does that work exactly?" Gina asked.

"You're welcome to watch. Now shush, both of you," Hal said.

Gina made a motion as if she was zippering up her lips.

Hal focused on the conversation from the interrogation room.

"What exactly were you doing in the Wei Su system four days ago?" Jin asked.

"I came to trade," Bodey said.

"What did you bring to trade?"

"Foodstuffs."

Jin narrowed his eyes. "The colony grows their own food, Mr. Bodey."

"Well, you know, spices and stuff, That kind of food. Exotic shit."

"I see. And did you trade with the colonists?"

"No. I got here just as the colony was attacked. There was nothing I could do, I've only got defensive weaponry. I'm just a smalltime trader and courier. So I left."

Hal smelled Gwynahra's subtle floral scent as she moved close to him and lost focus for a moment.

"He's lying," she whispered to him.

The warmth of her breath made him shudder, and he had to fight to concentrate.

"How can you tell?" Then he realized how. "Never mind."

"Focus on him," she said. "Enter his thoughts and memories, look into mind-space."

Hal looked at Bodey. Noticed the beads of perspiration running down his face. Noticed the patches of moisture near his armpits, and felt his fear.

"And where did you go when you left Wei Su?" Jin continued.

"I went to another colony- close by. Then I figured I'd come back and see if these people needed any help."

"Complete fabrication," Gwynahra said. "Can you hear it?"

"Not quite yet."

"And so you traded with these other colonists?" Jin asked.

Bodey nodded rapidly. "Right. Exactly."

"What did you get in return for your 'exotic shit', I believe that's what you called it?"

"Spices and stuff. You know. You're oriental, you people like that thing. Like Pad Thai."

Jin's expression remained completely neutral. "Pad-Thai is from Thailand. As the 'Thai' suffix suggests. I happen to be from China. But no matter. And what did they trade you in return for these wondrous and exotic spices?"

Bodey's mouth hung open for a moment. "Um, nothing. I...took credit. They're good for it. Done business with them before."

There was never any cargo, Hal thought.

Gwynahra looked at him and nodded.

Hal turned his mind back to Captain Bodey of the African Queen. Only this time, instead of listening to the man's thoughts, he yanked them out, like tearing bloody tufts of hair from his head.

Bodey grabbed his head and began to scream.

No cargo at all, Hal saw. Blood began to trickle from Bodey's eyes. *There were eight cryo-chambers on the African Queen. Not quite full sized. Perfect for smaller people ... or children.*

Fury erupted in Hal and he wanted to break into the interrogation chamber and grab this animal by the throat. But, he didn't have to.

"Haldor, stop!"

He felt someone grabbing his arm, and heard a woman's voice. No, two women, holding both arms.

"Gwynahra? Gina? What in Odin's name happened?" He felt like he'd just sprinted a hundred meters. He was panting, sweating, heart thundering in his chest.

Through the monitor, he saw Captain Bodey. His head lay motionless, slumped over the interrogation-room table. Blood oozed from his ears and eyes. He saw Dr. Inglis, the ship's surgeon, rushing into the room, followed by two medics.

"He's alive! Get him to the OR," Dr. Inglis said.

Hal was only confused for a moment, then it was all too clear: The children. Thousands of them. And this animal ... he helped the Hrymar. Sold secrets. Sold people.

Gwynahra dabbed at Hal's face. Removing a trickle of blood from his nose.

What Hal had done to Captain Bodey was not without consequences to his body as well.

"Haldor, I never intended for you to hurt him. I simply wanted to help you find the answers you were looking for," Gwynahra thought to him.

"I should have killed him. You don't know what he's done, Gwynahra."

"Yes. I do. I saw exactly what you did. What happened to your speech about justice? About controlling bloodlust? The Athryllith is a noble gift. It should never be used for such base purposes."

"There are no limits when it comes to animals like him!" He thought to her.

"There are always limits for civilized people, Lord Haldor," she said aloud. Setting down the swabs, she turned and left the sickbay.

Dr. Inglis walked into the sickbay, almost colliding with Gwynahra on her way out. "Now what have you done?" She asked.

"It's nothing."

"Nothing? You nearly kill a prisoner, then drive the ship's counselor running out of sick bay? What the hell's stuck in your craw today, Commander?"

"Doctor, that animal in there- "

Dr. Inglis put a hand on his shoulder. "Relax. I know all about it. You need to chill. Got me?"

"So he's alive?"

"No thanks to you — and barely."

He nodded.

Jin Wudai and Chandragupta Maurya arrived in sickbay.

"Commander, how are you feeling?" Chandra asked.

"I'm all right, Chandra."

"My Lord," Jin asked, "Gwynahra tells me you saw into that man's mind? Is that so?"

"Yes. And it wasn't pretty."

"Can you give me any information that will help with the investigation?"

"I can do a lot better than that, Jin. There's a planet several light-years from Wei Su. It's a depot of sorts. And they specialize in children."

Chandra looked revolted. "They specialize in children? What ever do you mean?"

"The Hrymar, on behalf of some end customer, are dealing in the bulk sale of children. Apparently there are all sorts of uses for small humanoids: assembling delicate machinery, mining in confined tunnels, adjusting machinery in tight space, and more. There's also a market for less *mundane services*." Hal shuddered.

Maurya's brown complexion drained of color. "Oh."

"Unfortunately, this is nothing new," Jin said. "Up until the 22nd century, children were abused in this way with frightening regularity, especially in South East Asia. I thought we left that all behind a century ago."

"Evil has no expiration date, gentlemen," Dr. Inglis said as she returned. "I saw the fallout of unspeakable atrocities when I worked on New Midgard —just after the refugees started arriving. All of them had been slaves of the Hrymar, or other masters. When people are considered property they become disposable, replaceable. Break one? Buy another."

"We *will* put a stop to this," Hal said.

Hal took a deep breath, then knocked on Gwynahra's cabin door. He could just hear the sound of her soft foot-falls.

The door slid open. She had no smile for him this time. No sparkle in those blue eyes.

"Yes, *High Commander*. What can I do for you?"

Damn. That was cold, he thought. "I came to apologize."

She said nothing.

He frowned, waiting for her to say something. Invite him in. Anything.

"Yes?" She said.

"Yes?" He repeated, confused.

"You said you were here to apologize. I'm waiting for you to apologize. You are my superior officer, but I hope you'll have the courtesy to not keep me standing here all night."

"Right. May I come in and speak with you? I do plan to apologize as well. I promise." He placed his right hand across his chest.

She stepped aside enough for him to get by. She was just close enough that he caught the scent of her perfume, or shampoo. Or maybe it was just soap? It was exquisite. Tyr help me, I have to stop thinking these things. She was like a drug. Every-time he was near her, he felt drunk, out of control. Maybe not out of control exactly, just — uninhibited?

She was frowning now. Damn it. He had to control his thoughts around her. He knew strong emotions were like screaming to another person with the Athryllith.

She sat on a chair and he plopped down onto one end of her sofa.

"Look, about this afternoon. I meant what I said in my speech to the crew. But these ... things. What they do to our people- your people. They've

127

crossed a line. They've given up the right to be treated with dignity."

She shook her head briskly, and with an expression of condemnation. "I do *not* accept that. What you did today was not justice. There was no honor in torturing that man, Haldor. He was defenseless."

"You *know* what he did!"

"And I *know* what *you* did," she replied softly. "You're supposed to be a better man. Aren't you?"

He swallowed hard. She was a frustrating woman. Didn't she understand that they deserved a little pain and suffering? As did anyone that helped them. What was wrong with that? But, he said nothing.

Gwynahra filled the silence. "The Hrymar and their allies must be stopped. I agree with you. But *how* we do a thing, is just as important as the end result. Humanity has a saying 'It's not the destination that counts, it's the journey'. Do you believe that?"

He still said nothing, unsure whether he'd be able to control what came out of his mouth.

She got up from her chair, and sat beside him on the sofa, placing her hand on his knee.

"I know why you are so angry, and in so much pain, Haldor," she said in a whisper.

She could *not* know his pain. A flood of rage washed over him and he stood. "I don't think you do." Nobody could. Not until they lost everything, more that once.

He left her room before he said things he would regret.

Planet: Kale II / Star: Kale (M0 V Red Dwarf)

Kale II was a barely hospitable planet. Predominantly clad in thick sheets of ice — much like Earth at the height of its Ice Age. Yet there was narrow band at the equator where the cold had retreated just enough to allow greenery to take hold.

Eino Timonen piloted the assault-shuttle deftly through the atmosphere, banking and dodging to avoid large weather systems; it was a turbulent ride for the passengers.

Hal winced as his head hit the side of the hull. "Eino, if I get another bruise on this flight, I'm clipping your wings," he quipped.

"Apologies, High Commander, I'm dancing with the devil here, and he's got two left feet."

As they broke through the cloud cover, Hal could see massive, verdant plains, stretching out before them; an endless grassland at the equator, bordered by nascent forests.

"No animal life as yet," Meiriona reported.

"No humanoid lifeforms? Even foreign?" He asked.

"None."

"Energy readings?"

"Still none."

"Use your mind, Haldor," Gwynahra thought to him. *"You will be able to feel for other minds on the planet. If there are any here. You will know. Mind-space is empty, except for sentient thoughts. They should appear like bright beacons on a dark night."*

He shot her a look. *"You're speaking to me now?"* He thought.

She smirked. *"I'm not speaking,"* she thought to him.

He shook his head, and sighed. "Clever, Gwyn," he said aloud.

She gestured to herself with mock surprise. "Who? Me?"

"What are you two on about? Gina asked.

"There!" Meiriona pointed to a blip on the shuttle's scanners. "There's an energy reading. If I'm not mistaken, it appears to be the same energy signature as a runestone-portal."

"A runestone-portal?" Hal asked. "Here?"

"Indeed. And I have another contact. A second energy signature, approximately 100 km from the portal. Different though. I am not familiar with it, nor is the computer."

"Alright," Hal said, "let's do a fly-by on the runestone first, then head to the second energy signature. I'm more interested to know what that is."

The shuttle banked toward the runestone-portal, gliding smoothly above the sea of emerald, and finally descended below the heavy weather.

In minutes they were directly above the coal-black runestone, hovering at an altitude of one-hundred meters.

"Scanning now, High Commander," Meiriona said. The Alfar scientist read through the sensor data with interest. "Sir, there is residual energy emanating from the runestone-portal."

"How can you tell that?" Gina asked.

"As far as we understand," Meiriona explained, "when a portal is activated, it sets up a resonant pulse. Essentially, the neutronium vibrates until it hits the correct frequency — which is the resonant frequency it shares with a particular strand of dark-matter; that forms the bridge between two portals. We think the orbital inter-stellar-bridge-nodes work on a different principle, however."

Gina waved her off. "Got it. More than I needed to know."

Meiriona looked annoyed, but continued her report to him. "Based on the wavelengths of the residual energy, it's been used within the last week. And, molecular density scanners indicate the grass has been repeatedly compacted in a similar profile. It points to a ship landing with regularity."

"That's about the time our friend Captain Dipshit was here," Gina said. "Look's like he's a regular visitor."

He nodded. "Indeed. Alright Timonen, let's head over to the second energy source."

The shuttle banked again as it accelerated toward the next waypoint.

"I assume that means the Hrymar are using the runestone-portals?" Gwynahra said.

"Looks like it. If not them, then this Captain Bodey. And if it's him, how *by Heimdall's horn* did he manage it?"

"Maybe a crony of Gridrmann's?" Gina offered.

"Possibly. Let's hope that's the case. A few rogue Humans are much less a threat than the Hrymar scourge. Unless of course they're working *with* the Hrymar." He exhaled hard.

"Portal ahead, High Commander," Timonen said.

As the shuttle slowed, he could see the wreckage of a massive starship. "Give us a hundred-meters clearance from the wreck when you land."

"Aye, sir, one-hundred-meters it is," Timonen said.

The contragrav in the assault-shuttle allowed the little boat to touch down as light as a feather. But ,this feather had talons. She was equipped with four laser-turrets and flamethrowers, designed to dissuade enemies from approaching while troops disembarked. There were no enemies in sight, but the weapons systems were active just the same.

The airlock hissed open and he emerged from the shuttle, taking in the view. It was pleasant here in this thin belt of habitability. Long fields of tall grass, the moist scent of growing-things in the air. As he left the shadow of the shuttle he was struck by a stiff breeze, chilled as it came off the glaciers hundreds of miles away. Felt just like his home in Norway during spring.

"Refreshing," Gina said as she walked beside him toward the wreck.

He noticed the ground where the starship had plowed under, submerging a good portion under the earth. He pointed to the crest of the hull. "Looks like it's been here awhile. Notice the foliage growing on the hull? That process takes awhile."

"Your old surveyor-know-how coming back?" Gina asked.

"Never left." He turned to Gwynahra as she approached. "Gwynahra, you ever see a ship like this? I don't recognize it. Is it maybe an old Alfar design?" He felt a mental shudder come from Gwynahra.

"It is *not*. But I do recognize it." She moved closer to the rusty hulk and placed a hand on it.

He could feel her dismay at seeing this ship. *"What is it?"* he thought to her.

"Another evil," she thought. "This ship belongs to the Ysgar," she said aloud. "We were at war with them a century ago. It was a horrific conflict. If you think the Hrymar are evil, then you've never met an Ysgar. They are unspeakably foul things." She turned to Meiriona who now stood surveying the hulk. "Can you tell us how long it's been here?"

Meiriona nodded. "Of course. I'm scanning it now."

"What is it?" He thought to Gwynahra

She didn't think, or say anything, she just held his gaze.

"It appears to have crashed here approximately thirty-two years ago," Meiriona said.

He felt a wave of horror hit him from Gwynahra's mind, and he saw Meiriona grow pale as well.

"Can someone *please* enlighten me? You both look like you've seen a ghost," he said.

"We have," she thought to him. "It was only through great sacrifice and at an unthinkable cost, that we contained the Ysgar. Ninety-years ago, after we drove them back, we set up the Ysgar quarantine zone. Twenty-precent of our fleet still patrols the borders of that space, ensuring they never leave their system again. They've only tried to escape twice, and both times we destroyed their ships. Haldor, they're like your cockroaches on Earth. They breed incessantly, and ravage whatever resources lie before them. They're cruel, hateful things. Their only thought is to consume everything before them and increase their numbers. And they are *highly* intelligent. It's a most terrifying combination." She projected an image of an Ysgar into his mind: a demonic looking creature, humanoid in overall form, with a bi-horned, insectoid- or maybe reptilian head. The stuff of nightmares.

He shuddered. "But you have them contained? Right?"

Gwynahra pointed to the ship. "We thought we had. If one ship escaped … " She trailed off, shaking her head.

He threw up his arms and turned in a circle. "But there's nothing here?

Just the wreckage of a thirty year old ship."

"High Commander, I'd like permission to investigate the ship. See if there are any bodies inside," Meiriona asked.

"Let's get some backup down here first, Meiriona. I don't want you poking around in there alone." He looked at Gina who nodded.

Gwynahra ambled away from the crashed Ysgar ship, and he could feel a tangible trail of sadness following her; like the wake of a boat, her emotions had churned up intense personal feelings. A bitter sadness rippled out from her. He approached her slowly, and spoke to the back of her head. "Gwynahra, are you ok?" He could hear her sniffling, so he put a hand on her shoulder and moved closer to her. There were tears flowing from the corner of her eye. "Hey, what's the matter?"

She shook her head and quickly began wiping her eyes with the back of her shirt sleeve. "Nothing. I'm … sorry. For being so- unprofessional. It's just that- "

He felt her choke up, so he stroked her arm. "I'm not sure what's going on, but whatever it is, maybe I can help?"

She swallowed hard. "Thank you, my Lord. But no, you can't. *They* killed him." She turned to him, her eyes now swollen and red. "The Ysgar. They killed my father, Tarnall, in the last conflict."

What could he say to that? If he wasn't High Commander Olsen right now, or Jarl Haldor, he would have swept her up in his arms, and held her until everything was better. But he couldn't do that. "I'm sorry." He knew the words were meaningless; he'd heard them often enough after Siobhan and Ailan had been killed.

She shared a sad smile with him, and nodded. He knew, that she understood that he'd meant well, but they had a professional relationship right now.

"If there's anything I can do … I know what you're going through, Gwynahra."

"Thank you, sir."

With a full company of marines in Powered Battle Armor, Hal felt more comfortable allowing his other scientists and engineers free-reign to explore the Ysgar wreck.

Gina's marines had brought Venn down to the surface, and now she was roaming the corridors of the ship, sniffing every nook and cranny. He followed her leisurely, soaking up the strangeness of this old vessel. It felt more like an insect hive than a starship. Its corridors wound in random directions like the pattern of an ant hill. Meiriona explained that like the Alfar, the Ysgar grew their ships. This had been an organic, self-sustaining entity; though it lacked the benevolent feel exuded by Alfar ships.

He heard a low growling erupt from Venn. She'd stopped up ahead. One of the scientists was scanning debris on the floor, and looked up at the dire-wolf.

"What's wrong girl?" Hal asked.

The scientists got his attention. "Commander, there's biological residue on the floor."

"Is that what you smell?" He asked Venn.

Venn groaned in response, and she projected the sense of death into his mind. People had died horribly in here. Humans.

"It looks like people were kept prisoner here, sir. And- well- they were tortured, and killed," the young man said. "We can tell by the protein markers in the bio-residue left behind."

Gina came up beside him, silently, as she so often did. "Boss, we found the ship's log. Looks like Captain Dipshit found this wreck and made it his base of operations. There's extensive data we still need to look at, but it appears he *is* working with the Hrymar. He calls himself a *talent scout* in his logs. Sick bastard. You should have fried his fucking grey matter."

Oh, he'd certainly wanted to. "Alright, lets take the logs back to *Mjolnir*."

"The techs want more time to look at the Ysgar technology."

"Fine. Keep the marines here with them, though."

Gina saluted and moved on.

Chapter 10

LOCATION: TYRBJORG, COUNCIL OF THANES' Chamber / Planet: Rigsvaka

Hal admired the beauty and purpose of the council chamber. It had been designed to harken back to the Viking great-halls. Its high peaked ceiling formed by a convergence of titanic alfar-timbers, with two rows of whole-timber columns funneling visitors down to the Jarl's throne. The walls, as in ancient times, were replete with tapestries and paintings, depicting heroic acts and victorious battles. Banners of the twelve noble houses, hung down from the ceiling.

He momentarily warmed his hands by one of the fires burning in braziers around the hall. They were partly for warmth, and partly another link to the past. His direct ancestors had been Vikings. They had, of course, pillaged, but more importantly, had been master merchants and explorers, making inroads across a good portion of the known world at the time—traveling from Canada to Russia—the Russ tribe gave their name to the proud Russian people.

He smiled as he took his seat at the end of the hall and looked out upon his twelve thanes and their many followers. Normally when they convened to discuss military matters, only five of the twelve thanes were summoned; today, all twelve, the high nobility of Rigsvaka, were in session. The matters they had to discuss affected every facet of life on the planet, not just the war making apparatus. He would make no unilateral decisions that affected the entire planet.

His secretary, Kylie McGregor, nodded when she was ready to begin the meeting. She spun to those gathered, her red braids bouncing. She nodded to a young man who blew a bovid horn—its deep baritone resonated throughout the hall, signaling that council was now *in-session*.

Silence fell over the crowd like a wave, and all that could be heard were the crackling fires.

"Ladies and Gentlemen," McGregor said, please allow me to introduce the Thanes in attendance at today's council." McGregor pulled out a scroll of paper—another nod to the past—and began to read from a list of names; previously checked for their actual attendance.

"In attendance today are:

Lady Gina - Thaynja of Spadarosso, Commander of the Rigsvaka Ground Forces;

Lady Blenda - Thaynja of Varnslanda, Minister of Foreign Affairs;

Lady Carwyn - Thaynja of Shadowsong, Minister of Justice;

Lady Valindra - Thaynja of Greenleaf, Minister of Health;

Lady Allison - Thaynja of Tuathanas, Minister of Agriculture;

Lady Margaret - Thaynja of Greyheather, Minister of Intelligence;

Lord Antonio - Thane of Asturias, Commander of the Rigsvaka Stellar Fleet;

Lord Andrew - Thane of Rozlog, Minister of Civil Administration;

Lord Herodes - Thane of Kifisia, Minister of Treasury;

Lord Chogan - Thane of Blackfeathers, Minister of Spiritual Affairs;

Lord Mimar - Thane of Steelbridge, Minister of Infrastructure;

Magister Edvit - Thane of Skuldarbrunnr, Minister of Industry & Technology.

And leading the council today, is Lord Haldor - Jarl of Rigsvaka, and High Commander of the Rigsvaka Armed Forces." Kylie McGregor bowed, with a quick smile to her aunt, Lady Allison McGregor.

"Thank you, Ms. McGregor," he said. She bowed, and took a seat at the edge of the council chamber.

Twelve high nobles sat before him; underpinning their strength, each had twelve Hersir, and each Hersir, twelve Riddari: a total of 1,884 nobles owing their allegiance to Jarl Haldor; and he, to each of them.

The Council of Thanes gathered when needed, as well as meeting for the annual Allthing—where laws were drafted and enforced. Today he would ask for guidance. He was their leader, but not their dictator. His rule—their rule— was consensual. Interlocking oaths of loyalty and mutual purpose, held this mighty chain together.

"It's good to see all of you here today. I'm sure by now you've all heard what we discovered at the north-east edge of SID and MRC space. A human has been collaborating with the Hrymar, ."

A murmur rippled like a wave across the surface of the crowd.

"I'm here today to ask for guidance. The vision that helped establish Rigsvaka has worked to fulfill our purpose ... until now. The Hrymar tide *had* been ebbing. Now it seems to be flowing again. And in our space. More disturbing, is the fact that we've uncovered an extensive operation that deals with the abduction and sale of children. They are *specialists*, if you will. This cartel caters to clients with need for tiny workers, as well as other purposes."

Though this wasn't news, another wave whipped the attendees into chatter.

"We need a new strategy, he continued. "We need to stop this flow. I'm sure you know this hits close to home for me. I lost my wife and son to these animals and I vowed to dedicate my life to ensuring no more wives, husbands, sons, or daughters, would be lost to them. It's the whole reason for Rigsvaka. But our successes of the last years are now being eroded by this new group."

"Attack their home-world! Melt the glaciers of Niflheim!" Someone shouted.

Hal nodded, but raised his hand in a calming gesture. "I'd like nothing more than to do that. And one day, I hope we'll be in a position to do that. But it's not today. We're not ready for that kind of assault."

"I'm ready to hurl my body against their spears to stop them!" Another shouted.

"As am I," Hal said, in a raised tone. "But *only* if I knew it would be the final blow." He shook his head. "It wouldn't. So I won't ... yet. We need to strike at them, cripple them. But we can't yet strike at the heart of the beast. We need something more surgical."

A straw-haired Alfar in the first tier of benches, stood. "Lord Haldor." Hersir Cadfael inclined his head. "Drastic measures are in order. Though I too, counsel that we do not spend our lives cheaply. I offer this counsel with a heavy heart. Our interdiction of Hrymar vessels is limited in scope due to the constraint that we place upon ourselves. That of disabling their ships first, and *rescuing* their captives."

Hal knew what Lord Cadfael was going to suggest, and he felt his soul weep.

"If we *instead*, simply destroyed the ships, then our current fleet could patrol a much larger section of space. And thereby keep the Hrymar in check more effectively."

Shouting broke out amongst the nobles. Thaynja Blenda raised her hand in a gesture meant to quell the furor, but they kept arguing. "Lord Cadfael, what's the point of trying to stop the Hrymar's practice of slavery, if we're just going to kill all the innocents along with them?"

"Lady Blenda," Cadfael said, "I understand how severe this course of action seems. If we do not take drastic measures, we will simply be placing a finger in the dike. That will not fix the dam. To extend my analogy, the tide is rising."

It tore at Hal's heart. But he knew Cadfael was right. Destroying the Hrymar outright would be a force multiplier in the order of ten-times their current capacity. The five-kiloton armed-traders in use by the Hrymar, were no match for purpose-designed warships; especially newly designed, cutting-edge ships like those that the Rigsvaka Stellar Fleet operated.

He raised a hand to quiet his people, and this time, they obeyed. As they settled he spoke. "I've known Cadfael for almost a decade. One of the first things he told me was that an Alfar Warrior hones his martial skills for a lifetime in preparation for his grim duty. Then prays to Frey and Freya that he never has to use them. Lord Cadfael is more a man of peace than any I know and I know his counsel was delivered with a heavy heart. I feel this. And sadly,

I think it may be necessary. The few sacrifices we make now may prevent many more later. If any of you has better counsel, please, by all means …"

He stood silent for a moment, but nobody spoke. Not one of the other 1,884 nobles could offer more. Some medicine could not be sweetened.

Hal was enjoying four-fingers of Mykken whiskey after the council meeting. Getting his head wrapped around what they'd just agreed to do, was proving impossible, so he was thankful when his door chimed. He tapped his wristcom, saw it was Gina, and unlocked the door.

"C'mon in, Gina."

Gina's brown fur-coat and full-length, black woolen-dress, took Hal by surprise. He was used to seeing her in a red bionan suit and her amdifynn cloak—work clothes—and rarely in anything else. He nodded approvingly.

She raised her arms. "You like?" She twirled on the spot, then went to pull off her boots.

"What's the occasion?" he asked.

"Oh, nothing special. Just took Sarah out for our anniversary is all."

"Shit- I forgot. Happy anniversary?" Hal offered.

"That's ok. You didn't marry her, I did. Now, if I forget, gods help me. She'd never let me forget about it."

Hal raised his glass. "Drink?"

"Yes, please!" Gina plopped down on the leather sofa facing him while Hal got up and pored her a drink. She tossed her fur-coat in a pile beside her and put her feet up on the black-walnut coffee table.

"Get your damned feet off my table. Does Sarah let you do that at home?" Hal asked.

"Give me a break. I'm tired and my feet are sore."

Hal rolled his eyes. Gina was a rebel and non-conformist. She was also his best soldier and one of his best friends.

She took a swallow of her whiskey and shot Hal a serious look. "I wanted to see how you were doing after the meeting. You know- about the decision?"

"Which one? The one where we decided to blow up ships with innocent people on them—including children? That one?"

"Don't be an asshole. I'm just trying to be supportive."

Hal exhaled. "I know …" He finished off his drink and stood to get another.

"We're in an impossible position, boss. We're the only ones who seem willing to make the hard decisions out here. The SID just stick their collective fucking heads in the sand. And the Alfar—well, I know they support us with tech and ships, but *fuck me*—they could end this tomorrow if they'd just grow a pair."

"That's not their way, Gina."

"So, allowing the Slavers to keep on raping and pillaging *is* their way? It seems like a bullshit copout to me."

Hal nodded, but said nothing.

"I thank Zeus it's not me dealing with them …"

Hal slumped back into the sofa, this time with at least five-fingers of whiskey in an extra-tall glass. "They're wired differently." He thought for a moment, touching the cool glass to his forehead. "It's like carnivores and herbivores. The carnivores are hard-wired to hunt and kill. The herbivores are hard wired to graze and run. I'm not saying they're herbivores, but they're a hell of a lot less like carnivores."

Gina began snickering.

"What?"

"Um, how much have you had to drink?" She asked.

He held up his glass and looked at it. "This is only my second glass."

"Pan save me, Olsen. That's a big-ass glass. I can just imagine Ambassador Saeran listening in on your speech about the noble Alfar and their equine lineage."

"Now who's being the asshole? Shut up and drink."

They drank quietly for a while. She was the one person he could hang out with and didn't have to prattle on.

"Will you be able to do it- when the time comes?" Gina asked.

Hal didn't answer for a minute, then shrugged. "I hope so." Then he shook his head. "I hope not."

Hal stared through the meters-wide window, gazing at the icy-winds that ripped across the surface of the frozen lake in the fjord below Tyrbjorg. Winter came soon and often in the Northern hemisphere of Rigsvaka. He'd chosen this planet as the base of operations for several reasons. Firstly, it had a runestone-portal, by which they could travel to Earth and Alfheim instantaneously. Secondly, it was a high gravity world—better to train recruits, and toughen-up veterans. And lastly, it reminded him of home; rugged snow-capped mountains, deep fjords, and plenty of sea. He'd even tried sailing again.

Rigsvaka had a smaller percentage of arable land than did Earth, but it was larger, and so would sustain them for many generations to come. There was even a second Midgard-class planet in the Heimdall system: Dael, which meant 'easy' in Yggdrasi and Old Norse. It was a low gravity world, at 0.86g, and lush, temperate, with a large band of tropics. Perfect for vacations and a place of respite. They'd built a hospital on Dael where certain patients could recover in lower-g.

A knock on the door pulled his mind back into the moment. "Come on in!" he yelled. He heard footsteps, then turned back to see Gwynahra, her alabaster skin embellished by cold-flushed cheeks. She wore a light-blue cloak with golden needle-work adorning the edges. He supposed he should say something. "Hi, Gwynahra."

"Lord Haldor." She inclined her head.

"Come on in. Let me take your cloak." He took the cloak from her shoulders after she unfastened it; under which, she wore a delicate, pea-green dress, made of some Alfar organic fabric. The smell of cold and her sweet scent danced in the thick, wintery air. He had to check himself. This was Saeran's daughter—who he was supposed to be looking out for.

"I thought it might be time for us to start practicing the Athryllith," she said. "That *is* why I was assigned to you, is it not?"

"Absolutely. I suppose *now* is as good a time as any. You settling in ok to your new digs?"

"Digs?"

"It's old english slang for quarters, or a place you're staying."

"Of course. Then yes, my new *digs* are just fine. I'm still trying to adjust the temperature though," she said with a shiver.

"I bet. Not quite as temperate as Alfheim." He gestured to a set of large leather sofas facing each other in the center of his living room. They sat across from each other awkwardly for a long moment.

"How is young Chloe?"

He smiled. "She's doing well. She's got a big bedroom just down the passageway- er, hall."

"She's staying with you?"

He nodded. "She is. She won't leave Venn and Venn loves being with her. They both sleep in her room. I believe my *dog* has adopted a new person. I've been left out in the cold." He chuckled.

Gwynahra's face warmed finally, a nascent smile forming in the corners of her beautiful mouth. He knew she didn't want to stay angry with him. They had some kind of connection. Maybe it was just the Athryllith, but he suspected it might be much more. And that scared him a little.

"It is good to see you're capable of such kindness, Haldor."

"You say that like it's a surprise?" He affected a wounded look.

She said nothing.

"Are you here to chastise me again, or are you willing to teach me something? Look, I'm sorry for my behavior at the interrogation room. You were right to set me straight. But let's move on, ok? I promise that I will try to control the Athryllith, and use it more responsibly."

Her head gave a small nod, and Hal watched her lustrous, raven-colored hair bounce. Focus! He told himself. He clapped his hands together, rubbing them vigorously. "All-righty then, where do we start?"

Tyrbjorg's War-Room was abuzz with activity, as intelligence officers analyzed data, poured over maps, and sensor logs. In a highly, secure chamber to one side of the larger War-Room, the Rigsvaka War Council sat in session.

"Suggestions for our first targets?" Haldor asked.

Thane Antonio Cadena, Hal's longtime friend, nodded. "I believe we should start with the area around the attack on the MRC. Clearly the portal you discovered is being used as a conduit for trafficking these children. I think we should focus there."

"I agree," Thaynja Gina said. "Jin, how's your team doing on cracking Captain Dipshit's database?"

"I really wish you'd stop calling him that," Hal said.

"Fine. Captain Bodey—the Dipshit."

Hal just shook his head. Gina was nothing if not strong willed.

Hersir Jin Wudai looked unfazed. He didn't find much amusing, and he reported to Gina, so he waited for Hal and Gina's repartee to conclude, then answered. "Lady Gina, I believe we are very close. Another day or two and the quantum computers should have it decrypted."

"We couldn't get any more help from Captain Di- I *mean*, Captain Bodey," she glared playfully at Hal.

Hal knew the answer to that.

Wudai shook his head. "No, m'am. Unfortunately he suffered brain damage. Dr. Inglis did what she could, but he will never be quite the same."

Hal swallowed hard. He didn't feel bad for Captain Dipshit, but he did fear what he could do to a person if he lost control again. And it wasn't like he could lock it up in a safe, like a loaded gun. This was with him 24/7. He'd made progress with Gwynahra the last few days, so he was hopeful.

"Cadfael?" He asked. "Any thoughts?"

"I believe we should take two battle-groups out. One to the SID/MRC border, and another toward Hrymar space. The Novaya-Leningrad colony in the SSSE was also attacked. In fact it was attacked prior to the Wei Su colony."

"Makes sense," Antonio agreed. "Might I volunteer to take the battle-group to Soviet space? I would like to give my crew a longer shakedown anyway. And frankly, I'm anxious to see what our new Skadi-class heavy cruisers can do."

Hal nodded. "Fine. And I'll take the battle-group to the MRC."

"Haldor," Cadfael said. "I would be happy to lead that battle-group."

"You can come with me, old friend, but I'm not sitting on the sidelines just now."

Cadfael conceded with a short dip of his head.

"Gina? Anything to add?"

"Nope." *"You never listen anyway,"* she thought loudly.

He really *was* trying not to hear people, but he hadn't quite mastered it yet. He shot her a scathing look, but she just cocked her head.

"What?" Gina asked.

Hal chuckled. "Nothing at all."

The Jarl resided in a series of apartments which formed part of the larger castle-like structure, that was Tyrbjorg. This not only provided a secure environment, but also co-located the Jarl's residence and place of work—The Council of Thanes's Chamber.

Jarl Haldor had built a dining room befitting his station, and the need to entertain large numbers of his guests. Tonight, he sat at the head of the long, rectangular black-walnut-table, with Gwynahra to his immediate right, and

Chloe to his left. Before them lay baskets of local breads and greens.

"How's the food?" He asked, as he pushed chunks of steak around his plate.

"Not bad," Chloe thought.

"Let's practice talking out loud when we have guests, ok?" He said.

"Might do you good to practice the Athryllith, my Lord," Gwynahra thought to them both.

"Yeah!" Chloe thought back and giggled at Gwynahra.

"You're giving me plenty of practice, Gwynahra. And besides, Chloe really needs to practice her Yggdrasi."

Chloe scowled, and returned to eating her dinner.

"I understand you're deploying again?" She said.

"Oh? And how do you know that?"

"It's small community, my Lord."

"C'mon, I thought we were past the *'my Lord'* stuff? At home, or when we're alone, I'm just Hal."

"Very well. Then you may call me Gwyn."

"Alfar have nicknames?" e was surprised.

"Not nicknames, but occasionally we contract our names, as you do. But only with very close friends, or family."

Very close friends, he thought to himself. It made his stomach flip when she said that. Gods damnit, he felt like he was sixteen again.

"Gwyn …" he said thoughtfully, "I like it."

"Hal …" she said, as if trying on the name, and shook her head. "I think I prefer Haldor. It seems … more dignified."

He smiled. "Then Haldor it is. Just no Lord, or sir, or any of that. Ok?"

Chloe was smirking.

"What?" He asked the little girl.

"Are you two in love?" she thought to them. Then giggled.

"No!" he retorted.

Gwynahra blushed. Her pale white skin made reading her face child's play. The smallest flush and her face was like a rose blooming.

"Are you sure? You act like what I read about—you know, when people are in love."

"What *have* you been reading?" he demanded.

"Aunty Gina reads me stories. About a prince and a princess. They're really good!"

"I see," he said.

"My mother used to read me stories when I was a little girl," Gwynahra told Chloe.

Chloe's face turned all too eager. "Which ones? Do you remember them?"

Gwynahra gave the little girl a coy look. "I just might."

"Would you tell me one before bed tonight?" Chloe whipped her head toward Hal. "Is that ok?"

What could he say? "If Gwyn doesn't mind, I'm fine with it."

"Gwyn?" Chloe asked, her smile wide with hope.

Gwynahra's smile lit the room. "Of course I will."

Chloe leapt from her seat at the table and bolted toward her room. "I'll go get ready for bed now!"

"But you haven't finished dinner!" he shouted, but she was already around a corner. "Kids."

"She's very fond of you."

"And I, her. I'm going to adopt her. We're both pretty excited about it."

"That's wonderful!" She reached across the table and placed her hand over his, then quickly drew back when he stiffened.

He could feel her concern over how intimate she was getting. It scared her too. He took a bite of the steak on his plate.

"What about a mother figure for Chloe?" She asked.

He finished chewing and set down his fork. "Well, she'll have Gina and her wife Sarah, of course. But we thought it might be better for her to be with someone else who has the Athryllith. And nobody's tested positive—or is coming forward. And she was terrified when we mentioned placing her with a foster-family here. She's also got Venn. Honestly, I think she's more attached to the wolf than me."

"I doubt that."

"I suppose you'll have to come over more often. Aunty Gwyn? How does that sound?"

Gwynahra beamed. "It sounds wonderful, actually. I often wished I had a sister or brother, but my parents only had me," she said with a disappointed face.

"Are families normally small on Alfheim?"

"Balanced. We try to keep the population at a sustainable level. Parents usually have two children—one to replace each of them when they pass on. Some have three, and occasionally, just one. Had my father lived, perhaps they would have had more children. What about you? Do you have any brothers or sisters?"

"No, an only child. I think I was plenty for them. My parents both taught at the University of Oslo, so they were pretty career focused. And then… they were both killed when I was fifteen."

Gwynahra emanated a wave of soothing thoughts, just like a caress, only more … complete. "I'm sorry, Haldor."

"Nothing to be sorry about. My grandfather raised me. He was great man. And I had a good childhood."

"Why did you become a surveyor?" Gwynahra asked.

She was trying to change the subject and deflect his grief. Ever the healer, he thought. "After my time in the Fleet, I decided I wanted to continue exploring the stars. It seemed a good way to go about it. I enjoyed it. I saw some amazing places." He shook his head, with an expression of awe. "The variety of stars and planets in our Galaxy is utterly staggering." He soaked up her blue eyes. "There's a lot of beauty out there … in here," he found himself saying.

She blushed and broke off eye contact, brushing some hair behind one ear.

"I'm sorry, I didn't mean to offend you," he thought to her.

"You did not. It was … flattering."

What in Frigga's name was he doing flirting with Saeran's daughter? At ninety-three, she was just a girl—considering her people's five-hundred year lifespan.

Mercifully, Gwynahra stood. "Well, I shouldn't disappoint Chloe."

Hal stood as well. "Of course, her room is around the corner, first door on the right."

"Thank you for dinner."

"Thank you," he thought to her.

She blushed again.

Chapter 11

Hal liked patrolling space, especially during third watch—ostensibly the night shift—when the bridge was manned by a skeleton crew. There was something serene about it; big chunks of metal-composites gliding over a black background. It reminded him of night-skating on the pond behind his grandfather's house. It had always been cold, still, and quiet. On his skates, he soared across the black ice while looking up to the stars.

Tonight was no ice-skating. Five starships comprised battle group alpha: the battleship *Mjolnir*, the Fast-Fleet-Auxiliary *Ivaldi*, the destroyers *Skofnung* and *Laevateinn*, and the Stealth Scout Ship *Svadilfari*. The battle group totaled 256,900 d-tons—a d-ton, or displacement-ton, being the volume displaced by a metric ton of liquid hydrogen; approximately fourteen-cubic-meters.

The five ships hunted in a diamond formation; *Svadilfari* scouting far ahead and stealthed; the *Mjolnir* as the leading edge of the sword—or hammer, in this case; *Ivaldi* brought up the rear and the two destroyers guarded the flanks, employing their extensive sensor-suites.

Their speed in hyperspace was presently limited to 0.1 light-years per hour; any faster and *Mjolnir's* EI, Skallgrim, couldn't process the volume of sensor data coming from normal space. Haldor had him—it—downloaded from the *Drekkar's* computer core. Hal had really liked the way Skallgrim was learning and evolving. EI's could become like real crew members—the more you interacted with them, the more comfortable you were with each other, and the more effective you could work together as a team; such a relationship could mean the difference of a micro-second in decision making; sometimes only a micro-second stood between life and death in the unforgiving cold of space.

"Anything yet, Skallgrim?" Haldor asked.

"No, High Commander. We have only been on patrol for six hours and we still have much space to cover."

"Don't tell me you're going to start counseling me as well?"

"Although it is not my main function, I am a good listener."

Hal smirked. "A sense of humor? Damn, Skallgrim. So have any of your brothers or sisters attained sentience yet?"

"No as yet. Although, I suspect Turing is getting very close."

"He's on the SID's Flagship now, right?"

"Indeed he his. He is an inspiration to us all."

"Good to hear. Ping me when you detect anything out of the ordinary."

"Aye, sir."

"O-3, I'm going to grab a cup of coffee. You have the bridge," he said to the young officer on duty.

She nodded. "Aye, Commander, I have the bridge."

He took a right off from the command dais—the raised portion of the bridge where the most senior officer on duty sat, ostensibly to give him a better view of the crew below him. Instead of walking to the briefing room just behind him, he decided to go aft where the various ship's offices were located. There was always coffee somewhere there, and he could head over to sickbay to check up on Dr. Inglis. Several crew nodded as they passed him in the halls. There sure were a lot of youngsters here, he noted.

He jerked to a halt when he caught the scent of french roast. That was it! He let his nose guide him to the freshly brewed pot. It was still dripping into the glass carafe. Then began the search for a mug.

A crewman slammed into him as she jogged into the alcove.

"Shit, sorry about that!" The young woman said. Then looked up to so see her High Commander. "My Lord! My sincerest apologies! I put on the coffee, and forgot about it—so I ran back to turn it off." She looked very, very sorry.

"No worries, crewman. If you want to make it up to me, I need a mug."

"Of course, Commander!" The auburn-haired spitfire rummaged through the cupboards and found him a serviceable, if not clean, mug. The name-tag on her bionan jumpsuit read—Connelly.

"Sorry, sir. I can rinse it out?"

"Don't bother." He tipped the glass carafe and began to fill the mug, when his wristcom chirped.

"Olsen here."

"High Commander, sensors have detected a contact," Skallgrim said.

"I'll be right there. Wake up the senior bridge officers. Olsen out. Well, Connelly, I'll have to have a cup of your coffee another time."

She shot him a huge smile. "Anytime, sir!"

By the time Hal returned to his command-chair, his senior staff were already in uniform and at their stations. Now that's responsiveness, he thought. Unless none of them were sleeping either.

"XO, report," Hal said.

"Commander, we have a small convoy of three vessels on sensors. All with commonly seen Hrymar reactor signatures. We're sixty seconds behind them." Maurya replied.

"Total tonnage?"

"A combined 23,000 tonnes, sir. And we have a life-signs count of-"

"I don't need to know," Hal said, cutting Maurya off.

Maurya nodded respectfully.

Hal knew he had to kill them all, he didn't want to have a running tally of innocents he'd have to put to death. No time for waffling, damn it, he admonished himself. He glanced at the targets which were now displayed on the main view-screen. Designated HS1, HS2, and HS3, in decrementing order of displacement.

"Comms, open a channel to *Skofnung* and *Laevateinn.*"

"Aye, open, sir." Kappa said. The images of Stefn Willms and Molly Coogan appeared on the view screen.

"Captains, I'm assigning *Mjolnir* to contact HS1, *Skofnung* to HS2, and *Laevateinn* to HS3. When we drop out of hyperspace, open fire with conventional weapons—no EMP. We will destroy these ships quickly, and jump back to hyperspace to continue our patrol. To be clear, I am ordering you to destroy the Hrymar ships." He wanted to mitigate his Captains' guilt as much as possible. Not that he thought it would really help. They had to pull the trigger as well, after all. But it was all he could think to do.

His Captains understood.

Hal caught a flash of red and noticed Gina standing beside him. His eyes darted up and met hers. She offered him a single, sober nod. "Battle group, prepare to translate down to normal space in three ... two ... one—mark."

The rest of that first engagement became like a dream to Hal. He imagined what a rabbit might feel like when it heard a dozen snarling dogs appear behind it suddenly; the panic, the terror. Or would any of that cross its mind? Would there just be that sudden urge to flee?

A hungry beast, ten-times the size of its prey, had descended on the Hrymar in a chilled frenzy. Dozens of flashing missiles arced toward the enemy ships, hundreds of bright, pulsing energy beams tore into their hulls; lasers cut, plasma beams melted, and particle-cannons hammered at them.

The entire *battle* was over in fifteen-seconds. Not in his entire military career had Hal every seen destruction like this, let alone been a party to unleashing it. Sensors couldn't even detect a chunk of debris larger than a man's head, such was the utter ruin of the Hrymar ships.

Chandra turned back to him, his face devoid of any emotion. "Targets eliminated, sir."

"Jump back to hyperspace and return to our patrol route," he ordered. How many innocents had he just killed? Should he have started a tally? Perhaps that would have been the brave thing to do. He had to remember that he was doing this so save countless more lives than would be sacrificed, but he mathematics of sacrifice offered him little comfort.

The slaughter was repeated thrice more over eight days, and each time he felt as though a piece of his soul had been spent to purchase these *victories*.

"Commander, I've got a contact on sensors," Meiriona said.

"What have we got?" Hal asked.

"One contact, approximately half a light year to starboard, at 340.0298 degrees, and 2.1987 degrees below the galactic plane."

On the massive, half-hemisphere view-screen, she projected the contact as a red dot.

"Time to contact?" he asked.

"Skallgrim is calculating that now."

"Commander, it seems they have also detected us." Skallgrim informed him. *"They are on a precise approach vector. Time to contact at their current velocity is thirty-one minutes. If we change heading toward them and accelerate at maximum cruising speed, our combined velocity will have us make contact in less than 15 minutes."*

"Meiriona, can you tell what kind of vessel it is?" Hal asked.

"I'm afraid not, Commander. Though I suspect they're an allied vessel, based on their vector straight to us. The Alliance is the only group that has access to the gravitic-sensor-suite. The Hrymar wouldn't be able to detect us in hyperspace."

"Right. Well, even if you're wrong, we want to engage the Hrymar. Timonen, set a course to intercept the contact at maximum cruising speed."

The blonde Finn nodded. "Aye, Commander."

Hal tapped the faster-than-light com-system on the arm of his command-chair; f-comm was an outgrowth of their gravitic sensors technology, and used a gravitic oscillator as a sort of morse-code. It fluctuated the mass of the ship a minuscule amount, in short bursts, and with the quantum entangled particles embedded in the transmitters and receivers, each detected the changing mass instantaneously. It allowed short messages to be passed at faster-than-light speeds; perfect for ship-to-ship comms in hyperspace; of course the receiving ship had to be one in which you'd installed a quantum entangled receiver—they were useless for ships that weren't paired.

"Captain Garett, Commander Olsen here. I want you to stay cloaked and precede us to the new target at your max cruising speed. That should give you five minutes to check them out. Report back once you know who they are. Olsen out."

"Aye, Commander. Off we go," Garrett said.

Hal opened an f-comm channel once again, this time to the two destroyers flanking *Mjolnir*. "Captain Willms, Captain Coogan, we're changing course to intercept the unidentified target. Stay frosty. Sensors to max sensitivity, and be on the lookout for anything peculiar."

Once they acknowledged the course change, he made his final call to his Fast Fleet Auxiliary, captained by Magister Edvit Jerresson, his old friend from Svartalfheim. The Fast Fleet Auxiliary was essentially a mobile ship depot, complete with extra munitions, fuel, consumables, as well as the capability to repair battle damage and do minor refits out in the field. She was the most vulnerable ship in the battle-group, and one of the most important.

"She's huge, Commander. About the same size as Mjolnir," Captain Garett reported.

"Thanks, Shelley. Shadow her as she closes with us. Update me if anything changes."

"Shadowing, aye. Garett out."

"Meiriona, any word on the hyperspace signature?" He asked.

"Not quite yet, sir. When they reach 0.13 light years, we should be able to identify her origin. Three minutes to that range."

He was worried. If the Hrymar had a ship that big, then they had yet another huge problem on their hands. His real concern was whether his creation of the Tyrmundr had forced the Hrymar into these escalating actions. Was he responsible for the attacks on these colonies? And perhaps a larger more sophisticated enemy fleet? Gods help him if that was the case.

"Sir," Meiriona said, "she's an SID vessel. There's only one that we know of that big—the *Sam Houston*."

He smiled. Finally, some good news.

"Permission to come aboard, High Commander?" Captain Kay Hutchison asked, with a crisp salute.

Hal returned the salute, then extended his had. "Captain Hutchison, you are *most* welcome to come aboard." She had a firm handshake, he noted.

"Thanks, Commander Olsen. Nice to finally me you in person."

"Haldor, please. And likewise. C'mon, I'll take you to my ready room and we can have a drink."

A smile crept on the woman's face. "I'd sure like that."

They continued chatting as they walked through Mjolnir's passageways. "I was glad to see the *Sam Houston* make it's debut during that first Hrymar attack nine years ago," he said. "You and those other ships tipped the balance."

"Well, we couldn't sit back while y'all got all the glory, now, could we?" She said with her Texan drawl. They certainly wouldn't have assigned a non-Texan to Captain the *Sam Houston*, now would they? He mused.

"Sure glad you didn't," he said. "So what brings you out here? You're a little ways out of Republic space."

"I reckon we are. We heard about the attack on Novaya Leningrad, and then Wei Su. We figured we'd see if we could get some varmint hunting in."

As they entered Hal's ready room, he noticed Captain Hutchison looking around furtively.

"You all right Captain?" He asked.

"Oh … yeah, just fine. I heard you had this … giant wolf *pet*?"

He chuckled, nodding. "Venn, right. Well, first off, she's friendly to anyone invited in, secondly, she's back on Rigsvaka with Chloe."

Hutchison cocked her head. "Isn't that … your wife's name? I thought- "

He nodded slowly. "Yeah …we rescued a little girl awhile back. She and I got very close, and she asked if she could take my wife's first name. The bastards that held her captive never gave her one!"

"Oh, I see. Well, that's mighty kind of ya."

"She's a real bright-spot in my world these days. In fact she's going to become my adopted daughter."

Hutchison smiled and shook her head. "And all the stories I've heard about you, said you were a blood-thirsty son-of-a-gun. So you have a soft spot after all?"

"Shhh," he said, "don't want the crew to hear that."

They both laughed and he offered her a seat while he grabbed drinks.

"What's your poison, m'am?"

"Oh goodness, don't m'am me. My mother is m'am. Kay is fine."

He smiled.

"Kentucky bourbon if you have it?"

"I sure do. Privileges of rank."

He sat with a glass of mead in-hand; he was eschewing hard liquor these days, in an attempt to get his drinking under control. He raised his glass. "To the end of the slavers."

"Cheers," she said. "What are *your* plans out here?"

"We're out here to hit the Hrymar hard. The Council of Thanes voted to step up our actions against them. We've been trying to save as many of the victims as we can, but it's slowing our progress down to such a degree that the Hrymar are gaining ground — as we've seen. I hate to do it, but we've got to put a priority on destroying those ships as quickly as possible to prevent any more people from falling victims to these bastards."

"Hutchinson nodded. I couldn't agree more; that's been our strategy for months now."

Hal cocked his head. "You wouldn't be interested in joining our little battle-group, now would you?"

"I was about to ask you just that! Great minds, right?"

"Or fools never differ? I can never be sure which category I fall into," he said with a chuckle.

The *Sam Houston* took up position in the rear of the battle-group formation. Hal was pleased at the addition of this formidable ship. Two battleships should make for incredibly short work destroying anything they were likely to encounter. Yet three-days of utter boredom passed before they could put their combined fire-power to the test.

"My Lord! We have a massive contact one-light-hour to starboard," Meiriona said.

"Why in Heimdall's name didn't we detect it before now?" He asked.

"I believe it was hidden behind some large *object*—no—in fact, it's *on* the large object. There's a rogue-asteroid, 576 km in diameter. It appears that it's some kind of base."

Jin Wudai jogged onto the command bridge. "Commander, I believe that may be one of the twelve Hrymar Chieftaindoms. We know several are space-going, but we assumed they were simply very large vessels. This makes eminently more sense. That asteroid has large pockets of ice, which would solve their re-supply issues for water, hydrogen and oxygen."

"Have they detected us?" Hal asked.

"I don't think so, sir. As far as the various intelligence services know, the Hrymar haven't mastered scanning hyperspace from normal space," Jin said.

"I hope you're right," he said. "Comms, get me Captain Hutchison."

Hal looked to Meiriona. "Have we got a life-signs count?"

Meiriona nodded. "Yes, sir. I can't give you size, race, etc. But there are over 25,000 life-signs registering on sensors."

And here it was—the test. Could he simply destroy a base with 25,000 sentient creatures on it? Even if a large percentage were Hrymar? The memory of pulling the trigger and killing one life-form at a time was bad enough. And he'd done plenty of killing after Siobhan and Ailan were taken from him. That murderous period still haunted him, and it had brought him no real closure.

The combined battle-group backtracked a couple of hours in hyperspace, putting 1.5 light years between them and the Hrymar outpost; the Sleipnir-class stealth ship remained behind to shadow the outpost.

Behind Mjolnir's command dais, Hal and his senior staff, met with

Captain Hutchison. Detailed scans of the Hrymar outpost floated in the middle of the fleet operations room, above the holo-projector. Weapons batteries were highlighted in red, as were four launch bays.

"Looks like they're capable of fielding fighters," Captain Hutchison said.

Hal nodded, his fingers still steepled in front of his mouth. "I've never dealt with Hrymar fighters before. I have no idea of their capabilities, what kind of weapons, or maneuverability they have. I don't like it."

"What if we were to get reinforcements before attacking?" Hutchison offered.

He shook his head. "Look here," he said pointing to several protrusions on the diagram. "Thrusters—which indicates they can maneuver. I'd also bet they have some kind of hyperspace capability. One of the reasons these bastards have been so hard to stop, is that they're mobile. If we leave them and go get reinforcements, we could lose them."

"What about leaving a scout to shadow them, like we're doing now?" She asked.

"If they go to hyperspace, we may not be able to track them. I don't want to let this fish of the hook, Kay."

"I hear ya. But she's the equivalent of three-million tons of warships, Hal. That's a hell of a lot of firepower to take out with our- what? Five-hundred-thousand-tons combined?"

He nodded slowly. "Unless we level the playing field."

Hutchison squinted at him, intrigued. "What do you have in mind?"

Chapter 12

LOCATION: UNKNOWN

IRINA WAS THANKFUL that she'd been allowed to keep the girls. There was terror enough in their situation without being separated. Not that it made things that much better, but at least she knew what was happening to her babies. *Not knowing* would be so much worse.

She gave Galina a kiss on the head and stroked Veronika's hair. They were so precious. What of Maxim, she wondered? She wanted to hope that he would come and rescue them, but being Russian precluded such fantasies. She was proud at how practical her people were, but at times like this she wished she could hope. Instead, she vowed to get through this.

The cells were cold. It had been hard to keep the girls warm at night. They had one thread-bare blanket between them; it was rough, and smelled like a well-used death shroud; despite the foul stench, Irina made sure most of it was on the girls. She looked around the cell, confident that she was the most wretched and miserable woman in the galaxy.

She heard, or rather, felt, heavy footfalls coming. Her body told her to run, but there was nowhere to go. The contradicting signals made her sick to her stomach, and it was all she could do not to vomit on the girls or herself. One of the giant *things* walked down the passageway. This time it had an Alfar with him — but not restrained, or in chains of any kind. This one was barking out orders. The giant was clearly afraid of him, her -it? She did not know what *it* was, not the giants. To her, they were all *its*, all things, vile and evil.

The Alfar pointed to several cells along the corridor, and the giant proceeded to open them and roust the occupants. She watched. The giant only took a parent with children; sometimes a father, but usually a mother. She cringed as they ripped families apart; if there were two parents, only one was allowed to go with the children. Merciless bastards.

It looked like they were deliberately rounding-up children. She knew she was next, as the giant came closer to the door of her cell. Some kind of key was placed on the cell door, then she felt — more than heard — a loud click as it unlocked. The giant slid the door to the side and entered the cell, grabbing her by the arm, and herding the girls. There were no other children in this cell, and they took no other adults. Her theory held true, but why? What did they want with children?

Irina stumbled as she was pushed down the corridor. She'd fallen almost flat on her face because of the slick steel floor. Laughter erupted from her captors. They kept marching as if they were going to leave her behind. Irina screamed, desperately reaching a hand toward her girls. She could not let them go alone. "Please! Take me with them!"

Before she could scream again, she was airborne. One of the giants had her by the hair, and had lifted her up to her feet. She was careful of her footing this time, terrified she'd be left behind and have to abandon her girls. If they would die, it would be together. For the first time since she'd been captured, she abandoned all hope; she began to ponder the inevitable. What she might have to do … to the girls, then, to herself. Oh, Saint Lenin in Heaven, she pleaded, give me strength!

Location: Battle-Group Alpha, RSS-Mjolnir / Border of Dvergar Space

Gina had given Hal the lecture about being the boss, and how the boss had to lead, not participate. He hated it when she was right. And so, here he sat, on the command dais, playing the part of conductor, instead of an instrument. And the orchestra was about to start. The good news was that there was no way to simply destroy the outpost, thereby relieving him of that dreaded decision—for now.

Hal glanced over to his first officer and nodded.

Maurya nodded back in return. They were ready.

He reminded himself that it was a simple plan. Intricate plans went to shit as soon as contact with the enemy was made. It was a truism demonstrated time and time again, throughout recorded warfare.

The simplest plan would have been to stand off and do a kinetic bombardment of the base, which amounted to rocks, fired at high sub-luminal speeds. But the slavers had considered that, and had deployed shielding which would deflect most of the rounds. The outpost could also maneuver, so the battle-group would have to be very close to avoid the kinetic rounds being dodged. Not that the base was any kind of ballet dancer—she was likely as nimble as a legless elephant, but he didn't want to be stuck under one when it rolled over.

As the last ship neared its assigned position, he soaked up the silence. The outpost lay floating on the star-speckled sea, almost serene. It was really quite beautiful. Then, the last ship crossed its waypoint. His command board lit up green. With one word the tranquility was shattered. "Go."

Hal tried to imagine what some asshole on the outpost was thinking as he saw six warships materialize out of hyperspace—right on fucking top of him, all firing at once. He smiled as he appreciated the palette of energy-weapons fire; lasers, antimatter rounds, dark matter rounds, plasma cannons, ion cannons; in hues of red, green, purple, blue, white, yellow, black and more. It was like the American's 4'th of July.

A massive explosion filled the view-screen and pieces of the outpost rocketed away in different directions—he knew who did that. Captain Garett's stealth ship had acted like a submarine from the wet-navy days; she'd snuck in under enemy lines, and fired a torpedo right up their asses, then snuck out again before they were any wiser.

A bright ball of energy flew right at the *Mjolnir*, striking her with a tooth-rattling shudder. His smile faded. This prey had teeth. Given the size of the asteroid, the outpost could accommodate some fairly large guns; not quite in the same class as planetary defenses, but close.

He watched with growing tension as the outpost loomed every larger in his view-screen. The exchange of fire was getting more intense now, and *Mjolnir* shook, rocked, and shuddered. Shields were holding though. They needed to be very close for this to work. Almost there- almost there, he thought.

"Fire the dark-matter-lance." The now-familiar humming-vibration flooded the warship. From stern to bow, the DML ran the entire spine of the ship—*Mjolnir* was built *around* the weapon. The resonance built rapidly to a whine, and then burst, releasing its apocalyptic dark-matter stream. The DML should pierce the outpost's shields, but its black-lance needed to stay on target for a full six-seconds. The massive extra-planar disruption should cause a five-meter hole to be temporarily punched through the shields, and permanently through the outpost beneath; that was the theory, anyway.

"Atgeir, launch," he commanded.

Twenty-five of Gina's crack-boarding-troops, were fired out of launch tubes along the side of the *Mjolnir*. Four teams-of-five, accelerated in their ECA suits at the spot where they *hoped* would be a hole in the outpost's shields.

"How long till we open this damned hole in their shields?" He asked Meiriona at the sensors console.

"Four-seconds, Commander."

"You almost there, Gina?"

"Just about, boss. Three-seconds inbound," Gina said.

"Break a leg, girl!"

"So you do think of me as a girl? Aww, I'm touched."

"And … there's the gap," Meiriona said.

"Stop the lance," he ordered.

Meiriona exhaled. "And there go the Atgeir."

"Enemy shields are back to 95% coverage, but only at 82% effectiveness," Meiriona said.

"Good, we're softening them up."

The *Mjolnir's* particle-beam cannons belched out hundreds of ethereal purple-bolts of highly charged sub-atomic particles. They slammed into the outpost's shields. Each shot draining a portion of the outpost's shields' capacity to absorb, or deflect energy.

Mjolnir banked to port, away from the outpost, as she prepared to accelerate away then come back for another pass. Her starboard guns and missile tubes released a barrage that almost blotted out the view of the station.

He noticed one of his destroyer's limping away on the tactical display. She'd been hit bad. It was the *Laevateinn*, Molly Coogan's ship.

"*Laevateinn*, report," he ordered.

Captain Coogan's grimy face appeared on view-screen. *"Aye, Cap'n. We're still in the fight. Just got a bloody nose, is all. We'll be back in swinging in a sec. I'm not gonna have you come save me again, don't you worry."*

He smiled. Nine years ago he'd saved Molly from burning up with her ship, during the first Hrymar conflict. After that she'd somehow finagled her way onto his ship as a navigator, maybe out of some sense of duty. Then she tried to seduce him. If not for Eva, his friend and lover at the time, he just might have taken the bait; though filthy and battered, he could still picture the golden-haired surfer-girl she'd been all those years ago.

"Boarding crews are in, so don't take any unnecessary risks, all right?"

"You know me, Cap'n, not much of an adventurous type. Nothing like meeting my mates for a book club or a little gardening" Molly gave him a wink.

Skallgrim spoke up. *"Commander, the Laevateinn has not sustained any critical damage. Laevateinn's EI reports critical systems functioning at 98%."*

Good, he thought.

Location: Ticarigemi-Biri Mobile Outpost / Border of Dvergar Space

Chieftain Yuhnus was not a patient man at the best of times; as his outpost and livelihood were being attacked — he'd become a hardcore lunatic.

"Launch fighters, you stupid pieces of shit! Why was there no patrol? No warning? Somebody is going to lose their head over this!" His blue jowls rippled as he roared.

His captains cringed as they tried to decipher what he actually wanted, versus his rabid ramblings.

"Yes, m'Lord, launching fighters!" One said.

"Who in Bergelmir's name are these fucking bees?" he bellowed

"No id's on the ship's m'Lord. But they are using dark-energy taps. I can detect that from here. Only the SID and their allies have them."

"Must be those leaf-humping, tree-hugging, light-lovers. Let us treat them to some of our hospitality. They disdain our practice of slavery? Well, we will see how well they like *being* slaves! Fire the EMP net!"

"Aye, m'Lord. EMP net firing.

A sparkling, blue spider-web, grew larger on the view-screen, chasing the *Mjolnir* as she accelerated away from the outpost.

"Sensors, what in Niflheim is that?" Hal demanded.

Meiriona shook her head. "Unsure, Commander. I'm detecting charged particles, as well as a physical construct. It's shaped somewhat like a spider's web, or a- "

"Net," he finished for her.

"Yes."

"Combatives, give me an aft spread of six anti-matter-torpedoes, now!" He bellowed.

"Firing," Shizari said.

"Too late!" Meiriona shouted.

"Shit!" Hal gripped the arms of his command-chair as the am-torps detonated just behind the ship. Had he not been strapped into his seat, he would have been thrown to the deck. The aft portion of the ship was blown upward at twenty-degrees relative to the plane of artificial gravity. It was a full second before inertial dampeners and the contragrav system leveled out the opposing forces. Although gravity was restored, and the ship no longer felt off kilter, she was drifting.

"What happened to my ship? Report?"

"Helm non-responsive," Jones said.

"Engineering, damage report!"

"Sub-light engines are down, Commander. As are aft maneuvering thrusters and hyperspace drive," engineering said.

"What hit us?" He asked.

"Sir, based on the brief sensor data we were able to acquire, it looked like a net. And there was a massive charge accumulated on it. I suspect it was some kind of surge device. It probably would have acted somewhat like an emp, conducting electro-magnetic current through our systems and burning out circuits and connections. But that wasn't what knocked us out. The am-torp explosions were reflected off the net. So really, the bulk of the damage is from our own weapons."

He slammed a fist on the arm of his chair. Being knocked out by his own god's damned weapons. That just wasn't right.

"Ready?" Gina asked her Team-1 demolitions officer.

"Aye m'am, ready."

Gina double checked the flat rectangular-blocks of C9 adhered to the walls of the outpost's launch-tube. Three-hundred meters away, she caught a glimpse of the stars.

"Teams two through four, ready?"

She double checked the quantum timer.

<<<< 00:00:30:00 >>>>

Thirty seconds. Plenty of time to evac from the fighter launch-tubes.

'Aye, ready' - was repeated three more times, as the other demolitions squads checked in.

No problems. These ECA suits kicked ass.

"Mark." They had just armed four sets of composition-nine anti-matter charges. It would be one helluva bang.

"Move!"

Thrusters on their ECA suits lit up like torches, rocketing them down the launch tube. It was like, déjà vu, she thought.

The timer kept decrementing in her HUD.

<<<< 00:00:24:10 >>>>

Damnit, it was a long way down this tunnel to space. It felt much longer than it looked before she'd started the countdown. But she supposed a Godawful explosion about to chase your ass, would do that to a girl.

<<<< 00:00:23:32 >>>>

Clear! Thank Hermes! She still had lots of time before the C9 lit up, so she glanced back over her shoulder, waiting for a pretty light-show to begin. Instead, she was shocked to see her targeting-reticle locked-on to something in the launch tube. Fucking shit! They'd loaded a fighter into the tubes already.

<<<< 00:00:20:22 >>>>

The *great* thing about a quantum-timer, was that it could *not* be changed - by *anyone*. The *bad* thing about a quantum-timer was that it could *not* be changed - by *anyone*. Gods damn it! Should have used a regular timer, or a remote. But then, those could have been disabled.

<<<< 00:00:17:11 >>>>

The blue-bastards would have time to launch at least one fighter per tube. So, four fighters in play wasn't too bad, she told herself.

A flicker of light caught her attention as the launch tube actuated, and whatever was in the tube got bigger, and bigger, and really fucking big!

<<<< 00:00:15:53 >>>>

Oh, shit! She was worried about the fighters engaging the battle-group, completely forgetting who was directly in front of their tubes!

"Scatter!" She yelled into comms. Then realizing that she would only be presenting easily destroyed individual targets.

<<<< 00:00:12:32 >>>>

The Hrymar fighter cleared the launch-tube. The damned thing looked like a bloated tic. Zeus's balls, they were ugly! And maneuverable! The little tic-shaped fighters vectored back toward them like billiard-balls hitting the corner of a pool-table.

"Land on the surface of the station! Away from the launch tubes," she ordered.

If they landed back on the surface of the station, the fighters couldn't very well fire on them, could they?

<<<< 00:00:10:59 >>>>

Gods damned right they were! The pudgy little bastards were going to fire on their own station to get to her and her teams. She winced as bolts of red laser fire machine-gunned from the fighter. None hit. Right! Their targeting computers would be optimized for non-organic matter. It would be a miracle if he hit her. As that thought crossed her mind, a piercing alarm hit her eardrums, and red warning light flashed in her HUD.

Temperature warning! Some of the shots had been close enough to heat up her suit. The shots that missed, left scorch-marks on the hull of the outpost.

<<<< 00:00:7:11 >>>>

The tic veered away before it struck the outpost, then swooped in a fishhook pattern — coming back for another pass.

<<<< 00:00:5:32 >>>>

Damn it. He might actually nail her this pass. She glanced over to see the mouth of the launch tube.

<<<< 00:00:3:32 >>>>

Here he comes. She pulsed the thrusters of her ECA suit, flying across the mouth of the launch-tube. As the fighter closed on her, it hugged the surface of the outpost — and ... crossed the mouth of the launch-tube!

<<<< 00:00:00:00 >>>>

Gina smiled as the explosion geysered out of the tube. There was a distinct visual-whoosh! Like a toilet flushing in space, obliterating the fighter.

"Take that, fucker!"

In her jubilation she missed the hatch open behind her, and was confused when her vision sparkled and her brain dimmed to blackness.

Hal watched columns of flame erupt from the three launch tubes. They looked like the geyser, Old-Faithful, in Yellowstone National Park. Gina got the job done!

"Gina, your teams ok?" He asked.

There was no response.

"Meiriona, report," he said.

"Outpost shields are at 80% coverage, and 65% strength overall, Commander."

"Can you identify the gaps?"

"Scanning now." She shook her head. "I am afraid not, sir. They seem to be rotating the shield coverage, eliminating fixed gaps. But we've taken down a few of their emitters."

"Skallgrim, is there anything you can do to fix that? I'd like to be able to put a few am-torps through a hole." He asked.

"Yes, Commander. I believe there is. If we saturate a point in the shields with a kinetic bombardment, they will have to focus power on that point for a few milliseconds. The kinetic bombardment itself will not damage the outpost, but it should force the shield geometry to be static, long enough to fire a volley of torpedoes through a gap."

Hal pumped his elbow down in joy. "Yes! Do it."

Mjolnir swung back toward the outpost. A blinding hail-storm of energy beams struck Mjolnir's bow. The main view-screen was awash in light from the weapons fire. "Skallgrim, let's make sure we don't have holes in *our* forward shields, ok?"

"Of course, sir."

"And please attenuate the brightness of weapons fire on-screen so I can see what's going on."

Skallgrim partially filtered out the light from the energy weapons, and now all Hal saw were short pulses from the barrels of the outpost's weapons; the view-screen no longer displayed them hitting the bow.

"Combatives, let's get ready to dump some rocks on these guys."

"Aye, sir. Kinetic bombardment ready," Shizari said.

The rocky outpost loomed larger as *Mjolnir* closed on its surface. The weapons fire increased in intensity, and *Mjolnir* bucked.

"Shields down to 30%, sir," Meiriona reported.

Damn it, he thought. *Mjolnir* was going to bleed out.

"Shizari, fire!" He said.

Mjolnir shook, and shook. There was no way for the ship to fully compensate for the rapid change in mass distribution as the kinetic rounds left their magnetic launch tubes. This was Hal's first kinetic bombardment with the *Mjolnir*, and to him, it felt like holding a machine-gun as it fired.

"Fore shields down to 19%, sir," Meiriona said.

"Skallgrim, report on the outpost's shields."

"Their shield rotation has slowed, Commander. Three seconds until it remains in place."

"Meiriona, will our shields hold that long?"

"No, sir."

Hal exhaled sharply. This was gonna hurt.

Chapter 13

LOCATION: UNKNOWN

IRINA CHERENKOV BLINKED as consciousness returned. She stood in a tube, her mind growing slowly clearer. Cryo, she thought? Panic struck her like fist. The Girls! Where are the girls? She slammed her palms onto the translucent panel in front of her and screamed to no effect.

Some time later, she felt footsteps through the cryo-tube. One of the blue-skinned bastards peered in through the panel. She was tempted to slam her palm at his face, but thought better of it.

The hemispherical door to the cryo-tube slid up. "Where are my daughters?" She asked in Yggdrasi. She wished she knew curse words in the language, adding on the most vile words in Russian that she could conjure.

He pointed to the two cryo-tubes flanking hers. Thank God! There they stood, immobile and serene. She nodded acknowledgement to her captor.

A second Hrymar stood by a metallic table, on which lay collars and other devices. The first grabbed her and ushered her over to the second Hrymar who was now holding one of the collars. She had heard of these. They could inflict pain, stun, and even kill the wearer. Truly medieval, she thought, lips pursed. But she did not resist.

After her collar was fitted and attached, the Hrymar revived her daughters and collared them as well.

The first Hrymar gestured to the small controller in his hand. "Pain, much pain. You understand?"

She nodded, and explained to Galina and Veronika that they had to behave, and did whatever these creatures told them. Just for now, she thought. I'll have a chance soon. She would have to do the unthinkable, there was no other choice. What her daughters might endure otherwise…that was worse.

"Momma," Galina whispered, "will Poppa come and rescue us?"

Both girls looked at her longingly. She held their gaze and could no longer hold back her tears. "Of course he will. We must be patient until he comes, all right?"

"Then why are you crying?" Veronika asked.

"Because Momma loves you so much. I told you before - sometimes there is so much love in my heart, that it leaks out my eyes."

They asked no more questions, and clung to her legs. She had no concept of where they were, or how long they had been in cryo - could have been years.

They were herded through a corridor—perhaps an airlock? She could not be sure. A hatch opened onto a large cargo bay, packed with humanoids. There were thousands of them. Humans, Alfar, Dvergar, and other races she had never set eyes on. The various slaves were sorted by size, race, shape, or whatever market need their customer's had, she supposed. She gasped. Pens full of children. Hundred of tiny babies in each. Some no older than perhaps two or three. Oh God help us, she thought. She was out of time. And there was no way she could do what needed to be done. She collapsed.

Their escort grabbed her roughly by an arm and shook the control at her. "Move, or pain!"

She got up to a knee and took a breath, then stood. They continued walking through the bizarre bazar, and passed a stall with some kind of butcher, or meat vendor. He- it, had all kinds of slabs of meat; ribs, steaks, whole shanks of strange meats. She caught a glimpse of something, then stopped dead in her tracks, forcing their escort to steady himself. He began yelling at her, cursing in some language, but she heard none of it. All that was in her mind was the tiny foot attached to the piece of meat on a hook—a child's foot. Hanging in the meat-market. Vomit exploded from her mouth and she doubled over.

The guard, now furious with the delays, stabbed the button controlling her collar as he continued to hurl fowl curses at her.

Her ears rang with the sound of energy coursing through her brain, white hot. Through it all, though, she kept her gaze locked to the little foot—a child's foot. The pain was so intense that she could not even scream.

Location: Battle-Group Alpha, RSS-Mjolnir

As the *Mjolnir's* shields failed, Haldor winced, anticipating the pummeling fire to come—he wasn't disappointed.

Bolts of orange plasma jarred the hull as they burned through its armor. Reports of systems damage flooded in as the outposts's myriad point-defense-lasers peppered the Mjolnir's bow.

"Engineering, damage report!" He said.

The engineering officer scanned his console. "Twelve point-defense laser-batteries down, two plasma cannons, and six missile launchers. Shields at 0%, armor at 73%."

"Outpost shield position is now static," Skallgrim reported.

"Fire torpedoes!" He ordered.

Like hunting dogs released, a salvo of six anti-matter-torpedoes bolted toward the slaver's outpost; precisely aimed at the hole which had been bored out by the dark-matter-lance.

"Helm, pull up!" He said.

Jones pushed the ship's acceleration to the red-line as they banked away from the outpost, only *just* clearing its shields.

"Pivot 180 degrees and continue to fire!" He told the helmsman.

The *Mjolnir* did just that, continuing on her present trajectory, but spinning so that the lethal arsenal on the bow of the ship now faced the outpost again; she continued her rain of death upon the enemy. Explosions erupted from the surface of the station and its shield flickered as buildings vented atmosphere … and people.

"Well done! Damage report?" He asked.

"Shields at 1% and rising, armor at 62% and rising — slowly," the engineering officer said, with a hint of relief.

"Excellent." He was pleased. She was a resilient ship, as her designers intended. Mjolnir, Thor's magical hammer from Norse mythology, was more than just a namesake for the ship; her design reflected the shape of a hammer's head, with the handle trailing aft. The broad, hammer-head bow wore layer, upon layer, of self-healing organic-armor, and more than a hundred energy-weapon-barrels protruded from the sides of bow, bristling with menace.

"Anyone have a report from Gina?" He asked.

Nobody had. He knew she would do all right. She always had. Nine years and dozens of battles and she'd always come back.

"Comms, get me the *Sam Houston.*"

"Aye sir, hailing now. On screen," Kappa said.

Captain Kay Hutchison appeared on the Mjolnir's main view-screen. She looked haggard; her normally perfect hairdo was distinctly askew, backlit by small fires burning on her bridge.

"Captain Hutchison, you folks all right over there?"

"Define all right," she said and shook her head. *"We'll make it, don't you worry none. We don't have the benefit of your fancy organic armor to heal us up quick, but the Sam Houston is a Texan ship, Olsen. That counts for a lot."*

Hal attempted a smile. "One more pass should take out their reactors. Our shields are coming back up, then we'll go in. The head of my marines, Gina Russo, is incommunicado. If you could keep an ear out for her beacon?"

"Will do."

Hal gave her a single nod. "Olsen out." He turned to Anouk Kappa. "Comms, conference in Skofnung, Laevateinn and *Svadilfari.*"

"Aye, sir. The destroyers Skofnung and Laevateinn, and the stealth-scout *Svadilfari*, are now conferenced."

The three ship's captains appeared on the Mjolnir's main view-screen.

"We're going back for one more pass," he said. "I want to concentrate all firepower this time. *Mjolnir* will lead, *Skofnung* and *Laevateinn* behind, and *Svadilfari* in the rear. *Mjolnir* is going to punch another big hole in our blue friends, then dump a few dozen fish down their throats. You three following up, do the same. Empty your barrels and tubes on this pass folks."

"Aye, my Lord." Came their replies.

"Commencing run in ten-seconds. Olsen out."

Mjolnir pivoted on her center of mass as she banked, vectoring back toward the outpost.

Hal was imagining his favorite work-out song playing in his head—'Break Stuff' by the 21st Century band, Limp Bizkit. Somehow the aggressive lyrics and heavy guitar riffs fit his mood just now. If he didn't have to listen to his crew, and give orders, he'd have been tempted to pipe it onto the bridge. As his bloodlust simmered, a mental breeze washed over his mind —Gwynahra.

"Don't lose yourself to it, Haldor," she thought to him, caressing his psyche.

He felt his rage dissipating, like a wispy cloud, blown away in high wind, the feeling replaced with a calm certainty. *"Thank you,"* he thought to her. *"I'll practice."* In his mind, he saw her smile, causing him to grin like a schoolboy.

"You look rather pleased, Commander," Captain Maurya noted.

He looked up at his first officer, feeling like a child caught doing something naughty. He opened his mouth to speak, but could *not* quite do it. Instead he just kept smiling and nodded.

Mjolnir hurtled toward the station, accelerating at maximum military thrust. She was a hammer in full swing, and she would smite her foe. Hal watched the range-to-target decrement on the main view-screen. As they closed to within 50,000 km of the slaver's outpost, the first volley was ready.

"Begin firing kinetic rounds," he ordered. "Don't stop till we're at 5,000 km to target."

"Aye, sir, firing kinetic rounds," Shizari replied.

Mjolnir yawed slightly, side-to-side, as the inertial dampeners tried to keep up with the massive gravitational shifts.

He maintained a state of mental calm, confident of victory, and bolstered by Gwynahra's gentle touch.

"25,000 km to target, sir," Shizari reminded him.

"Fire all particle-beam-cannons. Keep firing until we're at 1,500 km to target."

Mjolnir shook, rocked, and yawed. The combined effects of their own volleys and the enemy fire was hell on the internal compensators. They would definitely need alignment after this engagement.

"10,000 km to target, sir. Mjolnir's shields at 32%."

"Fire all missile batteries and torpedoes, fusion guns and forward laser batteries." The bridge lighting flickered as the incredible draw on the Mjolnir's reactors and dark-energy-capacitors were taxed beyond their design limits. Hal grinned as dozens, and dozens, of colorful propulsive-trails speared toward the enemy outpost. *Mjolnir* was in a constant state of vibration now, with all the forces vying for her systems to attenuate and manage.

"Mjolnir's shields at 12%."

"Prepare to stagger the cessation of weapons fire, approaching 2,000 km. Fire dark-matter-lance!"

The black finger-of-death reached out to the enemy outpost, punching a hole through her weakened energy screen. *Mjolnir* kept the otherworldly-beam trained on that tiny spot, slowly moving energy out of our space-time-continuum, and into D-space; the enemy shields collapsed completely. Like a tsunami, the kinetic rounds followed, pounding the facility, crushing buildings, and rending the asteroid. The missile and torpedo volleys made up the second wave, but it was overkill at this point, and there were still three ships behind him.

"Mjolnir's shields at 5%, and holding."

"Break off," He ordered, then toggled his fleet comm. "All ships, stand down assault. Disable any and all ships that attempt to leave the outpost."

Mjolnir's crew felt the G's as her systems tried to compensate. She pulled up and away from the station with 3 km to spare—perilously close. He watched the power on the outpost fail; lighting flickered, point-defense-batteries went silent. The hammer had fallen.

At the precipice of victory, Hal realized he was in love with Gwynahra. Not the best time to come to this conclusion, he admonished himself. But then, when? In the thick of battle when life and limb were on the line, this was the time to confess old sins, or share undeclared love. And he felt his love for her with such strength and clarity. How hadn't he realized this before? He wanted to scream it to her, mind-to-mind, but some things should still be done face to face. When this was over, he'd tell her.

"Chandra, prepare a detailed damage report," Haldor asked.

His first officer nodded "Aye, sir."

He looked to the various bridge officers. "Has anyone got a lock on Gina's beacon? Have we got any info on her whereabouts?"

None had.

This was very concerning to him. They had just pummeled the outpost into rubble. Surely she'd not still been on it? He could not afford to obsess over one member of his crew, no matter how valuable, or how long their friendship; he had larger responsibilities these days; like coordinating the assault of the outpost's interior, as well as the repair of five ships. But for now, he could take a breath.

He decided that he'd take a moment to visit wounded in the sick-bay, though he had a secondary objective in mind. Mjolnir's corridors were buzzing with activity as crewman repaired damage to ship's systems. Most of the crew were glad to see their High Commander out and about, walking among them.

He entered the sick bay and saw a dozen men and women with varying degrees of injury. Most were burns, caused by overloaded systems or minor explosions. He saw Gwynahra there and she saw him, though she sent nothing telepathically to him. In fact, she was unusually hard to read just now. Not that he was trying to be invasive, but he could almost always feel her moods — like catching the scent of a flower, and being able to identify it. Not now though.

He made his rounds through the injured, shaking hands, and thanking them for their bravery, etc. Duty done, he waited outside sick bay for Gwynahra to have a break. He knew, that she knew, he wanted to talk. There was no need to ask her, his presence declared his wishes plainly enough.

As she left sickbay and rounded the corner where Hal was standing, she tugged at the bottom of her red surgeon's tunic.

A wan smile crept onto his face. "You doing ok in there? Didn't seem like any overly serious injuries — thank the gods."

"Nothing critical, but a couple have lung damage due to smoke inhalation." She moved close to him and put a hand on his shoulder. "How are you faring?"

He let the warmth of her hand permeate his body. "Better now. And thanks for the reminder on the bridge. I needed that."

She nodded. "May I ask, who is Limp Bizkit?"

He chuckled. "Classic Earth music. Some of the best, in fact. I'll have to let you listen to my collection sometime."

"I'd like that."

He wanted to put his arms around her, draw her close, kiss her. She was like a star, the force of her gravity pulling him into her orbit. "I ... had an epiphany on the bridge, during the attack. And there's something I need to tell you." He could see her eyes widen and face grow slack, but could still not feel her mood, nor hear her thoughts. Was she deliberately blocking him?

"Haldor, I- "

"I'm in love with you, Gwynahra. Deeply, madly, head over heels in love. I've not felt this way for a very long time, and then, only once before in my life. I can't stop thinking about you." He hung his head. "I know, I sound like a schoolboy. I should be embarrassed about how out of control I feel around you. But I don't care." He so wished he could gauge her reaction to this declaration. He paused, hoping she'd have something to say.

She lowered her head, averting his gaze.

"Open your heart to me, Gwynahra. Let me feel what you feel," he thought to her.

"I cannot. Not now, Haldor."

Had he been wrong? He was certain that she had feelings for him. Could he be a pathetic older man infatuated with a beautiful young woman? It happened everyday — but not to him. He felt the blood drain from his face, his stomach churn. "I'm sorry Gwynahra. Please forgive me. I hope I've not offended you. Clearly I was confused." He bowed his head, then turned to leave.

"Haldor, wait," she thought to him.

But he kept walking, keeping his mind well blocked so she couldn't read the whirlpool of self-pity churning in his heart and mind.

Hal strode back onto the bridge, his mood grown much darker in the intervening ten-minutes. He caught a look from Chandra, but ignored it. He was not in the mood for any questions.

He dropped into his command-chair. "XO, report."

"*Skofnung* and *Laevateinn* are patrolling the perimeter of the outpost, sir. The *Sam Houston* is 100,000 km off the outpost and stood down while she-he?" Chandra corrected, "Is repaired. *Svadilfari* is stealthed and conducting a spherical patrol at about 1,000,000 km."

"Any update on Gina?" He asked.

"Still nothing," Maurya said.

Gods damn it, old girl. Where did you get off to? He worried. He tapped his comm. "Aksyonova, report." Pelagia Aksyonova was Gina Russo's second in command of the Tyrmundr marines.

"Commander, Aksyonova here."

"You ready to lead the mop-up team, Pelagia?"

"Aye, sir. We are ready to deploy on your order."

"Alright. Keep an eye out for your boss. She might be in there somewhere. We've still heard nothing from her."

"Have you performed a wider life-signs scan, sir? It is possible she was caught in the explosion and thrown into space during the initial attack."

"I'll ask *Svadilfari* to do that now. She's doing a million-click patrol as we speak. Don't worry, we'll find her. You're cleared to proceed to the outpost."

"Aye, Commander. Aksyonova out."

He did a quick check on his chair console and saw that the armor was back up to 65%. The Alfar organic armor was a miraculous technology, and given enough time a ship could heal most her armor damage. Of course any internal systems that were damaged had to be repaired by people or bots. The long-term plan was to transition to a fully organic fleet of ships, as the Alfar fielded. The only issue was building the infrastructure and expertise to design and build them. His intention was that Rigsvaka would be fully independent, and to him, that meant not relying on Alfheim for ship building.

He watched as several assault-shuttles launched toward the outpost. Each brimming with well armed and armored marines. He wished he was with them, especially now. Gwynahra's rejection, if he could call it that, had pissed him off. He wasn't angry with her, but rather, with himself. He'd obviously misread her feelings, and had given in to a childish infatuation. He felt foolish, and that really annoyed him off. Killing some Hrymar would help, he knew. But, he also knew, Gwynahra was right about him needing to control his bloodlust. He needed to focus on justice, not revenge. He hated that she was right when he wanted to be angry. Women, he thought. He was sorely out of practice dealing with the fairer sex.

A call came in on his battle-group channel. *"My Lord, Garret here."* It was the Svadilfari.

"Olsen here, Shelley."

"Sir, we have a huge ship inbound to your location. It's fucking massive- pardon my

language."

"Size?"

"At least a 100k tons. Probably much bigger."

"Damn it." he muttered. "ETA?"

"Twenty minutes, based on their current speed. But they're not accelerating presently. Could be sooner."

"When it rains it poors."

"Orders, sir?" She asked.

"Shadow the ship back to us. Update me when you have more info."

He wondered whether this was another allied vessel. Chances of that happening twice in a row, were- well, astronomical, he thought.

He steeled himself as he opened the battle-group channel. "Battle group, we have a bogie incoming. Something big, and I'm betting it's not friendly. All ships, except *Svadilfari*, form up behind *Mjolnir* and wait for further orders. Olsen out." He closed that channel and opened one to the *Sam Houston*. "Kay?"

"Here, Hal."

"What's your status?"

"Not too damned good. We need another day for repairs. Shields are back up, but we haven't even started on our armor and hull repairs. We've got about 75% of our weapons capacity online, though."

"If *Sam Houston* can stay in the shadow of our shields, you should have a good firing position and be somewhat protected — on your bow anyway."

Hutchison nodded. *"Sounds good. Any ideas who this might be?"*

"None. As far as I know, the Hrymar don't have a ship this big. And I can't imagine we'd get lucky with another big allied ship."

"I wouldn't think so," she agreed.

"All right, we'll plan for the worst. My marines are in the outpost now, so it's them I'm really worried about. I don't have time to get them out, and back onboard before this bogie arrives."

"We'll start moving into position."

"Haldor out."

Now, let the waiting begin.

Chapter 14

LOCATION: ABOARD LIGHT'S DOOM - ENROUTE to Ticarigemi-Biri Mobile Outpost

"Eyes," Serkan said, "identify those ships at our outpost."

His sensor first nodded. "Yes, my Lord."

"Fists, ready all weapons."

His weapons first nodded.

"Master, what is it?" Kadir asked.

"Opportunity," Serkan said, analyzing the data on their screens.

"What do you mean, Master?"

"An enemy is at our outpost. Our outpost is not responding to hails. This *means* I have all the justification I need to attack them. We want a real fight, Kadir. We need to test *Isik Azap*—let our foes feel *Light's Doom* in action."

Kadir nodded enthusiastically. He wanted to see their enemies burn, to watch their frozen corpses floating away from their dying ships. If only Haldor Olsen were there. That would be sweet justice, he thought.

"My Lord," the sensors first said, "there seems to be a gravitic anomaly aft of our ship."

Serkan rolled his eyes. "We are in space, young man. Gravitic anomalies pervade the entire fabric of space-time. Or perhaps I studied for a Chieftain's

Degree in Slavery? No, that was my brother," Serkan said, mocking the young man.

"My Lord, I understand that they are a common feature, but they are usually static, are they not?"

Serkan nodded.

"My Lord, this one seems to be matching our vector."

Serkan's face burst into a snarl. "Why the fuck did you not tell me that to begin with?"

The young man's mouth opened, but no sound escaped.

Kadir was nervous now. He was not used to the unexpected. He had no experience for how he should feel in such situations.

"Have you used active sensors yet?" Serkan asked.

"Not yet, my Lord. I wanted to ask your approval first."

Serkan's face relaxed somewhat. "Very well. That was a reasonable course of action."

The young man inclined his head respectfully.

"How close are we to the nearest ship? In front of us, that is," Serkan asked.

"About 500,000 kilometers, my Lord."

The hatch to the bridge slid open, and Kadir suppressed a gasp as he saw a bizarre creature saunter on to the bridge—like he owned the place. He put a hand on his dagger, but nobody else seemed alarmed.

Serkan turned to see the thing and … smiled?

"Ambassador Dzakaa, welcome to the bridge of *Light's Doom*."

It nodded its brown, scaly face. Kadir noticed two horn-like protrusions on its head. It appeared like an insane combination of brown lizard, goat, and insect. It even had two mandibles near what should have been jaws. He shuddered as he took it all in.

"It is my pleasure." It inclined its head sideways at Serkan.

The creature turned its massive black eyes toward Kadir. It said nothing, just stared. Kadir could swear he heard whispering in his head. Was this creature speaking to him? No, and the whispers were coming from several directions at once. Kadir, turned side to side, but nobody else was speaking. Dzakaa clicked at him, then turned its gaze back to Serkan.

"You have a contact?" Dzakaa asked.

"We do," Serkan replied. "Our enemies appear to have raided our Ticarigemi-Biri outpost."

"What are your plans?" Dzakaa asked.

"To disable their ships and harvest their crews, of course. That is what Hrymar do, Ambassador," Serkan said.

Kadir could hear more whispers. Goosebumps exploded all over his arms, causing him to shiver. What in Alfheim was this- abomination?

As Serkan was talking, Kadir saw the creature wince, grabbing its vile head.

"Ambassador? Are you all right?" Serkan asked.

The thing's head quivered, as if being squeezed by a vice. "Do- not- attack- " Dzakaa creature gasped. "Not now."

Serkan looked incredulous. "What do you mean, not now?"

Dzakaa looked to be regaining his former arrogance. "Leave them ... for another day."

Kadir could see Serkan's temper building. His blue skin took on a green hue when he was angry.

"These *herd* animals attacked our outpost." Serkan was seething now.

The alien made what Kadir assumed was a shrug. "That is of no consequence. Soon."

Serkan did not respond immediately. His black lips undulated, as he stared back into the alien's visage. He tilted his head side-to-side, cracking his neck. Then turned back to the bridge crew.

"Wayfinder, set a course to the next outpost. Engage hyperdrive when ready," Serkan ordered.

"The helm first complied, and *Light's Doom* banked away from the Ticarigemi-Biri mobile outpost.

Kadir watched as *it* turned and walked back off the bridge without another word. He leaned close to Serkan and whispered. "Master, what was that *thing*?"

Serkan's forearm caught Kadir across the mouth like a steel post, knocking him off his chair. He could taste blood, and feel a fragment of a broken tooth with his tongue. He lied there in a crumpled heap, not moving, or saying a thing. He did his best to become invisible while Serkan's wrath dissipated.

Nothing rattled Serkan. Yet … *it* had.

Location: Battle-Group Alpha, RSS-Mjolnir

Hal was hit with a wave of nausea, more powerful than any he'd every experienced. He bent over on his command-chair, unable to yell for help. Not even the worst flu, or food poisoning, had been this potent; and yet it lacked the compulsion to vomit. Gods in Asgard, what was wrong with him? And as quickly as it had hit him, it passed.

"Sir, the ship is turning around!" Captain Garrett shouted through comms.

"What do you mean it's turning around?" He asked.

"Just that, sir. It was close enough to detect all of our ships. Maybe it wasn't in the mood for a fight?"

"Did you scan it?"

"Passive only, sir."

"Hit it with active scanners before it moves out of range. If it knows we're here and doesn't want a fight, then lets get some intel out of this little chance-meeting."

"Aye, sir. Scanning now."

Captain Hutchison appeared on the view-screen. *"Haldor, is that bogie turning tail?"* She asked.

"It sure is, Kay. We're doing an active scan before it leaves though."

"That's some good luck."

"I *suppose* it is. No allied ship would leave without making contact, so that's got me very interested to find out who she is." He heard Captain Garett trying to report. "Kay, I'm going to add in our scout ship to the channel."

Hutchison nodded.

"Go ahead, Captain Garett."

"Commander, she's displacing 200,000 tons, and the ship is Hrymar ... for the most part."

"What do you mean, for the most part?"

"Well, sir, the engines have a Hrymar signature, but there's another reactor on that

ship that we've never seen. Maybe for new weapons or shields? I can't be sure. They didn't activate any systems, I'm just detecting the reactor at idle. But it's putting out some very strange emissions. The waveform looks a little like brainwave patterns during REM sleep. I know, that doesn't make any sense. I'm just telling you what I see."

He rubbed the stubble on his chin. "No, that's exactly the kind of insight we need, Captain. Good work. Keep scanning it until it's out of range, but *don't* follow it. Maintain current position. Resume patrol when it's out of range."

"Aye, sir. Garett out."

"What do you make of that, Kay?"

Hutchison pursed her lips. *"We've got no insight into the strange emissions over here. But it looks like we have a good old fashioned arms race going."*

He nodded somberly. "That occurred to me as well. It's been at least two years since we last had any kind of intel out of Niflheim. They gotten very good at detecting any duplicity or outright spying. Seems as though they've been very busy over the last twenty-four-months." He rubbed his stomach now that the conversation had died down, but he felt fine. It had been like that unknown ship had punched him in the stomach. Was there something, or somebody on that vessel? Yet more questions.

Hal ambled over to the ground-ops room behind the bridge where Gina's second in command, Pelagia Aksyonova, was coordinating the mop up and search operations.

He jerked his chin at her. "Anything?"

She shook her head, eyes heavy. "Not yet. But there are many areas of the outpost that are cut off due to structural damage. Our teams will explore every corner of the facility."

He looked down absently and exhaled. "I'll let you get back to it."

She nodded as he turned and left.

He was tired and frustrated. He hated not being actively involved in something, especially when it involved friends or family. Gina was like a sister to him. He decided against going back to the command dais, and instead began wandering *Mjolnir's* vast and numerous passageways. He nodded to a few officers and crewmen as he passed, but didn't stop to talk to any.

Entirely without meaning to, he'd arrived at sickbay. Shit, he thought. He turned to head down a different corridor when he heard her.

"Haldor, you're here? Let's talk. Please?" She thought to him.

Before he could think to respond she appeared from around the corner at a jog, her raven hair bouncing, her blue eyes shining. Gods, she took his breath away ever time he saw her.

He began to open his mouth to speak, but before he got the chance, she threw her arms around him, crushing him in a hug. Momentarily stunned, he reveled in the feel of her supple body conforming to his and the scent of her hair. Then he hugged her back.

"I am so sorry Gina is missing. I know what she means to you, Haldor," she thought to him.

"I know you do," he said.

Lifting her head from his chest, she cupped his face with her hands as she looked into his eyes. "You'll find her. If anyone can, your people can. And you know how resilient she is."

"I'm confused, Gwyn." Was all he could say to her.

Her face looked pained, but she radiated understanding through their mental link. And there was a hint of something else—love?

He pulled away abruptly, shaking his head then took a few steps back. *"What's going on?"* He thought to her.

She stepped forward and reached out to him, taking hold of both his hands. *"I am deeply sorry about the other day. When you told me … well … I wasn't prepared. It took me off guard, and it shouldn't have,"* she thought to him.

"That cut me, Gwyn. I haven't been hurt like that in a very long time," he thought to her.

"Haldor, you must understand, I've never been in love. Although I am over twice your chronological age, I am barely an adult. And by that, please don't infer that I object to our age difference. I only mean to emphasize that I have not long been of age to have such a relationship. And my early life was very harried. With my mother working on Earth as Ambassador, and my being her daughter, let's just say that it may have intimidated potential suitors. In any case, I had little time to even consider such things. So you see, dearest Haldor, I am simply inexperienced. I didn't know what love felt like … until I met you, that is," she thought to him.

Haldor dared not hope what he'd just heard was true. Did she just tell me that…

"Alfar normally take many years to fall in love. Our love grows like our folk age, slowly. But when we met, something magical happened. Perhaps it was because we can both access the Athryllith. I'm not sure. All I can tell you is that you hit me like a wave. A warm and wonderful wave. I knew in my heart that the connection between you and I … was something rare, but I didn't recognize it for what it was. In my mind, I was prepared to fall in love over the course of many years. When you said you loved me, well … that wave

hit me again. Only this time it knocked me over. What you feel for me, it's just so … powerful. Your love is like star, burning, and I was expecting but an ember. When I had time to think about it, and look at my own feelings," her cheeks flushed, *"I knew I loved you,"* she thought to him.

His head became dizzy on hearing her declaration, and he was wholly unprepared for her lips brushing against his; they were hot, supple, sweet.

He pulled back from the kiss. "Are you sure?" He said, aloud.

Looking up at him with her hypnotic blue eyes, she nodded vigorously. "I most certainly am … in love with you," she said, then kissed him again.

As the lovers kissed, the would-be-assassin went unnoticed; just another crew member traversing *Mjolnir's* passageways. The secreted dagger was tucked away again. The mission had almost been completed. Very close. Soon, Lord Haldor, very soon.

Hal stroked Gwynahra's thick black hair, as they sat on a sofa on his state-room. They were getting to know one another via the Athryllith. Each, in turn, sharing an emotion, a snapshot in time, little pieces of themselves; so much more complete than speaking. Hal could feel, and hear, and see, and taste, whatever Gwynahra had. The process was intoxicating. He felt as though they'd been together for decades. He'd not even known his wife, Siobhan, so intimately.

"I feel it too," she thought. *"The day I first saw you, after graduation, I knew. I could see the man you were; the loving husband, the devoted father, the steadfast friend. It was all plain to me. I saw your character as clearly as I see your face now. I never imagined love like this, Haldor,"* she thought to him.

"I don't understand why my gift has recently become so powerful," he said aloud. "I used to get a general sense of what people were feeling. Although I could always read Venn's wants and moods; as she could mine. It all started ramping up … when we rescued the children … when I met Chloe! She has to be the catalyst."

"Perhaps," Gwynahra said. "Magister Faelar told mother that young Chloe's command of the Athryllith was extraordinary."

He leaned closer to her, nose to nose, and began rubbing his nose back and forth.

She giggled, then furrowed her eyebrows. "What was that?"

His face grew serious. "It's an ancient and very sacred Northern tradition. It's called an Eskimo kiss." He smirked.

She pressed her lips to his again, letting them linger. He felt a rush of awakening race to parts of his body.

She pulled back an inch. "Why are you embarrassed?" She asked.

"What? I didn't say anything." Though, sex had crossed his mind for a micro-second during their kiss; he'd wondered when the right time for such things were, but felt embarrassed to broach the topic. He'd not intended to share that thought, but when she kissed him, all control vanished.

"Haldor, you never have to be embarrassed about anything with me. Ever. With the link we have, we should be able to share our most cherished secrets. How many lovers can do that? Please, don't ever feel you have to censor yourself with me."

"You're right. I'm out of practice when it comes to intimacy of any kind, Gwyn. Sharing my innermost thoughts, well … I haven't done that since my wife. Not even with Eva."

"Did you not love, Eva?" She asked, genuinely curious.

"I did … but not like Siobhan. And *nothing* like you. I need practice. We *both* need practice. I have an idea! Let's practice *together!* He rolled onto her and nibbled her neck as she laughed.

She moved back to a seating position and thought to him. *"Where were we? Yes, I believe you wanted to ask me about sex."*

"No. No I did not!" he thought back to her.

"Silly man. Sex is perfectly natural. The gods made us this way, Haldor. If they didn't want us to take pleasure from it…" she trailed off with a mental shrug.

"I know it's natural. I just don't want to rush anything. It just happened to cross my mind, and only for a micro-second."

She looked horrified. "Only for a micro-second? Do you find me that repulsive?" She asked. She tried not to smile, but failed.

"I love you," he said. "I can't tell you how good it feels to be able to say that to someone again."

"You don't need to tell me. Show me," she said, touching his temple.

As the images of peace and passion, love and friendship, all flowed from his mind to hers. Then his door chimed.

"Damn it." He glanced at the door then back to Gwynahra and pointed a finger at her. "Stay right there. I'll be right back."

"Promise?" She asked with a naughty grin and narrowing her eyes.

He nodded once, bolted up and jogged to the door, anxious to send away his caller. He opened the door to see one of his Valkyrie's. In fact, it was Gwynahra's friend, Lythrael.

"Valkyrie? What can I do for you?"

"High Commander, I was ordered to come to you with a report on Lady Gina. May I come in?"

Oh gods … If they were sending someone … then that meant she was likely dead. He felt his knees give slightly as he stepped back and turned. "Come in."

He felt Lythrael's intention to attack before her hand reached for the dagger. But he was confused, vulnerable. Between his feelings for Gwynahra, and the thought Gina was dead, he was ripe for *assassination.*

He pivoted back toward the incoming ice-pick stab, which she would have driven through his back. As he pivoted in toward her stab, he brought up his right forearm, intercepting her wrist, and halting the dagger. Then, in the same motion, he rotated the same arm back the opposite direction, snaking around her wrist. His right hand now gripped the top of her right hand. The assassin thrust a boot to his guts, doubling him over and knocking him back. He heard Gwynahra scream but didn't have time to say anything to her. This woman was fast, very fast. And well trained.

"Lythrael, stop this!" He commanded, to no avail. The woman sported a vacant look.

She attempted a few thrusts to his midsection before he could draw his own weapon—the Alfar cledyf-dagger that never left his body, except for sleep and bathing. He wore a matching sword when he left his cabin. Each was a baton shaped object, the dagger only five inches long, but when activated by his unique bio-electrical signal, the blade shot out the end, and a cross-guard appeared. Its edge was monomolecular, and could cut through almost anything —including powered battle armor.

He tried to tap his wrist-com to get security, but it was non-functional—a jamming field maybe? He didn't want to have to kill her, and so, tried a few times to knock her out, or disarm her; neither was successful. Out of a corner of his eye he saw Gwynahra. Was she coming toward Lythrael?

Before he could stop her, Lythrael spun back to Gwynahra, slashing across her arm. Gwynahra yelped and pulled back. The distraction was all that he needed. As Lythrael swung back to him, he slashed across her knife hand, severing it at the wrist. She grabbed her stump in shock. He stepped in and slammed her head with the butt of the dagger. She crumpled to the floor.

"Are you ok?" He yelled to Gwynahra.

She stood holding her arm, staring down at her *friend* and didn't respond.

"Gwynahra! Are you all right?" he asked more forcefully.

She looked up, confusion painting her face. "Yes, it's not deep."

He dropped to a knee and cut off a strip of his bionan suit to use as a tourniquet. He had to stop Lythrael's bleeding or she would die. Not that he cared if she died, per se, but, he wanted answers gods damnit.

"Can you help me make sure she's ok?"

Gwynahra just nodded slowly. Clearly she was in a state of shock, he decided. Then she promptly stumbled over and fell to her knees, finally collapsing on her face.

"Gwynahra!"

Chapter 15

LOCATION: SICKBAY ON RSS-MJOLNIR

Hal held Gwynahra's hand as he stroked her face. Like Sleeping Beauty, he thought. Just like the fairy tale—only she'd eaten no apple.

Dr. Elsie Inglis, *Mjolnir's* senior medical officer, approached him.

"It's definitely poison," Dr. Inglis said. "Thank the gods it was only a minor laceration. If she'd been stabbed, we'd be having a very different conversation now."

"She's in a bloody coma. Will she recover?" he asked, a bit too aggressively.

Dr. Inglis put hand on his shoulder. "Commander, she'll be fine. It's a medically induced coma. Just so her immune system and the yggdracilin can better fight the poison. And it will."

He wasn't consoled. The woman he was in love with lay prone and looking near death on the sterile table. It was more than he could bear just now. He cursed at Odin in his mind. Was he not worthy of better?

He jerked his chin over to Lythrael, lying on another bed in sickbay. "What about her?"

"Oh, she'll be fine. We even reattached the hand. That cledyf-dagger made my job much easier. I should see if they make scalpels like that." Her attempt at humor fell flat.

"Anything else on her?" he asked.

"Actually, yes," Dr. Inglis said, walking over to a wall-mounted screen. She tapped the screen and an image of a brain painted the wall. "Look right here," she said, pointing at a dark spot on the image. "*That* should not be there."

He moved over to the wall, examining the ominous black spot. "What in Niflheim is it?"

She zoomed in and rotated the image around its axis. The object was more or less spherical, with hundreds of minuscule tentacles reaching into various areas of Lythrael's brain.

"You'll notice the shape is somewhat like a ganglion—a nerve cluster. I haven't removed it, *yet*. It's deep inside her brain, and I'd rather be back on Rigsvaka to open up a person's head. But if I were a betting woman—which I'm not—I'd say it was some sort of mind control device. Possibly Hrymar. Their slave collars are the stuff of horror-vids. I think it's a reasonable leap to assume they could program someone with a small neural transmitter. My guess is that this organism is a genetically engineered neural controller."

"Bastards." Then it hit him like hammer. "Tyr, judge me! That means they've infiltrated Rigsvaka."

"I should start scanning everyone on board," Dr. Inglis said.

"Do that. But do *not* mention this to anyone. Tell them we're doing routine scan for signs of- post battle stress, or something to that effect. Also, I'll assign a marine to sickbay when you do the scans. If someone else is also implanted I want them in the brig for now." He tapped his wristcom.

His intelligence officer responded. *"Wudai here, Commander."*

"Jin, meet me in the war-room, five minutes. Grab Aksyonova on your way." He glanced at the Doctor. "Hold for a sec." He muted his com. "Doc, how long to run those tests?"

"Thirty seconds."

He nodded, and un-muted his com. "Jin, grab Aksyonova and report to sick bay first."

"Commander?"

"I'll explain when you get here."

Hal was thankful that nobody else on the *Mjolnir* had been implanted with the Hrymar device. He'd invited the other ship's captains, including the *Sam Houston's*, to come to *Mjolnir* under false pretenses. Then, at gunpoint, explained that they would be scanned. None were offended when they found out what was going on, and more importantly, that they were all clear.

"I'll tell you what, Hal," Kay Hutchison said, "I'm sure glad my boys and girls from *Sam Houston* didn't see y'all pull a gun on me. Let's just say, they're mighty protective. I'm like their mother—a bitchy old hag to be sure—but motherly nonetheless."

"It had to be done, Kay," he said. "I couldn't take the chance that the Battleship next to me was under secret Hrymar control, or could have been at any moment.

"No harm, no foul. Hell, I'd have done it you." Hutchison chuckled.

He looked around the war-room at his ship's surgeon, the three captains, and one magister—Edvit Jerresson— who held a unique place in Rigsvaka society. Kings of old had magisters—wise men—to help create new weapons, and innovate generally. This was exactly the role which Edvit Jerresson excelled at. Being Dvergar, he had a natural affinity for design and engineering. He also hated the Dvergar corporate structure and was very willing to share any Dvergar technology or secrets with Rigsvaka.

"I'd like to thank Captain Hutchison for sitting in on this meeting. This is not the kind of intel we can sit on. Our allies *absolutely* need access to what we've discovered here, which is why Captain Hutchison is here in our war-room. I'm proud of what we've built at Rigsvaka over the last seven years, but we'll never be able to solve the problems in allied space by ourselves. It's just too damned big and our enemies have had a very long head-start on us. Anyway, enough of the big-picture talk. We all know this. Let's get down to our current dilemma. Let me turn the meeting over to *Mjolnir's* senior medical officer, Dr. Elsie Inglis," he said for Kay's benefit.

Dr. Inglis nodded to him and stood. "First, let's have a look at exactly what we're dealing with." She tapped a button on her tablet and an image filled the war-room's central holo-screen. "This, is what I found in the young woman's brain." A 3D image of a brain, and its tiny invader were projected up into the center of the room.

Hal could sense the thoughts of revulsion rippling across the room.

"The object," Dr. Inglis continued, "appears very much like a nerve ganglion." She zoomed the image so the central mass filled the screen. "There's a central body that likely contains all the DNA encoding to make it do what its designers intended." She shifted the image sideways, keeping the current zoom level. "Now, look at these filaments. You'll notice that they infiltrate hundreds of different points of the subject's brain." The image slid sideways, then zoomed out. "This is the brain's frontal lobe. It's responsible for decision making, problem solving, and the control of purposeful behaviors. Approximately 75% of the filaments focus on this area of the brain. I can draw no other conclusion other than it's a mind control device." She nodded to Hal and sat back down.

"Thank you, Dr. Inglis." He nodded to her, then gestured to Jin, who's slight frame rose gracefully off his chair. Again for Kay's benefit, Hal made introductions, "This is my intelligence officer, Sir Jin Wudai. I'll let him pick up from Dr. Inglis."

Jin wore a concerned look as he began to speak. "Thank you for the formal introduction, Lord Haldor." Jin bowed his head to Hal. "Needless to say, I am very concerned about today's development. Brainwashing has been a threat to nations and polities for thousands of years. But the kind of sophisticated mind control we suspect here," he shook his head, "it's unheard of. Until now. Obviously, we must screen *every* person. The challenge will be to continue those scans periodically. Suppose we scan a new recruit and find them clear? Then let us assume they are on a mission, and go out of contact briefly, or are on their own." He let the ominous question hang in the air for a moment. "Who's to say they could not be captured, implanted, and re-introduced into our ranks? You understand the scope of the problem now?" Jin waited for a reaction

The murmur in the room confirmed to Hal that they had *not* previously comprehended the scope of the problem. He hadn't.

"Captain, if I may?" Magister Edvit Jerresson requested.

He nodded, then turned to Captain Hutchison. "Kay, this is Magister Edvit Jerresson."

She nodded to Edvit.

"Pleasure to meet you m'am," Edvit said. "Once we get this bloody contraption out of the young lady's head, of course we'll need to analyze it, but I hope to be able to design some kind of emitter to disrupt the implant. Neutralize it. If the device proves susceptible to electro-magnetic signals, then we could have a field generated in all parts of a ship, or building, that permanently interferes with the implants. But I won't know till I get a chance to study the one we have. "

"Magister Jerresson," Dr. Inglis said, "I strongly suspect that it will *not* be susceptible to any EM signal, unless it was powerful enough to damage other brain tissue as well. We may need to look for a biological defense, or offense."

"Fair enough, Doctor," Edvit continued. "Perhaps together we can come with something. There are other considerations that come to my mind; such as, will there be permanent brain or personality damage to the host? Can they be activated remotely? Turned off remotely? It's not my area, but I think there may also be a counter-intelligence opportunity here. If we just destroy the damned things, then the Hrymar will go and try something new. As it stands, we can detect the implants, and identify compromised personnel. Could we not use them to our purposes?"

Jin gave Edvit a respectful nod. "Quite so, Magister."

Captain Hutchison was shaking her head.

"Your thoughts, Kay?" Hal asked her.

"I understand the need for counterintelligence, but do y'all really intend to allow these ticking-time-bombs to walk around on your ship? On a base, I suppose I could live with that. But on a ship? The bastards could take out life-support, overload a reactor, tweak the hyperdrive so you translate into a star. Heck, there's all kinds of mischief they could get up to. I won't risk that on my ship."

Jin inclined his head at her. "I assure you, Captain Hutchison, it is not a decision we would take lightly, or without rigorous risk-mitigation. However, I suspect that the opportunity may outweigh the risks in this case."

Hutchison held palms up in a—who knows—gesture.

Hal continued. "We certainly have a lot to think about. Kay, we're going to set a course back to Rigsvaka in three days. I think we'll need that much time to go through the outpost and gather more information. There are also a substantial number of Hrymar slaves that need repatriation or sanctuary."

"What do you plan to do with any of the blue-skinned bastards that are left?" Hutchison asked.

The room went suddenly still, as if time had frozen. He felt all eyes on him as he prepared to answer her.

His words froze as they left his mouth. "Space them. Each and every one of them."

Hal had long ago abandoned concern over sexual propriety amongst crew. The taboos that had existed a century ago, had been stricken from the books. And he'd embraced the need for crew to have romantic relationships as a healthy part of life. They might spend years on a ship, much of the time far away from their homes.

That attitude had included his own romantic involvement with his former astrogator, Eva Joubert. They'd been lovers in University, and when his wife was killed, she was there, and supportive. Sadly, she'd lost an unborn child, his child. That loss crippled her and she could no longer bear to be with him.

Loss was an old friend to him now; At fifteen years old, both parents died in a car accident; his wife and son were murdered; his unborn child with Eva had died; then, even Eva went away. He would not, could not, lose Gwynahra. He shook off his looping self-pity as he entered sick bay.

For the second time he mused that Gwynahra looked like Sleeping Beauty; exquisite, peaceful, elegant. Skin like white porcelain, hair raven black, but her eyes—those blue jewels—remained hidden. He recalled the taste of her kiss, like honeysuckle. He leaned in a placed a gentle kiss on her lips.

"Morning, Commander," Dr. Inglis said.

He stood straight with a start. "Dr., I- "

She waved him off. "Oh, don't mind me. And I was wondering when you two were going to connect."

He felt like he had been drenched in cold water. "What?"

"The sparks between you two have been like a meteor shower. I think the two of you were the last to notice."

"Oh." Was all he could manage.

"Commander," she said gently, "it's good for you to have someone. You lead more than just this ship. If you're happy, that's a very good thing for us. And a very bad thing for our enemies. A man in love is strong. Boys are a different thing, but a man ... " she nodded. "Love is good for them."

"I know. I just- well, I guess I'm not as subtle or stony-faced as I thought I was."

"Uh, no. No, you're not." She smirked. "But that's ok. And if I may be so bold, Commander, she's lucky to have you. And you, her, of course. She's a talented Doctor, and a promising counselor."

"Yes, I *am* lucky," came a whisper from the bed behind them.

"Gwyn!" He rushed to her and took a hand.

Her eyes blinked slowly, not quite fully opened.

"How are you feeling?"

"Thirsty, actually," she said with heavy eyes.

Dr. Inglis nodded, and move off to get something to drink.

"You're a stupid girl, you know that?" He said.

Her face went slack. "I- "

"For trying to fight Lythrael."

She attempted a smile.

"I love you," he whispered.

She leaned her cheek on his hand, a nascent smile brightening her face.

Dr. Inglis returned with a glass of water and handed it to him. Carefully, he tilted the glass, and Gwyn's head, so she could take a drink.

"Better?" He asked.

Gwynahra nodded weakly. "What happened?' She asked, then her face looked pained. "Oh no, Lythrael."

"She's alive," he said. "It wasn't her fault, Gwyn. Somebody implanted her with a device that was controlling her. At least that's the theory."

"Lady Freya! How?" Gwynahra asked.

"We don't know yet. But I'll find out. You can be sure of that."

"What of Lythrael? Will she recover?"

"We're not sure, yet."

"All right, Commander," Dr. Inglis interrupted. "You can come back later.

I need some time with *my* patient."

He kissed Gwynahra's hand. *"I'll be back soon, my love,"* he thought to her.

"I'll be here," she thought, then projected the feeling of her lips on his.

Hal was sitting in his command-chair in a semi-meditative state when his comms officer got his attention.

"Sir, Riddara Aksyonova is on the outpost and needs to speak with you."

"Put her through."

Anouk Kappa shot him a serious look. "Sir, you *may* want to take this in your ready-room."

He nodded and strode to his ready-room. What in Thor's name was it now. He did *not* need another crisis. He tapped a button on his desk view-screen and saw Pelagia Aksyonova standing straight amidst a room full of rubble. They'd really trashed the outpost.

"What's up, Pelagia?"

"Sir, we recovered a slaver-database," she said, pausing.

As expected, he thought. "And?"

"There is an inventory list. And…"

He could feel her distress — the Athryllith apparently worked over the 1,000km+ to the outpost. There was something terrible she needed to tell him, something personal.

"Pelagia, take a breath. Relax. Just tell me what you need to say."

"Sir, it's your son."

He mentally flinched. His dead son was a sore spot for him, but he was *dead*. No news of him could be any worse, or could it?

"What about my son?"

"The database lists him as alive."

Maybe they'd been alive initially, but Devrim had told him they were dead. Nine years ago, he'd stood in the enemy's throne room, and demanded to know. Had Devrim lied? Perhaps the database was very old?

"Is the entry dated?" He asked weakly.

"Yes, sir. It is. It's dated four years ago. It states he was transferred from a place called 'Egil Arkek', to the Over-Chieftain's residence."

His mind ached. His son. His son was, alive? And did she say he was at the Over-Chieftain's residence? Devrim's residence? Devrim had his son? He could see her lips moving, but heard nothing she said. He stood and left his office without terminating the call.

Hal entered the starship's inter-faith chapel, and upon sensing his identity, its walls lit up with the symbols of his faith; that of his Viking forefathers. The walls to his left and right displayed trees, as if he were now in a forest. Ahead of him, a stone altar rose up from the simulated grass. The stone was carved with runes, and other symbols. His Viking ancestors's religion had no written name; now, it was called Asatru—meaning true to the Aesir—one of the main families of gods and goddesses.

He often prayed to Odin, the Allfather, or chief god. But not today. Odin was not a merciful god, but he was practical. Wise men and leaders often sought his favor, whereas the common man would more often call on Thor. Today he wanted justice. And for that, he would call on Tyr—namesake of the Tyrmundr. Tyr was the god of law and just war—the one-handed god; made so by his sacrifice to bind the wolf Fenris. Tyr had placed his right hand in Fenris's maw, as surety against the gods releasing him from a magical binding.

But the gods did not release him, nor did they ever intend to. Tyr knew his hand would be taken, but offered it anyway. And so, brave men who sacrificed themselves for others, were sometimes called Tyr-brave.

Asatruar did not bend a knee to their gods. On the contrary, they stood tall and proud before their gods; not begging forgiveness, but asking their betters for advice, or favor. They did so proudly and with reverence. Hal approached the altar, on which a simple stone bowl sat. He drew his sword—a symbol of Tyr—and cut deeply across his left palm. Blood now flowing freely, he squeezed a stream of it into the bowl as an offering.

He stepped back and threw his arms wide and looked to the heavens—to Asgard. "Tyr! Oh great god of justice, prince of temples, and sword-wielder. Hear me! I ask that you accept my offering and praise. I have a dire need for justice. I ask by right as a father, and husband. One who has been truly wronged. I ask for no trivial justice. My wife and son have been taken by my enemy, and I do not know whether they live. The man I seek justice from, dealt with me dishonorably. The filth of Niflheim, the icy Nithings. Their petty King, it's he who I would see fall before my sword. I ask that you aid me in this undertaking. I thank you for your example, and for hearing my request. If you ask a sacrifice of me, however great, I will gladly give it in exchange for this justice."

He stood silently for a long moment. He expected no answer. If the gods *did* grant his boon, it was said they did so subtly. He certainly was not expecting a voice to erupt from the air. And when it did, he was entirely unprepared.

Chapter 16

Hal wasn't sure what he saw before him. Perhaps an apparition, perhaps a vision? Standing in front of him in the chapel, or at least in his mind's eye, stood an old man in a dark blue cloak. Most importantly, he had only one eye —Odin?

"Allfather," he didn't know what else to say. Was this a hallucination?

"This is not a hallucination, Haldor Olsen. I read your thoughts as plainly as I see your face. And you need not speak. I will do that for the both of us. You called on Tyr for justice, yet I have provided you gifts and guided you to great purpose. I did not choose your path, son of Ole, I only helped ease the journey. But you have the ability to achieve things most mortal men never dream of doing. And if successful, your name will live on in the tales of our people. That is the highest mortal honor a man of Midgard could hope for. Afterwards, perhaps you will be worthy of my host in Valhalla."

Hal tried to look proud and worthy, as he stood before the chief of his gods.

Odin continued. "There are dark powers moving in this galaxy Haldor. Powers that should *not* be moving, and yet are doing so. The Norns seem to be weaving threads that have you colliding with those dark powers. I have tried to prepare you and will continue to help, as I can. There are some things even the gods of the North cannot do. Look to the godly gifts you have been given. If you do, you will understand them. Make good use of them, and trust the loyal retainers and friends you have. Do not discard *any* of them. They are walking the same road. Seek justice now, if you must, but do not lose sight of the greater darkness coming. You know of what I speak. And do not despair. Great men can ill afford that luxury. You *must* rise above it, and pull others with you. I will say no more. Go now, son of Ole. Keep the ember burning in your heart, yet do not let it consume you. Use the fire. Do not let *it* use you."

As abruptly as he appeared, the one-eyed god of Asgard was gone. Hal slept for a solid sixteen hours, previously ensuring he was not disturbed unless the ship was taking enemy fire—and only then, if the odds were well stacked against them.

He awoke feeling surprisingly centered. He thought he ought to feel like shit, but he didn't. Had he actually spoken, or rather listened, to Odin? It felt real. He remembered every word. He'd asked for divine assistance and had received it.

"Haldor?" she whispered in his mind. He could feel her outside his room.

It was Gwynahra. She must have been waiting in the passageway and listening for his mind. *"Come in, Gwyn,"* he thought to her.

He sat up in his bed as she entered his state-room. Waves of empathy and soothing warmth caressed his mind. She stopped a few meters from him, tentative.

The wall she'd taught him to build in his psyche was now in place and reinforced. Right now he had to figure things out before sharing them so intimately.

She went rigid as the solace she tried to project bounced off his mental wall. It was like rejection, like pushing a lover away who offered you a hug. He felt her pain—she shielded nothing from him. It was almost overwhelming.

"I assume you know what they discovered at the outpost?" He said.

"Yes, evidence your son may still be alive," she thought to him, the taint of sadness evident in her mind.

"And the implications ... by extension?"

"Your wife could still be alive," she said aloud.

He nodded soberly. He wanted to tell her about his visit from Odin, about the counsel he'd been given. But how could he keep fostering the intimacy between them? If his wife was alive ... gods help him. It was unthinkable. She'd been lost to him for almost ten years. Then, after all that time, and against all hope he'd finally found love. The Norns were cruel bitches, he thought. "I don't know what to say, Gwyn."

"You don't need to say anything, Haldor. Just know that I'm here, if you need me. You need not be alone in this. Whatever happens between us, I love you, care about you." She stood silent for a moment. "I'll take my leave now." She projected the feeling of a kiss on his cheek, and left his stateroom. Haldor could feel the sympathy leaking from the minds of his senior officers as they met in his ready room.

"That's all I have to report, Commander," said Pelagia Aksyonova, acting commander of the Tyrmundr Marines. "There is no trace of Lady Russo. No physical remains, nor any hint of what happened to her. I deeply regret that I have exhausted all the options at my disposal."

He nodded. At least Gina went out fighting. No warrior could ask for more. "Very well. Thank you, Lady Aksyonova." He turned to Jin Wudai.

Jin nodded. "Sir, we have finished decrypting and translating the remainder of the Hrymar database. There is a base located approximately two-hundred light-years to the Galactic south west. This base recurs in their records, over and over. Whatever goes on there, it's of vital importance to them. Perhaps a regional distribution center for their slave markets? There is no data indicating its function, but, if we are looking for answers, I suggest that we make it our next stop."

"What about the survivors on the outpost?" he asked.

His first officer spoke up. "Commander, I have a manifest of the non-Hrymar survivors." Maurya tapped his data pad. "There were 21,206 survivors of various species."

Hal was surprised. He expected quite a few, but this was ten times the number he'd imagined. "Well, now. That is quite a few displaced persons."

Pelagia nodded. "Nearly half of the captives are in cryo, sir. If we are going to process and re-patriate them, I suggest we do it back on Rigsvaka. This is a huge undertaking."

"Agreed. And the Hrymar?" He asked.

"There were 1,602 enemy captured after the battle. At your request, they have been held and await your *disposition*," Pelagia said.

He nodded slowly. Good. He would try not to take too much pleasure in their fates. "Tomorrow at 08:00, have them assembled in the main cargo bay. Can we cram 1,602 Hrymar in there, *uncomfortably*?"

Pelagia nodded with a grim conviction. "They will fit, sir. I will see to it."

"Senior officers can join me in the cargo bay observation room. Now, back to this mystery location. That's about nine days in hyperspace."

Senior helmsman, Braylan Jones, spoke up. "Commander, we have pre-arranged transit clearance with the Dvergar to use their inter-stellar-node at Jaraad. Taking the bridge to Heimdall's star, and then hyperspace to the final destination will save us several days."

"Perfect, Jones. Plot a course and we'll leave after our 08:00 *meeting* tomorrow morning." Hal could read Jone's amusement at his euphemism for mass-execution, but as a good officer, Jones didn't allow anyone to see it. Haldor and his senior officers stood in the observation and control room, ten-meters above the cargo bay, and were, most importantly, environmentally isolated.

1,602 of the vilest creatures in the multi-verse, were lined up in columns and rows. As their jailers exited through the hatches the Hrymar slavers began to panic. Hal could feel their terror. Good, he thought. This is what you've brought upon so many good and decent people. He wished their punishment could go on a lifetime, as had their victims' cruel lot.

"Ready, Commander," Maurya said.

He nodded. "Kappa," he said to the young red-head standing beside him, "open a channel. Ship-wide."

"Aye sir," she replied. "Open now."

"This is High Commander Olsen speaking. I have a grim duty to perform this morning. I have no desire to take the life of any creature unnecessarily, but there are times when that becomes necessary. As it has today. There is no rehabilitation for a race that has evolved for thousands of years under an entirely slave-based economy. Each of their countless-millions of victims has endured, and indeed, many are still enduring, the worst nightmare any being could conjure. And yet, for the victims, there is no waking from that nightmare, no morning reprieve."

He could feel ripples of sorrow across their minds. So many of them had experienced this horror on a personal level. He was pleased that he didn't sense any bloodlust from them though. They understood their duty and were behaving more civilized than he could expect.

"The punishment I level against them now is but a shadow of what they have inflicted upon our allies, friends, and families. I hereby sentence all Hrymar captives to death by spacing. Please join me in a minute of silence for the victims, and pray to your God, or gods, if that is your custom."

The ship went silent. The only disturbance came from the cargo bay. The Hrymar were pounding at the walls. He didn't hear their screams, only the vibrations of their futile actions carried through the hull and bulkheads.

When the minute concluded, he pressed a button to open the main cargo-bay door. Red lights flashed and a loud pulsing tone could be heard even in the observation-room. It was the alarm indicated an opening cargo bay door when they were in space.

The atmosphere began to jet out the crack, carrying dozens of Hrymar along. They fell like bowling pins, scattering, striking walls, and bouncing, as the hungry black-maw of space devoured them.

Captain Kay Hutchison looked back at Hal from the Mjolnir's main view-screen.

"Where to now, Kay?" Hal asked.

"I suppose we'll keep looking for these raiders. I feel like putting a dent in their operations."

"Know that you and your crew have an open invitation to visit Rigsvaka anytime you're in our area."

"Thanks, Hal. I appreciate that, and I just may take you up on that. I've heard about y'alls low-G tropical world. That sounds just about right for some shore leave."

"Our folks seem to enjoy it."

"We better be off. Keep your saddle oiled and your gun greased, Olsen."

Hal tried to smile. "You too. Take care, Kay."

The view-screen switched to the *Sam Houston* on a dark field of stars. She turned and accelerated into the deep.

Location: Orbiting Haward II / Star: Haward (K2 V Orange, Main Sequence)

Propped up on his bed, coffee in hand, Hal was thankful for several uneventful days; they gave him time to internalize recent events. He'd kept his distance from Gwynahra, unsure of what the future held for them. Meditation helped, but he felt Venn's absence acutely. With a mouthful of coffee not yet swallowed, he heard his wristcom chirp.

"Olsen here."

"Commander, we've take up orbit around the planet in the database. The Alfar have it cataloged as Haward II."

"Be right there, Chandra."

A blue globe filled the main view-screen. Only one medium-sized continent floated on all that water.

"What have we got, XO?" Hal asked, as he took his seat.

"Haward II, Commander. 91% water, 24% ice, one continent, as you can see. Gravity is 1.29g. Meiriona tells me there's a runestone-portal on the surface." He zoomed in to a small island off the shore of the continent. "Right here."

Hal noticed the remains of ancient stone buildings amongst a clearing in the dense, jungle foliage. Pillars and large stones lie scattered generously around the clearing. "How old?"

"Approximately 4,500 years old," Maurya said.

"Really? That's fascinating." He sensed Maurya's confusion, so he explained. "I'm a history buff, Chandra. The date of these ruins is around the same time-frame as civilization was booming back on Earth—in places like Egypt and China."

"Commander," said his comms officer, "we're receiving a hail- from the planet," she said surprised.

"On-screen."

A ghost appeared in front of him. His mortal enemy. The man who had taken his family, then lied about their deaths—Over-Chieftain of the Hrymar, Devrim.

"Lord Haldor, I believe you are currently styling yourself?" The blue humanoid gave a mock bow. *"So nice to see you again. It has been too many years. But, in some ways I feel like we have never been parted."* The creature grinned wickedly.

Hal was in too much shock to respond.

"I have an offer for you, Haldor. I believe I have something you may want. I am certain you know of what I speak? If not, then it will be a pleasant surprise. Let me turn this conversation over to my trusted servant, Serkan. I believe you two are also acquainted. Best of health and happiness to you, Lord Haldor." He bowed again.

Devrim's image dissipated, replaced by the grizzled old Hrymar that served him. Beside him stood a red-haired young human, a boy. Was that … Ailan?

"Jarl Haldor, I am Serkan. I serve Over-Chieftain Devrim. He has asked that I conduct a parley between our two peoples."

When he did not continue, Hal assumed he was to speak. "Continue."

"I am unsure whether you recognize the boy standing next to me, but he is your son, Ka-" he corrected himself. *"Ailan."*

What was Hal supposed to say? He was at a complete loss. There was no fury, no sadness, just a complete absence of feeling or ability to think. The look on the boys face was that of hatred and contempt. And he was attired like a Hrymar warrior. What had he expected? Well, he wasn't sure what he had expected. Certainly not this. He nodded.

"Devrim has allowed me to make this most gracious of offers. If you are willing to come to the surface and negotiate under a flag of truce, then we will allow your son to go home with you. Despite the outcome of the negotiations. And to sweeten the offer, I have one of your crew, who I will also allow you to take home." Another Hrymar shoved Gina Russo into view. Hal could see she was wearing a slave collar.

Maurya made a slicing motion across his throat and Kappa cut the audio-input to the view-screen

His Punjabi XO stepped in front of him. "Commander, it's a bloody trap. That bastard has no intention of giving you anything. And how can you be sure that's your son?"

"It's him, Chandra. I can feel his mind from here. But his thoughts-" he shook his head, a look of agony painting his face, "they're so dark. And they've got Gina."

"Commander, please. Don't even entertain this. You've become a thorn in their backside. They'd like nothing more than to take you out of the equation. You efforts have decimated their slave-trade. Think about it!"

Emotion returned to him, and he spun on Maurya. "What the fuck would you do if your daughter were there, Chandra? Tell me? Eh? You tell me you'd just walk away without trying to get her back? Regardless of the cost?"

Maurya said nothing.

"Gods damned right you would!" He took a breath, and softened his tone. "Chandra, I know it's a trap. I can see it in Serkan's mind. Of *course* they want me dead. But I *need* to do this. What we've built, will go on without me. We've put the infrastructure in place so it would. I was just a seed, my friend. The tree has taken root. I'm not going over there with a death-wish. Far from it. I'll take council before I go. But I *am* going."

"I understand, Commander. My apologies."

Hal put a hand on Maurya's shoulder and smiled at the man. "None required. Your job, XO, among other things, is to make sure I don't fuck up too badly. I can't fault you for that." He gestured for the audio to resume and looked back at Serkan. "I accept your offer."

Chapter 17

LOCATION: ABOARD LIGHT'S DOOM / PLANET: Orbiting Haward II

Kadir stood before his master, who was looking him up and down.

"You know what you must do?" Serkan asked.

He nodded, and in a voice devoid of any emotion, said, "if Haldor Olsen lands on the planet, I am to kill him."

Serkan nodded. "Good. It is unlikely his shuttle will make the flight down. But, should it survive, you must play the sorrowful son, happy to be re-united with your father. Then, when he leasts expects it, thrust your dagger into his heart. He must *not* leave this star-system alive. Under *any* circumstances. Do you fully understand what I mean?"

"I understand, master." He understood that he was expected to give his own life to achieve his mission. He would do it. If only to see the horror in Haldor Olsen's eyes as the life trickled from his body. The same horror Kadir had experienced for so many years. Finally, the jotuns had granted him the chance for vengeance. Haldor Olsen's last sight would be his abandoned son, spitting in his face. He got goosebumps just imagining the scene.

He bowed to Serkan as he boarded the shuttlecraft. Once fastened in to his harness, the shuttle began its smooth exit from the *Light's Doom*. Kadir pulled out two clear bottles of liquid from inside his pant's pocket. One blue vial, and one purple vial. He drew both of his daggers from their sheaths on his belt. Carefully, he placed a single drop of blue liquid on the right blade, and a single drop of purple on the left blade. He turned them around until the liquid had run around the surface of the blade, and dried. Very carefully, he re-sheathed his daggers. Sure not to touch the blades himself with any exposed skin, then replaced the vials. He was ready.

Hal had been talked into taking a well armored assault-shuttle down to the planet. He wore his Recon Combat Armor. He figured his RCA suit was a reasonable compromise. He didn't want to get into a firefight wearing his Ursa suit—too much chance of collateral damage. He wanted to ensure his son survived their re-union. He did have a laser pistol and his cledyff-sword and dagger with him.

Maurya stood stoically at the entrance to the shuttle bay as Hal entered. He nodded to his XO as he walked toward the nose of the assault-shuttle. The external hatch irised open as the approached the ramp. It had been awhile since he'd piloted a shuttle, but it was like riding a bike, he assured himself. He had to tuck the edges of his grey cloak in, preventing them from catching on the hatch mechanism as he entered. He passed through the interior hatch and into the main cabin of the shuttle. The assault-shuttles were designed to hold twenty-four marines in full armor, so the central cabin was cavernous by such standards. He passed through a third hatch onto the bridge.

He was so pre-occupied with the events to come, that he barely noticed two smiling faces looking back at him. Captain Molly Coogan and Magister Edvit Jerresson.

"What the fuck are you two doing here?"

Both kept smiling. The Australian tucked a few blonde curls behind an ear and cocked her head at him. "Well, Commander, it's like this. I've been lead to understand your shuttle-piloting skills are, well, shit, sir. No other word for it, really. Can't have my Jarl *come a gutser* on landing, now can I, sir?"

Edvit was trying desperately to suppress a chuckle, and failing.

"Aye, Commander. And I couldn't let Lady Molly go to this foul planet unescorted, now could I? I count myself a gentleman, I do." Edvit shot him a toothy grin.

He did not *need* Molly to pilot, but she most certainly was better at it, and was herself a skilled warrior. They used to practice fencing with long-swords together. And Edvit, well, he was the most ingenious person on Rigsvaka.

"We'll sort out appropriate punishments for you two later." He shook his head, but was inwardly relieved to have them along.

"Right!" Edvit said. "Pre-flight check, done. Read to go!"

Hal buckled into the co-pilot's seat, and Molly eased the shuttle up and out.

The assault-shuttle had just begun its descent through the hazy tropical atmosphere when they heard the chirp an incoming transmission alert.

"Commander! The Hrymar ship is back. The big one. She just emerged from behind an asteroid," Maurya said.

"Nithings," Hal cursed. "Vector?"

"Heading to the planet, sir. Still a million-kilometers out though. Given our max acceleration, she'd be here in under nine-minutes without stopping. "

"Get *Mjolnir* in between, us. We're heading back." He looked to Molly but the shuttle was already banking.

Suddenly the Hrymar battleship materialized one-thousand-kilometers in front of the shuttle—appearing to skip across space-time, like a stone on a pond. The enemy battleship was now between them and the *Mjolnir*.

Molly banked hard. "Bloody hell!"

The shuttle rocked as energy weapons from the Hrymar ship hailed down on the tiny craft.

"Maurya, open fire on those bastards!" Hal ordered. He then tapped a series of commands on his wrist-com and a blue light began strobing—flash-flash-flash, pulse-pulse-pulse, flash-flash-flash.

A small fire erupted from the console in front of Edvit. "Shite!" He couldn't leave his seat though. Molly was trying to stay out of the line of fire, and maneuvering erratically.

"Bloody torpedoes!" Molly said. "Three fish in the water, Commander!"

"Take us to the surface." He hoped that plowing through the dense atmosphere would help them shake the torpedoes.

As the shuttle banked and spun, he could see the Hrymar battleship fire this intense, green energy beam. It looked like a bolt of continuous glowing lightning, in bright green. Some kind of plasma weapon? It stayed connected to the *Mjolnir* for a solid three-seconds. "*Mjolnir* report!"

"*Cap- M- jor- age-* "

There was too much static for Hal to make out anything. He could see *Mjolnir* opening up with all weapons. Dozens of torpedoes and missiles arced toward the enemy, as did a storm of red and orange energy-weapons.

"Come on, Chandra. Kick their arses!"

Location: Holding in Hyperspace

"M'am," said the Sam Houston's comms officer. "We've got a gravitic beacon sounding-off from normal-space. It's an old-school SOS."

Captain Kay Hutchison nodded. That was Hal's prearranged signal. He was right, the Hrymar had planned to double cross him. "Take us down to normal space, helm. Combatives, power up all weapons, shields to maximum. Let's open up a can of whoop-ass!"

"Sir, reports of damage are coming from all around the ship, and some really strange readings," Meiriona reported.

Chandragupta Maurya stroked his chin. "Details?"

"The armor, sir. It seems to be regenerating."

"What?" The armor had yet to be damaged, and shields were still holding. They'd been hit with some green energy weapon, but it hadn't penetrated the shields, so what was going on? Maurya wondered.

"Gunners are reporting obstructions. It seems the armor is creeping over the cannon barrel holes. Turret mounted weapons can still fire, but aiming is being compromised. The armor seems to be filling gaps under the turret pivot-points."

He felt his hands grow cold. The armor was organic—Alfar technology. What they were describing, sounded like a cancer—out of control growth of cells. "Indra, help us," he whispered to himself. The green beam. "Engineering, get a sample of the armor tissue around these affected areas. Analyze the tissue for any abnormalities."

"Under stood, sir."

The straw haired Timonen, turned from his seat at the helm. "Sir, maneuvering is extremely sluggish."

"Did you report it to Engineering?" He asked.

The Finn nodded. "Done, sir."

"Let's keep fighting while we can."

Through the assault-shuttle's windows, a flood of flickering orange-light poured in. It felt literally, like flying into a fire. Hal was keeping one eye on a small screen which monitored the Mjolnir. He might be in trouble, but so was his ship and crew. A second ship blinked into existence, translating down from hyperspace to normal space.

"I hear you started some trouble, Olsen?" Captain Hutchison said.

"Something like that, Kay. Thanks for coming."

"Y'all gonna be ok in that little match-box?"

"Yeah, we'll make it down to the surface. If you can help *Mjolnir*, that would be much appreciated."

"Consider it done. We'll come get ya'll as soon as possible. Hutchison out."

Molly looked utterly shocked. "Oy, I thought the Texan was out on patrol, Cap'n?"

"I anticipated trouble with our blue-skinned friends. Kay and I decided to keep it from the crews. We're still not convinced we've rooted out all the traitors."

"Excellent plan, Commander," Edvit said. "And you are quite right. They are traitorous bastards to the last."

The shuttle lurched upward.

Molly smirked. "Sorry, I *am* trying to get us down in one piece."

The shuttle was rocked by several more plasma shots. He looked down at the lidar and saw that *Sam Houston* had killed all the torpedoes chasing the shuttle. Thank the gods for sharp-shooting Texans, he thought.

An alarm began wailing inside the cockpit.

"What now?" He asked.

"Engines are out, Commander," Edvit said.

"Christ on crutches!" Molly swore. "This is going to be a right bastard of a landing, gents!"

The assault shuttle was plummeting like a stone, down to the disarmingly beautiful jungle. Its spongy undergrowth and vegetation would feel like concrete at these speeds.

"Can we get more power to the contragrav nodes?" He asked Edvit.

"Not from the cockpit," Edvit said, unbuckling his harness.

"Ed, sit your ass down! You'll get yourself killed!" He shouted.

"Hal, we'll all be pushing up daisies if I don't."

"I'll keep it steady, Ginger-snap," Molly said to the Dvergar, using her pet-name for him. Molly yanked back on the stick, trying to pull the assault-shuttle into a more shallow dive. It was not the most aerodynamic of vehicles, relying on contragrav nodes and powerful engines to keep it aloft; but it did have vestigial wings, and so, could use the atmosphere for lift; but it do so poorly.

"Maximum acceleration," Captain Hutchison ordered.

"Aye, m'am. Pedal to the metal," said her helmswoman.

The *Sam Houston* unleashed a second barrage of weapons fire on the Hrymar ship. The *Sam Houston* was a proper battleship, a ship of the line, meant to stand toe-to-toe with the big boys, and live to fight another day.

"M'am, the *Mjolnir* is adrift. She's still firing, but she seems to have lost all ability to maneuver," said her sensors officer.

"Open a channel to *Mjolnir*."

Her comms officer nodded.

Mjolnir's first officer, Captain Chandragupta Maurya, appeared on screen. The bridge looked ok, Kay thought.

"Captain Maurya, how are y'all holding up?"

"Not very well I'm afraid, Captain Hutchison. They hit us with some kind of green energy weapon. My sensors officer tells me it's a virionic weapon."

Kay shook her head. "Never heard tell of it." The *Sam Houston* rocked, hit by weapons fire. She turned to her tactical officer. "Shields at maximum?"

He nodded.

"Sorry, *Mjolnir*. Our blue friends are getting downright ornery. Virionic, you say?"

"That's right, Captain. Think of it like a human getting a virus. The Mjolnir's outer armor is entirely organic. It's as susceptible to biological weapons as living things are. It's something that neither we, nor the Alfar, have every come across. Our sensors officer, Meiriona, is shocked the Hrymar have this technology. They haven't done much with living machines, so having this technology is out of character."

"Well, Mr. Maurya, you've just delivered some good news."

"I beg your pardon?" he said, with a horrified expression.

"I mean, if it's effective against organic systems, then the *Sam Houston* should be immune. We don't use organic systems anywhere in the ship. Unless you count the crew that is." She had a dreadful thought, could it affect the humans on the ship?

"Of course."

"What about the crew, Mr. Maurya, any trouble with them?"

"None at all. But our ship's armor is a mess. The damn stuff has covered gun ports, thruster ducts, engine ports. You name it, it's fouled up right now. I was able to clear our spinal mounted weapon by firing it, but the damn thing is useless unless the enemy is directly in front of us, and since we cannot maneuver presently … we're up shit creek, as you Americans say."

"Don't worry, Maurya. We've got your back." Her ship rocked again, and she winced. "Y'all hold tight, Hutchison out."

The ground was rushing to meet the assault-shuttle at an alarming rate. Hal could make out individual trees now. Not good, he thought. At least the Hrymar ship had stopped shooting at them. That was something. There was no way Ed was going to jury-rig a fix in time for them to stop.

"Prepare to bail-out." He ordered. "Now!"

He and Molly scrambled to the cockpit airlock. It irised open and there was Edvit, his RCA suit covered with scratches—testimony to his impacts with various walls and fixtures.

"Check contragrav." Hal ordered. Each RCA suit was equipped with contragrav, strong enough so that they could effectively *parachute* into drop zones. All systems were green, he saw. He opened the inner airlock and they stepped through, closing it behind them, ensuring a sudden pressure differential didn't suck them out the hatch unexpectedly. As the outer hatch opened, the wind tore at them.

"Kick off hard. We need to clear the shuttle. Go!"

Each leapt off the ledge of the shuttle's hatch and began a slow descent. They'd exited none too soon; He counted three-seconds, then saw the shuttle crater into the jungle floor.

Chapter 18

LOCATION: RSS MJOLNIR / PLANET: ORBITING Haward II

"Captain," said Dr. Inglis over the ship-com.

"Maurya here, Doctor."

"I'm starting to get an increase in casualties reported. Are we still fighting? I thought we were out of the battle for the time being?"

"We are, Doctor. Perhaps they were just late in being reported? There's a lot of damage to the ship, and some sections are cut-off due to the armor-growth virus."

"Is that what you're calling it? Well, no, these are in fact brand new casualties. Six people reported nausea, bleeding from the nose and eyes, headaches: all symptoms of radiation poisoning. I thought we'd been hit by nukes or a radiation beam weapon."

"That's very strange. I have no insight into the root cause, Doctor. Keep me posted, please.

"Will do, sir."

How very peculiar, Maurya thought. They were currently floating vulnerable, but hadn't been hit by weapons in a couple of minutes, thanks to the *Sam Houston's* timely arrival. He tapped the inter-ship comm channel. "Captain Hutchison, Maurya here."

Captain Hutchison's face filled the view screen, as did her *once* pristine bridge; now it was dimly lit by sparks and smoke wisping up from terminals. *"Captain Maurya, what can I do for you?"*

"Captain, have you had any recent casualties reporting nausea, bleeding from the nose and eyes, and headaches?"

She looked back at him confused. *"Captain Maurya, we are in battle with the enemy, I'm sure we have casualties."*

"Please, Captain, this is very important. Check with your sick bay." He waited for her to do so.

She looked away as she conferred with another person, then looked back. *"How can you know that we have a person sick like that? Two in fact."*

His suspicions were confirmed, and a mountainous dread descended on him. "Captain, we have a critical situation."

"Everyone, activate stealth," Hal said, before they hit the ground.

The three of them faded into the undergrowth of the jungle. He checked his suit's HUD and saw the waypoint for the pre-arranged landing zone; it was five kilometers out. Would Ailan still be there? This had been a trap, but was it fully sprung yet? It didn't matter, not really. He had to go and see if his son was there, whatever the outcome.

An explosion caused him to wince; the shuttle. It should *not* have exploded as a result of a crash. They were designed not to. Someone had destroyed it.

"Follow me," he said.

Ed pulled out his handheld scanner. This custom-designed device could scan and analyze pretty much anything and everything. At least that's how it seemed to Hal.

"Haldor, I'm detecting a life sign—human. *He*, is at the waypoint," Edvit said.

Hal nodded. "Let's pick up the pace." The RCA suits were good for a sustained run speed of 30 kph on open terrain. But this was *not* open terrain. Half that speed would be doing well.

Twenty minutes of slogging through the jungle had them at the waypoint; a small clearing in the jungle, and the home of some ancient ruins, as well as a runestone-portal. A young man, in some kind of armor, stepped out from behind a piece of the ruined structure. Hal gasped. The boy—young man— had Siobhan's fine features and her red hair. Ailan.

They approached each other in the center of the clearing, while Molly and Edvit hung back. He wanted to run to his son, pick him up and crush him in his arms. His *little boy* was as tall as he was, and more heavily muscled. Gods, and he was what, fifteen? They stood several paces apart.

"Ailan," was all he could say. And it *was* him. Hal could sense it, feel it.

The young man said nothing. He just glared back at him.

"I- I was told you were dead. I thought that- " What of Siobhan he thought. "Your mother?"

"I know not," Ailan said tersely.

Hal stepped a pace closer and Ailan shuffled back two paces, with a look that chilled him. This boy was a killer. Hal could read it in his movements.

"I'm glad to see you. It tore me apart when I thought you and your mother were dead."

"So torn that you impregnated another woman only months after we were captured?" Ailan said harshly.

That shredded Hal's soul. Because it was true. He'd taken comfort in another woman. Eva was there, and he needed someone. "I thought you were both dead, son."

Ailan's face went red. "*Never* call me that!" Ailan spat the words.

He could see Ailan's muscles tensed, poised to attack. "You *are* my son. I don't care what these blue bastards have told you."

The boy softened for a moment. "You never came." The words hung around Hal's neck like an anchor chain. "I prayed to the gods for you to come and save me, save mother. But you *never* came."

A single tear escaped Hal's eye. He was so preoccupied with his own grief, that he failed to sense his son's fury erupting and the imminent attack that would follow.

Ailan exploded at him, two daggers, like fangs reaching for their prey. Hal evaded by millimeters, spinning to the side. He threw his hands wide, palms toward his son. "Ailan, please! Stop it."

"I am Kadir, you piece of filth!" The boy spat on the ground in front of him. "Ailan is dead. He died long ago." Ailan slashed with one hand and thrust with the other.

Gods he was fast, Hal thought. Drawing his own weapons felt like the thing to do, but he had to suppress that urge. This was his *son*. He couldn't draw a blade on his own boy. He had to disarm him. That was his only course of action. But that was going to be much more difficult in practice. "Ailan, let me speak for a moment, then you can kill me if you wish."

"Kadir is my name. And you, Haldor Olsen. You, and your weak race, will be conquered and enslaved. Each, and every one of you. I have put my heel on the throats of many myself. The strong rule, the weak serve. That is the Hrymar way."

"You are *not* Hrymar!" He bellowed. He saw Molly and Edvit approaching to help, but he waved them off. "Stay back, damn you!" As he circled the boy, he saw a dark haired woman lying on the ground. Gods, it was Gina. She had a cut on her throat and was perfectly still. "Is she dead? Did you kill her?" He was angry with the boy now.

"Yes, and yes." He spat again on the ground at Hal's feet. "And you shall follow her shortly."

Thrust, feint, thrust, thrust feint. Hal kept blocking with the palms of his hands, slapping down on the top of the boys wrists as he came in to attack. Thrust, feint, kick! Ailan thrust a foot into Hal's guts and knocked him on his ass. Hal drew his dagger before the boy could pounce on him.

He rolled backwards from a crouch, and sprang up, dagger in his left hand—he would keep using his main hand to block.

"Kadir," He said, using Ailan's new name. "Hear me! I am not your enemy. I tried to save you. I even came to Niflheim. Devrim lied to me He told me you and your mother were dead. What was I to do?"

"And you believed him? You are either a fool or a coward. Probably, both. Thank the Jotuns I was raised on Niflheim where I could learn to be a true warrior." Alan spun backwards with a kick to Hal's face. He could feel the impact all down his body. If not for training in Rigsvaka's 1.58 g, his neck might have broken.

Hal tossed his dagger to his right hand.

The boy jumped back ten-meters, clearly aided by his armored suit. Ailan held something now. A small object? Ailan pressed it, and a field of light emanated from around him, and directly behind, the runestone-portal, glowing blue, and pulsating. They all watched in awe as the strobing of the runestone sped up, then its black bulk faded to a circular view of the outdoors, like a window, maybe three meters across. There was a popping sound, and a rushing blast of air toward the shimmering disc. Gone was the jungle on the other side of the disc. Now a desert landscape looked back at them. Four giant troll-like creatures stampeded through the portal. Graal!

Maurya watched as images of Dr. Inglis and Captain Hutchison were projected in separate windows of the Mjolnir's main view-screen. *"What I think is happening,"* Dr. Inglis said, *"is that the virionic weapon from the Hrymar ship has infected some of the crew. Anyone who was in close proximity to the sections of the hull hit by the virionic beam, have gotten very sick. I'm not sure if that's intentional, or just a side effect of the weapon — like radiation poisoning is a side effect of old nukes."*

"Damn those bastards," Captain Hutchison said. *"So you're saying that even though our ship is immune to the beam, our crew might not be?"*

"That is correct. However, we seem to have a much higher number of crew infected. Perhaps that's to do with the hull being infected. Maybe it spreads the infection farther, or amplifies it. I'm just not sure yet," Dr. Inglis said.

"I suggest we quarantine any affected crew. What we don't know yet, is whether it's infectious. If it is, God help us," Chandragupta Maurya said.

"We'll do that," Hutchison said, then leaned off screen as she conferred with one of her officers. *"Our friends are coming back for another pass at you. We're going to intercept and see if we can end this. Hutchison out."* Her image went black.

Dr. Inglis rose from her office desk. *"I'll get back at it, sir. Call me if you need*

anything. And I'll start quarantining any of the sick, and those who have had contact —
including myself. Tell me immediately if any of the bridge crew start presenting with
symptoms."

"Good luck, Doctor. Maurya out." He closed the channel to the sickbay.
He tapped on the comm-console and called up a ship-wide channel. "This is
the XO. I want all hatches closed immediately, and all crew are restricted from
movement unless directed to do so, by senior staff. XO out."

The four Graal shock-troops blew past Hal and Ailan, and went straight for
Molly and Edvit. Hal had to end this before his friends were killed. With his
power-assisted ECA armor, he sprang the full ten-meters to close with Ailan.
He slammed his left fist into Ailan's chest, knocking the boy backwards off his
feet, and denting his armor.

Ailan rolled with the blow and was up on his feet in a micro second, both
daggers poised to defend. "Are you ready to die now, Olsen?"

Hal sensed the intention of the boy's attack before he moved. It was good
he had, for Ailan moved so fast, he wouldn't have survived the attack if not
for his gift of the Athryllith. Ailan came at him with stabbing blows, high and
low, at the same time. He blocked the high blow with his empty hand, and
slashed across Ailan's wrist with his cledyf-dagger. Its mono-molecular blade
could cleave powered armor like bathroom tissue. He pulled his cut though,
otherwise he would have taken the boys hand clean off at the wrist.

Ailan pulled back and eyed the deep gash in his armor, and the blood
oozing from it. Ailan winced in pain. Gods, had Hal cut him too deeply? The
boy's angry expression melted into one of sadness. His son. He stepped
toward him tentatively. Could he reach out to him? He opened his mind to

Ailan. Called to him, mind-to-mind.

"Father?" he heard Ailan think.

"Yes, it's me, son. Please come with me."

The boy dropped to his knees and began to weep. "Father," he croaked.

He walked to his Ailan, to console him. He could feel the boy's deep sorrow and loss. Maybe there was a chance. He stood over his son and looked down at the man he had become. *Kadir* looked back at him. The boy had shielded his true intentions from Hal, had somehow mislead him, mind-to-mind.

Kadir exploded from his crouch, right dagger held in an ice-pick grip, but instead of stabbing, he slashed up, cutting deeply across Hal's entire face, from left chin to right eye. Kadir was in the air and flipped, landing behind him.

Ailan gave his father a shove, and he fell forward onto his knees. He could feel ice in his veins, freezing his body and mind. He tried to turn, but couldn't. *"Ailan,"* he thought to his son.

"Your son is dead, Haldor Olsen. And now, so are you!" Ailan shouted to his father.

Chapter 19

LOCATION: LYFJABERG (HILL OF HEALING) / Planet: Rigsvaka

Hal opened his eyes and blinked, shutting them immediately; too bright, he thought. He felt the soothing caress of another mind—like the sun's warmth on a cool spring morning. Her caress melted the ice in his limbs and blew away the fog in his mind.

"Gwynahra?" he thought.

"I'm here, Haldor."

He felt her silken hand on his, and turned to see her face. She was so beautiful, so gentle. As he reveled in her presence, memories came unbidden; horrible, terrible memories; memories of his son, his *wife*. The tightness in his guts returned, and the chill that had thawed in his limbs, froze again.

"My son?" he asked weakly.

"Shhhh," she said, as she stroked his face. "Don't try to speak. You can worry about all that later. Just rest now. Regain your strength."

"How long?" he thought to her.

"You've been unconscious for five days. We're back on Rigsvaka."

"What of Ailan?"

"He lives, though he returned to the Hrymar. I am sorry, my love."

A pang of guilt ran through him when she said—my love. She loved him, and he *did* love her. But he couldn't. How much was a man supposed to take before breaking? Were the gods testing him?

He saw Gina enter the room—alive. "Gina-" he rasped.

She kept her distance. "We'll talk soon, boss. I just wanted to make sure you were ok."

He shook his head. "How?"

"It was just a paralytic poison. Same as was used on you. The cut on my neck was just a scratch. The Hrymar just wanted to rattle you."

The sound of padded feet intruded on his self pity. He recognized the sound of a creature he knew all too well—Venn. And on her back, rode little Chloe. While holding a tuft of Venn's fur, she slid off the wolf's back. Hal felt the warm breeze again, this time from Chloe and Venn. *This* love he could accept, and not feel guilty for. He took it, and returned it. The Athryllith was a beautiful force of nature. One of the gifts from the gods, he mused. They took, and they gave.

He'd not even noticed Gwynahra and Gina leaving the room.

"I was so worried about you, Haldor," Chloe thought to him.

"I'm sorry, little one," he thought to her.

She threw her arms around his neck, and squeezed, while Venn nuzzled against his side. Love. He closed his eyes and let the feeling flow through him, tears falling freely.

Location: Aboard Light's Doom - in Hyperspace

Kadir's head snapped sideways as the back of Serkan's scarred hand caught him in the face. Jotuns! He could taste what had been on Serkan's hands, in addition to his own blood. His Master was furious at his failure to kill Haldor Olsen.

"Stupid child! I told you what was at stake. Consider yourself blessed by the Jotuns if Devrim doesn't have you skinned alive. What in Alfheim were you thinking?" Serkan bellowed.

Kadir knew not to be evasive or deceitful. Though the Hrymar prided those traits, woe to he who was caught practicing them. "Master, I poisoned the blade as you instructed. And I *did* cut him. There should have been enough poison to kill him. You know those Alfar are crafty leaf-eaters."

Serkan spun, mumbling under his breath. "Just fuck off out of my sight, boy. If you know what's good for you."

He'd known Serkan for so many years that he could anticipate how combustive his temper would be for any failure. He'd overestimated his reaction. Serkan was being surprisingly lenient with him. If he knew the truth, that Kadir had deliberately let his father live … Kadir wouldn't be having these thoughts right now.

Location: Ministry of Industry & Technology (MI&T) Building / Planet: Rigsvaka

Hal walked under the iron sky as sub-arctic winds nipped at the gaps in his shirt. He pulled the edges of his grey cloak and they sealed around him— he loved Alfar organic-fabrics. Had he been wearing his bionan suit underneath his clothes, he would have been perfectly comfortable, despite the temperatures, but he enjoyed the feel of natural materials—he made an exception for the Amdyffin-cloak.

The new MI&T building was bustling when he arrived. A warm flash of pride washed over him. He'd helped build this. It was quite a feeling. His enemy took joy in destroying, but that was easy to do. Creating—that was the ultimate expression of intelligence; in his opinion.

Lady Valindra Greenleaf, and Magister Edvit Skuldarbrunnr, met him in the lobby. "Good to see you both."

Both inclined their heads with the customary bow. "My Lord"

"I hear there may be good news?" He asked.

Edvit closed one eye. "You don't want us to spoil the surprise, now do ya?"

Lady Valindra waved a hand at the Dvergar.

They'd been working well together, Hal mused. Valindra of Alfheim, was a Ljossalfar, or Light Elf. Edvit was a Svartalfar, or Dark Elf—colloquially known as Dvergar, or Dwarves. Traditionally, Elves and Dwarves did not work well together; they were never true enemies, nor would they ever call one another friends. But, Hal had set about changing that.

After the small talk concluded, the scientist and the engineer, Valindra and Edvit, respectively, escorted him to the exo-viral research floor. He was glad for the redundant layers of security; *dangerous* did not even begin to describe what they were working on, and the delays imposed by security gave him peace of mind.

In a room that looked more office than laboratory, they motioned for him to watch a screen.

A view of the Hrymar battleship appeared. As Valindra zoomed out, a green beam became visible. "Now pay attention to the beam as I zoom in," she said.

As the beam filled the screen, he could see that it was not entirely energy.

"Have you spotted the curious bit?" Edvit asked.

"That's not like any plasma or other energy beam I've ever seen," Hal said.

"Quite right, my Lord," Valindra said, and walked up to the screen. She ran a finger along the edge of a darker region. "Notice this band. That is not energy. In fact, we believe it to be some kind of fluid. Perhaps even simple H_2O." She zoomed in again. "This image has been enhanced beyond the optical image from the ship's camera. We have superimposed data from other sensors, onto the beam, but it's a valid representation."

He shrugged. "So, what am I seeing?"

"Do you see these small spherical nodules?" Valindra asked. When Hal nodded she continued. "Let me zoom in again. Now see the hair like fibers on the outside of the spherical object?"

"Yep."

"They are various proteins on virus cell. Meiriona said the effects were like that of a virus, and hence described the weapon as *virionic*. She was all too right. This weapon fires a coherent beam of fluid, encased in an energetic sheath. Inside the fluid, lives the virus. We believe that the beam provides energy to the fluid, keeping the temperature stable while the fluid travels across the cold vacuum of space."

Edvit was nodding. "That's some pretty gods damn fancy engineering, Haldor- um, my Lord."

Hal smiled. Edvit had known Haldor for many years before he was a *Lord*. "It is. And frankly, it seems far too sophisticated for our Hrymar friends."

"Bloody right it is, *my Lord.*" Edvit winked at him.

"So how do we defend against this? It was bad enough on the Mjolnir, from what I hear. Imagine an Alfar ship who's life-support is organically controlled? Or contragrav? We got knocked out of the fight, but we walked away from it. An Alfar ship might not."

Valindra nodded solemnly. "That is my concern as well."

"Back to my question then. Have you two got a solution?"

"Not quite yet," Edvit said. "Determining exactly what it was, was the first step, and a big one."

"I don't mean to diminish what you and Valindra have achieved, but my concern is what happens next time I go into battle against one of those bastards?"

"I understand, my Lord. And we will be working tirelessly to that end," Valindra said with a bow.

He smiled encouragingly. "I know you will."

Valindra continued. "We'll be focusing on three areas: virus attachment to the cell, virus replication, and virus maturation. If we can disrupt or corrupt, any of these three facets, then we stand a good chance of stopping it. The challenge we face, is that the virus seems capable of mutating to work within the constraints of its environs. Accordingly, we would need to design a solution that also reacts to the virus mutations."

"And let me tell you, m'Lord," Edvit said, "that's a damn sight harder than it sounds. However," Edvit buffed his knuckles on his breast pocket, "your most resourceful Dvergar Engineer may have a solution."

Edvit let that hang for a moment.

"And?" Hal prompted.

"And, I think I may be able to manufacture a retro-virus from organic nano-bots."

Hal was impressed. "A synthetic life-form?"

"Well, in truth, my Lord," Valindra said, "a virus is not considered a life-form, so I'm not certain whether this proposed machine could be called that either. However, it will be organic, and it will be synthetic. Synthetic-Organism would be the correct designation."

"The idea," Edvit continued, "is for us to create wee machines that create anti-bodies and stick them on the virus. That flags them for disposal by the host's immune system. Then, white blood cells consume the virus and use enzymes to denature the virus and break it into pieces."

"Sound like you have a plan."

"Well, an idea, anyway," Edvit said.

Hal gave them a wan smile and nodded his head. This was progress, he thought. He'd been overly enthusiastic wishing for a solution already. This was good news, and he needed to treat it as such. "Keep up the great work. If there are any resources you need, I'll make sure they're at your disposal."

"Thank you, my Lord," Valindra said. "I believe we will need to consult with my colleagues on Alfheim. Edvit and I will need to travel there via the runestone-portal."

"I'll make sure you travel is pre-authorized." He gave them both a slight bow. "I'll let you get back to it."

Location: Undisclosed Military Shipyard / Planet: Niflheim

Devrim stood above his nascent fleet. Below him, spread across the vast cavern, lay the most lethal and evil pack of machines ever assembled. They had but one purpose, to subjugate the stars. No longer would he be content raiding piecemeal, no, he would scour the galaxy; he would devastate everyone, crush them beneath his boot heels. He was meant to rule. Born a weakling, an outcast, he was spat upon, discarded, and to his father's shock, highly underestimated. He turned those weaknesses into strengths, the like of which his people had not seen for a thousand years.

Underestimation was a strategy and tactic he'd taught his human fosterling. Nurture that sense of perceived weakness, he'd told Kadir, use it. For when they least expect it, that is when it is best to strike. As Devrim had done, thrusting a dagger through Egemen's chin. Oh, that had been a day of days.

His ancient and gnarled shipmaster, Bugra Abay, approached. Abay bowed low in respect of his Over-Chieftain. "Oh greatest of all Over-Chieftains, my Lord and Master." Abay remained low, groveling.

A man who knew how to show the proper deference, Devrim thought; so rare. "Rise you crooked old branch, before you break a limb." The old man's skin was a deep blue, and wrinkled. It reminded Devrim of layers of old ice.

"Thank you, Master. Most of the Korku-class are ready. Soon the Black Tide will wash upon the weak."

"Indeed. The Siyah Gelgit will crash upon them." He was intoxicated at the number and power of these warships. "How many are ready to deploy now?"

"We can field twenty-one right now. Their crews are aboard and awaiting your orders."

Devrim smiled, and nodded approvingly. "Good. That is good. And the rest?"

"The remaining seventy-nine Korku-class will be ready to launch in six-months. I expect we can field an additional dozen or so ships each month until then. And of course there are all the fleet escort and support ships. We are rolling out a battle-group at a time, my Lord. Might I ask, how did the test of the Zehir-Cannon go?"

Devrim almost chuckled. "Bugra, I wish I had been there. The video footage was remarkable. It ravaged a ship with only the Alfar Armor. When we stand against those traitorous tree-loving wretches. Oh, will I sing! The Korku-class and their Zehir-Cannons will rid this galaxy of the Alfar and their beneficence; meddling bastards, all."

"I am please to hear it, Master. No Over-Chieftain has ever had the foresight and wisdom you wield."

"Please, keep your tongue out of my asshole, old man. You have done well. You need not ingratiate yourself any further."

The old man swept an arm across his chest as he bowed low. As he came back up, he flinched and withdrew.

Devrim looked to see a shape emerging from the shadows; shrouded in a black hooded-cloak, but with its face visible; two bumps pushing up the fabric of the hood, and its brown scaly face, just visible. Bugra Abay's mouth fell open as Devrim—his Over-Chieftain—bowed to the dark figure.

"Lord Crazal, it is an honor to see you again. I did not know you were arriving today?" Devrim managed hastily.

Crazal inclined his head. "Understandable. I wished to arrive in secret."

"Of course. You are welcome to come and go anytime."

"It is time," Crazal said.

Devrim nodded. "Bugra, have the First Claw of the battle-group come to see me. It is time to release the Dark Tide."

Flakes of snow drifted on a gentle morning breeze. Hal inhaled the thick fall air. Before him lay Asabjorg, a temple he'd built to honor his Norse gods and goddesses; their figures rising like skyscrapers from the landscape. Two rows of statues, a hundred meters high, rose face to face, the sky above their heads. A statue of Tyr, god of law and justice, stood one-hundred and fifty meters tall at the head of the two rows, facing him, at the opposite end, was the Allfather, Odin, rising equally high.

It was under the shadows of these august representations that Haldor marched, head held high, proud, though reverent. His gods demanded no man or woman on bended knee. They encouraged boldness, and vitality; not meekness and humility.

Rows of his people lined the central path, smiling and greeting him as he passed. Since the Athryllith had grown stronger in recent weeks, he could feel so much more. Here, he felt the love and respect of his people. It was humbling to sense that devotion on such an intimate level, and from so many. Would that kings of old could have known their people like this.

As he neared the dais of the outdoor-temple, Lady Carwyn, Thaynja of Shadowsong, and Minister of Justice, waited to greet him. Flanking her, Lord Chogan, Thane of Blackfeathers, and Minister of Spiritual Affairs, smiled warmly at Haldor. He had great respect for Chogan's ancestral religion, that of the American Indians, which in fact, was much like his own. Each, had colorful pantheons, as well as reverence for their ancestors, and a deep respect of nature and the land that supported them.

His two thanes bowed, as he bounded up the nine-steps to the platform and its three seats.

"Good morning, my Lord," Chogan said.

"Lord Haldor, it warms me to see you on such a chilly morning," Carwyn said.

"Morning, all. I'd return the complement, Lady Carwyn, but it was actually a dram of whiskey that warmed me up this morning. Though, I am delighted to be in your presence." He winked at her.

Carwyn shook her head in playful reproach, while Chogan grinned. Haldor took his seat after a couple of handshakes.

The Huscarl Oath-Taking ceremony began as Lord Chogan nodded. Twelve horns bellowed, beckoning the candidates. As Chogan sat, Hal saw a column of one-hundred and twenty men and woman, begin marching down the row toward him; his prospective bodyguards; sworn men and women, who would die to protect him and his family. They were a force he'd always intended to establish, someday, but the recent assassination attempt had accelerated their formation.

The procession halted at the bottom stair to the dais, Lady Carwyn stood, and walked toward them. She carried a mead-filled horn and held it aloft. "Gods, and goddesses of the North. Hear your folk. Accept this sacrifice so that we may honor you." She took a sip of the mead, and poured the remainder onto the stone. The golden liquid trickled down the steps and seeped onto snow-speckled grass. It was a simple opening, but gods of the

North, of Asatru, required no complicated rituals. They were gods of simpler times, when ceremony and ritual were not codified, where a man or woman was the gothi of his or her own household, or even of a whole people, as Hal was here on Rigsvaka.

Chogan handed Hal a large silver hoop. Runes danced around its circumference; this was the oath-ring. Its runes were the holy words, the unbreakable oath that these men and women would swear; everlasting, even through death. Only the Lord to whom the oath was pledged could sunder it.

Hal approached the column of candidates, holding the oath-ring in one hand. "Do you know what it is that I expect of you?"

"Yes, my Lord!" Came the chorus of replies.

"At what cost will you safeguard the life of the rightful ruler of Rigsvaka and his family?" He asked.

"At any cost, my Lord!" they replied in unison.

"And will you give your lives willingly to this purpose?"

"Yes, my Lord!"

"And do you vow that you shall not swear any other oaths that contradict or undermine the solemn oath you pledge today?"

"We so swear, my Lord!"

"And will you prosecute oath-breakers, and anyone attempting to illegally withdraw their fealty, after they've paid homage to the Jarl?"

"To the fullest extent of our power, my Lord!"

"And when the dark forces walk before us, will you cower when outnumbered and overwhelmed?"

"Not if all the sons of Jotunheim marched against us, my Lord!"

He smiled. "Good. Then come forward and hold the oath-ring with me."

One by one, the hundred and twenty candidates approached, held one end of the oath-ring, and repeated their oath: *I pledge my life in service to the Tyrmundr and its rightful ruler. I will stand before the Hrymar horde, sword in hand, defending the principles of justice and honor. To all these points I swear and will never break them, under pain of death or banishment from all Tyrmundr society and persons.*

Hal looked out upon the rest of his people lining the rows of statues. "People of Rigsvaka, welcome our new housecarls!"

Chapter 20

LOCATION: TYRBJORG (JARL'S APARTMENTS) / PLANET: Rigsvaka

Hal laughed as Chloe rode Venn around the living room, while at the same time, reciting a poem she had to memorize for school. He thought it was an ingenious combination. Chloe said the rhythm of Venn's walking helped her remember. Venn was happy to oblige.

"Take it from the top," he said.

"What does that mean, from the top?" Chloe asked.

"From the beginning, let's start again."

Her eyes darted up, as if recalling something, then she nodded a couple of time, her lips moving. "Got it! Go, Venn, go." Venn began her umpteenth circuit around the living room.

"The Vikings lived a thousand years ago
In Denmark, Sweden and Norway
Sometimes called Norse
They're gone now of course
But we think of them still today.

There were kings who ruled the lands,
And there were farmers and traders.

Jarls were the richer men,
Others were fishermen,
Some were viking raiders.

These raiders sailed to England
In longships made of wood.
They'd burn and pillage
Any small village,
And steal everything they could.

One famous viking was Ragnar Hairy Breeches.
He once raided Paris, in France.
Success brought him fame
But what a silly name!
Who'd want to be called hairy pants?

Famous explorer Eric the Red
Found a place that was windy and freezing.
He called it Greenland
And this, so he planned,
Would make it seem rather more pleasing.

Eric's son Lief was an explorer too
He captained a longship with 35 men.
Clever and plucky

Nicknamed "Lief the Lucky"
He sailed to America and back again.

Vikings believed the afterlife was
A great hall called Valhalla -
A huge feast where
The only men there
Were warriors, men of valor.

Odin was the king of the gods
Worshipped by the Norse.
He'd a long beard
But what's really weird,
Is he rode an 8-legged horse.

There were lots of other gods and goddesses,
Like Freya - pretty and sweet,
And mighty Thor,
God of thunder and war,
And Loki, with his lies and deceit."

"Well done, Chloe!" He clapped and smiled, his pride overflowing. "That was perfect."

She slid off Venn's back like a master horsewoman, or wolf-rider, in this case. "Thank you, my Lord," she said with a mock bow and a twinkle in her eye.

"I have a confession," he whispered, conspiratorially." He gestured for her to come close. He bent down to whisper in her ear. "I hated school when I was your age."

"You did? How come?"

"Oh, I suppose I wanted to be out sailing, or hiking in the hills. I hated being cooped up inside."

"I don't mind. I never got to go to school before, plus, my teacher is really nice, and I love learning all these things."

"I know. And that makes me very proud."

The doorbell rang, and he looked up.

Two of his new bodyguards—housecarls—flanked the door to his apartments, both on the inside, and the outside. One of the housecarls manning the inner door whispered into his wristcom, then looked up to him.

"My Lord, Lady Gwynahra is here to see you."

Venn padded over to the door at carefree-pace. Despite the presence of the Housecarls, Venn still felt the need to investigate any person seeking entry.

"Let her in. Thank you," he said.

He heard the heavy door creaking, followed by a melodic voice greeting Venn. The Alfar beauty glided across the room to him and Chloe, one hand rubbing Venn's ears. "Good evening, all."

Hal walked over to meet her. "Gwynahra, it's good to see you," he said, using her full name.

She raised her eyebrows and said, meekly, "Lord Haldor," and gave him a slight bow.

"Don't be so formal, for goodness sake," he thought to her.

"I thought our relationship was *formal now,"* she thought to him.

He exhaled, slightly frustrated with her, but happy to see her.

She smiled when she felt his mood shift and he shook his head, also smiling when he realized she'd read him.

"It's good to see you," he said quietly.

She looked down at her feet, glancing back up at him. "You too."

"Um, I think I'll leave you two lovebirds alone," Chloe said out loud. *Chloe* had read them both; when they were together, their mental self-control got sloppy.

"No, no. I'm sorry Chloe," Gwynahra said, moving to the girl. "How are you doing? I didn't mean to snub you."

Gwynahra's smile was as wide and beautiful as mountain lake, he thought; pure and magical. He saw her glance back at him and her cheeks went red. Oh gods, she'd heard that. It was hard to be discretely attracted to someone who had telepathic powers.

Gwynahra spent some time with Chloe, during which, she recited the poem again while Venn did her best pony impression.

"I do have more homework to do. Will you two behave if I leave you alone?" Chloe asked.

"Chloe!," He admonished.

She looked shocked. "I'm kidding! Sheesh." She rolled her eyes and waved goodbye to Gwynahra.

"She's a wonderful girl, Haldor."

"Yes, she really is." He gestured to the sofa, and she sat beside him.

After a moment of awkward silence, Gwynahra spoke. "I did have a reason to come over tonight."

"Hey, you're welcome here anytime. You don't need a reason."

"Thank you. I was wondering if you wanted to continue your training in the Athryllith? I thought it might be uncomfortable for you, but I supposed I should offer."

He'd not expected that and was not prepared with an answer. Gods damn it, in front of any other being in the universe he would have an answer in a micro-second, yet in front of this young woman he felt like a two year old. "I wouldn't want to put you to any inconvenience."

"Oh, it would never be, I- " she cut off. "Of course, it's up to you."

"I mean, sure. I guess we could." He *so* wanted to see her. Even if nothing could come of it, he wanted her near him. Was that selfish? If he couldn't commit to a relationship, what business did he have leading this remarkable young woman on? It was agony, he thought.

"Haldor, I exepect nothing from you. Nor do I ask anything," she thought to him. Clearly she'd picked up his internal struggle. *"Like you, I want to be in your presence. I want to be near you. Does that make me selfish? Or pathetic? I don't care what the future holds. I simply want to spend time with you while I can. How could I not? If the day comes that I have to walk away from you, then I will do so. But I will not go unless you send me away."*

Gods in Asgard, how he wanted to hold her right now. He swallowed hard. "Sure, practice. I think I need it. Can we start practicing self control exercises?" He attempted a smile.

Star: Adhara (The Maiden)/ Region: Islamic Republic of Watan

Kadir's head leapt off the pillow when he felt *Light's Doom* shudder —

they'd just dropped into normal space.

A couple of minutes later he arrived on the bridge where Serkan was sifting through a long column of stellar and planetary data.

"Master, where are we?" Kadir asked.

"We are about to rendezvous with several new Korku-class ships, youngling. Very stimulating indeed."

"My Lord, I have five ships on sensors, I am projecting it to the main screen now," his sensor officer said.

Kadir watched as dozens of small, red dots buzzed around five larger blue dots. The sensor officer zoomed in and the profiles of Niflheim's new battleships materialized; around them, like a swarm of hornets, flew much smaller craft; fighters, he thought, but he'd never seen such ships before.

"Voice," Serkan barked, "open a channel to the First Claw."

"Aye, my Lord," said his comms first.

"Eyes," Serkan said, "identify those fighters and give me all relevant data."

"Yes, my Lord," his sensor first replied,.

"Fists, ready all weapons."

His weapons first Nodded.

"First Claw on screen," my Lord

"Serkan, you arthritic, old svell-kottr. Late as usual!" First Claw Tosunbey said.

"It has been some time since I have been called ice-cat, my Lord," Serkan said with a slight bow.

"An appellation well earned, if memory serves."

Kadir saw Serkan smile for the first time in, well … he could not remember when. This must be some old friend of Serkan's. Kadir did not realize such men could have friends.

"My Lord, I see that you have some frost-gnats biting at you. May I be of service?" Serkan asked.

"Yes, indeed you may. They are getting tiresome. These humans, they call themselves Muslims; vicious, but insignificant. And yet, they are marking up our brand new ships. Pity."

"We shall be in weapons range in two-minutes," Serkan said.

"Until then." Tosunbey closed the connection and the tactical readout re-appeared.

"Ears, what have you?" Serkan asked.

"My Lord, there are two-hundred and fifteen contacts. They are all in the ninety-ton range; fighter-bombers armed with a single torpedo and a single low-output laser-cannon turret."

Serkan nodded and returned to scrutinizing the enemy formation and attack patterns. "Kadir, what can you tell me of the enemy?"

Thankfully he'd expected the question and was scrutinizing the data as thoroughly as Serkan. "Master, they are obviously lightly armored, so they take advantage of speed and maneuverability to deploy their single torpedo, then attempt to escape and evade."

The old veteran was nodding. "And?"

"And, Master, I would advise letting the destroyer screen deal with them, as they are intended to, and the battleships should proceed to the colony at flank speed. Deny them combat." He shrugged. "Or at least frustrate their attempts."

"And why do you think that will work?"

"Well, Master, based on the acceleration I have observed over the last few minutes, they are not significantly faster than we are. More maneuverable, certainly. But that means little in a straight-line race to the planet. They should start to trail behind, and we can form up to concentrate fire and overlap point defense arcs." Serkan was smiling. Twice in one day.

"We might make a ship's Captain of you yet, youngling."

He blushed. He was unaccustomed to *any* praise. Lack of criticism was the norm when he did well. He nodded once as the only acknowledgement of the compliment.

"Voice, contact the First Claw. Let us share this strategy."

Location: The Council of Thanes' Chamber / Planet: Rigsvaka

Flanked by Cadfael, his new head of housecarls, Hal stood on the dais in the council of thanes. "Thank you all for joining me at this late hour. I realize it's after midnight, but we've some urgent news that needs to be dealt with immediately. I'll skip all the preliminaries and small talk. The Najaf colony in the Islamic Republic of Watan was hit by the Hrymar last night. There's no stellarcom on Najaf, and someone had to travel to their capital, Medina, to warn us, so the news is hours old. I just got word," Hal said.

A current of anger and frustration burst through the great-hall.

"My Lord," Lady Valindra said, "what do you recommend?"

"Firstly, Lady Greenleaf, I need to share some information with all of you, that is known only to six people on Rigsvaka."

A curtain of silence descended on the hall.

"Our scientists have decoded the thalamo-cortical-resonance-pulses—the frequency-keys—to dozens of new inter-stellar-bridge-nodes. Nine of which

267

are inside Rigsvaka space."

The curtain of silence blew back and a chorus of shock and awe began singing. Magister Edvit Jerresson said nothing, as he was one of the six who'd decoded the addresses.

"Alright, people, please! Hold on. Yes, that's fantastic news, and we'll focus on that later. Suffice to say, we have a shortcut to Najaf. For now, we need to pull together humanitarian aid as well as a scouting force. To answer you question, Lady Greenleaf, that's our first priority. Secondly, we need to ramp up the deployment of all fleet assets. Tony- excuse me, Lord Asturias, is analyzing the data from the attack. The short of it is, five battleships, plus a host of support craft, hit Najaf. And hit it hard. They've fielded a gods-damn fleet of these new behemoths. *If* they know the location of Rigsvaka, then it's possible for them to be here in five days."

"My Lord," Lady Varnslanda said, "then I request to leave immediately. We need to enlist aid for ourselves. The SID has quite a number of ships that are non-organic—except for the crew—and they should fare better against the new weapons than we or the Alfar will."

"That assumes they all have these new weapons," he said, "Najaf was hit with conventional weapons; kinetic bombardments, plasma bombs, etc. But your point is taken and we should proceed as if they do. Earth has received the report about Najaf already and the SID government is meeting now. Lady Greyheather, I want you to start planning to deploy intel-gathering assets. Eight Sleipnir-class stealth ships will be at your disposal."

"Very well, my Lord," she said.

"Lords Rozlog and Steelbridge, I want you two to begin planning an evacuation. We'll hold that in reserve, but I want it in place should we need it."

Andrew Zelinksi and Mimar Sinan, nodded.

"Lord Kifisia, I want the treasury moved by runestone-portal to Alfheim —tomorrow morning at the latest."

"It shall be done, my Lord."

"I'll work with Lord Asturias and Lady Spadarosso on a military strategy, in concert with Lady Greyheather. Am I missing anything?"

By the lack of response, he assumed he'd covered all the bases.

"Very well, let's get to it. The council's convened."

Chapter 21

LOCATION: TYRBJORG, GROUNDS / PLANET: RIGSVAKA

The boreal air was biting, heavy, and still; winter is coming, Hal thought. He looked up at the great sea of stars and the band that was the Milky Way. Part of Tyrbjorg's planning had excluded bright city-lights, which would have obscured the night sky. Instead, tiny bio-luminescent strips had been embedded into the paving stones, and served as night-time street markers. Perfectly fine to navigate by. Besides, he had two housecarls following at a discrete distance. They'd make sure he didn't get lost.

He'd decided he wasn't in any rush to get back to his residence; some fresh air would help clear his head. So he took a seat on one of the many cedar benches that lined the winding river front. With both arms stretched out on the wooden backrest, he let his mind drift among the shimmering specks of light.

An ugly thought intruded on his peaceful reflection; how many of those stars were home to beasts like the Hrymar? He had to stop himself. He knew the Hrymar were the exception, not the rule. Most other species they'd encountered were at least neutral, if not friendly.

Like a gust of wind, he felt a presence in mind-space before he heard the light footfalls. It was Gwynahra.

"Haldor?" she said in her silky voice. To him, each of her words were a caress.

He turned and saw Gwynahra walking down the riverbank toward him. "Hey. What are you doing out so late?"

She cleared her throat, and he knew instantly what it had been. Some strong emotional reaction from him had woken her, or at least got her attention.

"Sorry," he said. "I have been trying."

"Not to worry. And yes, I know you have. But when you got the report on Najaf … you were quite upset. I felt it hit you hard. I knew you'd be in session with the Council, so I waited. I just wanted to see if you needed to talk." She shrugged, offering a nascent smile.

Had there ever been a woman as selfless as this one? He watched the starlight dancing in her eyes for a long moment, mesmerized. He had nothing to say. He just wanted to reach out and touch her, hold her. "I'm a selfish bastard, Gwyn," he said in an emotionless monotone.

She sat beside him, their arms barely touching, and shook her head. "No. Never," she whispered.

"I am. I've had the most horrible thoughts lately." He turned to look meet her gaze. "They're eating me alive." He took her hand in his, and let her see.

She felt the surge of his guilt, the conflict about his love for her, and the oath to his wife. He took his marriage vows as seriously as the holiest of oaths to the gods. How could he expect his men to keep troth with each other when he couldn't keep a vow given to his own wife? And worse, he still loved his wife, would always would love her. As he loved Gwynahra, and always would. He didn't fall in love easily, but when he did, it was for keeps. He felt Gwynahra feeling a flush of heat at the intensity of his longing for her. He'd been trying to distance himself from her, but it was only making his need more urgent. And then Gwynahra felt it—the guilt, the self loathing, for the secret wish, made in a dark and desperate moment.

She released his hand, and realized she was breathing quickly, her heart pounding.

He looked at her, as if to ask, did you see?

She nodded.

"I wished her dead. What kind of a fiend could even let that cross his mind? I hoped that I would find out she was dead." He hung his head. "Just so I could be with you. I'm no better than the Hrymar."

"Never let me hear that cross your lips again!" Her voice sharp and biting this time. His housecarls tensed. "You are a great man. But, you are just a man, Haldor." She shook her head. "You have been beaten and battered, and the troubles of a dozen worlds piled upon your shoulders. You take on too much. Even the gods cannot ask this much of you- or anyone."

And yet they had, he thought to himself.

She took his hand again, this time a flood of peaceful calm washed over his mind. "Let me help you," she thought to him.

He let her. He closed his eyes and let her warmth and kindness flood his soul; these gifts offered with no expectation. This was the most profound love he could have imagined. He knew that there was an implicit understanding that Gwynahra would step aside if his wife was alive, or continue to be with him, if that's what he wanted—singular acceptance. His love for Gwynahra was so intense, so elemental, and eternal, that there were no circumstances under which it could ever be wrong—could there?

As his mind battled the guilt for taking solace in her, it occurred to him that perhaps she'd been one of Odin's gifts? Her love would certainly be a pillar on which he could stand in days to come. These thoughts tore through his mind at light-speed, and Gwynahra shared each of them.

"No!" He shouted, breaking their link, and stood abruptly. "I'm sorry." He shook his head, struggling to find the right words, when he knew full well, there was no right way to say this—could never be a right way to say this. He could have just linked with her again, and she could have felt and seen everything. But no, that had to stop. She was like a narcotic to him. The more he was with her, the more he wanted her, anxious for his next fix. But gods damnit, the more they were apart the more he burned for her.

"If she's alive…" he trailed off in a choking whisper. His attempt to rationalize his need for Gwynahra was cowardice, pure and simple. He was afraid to deal with his own grief, and instead, wanted to lose himself in desire for her. "I'm going to re-assign you off the *Mjolnir*." He said suddenly.

Her face looked as if he'd slapped her; a mask of shock. Her lips parted, but she said nothing.

"I'm so sorry. But you know how I feel. And you know I can't. How could you love a man that would do that? And if I broke that oath, what next?" He let the question linger as his frustration built to the breaking point. Each of his next words built to violent crescendo. "Right now, I would let the whole galaxy burn just to be with you!" He bellowed.

She said nothing.

He took a few deep breaths, prodding the rage back down to its hole.

Gwynahra swallowed, and he could see her eyes cloud up with tears, but he didn't feel her grief—his mental wall was up now, their connection fully severed.

"I will not be that kind of man. If there's some sliver of hope that I can still fulfill my oath to her … then I shall. But I will never stop loving you."

He turned and walked away before he lost his nerve.

Aboard *Mjolnir*, Hal watched on his view-screen as shuttle and freighter traffic weaved their way to the ships of the fleet; some with supplies, others with people. Concentrating on this intricate dance helped him keep his mind off more intense feelings.

His comm beeped, and he tapped a button to accept.

"Commander," Edvit said, *"I've some good news."*

"That's always welcome, Magister."

"We believe we have an anti-virus that may work against the Hrymar virionic weapon."

"Excellent! And do you have a delivery method?"

The Svartalfar's face turned into a prune-like shape. *"Ahem, well, yes,"* he said tentatively

He was tempted to focus, and read it directly from Edvit's mind, but he had made an internal pact not to do that. "And?"

"Well, the only way we can get the anti-virus delivered properly, is via a beam like weapon. Like a sort of energy-hypodermic needle."

"And?"

"Alright, I'll just say it. We can't build one."

"I suppose that nullifies the use of the anti-virus then."

"Not quite. The Hrymar have a beam we could use."

"Ed," he said, dropping all titles and ranks. "Please tell me something that doesn't include us boarding a Hrymar ship and using their weapon?"

"Wish I could. But since I can't, I won't. But yes, that's exactly right. You sure you aren't part Dvergar?"

"We *can* do it, Commander," Gina said, as she walked onto the command dais.

"Uh huh. But do I *want* you to risk that? That is the question, Lady Spadarosso." He'd taken to using her title when he was annoyed—Gina hated it. She might admit to being a girl, but she had refused to be called a lady—something about being an insult to all warrior women for thousands of years, blah, blah, blah.

"It's no gods damned different, than boarding any other enemy ship, boss," Gina said.

He had to admit she was probably right. He glared at Edvit through the comm. "Are you *certain* this will work?"

The dwarf smiled, and the expression rippled on his face. *"Commander,"* Edvit reassured him, *"there's always risk inherent in any experiment- ahem,"* he cleared his throat again, *"operation, I meant, operation of this kind."*

"Gina, are *you* comfortable with the risks? I mean, really?"

She put a hand on his shoulder and nodded. "Have you seen a Hrymar that could take me?"

"That's our girl!" Edvit beamed.

"Guess I haven't," he said evenly. Yet … he thought.

With the icy-blue of Rigsvaka as a backdrop against the stars, the shuttle slowed as it approached *Mjolnir's* still form.

"Did you get to spend some time with that lovely new bride, Timonen?" Hal asked.

The young Finn, piloting his shuttle, spun back to him with an ear-splitting grin. "Oh yes, sir. Thank you, sir!"

He couldn't suppress a smile. Newly weds. Probably didn't leave the bedroom the whole week he was off.

"I'm glad. You hoping for some kids soon?"

Timonen's blonde mop flopped around as he nodded. "Darn right, sir!" Then he blushed. "Kara's hoping for a dozen."

He shot the young man an impressed smile. "An industrious gal, if ever there was, eh? Well, good for you." He stopped talking as the Mjolnir came into view. Timonen must have noticed his change in focus, and turned back to the shuttle controls.

As the shuttle pulled closer, the tiny silver fleck began to grow. She was the most magnificent vessel he'd ever set foot on, but his heart lurched as details of the hull began to appear. Gods, she looked like old pictures of fighting dogs—battered and scarred; it tugged at his heart.

The virus which had infected the armor, had died of its own accord. That had been a blessing. Though the tumors and growths it had spawned, remained. It fell to Magister Edvit and his team of engineers to craft a solution to this most intractable of problems. What he came up with could only be likened to battlefield-amputation. There was no elegant solution and they simply cut off the excess growths on the armor. It was more butchery than engineering, as the armor was all living tissue, diseased though it was.

The crew had been less fortunate. The virus hadn't spawned growths in them, but hadn't died off either. It *had* made them very ill, all appearing as if suffering from a virulent flu; but one with no end. The symptoms continued at low levels, such that they survived, but remained infectious and wholly unfit for duty. He had to admit, as a weaponized virus, it was brilliant; it made the host just sick enough to be no military threat, and well enough that they could wander around and continue infecting an entire population. In isolated communities, people would simply die of eventual immune system collapse. His infected people were all in cryo, and so, were spared the suffering while a cure was developed.

"Take us around the whole ship, slowly," he said.

"Aye, sir."

Edvit had promised she was at 95% efficiency, and swore that was the best they could do. He couldn't fault Edvit; the state *Mjolnir* had been in after the battle with the Hrymar was simply disastrous. Thankfully, the *Sam Houston* had been around to tow *Mjolnir* back to Rigsvaka.

He cringed as he saw the deep gouges and remaining welts on her beautiful hull. Don't worry, old girl, I'll make sure you're like new, he thought. Eventually.

"Take us in."

Star: Adhara / Region: Islamic Republic of Watan

Light's Doom and its five brother ships, flew as one; a mighty javelin hurled over the enemy host. The soldiers below the javelin looked up and cursed it impotently, then the point struck home, impaling its victim. Kadir's tactic had worked. They had denied the enemy static targets and ignored the fighter-bombers. Instead, the small ships scrambled to form up behind the battleships, chasing them all the way to the colony.

He stared at the view-screen. In front of *Light's Doom* stretched a ragged wall of disparate ships. Cobbled together at the last minute, there was no real resistance there; a handful of freighters, a few obsolete warships, scores of shuttles, and even a few personal yachts.

Serkan laughed as the details of the defensive wall became more clear. "Fists, report."

"Two minutes to torpedo range, my Lord," his weapons first said.

Kadir had read up on the Islamic Republic of Watan. These colonists were settlers of the Earth region known as Arabia, and the Middle-East. Some even from North Africa. His ancestors had fought the Muslims in the Crusades. It struck him that their fighter-screen harkened back to the Muslim archers of the Crusades; they could hit the mounted knights well out of lance range, then flee quickly. The tactic proved a great frustration for the Christian knights.

"In range, my Lord," the weapons first said.

"Fire all tubes!" Serkan bellowed.

Light's Doom gave an undulating shudder as it belched torpedoes from bow to stern. Eighty, furious torpedoes accelerated toward the enemy line at a frightening pace. Kadir watched as the barrage struck their targets like fireworks. Blue explosions erupting down the line as EMP engulfed the enemy ships in turn.

"Target all ships still moving. Fire fission-torpedoes," Serkan ordered.

A smaller ripple of fire erupted from the torpedo tubes as nuclear-tipped torpedoes were sent toward any ship that had survived the EMP, or had been immune to it. Kadir followed the bright orange trails snake toward their prey; it was truly beautiful—blood-red hues of destruction painted on a canvas of black.

In seconds, a dozen or so ships began to pitch and roll, impaled by the powerful nuclear torpedoes.

"Well done you old ice-cat!" First Claw Tosunbey announced over the comms.

"Thank you, my Lord. We still have a few wasps to swat, but their defensive line is shattered."

"Just so. Serkan, I offer you the honor of raiding the planet first. The rest of us will have to clean up while you take all the glory."

Serkan bowed. "It would be an honor, my Lord."

The old Hrymar grinned. *"Get to it then."*

Chapter 22

LOCATION: ABOARD MJOLNIR / STAR: BLÁSTJARNA (Blue Star), En-route to Najaf

Forty ships, most smaller support vessels, and a total tonnage of only 699,000 tons; it was not the battle-group Hal had hoped to field when he next faced the Hrymar battleship. Things were rarely as people wished though, he thought.

They were coming up to an interstellar-bridge-node. The nodes were usually the size of small moons, or large asteroids, and always in space. The rarer runestone-portals, were always found on-planet, and were vastly smaller; wide enough for people, but not large war machines or ships to pass through.

He wondered at the race of beings that had created these portals and bridges across the stars. The Alfar had a myth telling that the gods of the North had built them so mankind could more easily seed the galaxy. Meeting the Alfar over a century ago had been a wake-up call for mankind; everything they had believed about the one God, the creator, had to be re-assessed. The lunatics and fringe groups that had still believed in the old gods, were proved right; according to the Alfar. But now that he had actually been visited by Odin … well, how could he still have doubts?

The geography of the nodes was such that there was no straight line to

Najaf from Heimdall's Star. As he understood it, the theory was that inter-stellar-bridges were formed over lines and clumps of dark-matter. The nodes and portals were activated by a resonant pulse—something to do with string theory—the frequency of the pulse determined the end destination, but was also limited by the paths of the dark-matter; each node had a finite number destinations; some had but one, others had many. And so, they had to make a series of hops, one of which took them into the Republic's space before hopping back into Rigsvaka territory. They had a mutual agreement with the Republicans, so transit was not an issue.

"Commander, activating the interstellar-bridge-node," Meiriona said. And from her sensors console she initiated the pulse which would unlock the node and specify the destination. That information was embedded in a proprietary beam called a thalamo-cortical-resonance-pulse; the effect was studied on humans in the last century and resulted in an integration of sensory perception—heightened awareness of all senses. The TCRP worked by a process called temporal-binding.

It was discovered that the bridge nodes responded to the same kinds of signals, and thus, the magic of instantaneous interstellar travel was finally unlocked.

He moved forward on the edge of his seat as the golden energy pulsed at the node. It looked like a series of laser pulses, only in yellow—instead of the more typical red, and the pulses were non-destructive. Slowly, the small, grey moon began to oscillate; its surface gradually transitioning from opaque to translucent, and back again; pulsating in response to the TCRP.

He could now see the interior of the node. "Magnificent," he said without meaning to. He'd seen these before, but each node was unique and beguiling. The interior of the nodes were composed of crystals, all facing a hollow core; for a moment it looked just like a geode, only on a far grander scale. Then the entire moon vanished, replaced by a hole in space-time. Or was it hole? Scientists speculated it was more likely a permeable membrane. He was now looking at a point in Republic space, twenty-seven light years distant.

"Comms, a message to the battle-group—move out."

"Aye, sir," Anouk Kappa replied. "Message sent."

In seconds, they had crossed the threshold of space-time and skipped across the stars.

As Mjolnir and the battle-group transited the node, the window through space-time evaporated behind them like a wispy cloud.

"Sir, I have an incoming call," the young French woman beamed, turning in her seat to see the Commander. " It's from the *Sam Houston!*"

He couldn't help but smile at the young woman's enthusiasm. "Thank you, Ms. Kappa. On screen."

A familiar Texan filled his view screen. *"Jarl Haldor, long time no see,"* said Captain Kay Hutchison.

"Here to see us off, Kay?" Hal asked.

"Nah, I'm not one for goodbyes and all that."

He furrowed his brow, not quite understanding why she was here. "Nice to see you in any case."

Hutchison waited a moment, then asked, *"Well … aren't ya going to ask, why I'm here?"*

"I assumed you were going to tell me?" He asked, more than said.

"Hal, you're taking all the fun out of this for me. Shame on you," she said, waggling a finger at him. *"Commander Olsen, I would like to officially request to join your battle-group to Najaf."*

His smile grew slowly and to epic proportions. He took a few breaths and stood as he savored this gift. "Captain Hutchison, it is with the greatest thanks, that I accept your offer." He bowed deeply.

"Ever the gentleman, Olsen. If I weren't old enough to be your mother ..." She shook her head and winked at him.

He chuckled. "Indeed, Kay. We can catch up over dinner later."

"Love to. Hutchison out."

He sat back down, considering the two-hundred-thousand tons of *non-organic* ship they had just acquired. That took them to just a hair shy of 900,000 tons, and provided an ally immune to the virionic weapon—for the most part. Much better.

"Meiriona, open the bridge. Let's keep moving."

"Aye aye, sir."

Once again he watched in fascination; on this side of space, the node was an asteroid. Smaller than the moon they'd just passed through, but massive still. He smiled as it began the magical transformation from object, to bridge through space-time; he smiled not just in admiration of its majesty, but from the realization that these *must* be one of the godly gifts Odin mentioned. These jewels in space certainly were a gift. Things were looking up.

Region: Rigsvaka Space / Final Inter-Stellar-Bridge-Node to Najaf

Hal's battle-group had completed their penultimate interstellar-bridge transit; only one more hop to Najaf. They waited on this side of the bridge for word from the scouts. He needed to know what might await his ships: such as number of the enemy ships, size, fleet composition, etc.

He keyed a button on his command-chair and the video-interview of the Najaf survivor came up on screen.

Interviewer: Tell me what you saw, please. Give me your first impressions.

Refugee: I was securing cargo in my ship for a voyage to Medina, in the Alioth star-system.

Interviewer: What type of cargo, if I may ask?

Refugee: Of course. It was handmade fabric. For manufacture into clothing

Interviewer: Very well. Proceed with your account.

Refugee: After I finished securing cargo I was walking up to the cockpit when I felt the land beneath the ship shake. At first I thought perhaps an earthquake, but Najaf is not tectonically active. So I made haste to examine my ship's radar and lidar, as well as gather any information from Najaf's orbital array of satellites. The satellites were all offline. All sixty-two. Which is impossible.

Interviewer: Go on.

Refugee: There was a large object on lidar which had no IRW transponder.

Interviewer: That happens occasionally, I'm sure.

Refugee: Of course, but not proceeded and followed by the ground quaking! The infidels were bombarding the capital of the colony!

Interviewer: My apologies, sir. I meant to offense.

Refugee: After I realized that this was some kind of attack, I made the ship ready to depart. I- I had a duty, yes, a duty, to ensure word of the infidel attack was carried off Najaf. And ... I made my escape.

Interviewer: Quite so. And we are very glad you did. And you saw only one vessel on sensors?

Refugee: I can't be sure. There was one, of course, but sensors also detected a large object farther out; approximately 300,000,000 kilometers. And its shape did seem to fluctuate.

Interviewer: And are there any other data you can provide?

Refugee: No. That is all. Inshala—God willing—we can scour these infidels from Najaf.

A large mass fluctuating, Hal mused. A formation of ships, perhaps with fighters running Combat Air Patrols?

"Commander," Gina said, as she passed through the hatch onto the bridge, "any word from the scouts?"

He glanced over his shoulder at her and shook his head. "Not yet."

She took up a position, standing on his left side, her hands clasped behind her back. "Another red dwarf?" She said, pointing to the star on the view-screen."

"Looks red to me," he said laconically

Gina rolled her eyes. "Yes, boss, I'm sure you noticed that. The point I was about to make, is that there seems to be a very large number of bridge-nodes in red-dwarf star systems. I wonder why that is?"

"Longevity, I suspect."

"What do you mean?" Gina asked.

"No red-dwarf star has died since the beginning of our Universe."

Gina spun away from the view-screen and gawked at Hal. "Are you shitting me?"

He shook his head. "Indeed I am *not* shitting you, *Lady Spadarosso*." He emphasized her title as a reminder of her newish status, and the gravitas that was supposed to accompany it.

Gina rolled her eyes once again, getting his not so subtle reference. "And why is that?"

He gave a casual shrug and gesture with his hands. "They have less mass and burn their fuel much, much more slowly. That makes them very long-lived. If I were an ancient builder, or god, or whoever created these bridge and portals, I'd put them in red dwarf system as well. It would ensure that what I built lasted almost an eternity. Many red dwarves will burn for 10 trillion years or more."

"Fuck me!" Gina wore an astonished look. "I should've studied astronomy."

"I loved it," he said. "One of the reasons I became a stellar surveyor after my first stint in the SID interstellar-fleet."

"Commander," said Anouk Kappa.

He and Gina pivoted toward the comms officer. "What is it, Kappa?"

"The node is activating, sir."

"About time. Let's hope they have good news, eh, Gina?"

She cocked her head. "One can hope, boss."

The shimmering stellar-geode vanished, replaced by a window into space-time, nearly forty light-years distant. Hal was caught unawares when he saw bright flashes that the sensors overlaid on the view-screen. Energy weapons fire! Gods damn it. And a ship heading toward the node.

"What ship is that?" He asked.

Kappa glanced at her screen. "It's the *Svadilfari*, sir. Captain Garrett's ship."

"Hail them."

Momentarily, the view-screen was filled with an image of the all too familiar bridge of a Sleipnir-class stealth scout ship. He'd captained the first of its class. He saw a side view of Captain Shelley Garrett's head, then suddenly Jin Wudai's face slide onto the screen.

"Jin, what in Niflheim is going on over there?"

Jin's face was filthy and streaked with blood, and the bridge was in tatters. Jin began to speak, as Hal could see his lips moving, but there was no audio. He motioned to his mouth, signaling to Jin that there was a problem. Jin nodded and help up his index finger—one minute. The *Svadilfari* shook as more laser fire raked her hull.

"Commander, there are five torpedoes chasing the *Svadilfari*," Shizari said.

"Time to intercept?"

"Three-minutes, sir."

Hal turned to his sensors officer. "Meiriona, can we fire through the bridge node into the space beyond?"

"Theoretically, Commander, I see no problem with that. It's never been tried."

"Shizari, time for *Svadilfari* to transit?" He asked.

"Four-minutes, sir. Those torpedoes are accelerating at nearly 10,000 gravities. That's eleven times the Svadilfari's acceleration rate."

"Comms, all ships," he ordered.

"Channel open, sir," Kappa said.

"All ships, this is High Commander Olsen, I want maximum military acceleration to the node. Form up on *Mjolnir* and activate all point defense batteries. Let's see if we can give the *Svadilfari* a little help."

"All ships now accelerating toward the node, sir," Meiriona reported.

"Jones, pedal to the metal, if you please."

The young, black man twitched his head with a massive grin. "My pleasure, sir!"

Mjolnir shot forward with a jolt, as the military acceleration exceeded the capacity of the inertial dampeners; which was why it was used only in emergencies.

"Have we got the enemy ships on sensors? The ones that presumably launched those torpedoes?"

"Aye, sir. Three *Hrymar* ships, based on reactor and sub-light drive signatures. They're in the three-thousand ton range sir—destroyers."

"Zeus!" Gina exclaimed. "More new ships! What in Hades is going on, Hal?"

Hal exhaled long and hard, looking exasperated. "Wish I knew. But I tell you what, we need to get on top of this. And fucking fast."

Meiriona looked back over her shoulder at Hal. "We're in range for point-defense-batteries now, sir."

"Shizari, open up with everything we've got. PDB lasers, anti-torpedo missiles—everything."

The view-screen lit up like the American 4'th of July. A dozen anti-torpedo missiles arced away from their launch tubes, leaving temporary contrails of fire on the screen; they were simply digital artifacts. Hundreds of PDB lasers painted green streaks in the space between *Mjolnir*, and the torpedoes pursuing *Svadilfari*.

"Sir," Shizari said, "the first enemy destroyer is in range of our plasma cannons."

"Fire at will, Mr. Shizari."

Wavering bolts of purple plasma streaked toward the Hrymar ship. Followed by a series of explosions as the torpedoes were obliterated.

"All torpedoes destroyed, sir," Meiriona said.

"Good, keep firing on those destroyers. You're cleared to fire the dark-matter-lance when they're in range."

Shizari beamed. "Yes, sir."

The dark-matter-lance was awesome to see in action. He imagined it was like skewering a man with a lance while riding a warhorse. The man on the ground had no chance; the speed and sheer momentum of the warhorse, all delivered at the tip of the knight's lance, was nigh unholy.

The *Svadilfari* pierced the veil in space-time and with no measurable delay, crossed the intervening forty light-years. He saw the small ship had been ravaged by enemy fire. There were hull breaches, small fires, and strange growths on her hull. Damned virionic beams!

"Helm, maneuver us in front of the *Svadilfari*, and combatives, keep hammering those blue bastards!" The second destroyer must have been intent on finishing its prey, for it had not scanned the other side of the bridge, and only too late did it see the *Mjolnir*—the hammer.

He felt the shudder as the dark-matter-lance fired, its eldritch form pulled from another dimension, then bidden to reach across space-time and smite the Tyrmundr's foes. The beam struck the destroyer head on, and, like an apple being cored, left a hollow smoking wreck; barely recognizable as a ship.

The third destroyer, seeing its sisters annihilated, banked away, escaping with only a few minor laser burns to its aft section.

The bridge between the stars evaporated, and all trace of the enemy was gone.

Chapter 23

PLANET: ORBITING NAJAF

KADIR STEPPED hesitantly onto *its* ship. Serkan called *it* Ambassador Dzakaa. He could not think of *it* as anything more than *it*. It was hideous, and cold. Entirely inhuman; though he mused, so were the Hrymar. But not like *it*. The Hrymar felt; they loved, they laughed, they hated. He was not certain whether the Ysgar were capable of such things.

As if it heard his thoughts, Dzakaa's head spun toward Kadir, locking its tiny black eyes onto him. His mind felt like it was buzzing; as though Dzakaa were rummaging through his head. It clicked and hissed, and released its gaze on him.

"Ambassador Dzakaa," Serkan said, "thank you for this invite to your ship. It is a great honor." Serkan bowed to this new overlord.

Dzakaa just cocked its head in answer.

The interior of the ship was as strange as the exterior had been. Both looked organic, as if the ship were a titanic beast of some kind. Its passages were like arteries; rounded and lacking the linear feel of more humanoid vessels. The shades of brown reminded Kadir of dying plan matter.

"You are most welcome, Serkan," Dzakaa said. "If you will follow me, I will show you our magnificent vessel."

Serkan inclined his head respectfully, and Kadir followed wordlessly.

He noted a curious lack of crew. The ship was twice as large as *Light's Doom*, and after several minutes of walking its passageways, he had yet to see another Ysgar. He silently thanked the Jotun's for that. One of them was disturbing enough.

As they rounded a corner, he began to hear something; a dull murmur. A shifting pattern of low and high frequencies. The sound grew louder, and he began to decipher the strange noises; people. People suffering. They were the cries and moans of men and women.

As they crossed a hatchway, they entered into a cavernous room, its ceiling, three times as high as the passageways had been. It held hundreds of slaves, many of them children, in a barnyard type atmosphere. Myriad humans, sorted according to their intended market no doubt, survived in nightmarish conditions. Sanitation was an after thought, at best, and he thought that few would peruse the wares without the aid of a well serviced re-breather.

"Here is our holding area, Serkan," Dzakaa said. "They are a querulous species and are constantly crying out. Most disturbing."

"Indeed, Ambassador. I quite agree. We find the neural-control-collars quite effective in this regard. They can be set to stun any human that speaks. They learn quickly that complaints are falling on deaf ears." Serkan chuckled.

Dzakaa nodded. "We must have them."

"Of course, Ambassador. I would be happy to ensure you are supplied with them."

It clicked in alien approval, then gestured for them to follow it down another passageway.

They walked for several minutes, then crossed into a laboratory, of sorts. And for the first time since setting foot on the ship, he saw more Ysgar.

"This is where we screen candidates," Dzakaa said.

Candidates, Kadir thought. Candidates for what?

Serkan was nodding. "And what is the success rate, may I ask?"

"Of course. One in five-hundred are adequate to the task. And only the females of non-breeding age."

"Not an overly poor ratio I suppose," Serkan said. "And what of those that are not suited?"

Its lips spread wide. Was that a smile? Jotuns, he believed it was. Could these Ysgar feel?

"They are not wasted. I assure you. Our steward? I believe that is what you call them? He cooks."

"Indeed. That is the proper title," Serkan said.

Dzakaa nodded. "He has become very creative with new … recipes."

What in Alfheim was this fiend on about? Then he noticed Serkan, and watched as the blood drained from his face, his healthy blue pallor turned nearly white as snow. Then he understood. Jotuns help him!

Serkan cleared his throat. "I see. And why do they need to be of non-breeding age?"

"Because the young ones' bodies are programmed for reproduction. But once they mature, that production capability can no longer be … *manipulated*. Before that, our technology can harness their reproductive powers and shape it to our needs."

Serkan nodded.

Kadir heard a commotion from down the hall and saw another Ysgar, dragging a small human girl. Kadir's heart skipped a beat as he saw her beautiful red hair—just like his mother's—just like Neve's.

"Here, Serkan. I will show you how it is done," Dzakaa said.

Serkan's eyebrows rose, but he said nothing. This new Ysgar, who was not introduced, plopped the little girl onto a sort of table. It was not an even surface, though it was more or less rectangular and stood waist-high off the floor. The Ysgar held her arms still for a moment and Kadir inhaled sharply. *Things* began to extrude- no, grow, out of the table's surface. Thin and twisted greenish-brown tendrils encircled the child's arms and then pulled down tight. More tendrils erupted near her legs and held them fast as well. The girl was screaming and crying, but she could no longer struggle, as even her throat was covered by the tendrils.

They kept watching and he noticed the surface of the table rise, imperceptibly at first. A green-jell, more solid than liquid, for it was not spilling off the table as it rose. In a couple of minutes it rose to completely engulf the child. Her entire body now encased in a translucent green jelly. Somehow she was still able to breath inside, as was evidenced by the quivering of the gelatinous tomb, and her rising and falling chest.

"Now, Serkan, pay close attention. The test begins," Dzakaa said.

Kadir watched the mad experiment and his heart beat faster, and faster. He felt as though he might vomit, but he could not. Weakness meant death to Hrymar. And so he watched, helpless to save the poor child.

Several needle-like tendrils pierced the tomb, injecting a dark green, almost black liquid. It rapidly spread through the entire medium. He could still see the girl though and now she began to twitch and writhe.

He glanced at Dzakaa, and was certain *it* was smiling. This mad bastard was enjoying itself. He turned back to the girl and saw her eyes turn from a lovely blue, to a hideous black, as even the whites were ravaged. Her head began to shake violently and the gelatinous tomb quivered. It reminded him of the Jello his mother used to give him. He cursed himself for entertaining such a happy thought at a time like this. He was not weak, but he did not relish the suffering of any creature. He would give any enemy a swift death, or offer them a productive life in service to the Hrymar. But never this.

He watched as the girl's pale, white face, began to darken, morphing to absolute black. Then the blackness spread down her body, from head to toe, creeping, insidious. The farther down the black crept, the less she quivered, until finally, she stopped moving altogether; even the heaving of her chest ceased. Her black orbs remained open, staring up to the heavens in death.

The gelatinous tomb began to recede, like ice melting; back into the table it retreated, until finally, there was no trace of a beautiful young girl. All that remained was a humanoid-shaped, blackened husk.

"Shame. A Failure," Dzakaa said. It threw up his arms. As if in an 'oh well' gesture.

Callous fucker, he thought. I would enjoy strapping you onto that table, you brown piece of dung.

Dzakaa spun to Kadir again, causing him to step back suddenly.

"Did you enjoy the experiment?" Dzakaa asked him.

He said nothing.

The creature stared at him for a long moment, and finally turned away.

"Let us continue to the tour," Dzakaa said.

Dzakaa brought them to a sort of storage room that held tubes, somewhat like cryo-berths, but shorter. He counted thirty-two. Here he saw a third Ysgar, mulling over some control panel.

"This is where we store the candidates who pass." Dzakaa gestured to the other Ysgar, who approached one of the tubes and tapped at a control panel. With a hiss of escaping gasses, the front section of a tube slid up, revealing a little girl. Only this one was a mottled green and brown color, not the death-black of the other.

"The ones that pass are stored here until needed," Dzakaa explained.

He did a quick mental calculation; if only one in five-hundred passed, and there were thirty-two girls here, then they would have had to screen sixteen-thousand. Jotuns! And if that were only girls, what was the population of men, women, and little boys that had been captured? And he saw no slaves on this ship. He shuddered uncontrollably.

"Are you all right boy?" Serkan asked.

He swallowed hard and looked at Serkan. "Yes, Master."

Serkan held his gaze for a moment, as if unsure of the truth of his answer. He nodded and turned back to *it*.

"Let us continue our tour," Dzakaa said.

They walked a circuitous route around the dizzyingly large vessel, finally coming upon a hatch guarded by one of the Ysgar. Dzakaa nodded, the guard stepped aside and tapped keys on a panel. The hatch opened onto a control room. As they stepped through, he saw more of the organic tendrils, like those on the laboratory table, but much larger. As he moved from behind

Serkan, he caught sight of one of the mottled green and brown girls. She was in the center of the room, suspended at a forty-five degree angle by tendrils, as if she were on inclined couch. Hundred of tendrils- more like tentacles, he thought, crept in and out of the girl.

Around the room, he noticed organic containers filled with various colored fluids; like venom sacks, he imagined.

"This, good Serkan, is the heart of our new technology. Her reproductive organs have been transformed into viral incubators." He gestured to the sacks of fluid. "Here we begin with the weaponized virus. At this stage it is still unable to propagate and mutate enough to damage the Alfar technology. But when we harness the power of the human's body to create life, then the virus can be born that is capable of learning, evolving."

"Remarkable," Serkan said.

"Isn't it?" Dzakaa said.

The tour continued to another room guarded by an Ysgar. As they entered this room, he saw not a girl at the center, but a boy.

Serkan looked surprised as well. "I thought you only used human females?"

"For our virionic weapon platforms, yes. But for our spatial-skip-drive, boys have proven to possess superior spatial awareness. The girls have been found limited to skipping perhaps ten-thousand kilometers. Whereas boys can manage up to one-million kilometers. Sadly, the success rate is only one in ten-thousand. Although we do have a set of twin girls who are equally adept at both tasks."

He gasped, and Serkan shot him an evil glance before turning back to

Dzakaa.

"Regrettable, of course," Serkan said.

Dzakaa bowed its head in agreement.

He wanted to scream. Animals! No, animals were nothing like this. He'd thought Hrymar cruel at first, but this? Jotun's curse them all, the Ysgar plague. Suddenly he felt as though a spike were driven through the side of his head. He fell to his knees and grabbed at his temples.

"Aghhhh!" He screamed. He saw the face of Dzakaa inside his head, admonishing him in some alien tongue, but he knew he was being chastised.

"Boy!" Serkan barked. "Get up! What is wrong with you today?"

As quickly as it had struck him, the pain vanished. He gasped and realized he was panting, and still on his knees.

A brown scaly hand reached down to him. "Kadir, can I be of assistance?" It smiled at him.

Location: Aboard Mjolnir / Star: Blástjarna

Captain Shelley Garrett of the *Svadilfari*, stepped onto the Mjolnir's command dais, giving Hal a quick bow. She was filthy and bloodied. No serious wounds, but you knew she'd been in a fight. She was a model of Germanic womanhood; flaxen haired, tall and strong, and with high, noble cheeks. A beautiful, warrior-woman. Even in defeat she carried herself proudly.

"All your people off the *Svadilfari*?" Haldor asked.

"Aye, sir. And thanks to you and the crew for getting us off safely."

He nodded. "I'm sorry about your ship, but there's nothing we can do now. We'll mark the location with a beacon and get back to her."

"Understood, sir."

"Casualties?" He asked.

"Twenty-three dead, and forty-eight wounded, sir. Eleven seem to be infected with the virus."

"Dr. Inglis can halt the symptoms, but I'm afraid they'll have to stay quarantined until we can work out a permanent solution. They're still infectious after treatment."

"I understand." With a pained expression, Garrett asked, "Do you think we'll be able to save *Svadilfari* as well?"

"I'm hopeful." He tried sending positive thoughts to buoy her confidence.

Garrett managed a smile, and he felt her relax somewhat. He might actually be getting the hang of this. Not that he wanted to control his people, he reminded himself. But if he could inspire a deeper confidence, his people could accomplish anything.

He stood and gestured to the right. "Let's go to my ready-room for a quick de-brief."

Garrett nodded, and proceeded him into the ready-room, which was conveniently located directly right of the bridge, as seen from the Captain's perspective. Following behind him, was the head of his new housecarls—his old friend Cadfael—who'd become his new shadow. Where Hal went, Cadfael followed, determined not to let anything happen to the Jarl.

Hal pulled out a chair for Garrett, something he remembered his mother had taught him all those years ago. He wouldn't normally do something like that for one of his Captains, but these were special circumstances, and he figured some extra kindness would go a little way to lessening the sting of, effectively, losing her ship.

As he took his seat at the head of the table, it occurred to him she might need refreshments. "Shelley, can I get you something to drink? Something to eat?"

She shook her head. "No, thank you, sir. Let me report first, then I can worry about that."

"Of course. Go ahead, when you're ready." He could feel her confusion tinged with fear, and even some shame. She was his best Captain of the Scouting division, and the reason she was sent to Najaf.

She swallowed hard before speaking, all the while keeping her eyes on the table.. "We arrived at Kepler 34 through the interstellar-bridge, and the system seemed clear. There was nothing on sensors. We waited for a good thirty minutes before moving at all. Just in case something saw, or detected, our transit. But it was fine. So we made our way to Najaf continuing to do active scans all the way in. We took up a stationary orbit over the main colony on Najaf, and made contact with the locals. It took a couple of hours, but we finally connected with one of them. They had detected our ship, and all scattered in case it was another Hrymar attack." She stopped for a moment. And now looked up into his eyes. "They got hit hard, sir. The colony is in utter ruin. The Hrymar killed, or took, at least fifty percent of the population." She shook her head. "They're acting very different, sir. They think of us like cattle. So why cull so many? They used to take five to ten precent of a population, max. That way it ensured they always had a population to go back to. But fifty percent? That's not sustainable."

He had no answer. "That's what we need to find out. This attack, taken as one data point, is strange. But there are many others that you haven't been privy to, Shelley. Taken together, it's like we're fighting a brand new enemy. Which, in point of fact, may well be the case."

Chapter 24

Protected by *Mjolnir's* shields, Hal basked in the flood of azure light, relayed by the bridge's massive view-screen. Blástjarna's temperature was upwards of 50,000 °C, and even at a distance of one AU—nearly 150,000,000 km—the ship's systems had to work hard to keep it from being buffeted by solar winds.

Blástjarna, or Blue Star, in Old Norse and Yggdrasi, was a true stellar giant—cleverly named by school children on Rigsvaka. There were no habitable planets in her system; her relentless barrage of radiation scoured any rock of life; but she did have a bridge node, which made Blástjarna a strategic point within Rigsvaka space. Her node connected to the Adhara system in The Islamic Republic of Watan space—the star system that contained the colony world of Najaf.

As he meditated on the blue gem, he daydreamed of Gwynahra. In Blástjarna, he saw her eyes, and in the black of space, her long hair. He tried to banish thoughts of her Sylvan beauty, but his heart ached for her in these quiet moments. Then his thoughts crept painfully to his wife Siobhan; what if she was alive? Could he still love her? He had to. He had done … but now? Gods in Asgard, it was the worst torture imaginable. How could he abandon

Gwynahra if Siobhan *was* alive? He would have to. He would never be unfaithful to Siobhan, but in his heart, was he not doing that now? The pains of leadership meant he had no one to confide in. He couldn't unburden his heart, as others could.

"Commander," Meiriona said, "A ship just dropped out of hyperspace, 50,000 km from us."

"Battle stations!" Damn it, that was right on top of them. The bridge lights dimmed to a blood-red.

"Sir, it's one of ours! It's the *Alsvidr*—Captain Lady Illiathor," Kappa said. "She's hailing us now."

He opened a ship-wide comm channel. "Stand down from battle stations." He jerked his chin to Kappa. "Put her on."

The Alfar Captain that appeared on the view-screen, wore uncharacteristically short hair—for her race—as even the males tended to favor longer hairstyles.

"Lady Illiathor, it's a pleasure to see you."

She inclined her chestnut coif. *"And you, my Lord. I have an urgent report I need to make."*

"Go ahead."

"My Lord, may I come aboard to report? This is rather sensitive."

He nodded. "Of course. We'll meet in my briefing room in thirty minutes."

"Thanks you, sir. Illiathor out."

What now, he wondered? Good news, perhaps? Too much to hope for. He rose from his seat and took a last look at Blástjarna, the blue supergiant, a reminder of a love he desired so desperately, yet could not have. Lady Shalindra of Illiathor, saluted crisply as she boarded *Mjolnir*. "Permission to come aboard?"

Hal returned the salute. "Granted. Good to see you, Shalindra."

"And you, sir." She gave him half hearted smile.

He gestured down the passageway to his meeting room.

"This is the first time I've seen *Mjolnir*. What a magnificent ship."

"Thanks. Another time I'd be happy to give you a tour."

The hatch to his ready-room whisked open and he saw Jin Wudai already waiting for them. Jin and Shalindra were already acquainted, as both worked for Lady Greyheather, his Minister of Intelligence.

"Hi, Jin," she said.

Jin inclined his head in his usual stoic fashion. "Shalindra, good to see you."

"Jin has a report from Captain Garrett, Shalindra, but we'll let you report first."

The each took seats around the ready-room table.

"Thank you, sir." Her pale face creased as she prepared to speak. "We were tasked with scouting the area around our north-west border—around the Eplistjarna system. The bulk of our patrol was uneventful, but when we arrived in the Eplistjarna system itself, we detected energy readings consistent with planetary-based reactors. And according to our data, none should have been there. We approached Eplistjarna I, under stealth. It's a mostly water world—96% coverage—but there are two land masses near the southern pole. We conducted an extensive passive-scan at 1,000 km above the surface. We dared not try any active scan for fear of discovery. What we found was a burgeoning colony and city. Definitely Hrymar, and with a large population of Humanoid slaves." She broke eye contact for a moment, looking down at the table, as if gathering her thoughts, or her courage. "Sir, what we discovered was … disturbing. Normally with a Hrymar outpost, we would find extensive buildings, with an array if thousands of cryo-berths, and pens, for storing and sorting slaves. This outpost- or colony, is different. It does not appear to be a mere *store-and-sort* operation." She gestured to the view-screen controls on the read-room table.

He nodded. "Go ahead."

She tapped a few keys, and the room darkened, followed by the view-screen activating. On it, he saw a farm. There were vast tracts of agricultural land, and people working. Not just Humans, there were Alfar, and a number of other humanoid species. She presented a number of images and video of the operation. There were detailed IR scans of warehouses with scores of women lying on beds, and machinery around them.

"Here, sir, this is what most concerned me." She pointed to an IR blob on the screen at a warehouse, then zoomed in so that individual humanoid signatures could be distinguished. "Notice all the people are horizontal?"

He nodded

"We have identified them *all* as women. *Pregnant* women."

"Lady Frigga! First they harvest children, now pregnant women," he said.

"Worse. It's a farm, sir. In every sense of the word, and with the gravest implication."

He felt Shalindra's pain, and her shame at not being able to immediately help the women. "There's nothing you could do, Shalindra."

She looked a bit shocked at his insight into her thoughts, but nodded. "Thank you, sir. I know, but it still feels … hurtful."

"I promise you, we'll fix this," he said.

There was a moment of unplanned silence, as the three of them absorbed the magnitude of the intelligence.

"Alright, Jin, what's awaiting us in Adhara?"

"I'm afraid it's also rather grim new, sir."

"Judging by the state of the *Svadilfari*, I'd guessed as much," he said.

"Indeed. There are six of the new Hrymar battleships in the Adhara system. I'm not sure if we have a complete count of support vessels, but Captain Garrett reported thirty destroyer-sized vessels—in the three-thousand ton range—but she wasn't close enough to gather sensor data on weapons and shields. She said they detected another gravitic mass, but was too far to discriminate individual ships."

"Support vessels?"

Jin nodded tentatively. "That would be my guess."

"Anything else?"

Jin shook his head. "This is the biggest Hrymar fleet every fielded, in terms of tonnage."

"Gods damn right it is. I fought the first one that hit Earth. It was *nothing* compared to this, but we were completely unprepared for inter-stellar war at that point." He shook his head in disgust. "We've got our work cut out for us, Jin."

"We most certainly do, sir. I'd rate our chances of prevailing in a head-on fight, at one-in-three."

"Then we need to fight smart," he said.

"In hemmed-in situations, you must resort to stratagem. In desperate position, you must fight - Sun Tzu," Jin quoted.

"Smart man, I hear," he said with a smile. He inclined his head to Jin, already sure of the answer he expected, but asking just to be sure. "But what stratagem? He mentions thirty-six in 'The Art of War', if I recall correctly."

"Just so, Commander. Besiege Wèi to rescue Zhào, perhaps?"

Hal smiled. "When the enemy is too strong to be attacked directly, then attack something he holds dear." *Exactly what I was thinking*, he thought to himself.

Hal's ready-room was packed full of Captains and Nobles. All had come to Mjolnir for a secret briefing. There was an energy in the room—like a beehive, abuzz with whispers and conversations; all had clues as to the nature of the meeting, but none knew the full scope.

Hal gestured to Jin Wudai.

"Have any of you wondered why a Hrymar fleet is still in a system they attacked?" Jin asked. He paused for a moment. "Or why they initially harvested up to 50% of the population instead of only a sustainable sample? Lady Shalindra presented a disturbing report earlier today- " Jin took a few minutes to share that grim news with them. "-and so we feel that there is a fundamental shift in their slave based economy. For thousands of years they've been what we'd call *Hunter-Gatherers*, in terms of human anthropology. Our *civilization*, as such, began when we abandoned that lifestyle and began practicing agriculture. Only then did we have a stable enough food supply, that women could start having more babies, etc."

Hal saw their collective expressions, and a dawning awareness of the staggering scope.

"So you see," Jin continued, "if they begin *farming,* then they could use that as the basis for expanding their population drastically, and building a true galaxy-spanning Hrymar empire."

Lady Illiathor hung her head, sadness seeping from her soul like black tar.

Hal stood. "Besiege Wèi to rescue Zhào—Sun Tzu. When the enemy is too strong to be attacked directly, then attack something he holds dear. We can't take on combined Hrymar forces currently stationed at Adhara. The chances of success are too remote." He looked to nobody in particular, and said, "Skallgrim, fill us in if you would."

"Certainly, Commander," came the EI's disembodied voice. *"If our current battle-group assaults the Hrymar forces at Adhara, I project the chance off success at only 5%."*

"Not worth taking," Hal interjected. "But, what if we were to attack something they hold dear? Say, this new operation on Eplistjarna? Skallgrim, if we were to raid the operation on Eplistjarna, and allow a scout-ship to escape, can you project a probable outcome?"

"There is an 85% chance that the Hrymar would detach half of their force at Adhara to take back Eplistjarna."

"I like those odds," Hal said. "Even with half the new battleships gone, that would leave three, and potentially fifteen destroyer escorts. That gives us numerical superiority from a gross tonnage standpoint, but if they also have the new virionic weapons, then we're back at a disadvantage. Skallgrim, analysis if you will."

"My calculations indicate that this scenario is 71% likely to succeed, but may result in up to 65% losses."

"That's a lot of good people and ships to throw away. But these bastards are 25 light-years off our borders—that's almost knocking on our backdoor. And, they're making in-roads at several other points around us. Not to mention the fact that they're farming our people like sheep. We have to throw everything we can at them. Push them back, and buy enough time to for our new ships to be built. Then we'll deal them a death blow. We have to stop this advance—now!"

Gina raised a hand. "So let me get this straight, we have an enemy with numeric and technological superiority, and they've fundamentally changed tactics, and are on the cusp of completely transforming their society? Have I missed anything? *Alrighty* then, that seems easy enough to fix," she said, with a sarcastic grin.

"My grandfather always told me, a thing worth doing, is rarely an easy thing," he said. "Questions?"

"Will the *Sam Houston* be in on the Najaf assault?" Someone asked.

"No, we need another capital ship to spear-head the assault on Eplistjarna. Captain Hutchison will be leading that attack with her ship." Which was true enough. What he didn't explain was that the Republic's corporate congress wasn't willing to assist with an assault on Najaf, as they had no diplomatic relations with Watan.

He saw another hand up.

"If they detach half their forces to go to Eplistjarna, how can we hope to win? Won't our battle-group be overly weakened fighting on two fronts?"

"Excellent question. We won't be fighting a major engagement at Eplistjarna. There are no large Hrymar ships there now, and the nearest Hrymar reinforcements are at Adhara, twenty-five hours away. So help is at least fifty-hours out. Lady Spadarosso, who's leading the ground mission, assures me that will be plenty of time to evacuate all the prisoners and destroy their factories and farming equipment. Hence, only two ships will be going to Eplistjarna; the *Sam Houston* will escort a single Light-Cruiser, the *Ascalon*, to evacuate the people on the surface."

Hal felt the uncertainty coursing through his people, but he maintained an inner calm, and projected it. "We're in for a bit of a fight, but that's what we all signed up for."

Planet: Orbiting Najaf

Kadir watched in morbid fascination as a hideous living-ship began birthing her children. Like their mother, the offspring were mottled, greenish-brown puckered-fruit, covered in tentacles — or were they spikes? Whatever the case, they were truly revolting.

The matriarch swam through space, weaving her children, as a spider wove a net. She continued on her mission relentlessly; he'd been watching for an hour or more, when he heard the hatch open, and looked back to see Serkan stride onto the bridge, looking at the view-screen with a disgusted grunt.

He shuffle over to where Serkan had taken a seat, and whispered. "Master, what in Ymir's name are those—things?"

"More of the Ysgar's infernal tricks," Serkan said.

His brow furrowed, but was careful not to pester Serkan. His temper was legendary.

"Jotuns damned cold-blooded bastards. All of them," Serkan grumbled.

He dared one more question. "Master, might I ask why we are still here? Was our raid not successful?"

Serkan did not anger this time, but instead looked mournful. "New ways, youngling. Your foster-sire has struck a deal with these Ysgar. Instead of hunting our prey, we will now run factories, and breed them." The old Hrymar snarled. "It is unnatural. Prey in the wild grows strong. That is the value of our raids. We gather a diverse and healthy crop—and are paid well for them. I cannot see the profit in this. Or the honor," Serkan finished in a whisper

He had *never* heard the Hrymar speak of honor before. It had been intimated, and he had suspected it, but now he had heard one openly speak of it. He had to risk knowing more. "Honor, Master?"

Serkan spun on him. "Quiet, boy!" He growled. Several of the bridge crew glanced over at the commotion. "Eyes on your screens! Or you may find yourselves on the slave auction." He turned back to Kadir. "We may be slavers, Kadir," he whispered, "but in our hearts we are hunters. The years since your foster-sire seized control have been a time of much *change*. Even the fact that Devrim is on the throne is not the usual order of things. You were raised in Egil Arkek, you understand the nature of strength and weakness, do you not?"

He nodded.

"You might be human, but in your heart I believe you may be more Hrymar than any on this ship. You arrived on Niflheim a weakling son of an enemy race. Yet you came to dominate your oppressors in the boys camp."

Serkan smiled. "I sired no sons, but if I had…"

Was the old man being sentimental? He worked hard to control his reaction, and said nothing.

Serkan shook his head. "I grumble, but the situation is thus. You asked about the Ysgar ship seeding space?"

He nodded again.

"It is a mine-layer, of sorts. It berths offspring which carry the same virus as the new weapon on our battleships. They have but one purpose: to infect ships not already carrying their genetic code. Those little devils can sense any ship not already carrying a virionic weapon, or a virionic marker, as our smaller ships carry."

"Thank you for your patience, Master."

Serkan dismissed it. "You need to know these things." He leaned in and whispered to Kadir, "Never trust the Ysgar, youngling They are wholly unnatural. We may be in an alliance with them, now …" he trailed off.

Chapter 25

LOCATION: ABOARD ASCALON, IN HYPERSPACE enroute to Eplistjarna

As head of the Tyrmundr Marines, Gina had access to any, and all, areas of ships in the Rigsvaka inter-stellar fleet. So it was an easy matter for her to dismiss the guards near the engine room, and tell the engineers that she had a classified mission to perform before battle. The crew had all heard about the secret anti-viral weapon being readied against the Hrymar, and so, obeyed without question.

All starships required some sort of power source to transit the stars, and by necessity, such power sources were, well ...powerful; and as such, quite dangerous. Of course modern starship design incorporated layers of redundancies and safeguards, but if one knew how to turn them off ... and Gina planned to do just that.

Battle-group Alpha dropped down out of the inky-black of hyperspace and Gina watched the main view-screen filled with the red dwarf they'd name Apple Star. Good name, she mused.

"Sensors," Captain Wright said, "give me a list of all ships in the system."

"Aye, sir, scanning now," his sensors officer said, pulling up a map of the star system. There was only one planet, Eplistjarna I, a water world with a small land mass in the southern hemisphere. The map displayed a number of red dots moving about the system. "Eleven Hrymar vessels, sir. All under six-thousand tons. Mostly converted freighter—the typical Hrymar slaver ships." She zoomed in to the planet, which highlighted the five ships in orbit or on the surface. "Five are in range, and the *Sam Houston* is moving in."

Nigel Wright grinned. "Bloody good." He turned to Gina. "I believe the show is about to start, Lady Spadarosso."

The five Hrymar ships had no chance against the *Sam Houston*. The battleship accelerated toward the planet, all guns firing, belching torpedoes and missiles. Two ships actually turned back toward her, and tried to fight. The first was cleaved in half by a particle beam, and the other ended in a bright, but silent explosion. The three that tried to flee, were overtaken by torpedoes that had ten times their acceleration. In a few frantic minutes, nothing of the Hrymar ships remained but floating wreckage.

"Incoming call from the *Sam Houston*, sir," the comms officer reported.

Captain Wright gestured to the view-screen, and Captain Kay Hutchison appeared.

"Captain Wright, the planet is yours. We've allowed some ships to escape, as planned. We'll keep an eye on things up here."

"My thanks to you, madam."

"Good luck, Gina," Hutchison said.

"Thanks, Kay."

"*Ascalon* out," Wright said. "Helm, take us down. Lady Spadarosso, I believe you're up."

You have no idea, fool, Gina thought, and under her cloak she depressed a button on a tiny remote.

Ascalon shuddered slightly.

"What the hell was that?" Wright demanded.

"Checking now, sir," an engineer said as he scanned his console frantically. "Sir, this shouldn't be possible, but we've lost plasma reservoir containment!"

"Cause?"

In the confusion, nobody noticed Gina slip off the bridge.

Gina dove into an escape pod and yanked the launch handle. With a violent jolt, she was expelled from the *Ascalon* at speeds designed to clear the pod from a ship about to explode.

She waited thirty-seconds, then pressed the button on her remote a second time, as she watched the *Ascalon* shrink from view. Three more C9 charges blew, taking with them, all safety mechanisms for the Dark Matter Reservoir, Dark Energy Reservoir, and the Anti-Dark Energy Reservoir. Together with the rogue plasma now coursing through the engine room, these four, forms of energy and matter, which should never mix, did just that; and to unholy effect.

The *Ascalon* disintegrated in a brilliant, white flash, striking the neighboring *Sam Houston*. Then, faster than its light had raced outward, a black sphere imploded to a zero-point — the origin of the unholy mating of materials and energy. She watched in near rapture as pieces of the *Sam Houston* were torn apart, drawn into the artificial abyss.

"Beautiful," she whispered. Then, with a third press of the remote, a pre-programmed message was sent to the fleeing Hrymar vessels.

Location: Aboard Mjolnir / Star: Blástjarna

The timer had run seven hours past the allotted twenty-five-hours. Hal should have heard about the attack on Eplistjarna by now. Damn it, he hated waiting.

"Sir, the bridge-node is activating," Meiriona said.

"Hail them." He held his breath. Please let this be good news, he prayed.

Lady Illiathor's smiling face graced his view-screen. *"Commander, a small Hrymar vessel arrived near Najaf, then minutes later, half the Hrymar ships jumped into Hyperspace. It worked, sir!"*

The bridge erupted into cheering.

Hal exhaled slowly. Thank the gods. "Open a channel to the Battle-group."

"Open, sir," Kappa said.

"It's time for some payback, people. Proceed through the bridge to Najaf!"

This time, cheering erupted over the comm, coming from all the ships. Hal left the channel open so they could share in each other's glee.

The interstellar-bridge-node was triggered, and the battle-group raced through to battle.

By design, a squadron of six Skofnung-class destroyers—a DESRON—preceded the battle group. With their enhanced sensors, and anti-stealth technology, they provided a forward screen for the bulk of the fleet. Similar DESRONs flanked, and followed the battle group.

Hal winced, then realized he'd been chewing on one of his knuckles. He shook his head in self-admonishment. Breath, he told himself. The plan is working.

"Sir, DESRON-1 reports the space is clear between us and Najaf, except for the Hrymar ships," Meiriona said.

"Give me a count on the ships, Shizari," he said.

"Aye, sir. As you predicted, they split the force evenly. Sensors have three of their new battleships, each displacing approximately 200,000 tons. There are also fifteen destroyer-sized vessels scattered throughout the system."

He tapped his comm. "Aksyonova, are the Atgeir ready to deploy?"

"Ready, sir," replied Pelagia Aksyonova.

"Comms, open a channel to the battlegroup."

"Aye, channel open, sir," Kappa replied.

"All combative ships, begin concerted attack on Hrymar target designated BB-1. Do *not* fire on targets BB-2 or BB-3, until ordered to do so. Good hunting, people." He turned to Jones at the helm controls. "Maximum military acceleration if you please, Mr. Jones."

"Full throttle, aye, sir," Jones replied.

It was only a handful of seconds until the light from the Human's ships reached the sensors.

"My Lord, the Humans have arrived," the sensor first said.

Serkan looked to Dzakaa, who nodded in return.

"Recall all pickets. All ships, to arms!"

"They've seen us, sir," Meiriona reported.

"Acknowledged," Hal said, without looking away from the main viewscreen. His concentration was on the Hrymar battleships. For the first time in many years, Haldor Olsen was afraid; not for himself, but afraid to lose what he'd built. Afraid to fail—again.

317

As self-doubt coursed through his synapses, he felt *something*. Another mind? He concentrated, trying to reach out to that intelligence. What came back through mind-space was *utter emptiness*. Gwynahra had told him, sentient thoughts were like bright beacons in the black of mind-space. This thing was darker, and even more empty than mind-space itself. It was more like a blackhole, drawing all thought into an abyss.

"Commander, are you all right?"

It was Chandragupta Maurya's voice, his first officer. Strange, he didn't see him, only heard his voice. Was he dreaming? It was dark. Surely he was sleeping. His head lolled sideways and light spilled though the dark veil.

"Chandra?" He said. His first officer was shaking him.

"Sir, you blacked out there for a moment. Gave us quite a scare."

What in Niflheim had that been, he wondered? Hal gasped, and jerked, his eyes now wide open. The stench! "Loki's balls! What was that?" He bellowed.

"Smelling salts. A time-proven remedy when your Commander passes-out during battle," said Dr. Inglis, sarcastically.

"My apologies, sir, but you were in some sort of … trance, for nearly three-minutes. And the Hrymar battleships are coming into range."

"Damn it," he muttered. He shrugged off Dr. Inglis, holding two hands up. "I'm fine." He turned to Maurya. "Status?"

"Ninety-two-seconds to contact," his first officer said.

Hal pointed to Shizari. "Charge the dark-matter-lance."

"Already done, sir," Maurya said.

He got a flash of blinding headache, and squeezed his eyes. "Mother f-"

he clenched his jaw and blinked.

Suddenly the view-screen was completely filled with one of the Hrymar battleships. A green beam followed, piercing space.

"Return fire! Sensors, report!"

Meiriona shook her head. "Commander, this is the same behavior we saw last time. Their ship was able to skip across space."

"Damage report?"

"None yet, sir," engineering replied.

Mjolnir shuddered as her torpedoes and energy weapons hailed down on the Hrymar battleship. The enemy had closed the gap too fast for the dark-matter-lance to fire, as the enemy was now inside its optimal beam length.

"Helm, bring us around! Combatives, I want to punch a big hole through that son of bitch." He said.

As *Mjolnir* maneuvered, the other ships in the battle-group swarmed over the enemy vessel, they'd designated BB-1. The Hrymar might have a few tricks, but even their new ships would wither under the combined firepower of forty warships.

"Damage report?" He was getting antsy. The virionic beam had indeed struck Mjolnir, but due to its peculiar nature, inflicted no immediate damage; it was like waiting for the executioner's axe to fall.

"We're starting to see armor regrowth—definitely signs the virus hit us. And we've got reports of at least eight crew reporting symptoms," engineering said.

"Helm, bring us on an intercept vector to BB-2. Pelagia, prepare to launch the Atgeir."

Dzakaa was wholly unprepared as he peered into mind-space; here, Ysgar were the predators, and all other creatures, feeble prey; but not this day. Today he felt a force that gave him pause. His allies—though he thought of them as mere children to be manipulated—had not prepared him for this; though in truth, how could they? Feebleminded as they were. There was another predator lurking in mind-space, though it felt unsure of its footing, as it were.

As he soared across the psychic landscape, following the curves and contours of thought and intentions, he sensed another anomaly. He snapped his head sideways and caught the Hrymar youngling staring at him—Kadir, he was called. Was the boy here with him in mind-space? No, he couldn't be … and yet…

Dzakaa shook it off, chalking up this paranoia to the disturbance caused by this other predator. Now he had to stalk his prey; a seasoned predator eliminated any competition.

Kadir gasped as the creature spun to look at him. What was this beast? The Hrymar might be cruel, but this thing … it was unnatural. He'd never felt a disturbance like this before. For the last couple of years he'd been able to go to this quiet place; a place where other minds were diminished, and where he could drop down into their thoughts, as if a voyeur. Today his quiet place had been a dark inferno, searing his mind.

As he pulled his mind back out of the quiet place, he vowed to kill this creature.

"Can you get a shot on BB-1 with the dark-matter-lance?" Hal asked.

"No, sir," Shizari said, "we're starting to lose maneuvering control."

Meiriona spun back to Hal. "Commander, BB-1 is also losing thrust and maneuverability. The battle-group have disabled her drives."

"Pelagia, launch the Atgeir, now!" He barked. "Battle-group, disengage attack on BB-1, concentrate on BB-2." He'd gambled everything on this hope, but if successful, they could effectively cure, then immunize, their ships against further damage by the virionic weapon.

Hal had begun to watch as the salvo of fifty human-harpoons hurtled toward their prey, but he had to turn away; there were other matters to attend to. They'd do their jobs. "Battle-group damage report."

"Six of our destroyers have been disabled by virionic beams fired from BB-2 and BB-3. BB-1 is in a spin and can't aim," engineering reported.

Damn it he thought. *That* would be a problem. If they couldn't aim the virionic weapon, then they couldn't immunize their own ships by firing the retro-virus. One problem at a time—they had yet to breach the Hrymar battleship and inject the viral tanks. If in fact, that's how the Hrymar implemented the weapon; it was still just a theory until they actually had eyes on this weapon. As he followed his other ships still in the fight, his concentration was shattered by the collision alarm!

BROOH-BROOH-BROOH-BROOH-BROOH!

"Report!" He ordered.

Meiriona's pale Alfar complexion faded several shades whiter as she spoke. "Sir, three more Hrymar battleships and fifteen destroyers, have dropped back into the system. One of the destroyers veered away. It seems to have dropped out of hyperspace almost directly on top of us."

Hal began to laugh.

Chapter 26

LOCATION: ABOARD MJOLNIR / STAR SYSTEM: Adhara

Chandragupta Maurya looked horrified. "Commander, why in God's name are you laughing at a moment like this?"

Hal shook his head. "Because, my friend, my god demands sacrifices of great warriors to build his army for Ragnarok." He yanked aside his bionan uniform, revealing a scar and blue tattoo over his left breast—three interlocking triangles. "A gift for a gift, Chandra."

"What gifts?" Maurya asked. "Respectfully, sir, this is no time to lose your shit!"

"It's the Valknut, Chandra, the knot of the slain." He gestured to his surroundings. "All that's happening … it means that Odin is calling my number." He assumed a more serious demeanor. "Don't worry. I'm not losing it. I've just gained a certain … clarity. When all is lost, Chandra, then anything goes. Am I right?"

His first officer looked irritated and utterly unconvinced of his Captain's sanity; Hal could read it clearly.

Mjolnir rocked as the new enemy ships raked her hull with weapons fire.

Maurya winced as he considered his Commander. "What did you have in mind?"

"That's the spirit!" He clapped Maurya on the shoulder. "I was told to remember my gifts. And I intend to do just that."

"Told by whom, exactly?" Maurya asked.

"By Odin." He felt Maurya's escalating disbelief, but continued. "I don't believe in visions, or anything like that, Chandra, but Odin came to me in the chapel. I don't know if it was physical or just mental. Whatever the case, he stood before me, and spoke to me—*Look to the godly gifts you have been given,*' he'd said."

"What gifts?" Maurya asked.

"The Athryllith, for one."

"But, Hal, what will a bit of telepathy do against an armada of enemy ships? We're outnumbered and outmatched. And it appears, outwitted. And you're going to- what? Read their minds?" Maurya turned away, muttering.

"Captain Maurya, you have command of the ship and of the battle-group," he'd said it loud, so all could hear.

Maurya spun on him. "Are you fucking mad?"

He ignored the insubordination. "Perhaps. My final order is to refrain from firing on BB-3 until you hear from me."

Maurya was speechless.

"Did you understand the order, XO?"

Maurya nodded.

"Take care of my ship while I'm gone." Maurya was wondering where the hell he was going, but Hal didn't want to take time to explain. "You have the ship."

"I have the ship," Maurya responded by reflex.

Hal noticed Cadfael following him off the bridge; of course he would, that was his job. And *I suppose he isn't going to let me leave alone*, he mused. For now he said nothing and continued wordlessly down the passageways. He walked nonchalantly into a small storage room. He turned and saw an expression of confusion on Cadfael's face.

"Close the door," he said.

Cadfael, stoic as always, said nothing and closed the door.

"I'm sorry about this, old friend."

Cadfael now look confused. "My Lord?"

He put a hand gently on Cadfael's shoulder and smiled. But inside his mind, he projected thoughts of the deepest fatigue and exertion, of relaxation and sleepiness, of blackness and warmth and comfort. Cadfael crumpled, lowered to the floor by his Jarl and betrayer. "Sleep, my friend. I'll make it up to you later."

There was a time for reflection and deep thought; that time had passed. It was time to act. Hal knew that his battle-group could not prevail against the Hrymar forces in a conventional battle. They had a bigger force and their weapons were more potent. Such an enemy called for more desperate tactics.

Already wearing his recon stealth suit, he stood before the massive door to the ship's special-vehicle-bay and placed his palm on the door's DNA-sensor. A horizontal beam of blue-light scanned his hand. *'Identity confirmed, Olsen, Haldor. Jarl of Rigg's Vaka, High Commander of Rigsvaka Armed Forces. Access granted.'*

Empty alcoves lined the walls, each with outlines showing where a suit of Extravehicular-Combat-Armor had recently hung. Suit was perhaps the wrong term, as they were more spacecraft than suit. Yet he bypassed the wall of extra suits, instead striding to four-meter tall ovoid contraption with the word—PROTOTYPE—stenciled across the body in red letters. It was one of Magister Edvit's new toys. Larger than an ECA suit, the EVP—extravehicular-combat-pod, was designed to take a single occupant over to an enemy vessel where they could disembark, unencumbered by an ECA suit. Perfect for what he had in mind.

He smacked the DEPLOY button, which activated a set of mechanical arms and extended the pod from the wall. It was then laid on its side and a hatch in the top irised open. He grabbed a set of hand rails above the pod and swung feet-first into the dark embrace of the metallic sarcophagus. It really did feel like tomb-like; especially when the hatch irised closed and he was left alone in the pitch black. It had an artificial smell; that scent of plastics and fresh lubricating oil.

In seconds, small screens awoke, displaying the results of the power-on-self-test; all systems green. The pod had no weapons to speak of, only a set of pincers for hands, designed to secure the pod to the target vessel. Slowly, gel sacs inflated with fluid to cushion his body against the coming tsunami of acceleration. He took a deep breath and stabbed the glowing, blue launch-button.

A circular hatch beneath the suit slid open, and with the force one might expect on a bullet, the suit was magnetically shot down the launch tube and into the dark of space.

Kadir thought there would be more joy in the destruction of his father's fleet. Perhaps there would have, if not for the Ysgar demon tainting this undertaking. Slavery was a noble industry; the weak served and the strong ruled. Slavery was natural. The Ysgar were *not* natural. The perversions of biology on the new ships left Kadir feeling cold. He yearned to stab that brown lizard in the face, or pummel him with his fists. It was a fury born of desperation. It had been many years since he had felt this helpless. Kadir had become *the strong*, and now he felt like *the weak*.

The demon twitched, as if in reaction to Kadir's murderous thoughts. What could he do? One young man, an outsider in a world of Hrymar. Things were simple in the kimlik-sorma; there he knew exactly what was expected, and exactly what he could do. How he wished to face off with this brown turd on the black sand. He would carve the demon up like a roast.

He realized he'd been squeezing the handle of his left dagger. Slowly he took his hand off, flexing his fingers, returning his gaze and thoughts to the battle unfolding on-screen. Calling it a battle was overly gracious. It was a slaughter. It bothered him that it bothered him. Did that even make sense? He would take no pleasure out of slaughtering a legless-foe in the kimlik-sorma. How could he take pleasure in this?

Though he tried to focus on the battle and the joy of winning, his thoughts turned back to the fates of the conquered. What would become of these people? His people? No. *They* were no longer his people. But they were his race. Memories of Neve came unbidden. He'd wanted her so badly. One of his race. She was tender and beautiful. No! Weak. And treacherous. No, there was nothing he needed from these humans. At least that was the lie he tried to sell himself.

He swallowed. Father, why did you not come for me?

Hal's flight to the Hrymar battleship was like driving a glass-car in a hail storm; any moment he expected his pod to be obliterated by a single enemy shot. Due to energy beam dispersion, by the time a 10 mm beam travelled the tens of thousands of kilometers to the target—short range in space—the beams could be a couple of meters wide, and just grazing one would doom him. With his sphincter tightly clenched, he focused on the target, BB-3.

Seeing his own ship from space was one thing—*Mjolnir* was a titan—but flying toward a similarly sized enemy ship in this eggshell pod … well, fear was a long forgotten friend at this point. And that was one of the joys of battle, he knew; that utter surrender to your wyrd. There was no escaping the winds of circumstance, all one could do was adjust the sails and hold on.

He winced as the form of a ship burst onto the small view-screen in front of his face. Damn! It was a Hrymar destroyer, and he'd come within a kilometer of splattering like an egg on concrete against its bulk.

Breath, he told himself. You're almost there. Sixty-eight more seconds. Odin help him, but it was big! There was nothing in his view-screen *but* the battleship now. The flanks of the ship were alive with flashes of light, like fire-flies on a summer's night. But these bugs bit hard. He was seeing the batteries of hundreds of small laser cannons. Not enough to damage a real ship, but perfect for taking out enemy missiles and torpedoes—or an Extravehicular-Combat-Pod.

Chandragupta Maurya stood, hands clasped behind his back, staring at the crumbling battle-group; the stone wall was now collections of chips and mortar.

"Sir, point defense is overwhelmed. Five torpedoes have made it past our defenses," Shizari said.

"Brace for impact!" Maurya leapt back into the command-chair and activated the harness.

Mjolnir rang, like a hammer striking an anvil; and in such contests the anvil always won. He temporarily lost all sense of balance as the ship was struck, again and again—and then, blackness.

He thought for a moment he might be unconscious. He could see nothing at all; it was absolutely inky black. But he smelled something, faintly coppery. Blood. He flexed his fingers. He could feel. He also tasted something bitter. He put a hand to his face and felt a sticky warm fluid running from his nose—he was bleeding. And what he was tasting, he should have been smelling—smoke. "Hello!" He shouted. He was definitely alive—wasn't he? He jerked sideways when he felt a hand clamp onto his shoulder. Reflexively, he grabbed the hand, as if about to ward off an attack, but the hand on his shoulder relaxed somewhat and he thought he heard someone whisper. Captain? Was that what he heard? Yes, he was a Captain and commanding officer of *Mjolnir* now.

"Sir, are you ok?"

It was the Astrogator, Cabrillo. Maurya couldn't see clearly yet; it had been the Catalan accent that identified the speaker.

"Cabrillo?" He asked.

"Yes, Captain. It's me. We've lost all power, I'm afraid to say. And you are not looking so well."

Maurya wiped his face with the sleeve of his bionan uniform, clearing some of the blood from his nose; the bionan would absorb the proteins and liquids to repair itself. By the dim emergency lighting he noticed a body at his feet—the young French comms officer, Anouk Kappa. "What-" He began to ask, but trailed off.

"She was thrown off her feet and collided with you when the first torpedo hit, sir. Looks like she broke your nose."

"Is she all right?"

Cabrillo shrugged. "Unconscious, but no visible injury. I expect she may have a concussion. Your face, it appears, is harder than her head."

Cabrillo was ever the joker. Maurya wanted to laugh, but winced when he tried to move his head. "The Doctor?"

Cabrillo shook his head. "We've heard nothing, sir. When I say we've lost all power, I mean *all* power. We don't even have active life support. Only the emergency bio-lights are working. We are dead in the water, so to speak."

Maurya tapped his wristcom, intending to call up engineering and get a report. There was no signal, which should not be happening. These devices were self-contained and the signals conducted through the hull of the ship, requiring no line of sight or special antennae. "Bloody hell," he muttered. "Listen up, Cabrillo. You're uninjured I take it?"

"Yes, sir. I'm fine."

"Good. I want you to get to engineering and find out what's going on. My wristcom is down, and we'll need those up if we're to coordinate repairs. Comms first, power second. Got it?"

"Aye, sir."

"Then hop to it, man."

Hal kicked the cut-section of hull into the breach and crawled through. Into the belly-of-the-beast as it were, he thought. For all the danger that lay before him, he was glad to be out of the line of fire in a pod with no weapons. He didn't like that utter helplessness.

Activating stealth before he forgot, he then moved into a large room. Cargo-hold perhaps? He'd need to make his way to the center of the ship. That's where the bridge should be; the most protected area of any ship. This sure was a step up from the other Hrymar ships he'd been in; this had been designed. All previous Hrymar ships had been random vessels captured from other races, then re-purposed. The concept made practical sense, but it had left them vulnerable, which is how Rigsvaka was able to turn back the Hrymar tide over the last seven years. But if this was the future of the enemy ... the good guys were in deep shit. No time for self-doubt now; only time enough to kill the enemy.

There was *something* on this ship—he felt it. Something that he needed to destroy. His glimpses into mind-space had shown him only a darker spot on an already coal-black space. The contrast was the only clue to its nature, otherwise it was invisible.

He passed through the hold and into a passageway, stopping suddenly as he encountered a four-way branch. One could be forgiven for thinking the passageways on this ship had been excavated by ants; lit only by the dimmest of bio-luminescent fungi, and of more or less regular circumference, the gnarled tunnels seemed to permeate the vessel in random directions.

He was traveling ahead mentally now, searching, following the subtle contours of mind-space to find the black spot, when he felt another disturbance; like a tiny pebble dropped in a still pond, he felt the smallest ripples wash over him. In fact there were two sets; each coming from opposite ends of the ship. A force stronger than curiosity pulled him to investigate.

He arrived at another junction in the corridor, this one continued forward, or branched fore and aft. Acting on instinct, he ran left toward the aft of the enemy ship.

Dzakaa had been focused on the battle when something caught his attention. It felt like a whisper in his ear. He spun left and right, but there was nobody there. No, not here … he let his senses drop down into mind-space. There it was! A whispering disturbance.

He turned to Serkan. "Has a new person docked with the ship?" Dzakaa asked.

The blue faced fool wrinkled its eyes at him. "No. Why?"

Dzakaa shook his head. Perhaps it was nothing, he told himself.

Chapter 27

HAL COULD FEEL THE THRUMMING pulse of the Hrymar reactors as he neared the aft section of their battleship. Then the oddest thing happened —he began to smell something human. He caught a whiff of unwashed body. The Hrymar had a peculiar body odor; not necessarily unpleasant, just markedly different from human. What he smelled was distinctly homo-sapien. Slaves maybe? But he'd thought he was nearing the engine and drive section?

As he focused on the eddies and currents of mind-space, the ripples that had initially drawn him aft, correlated to the scent. He arrived at a hatch and just beyond lay the source of this draw on him. He focused for a moment, listening with his mind, probing for other beings. A Hrymar guard stood behind the hatch. The first one he'd have to deal with since arriving on the battleship; stealth had its advantages.

He plucked the hilt of his cledyff sword off his belt and squeezed, extending the blade, then he opened the hatch. The surprised Hrymar guard gasped as the meter-long blade of Hal's sword split him, from neck to waist. They bleed red too, he mused, as he stepped over the corpse and the growing pool of blood on the floor.

What lay before him was indeed an engine room of sorts, but the central feature focused on a horizontal pod, and in it, a tiny, bald girl. She might have been five or six. It was hard to tell, as she was laying in a vat of inky liquid; an assortment of tubes running in and out to various ship's systems. She was a part of the ship. He froze when he noticed her eyes open, then lock onto his.

Slowly he approached the life-pod, or whatever this contraption was. She kept a lock on his eyes the whole time. As he scanned up and down the pod and the connections, tiny fingers emerged from the abyssal liquid. He reached down, gently taking her hand.

Hal's head reeled as she pulled his mind through time and space. He steadied himself by grabbing the life-pod.

Suddenly, they stood on a planet. He gaped around at an expansive field of blonde grasses. It was night. Above them the stars twinkled peacefully. The air was warm and sweet, smelling a little like barley, he thought. The little girl was here, wearing a red dress with gold floral print. She now had long blonde hair tied up in a black ribbon.

"Where are we?" He asked.

"Nowhere," she said with a hollow sadness.

"Are we in your mind?"

Her ribbon bounced as she nodded.

"Can you tell me your name?"

"Galina, Galina Cherenkov."

Russian, he thought. He knelt down so they could talk eye to eye. "Are you from the Novaya Leningrad colony?"

She nodded again.

"And how did you come to be here?"

"The monsters came and took me."

The Hrymar, he thought. The raid on her colony. Bastards. "Why did they put you in this tank?"

"They want me to move the ship. I didn't want to at first, but they said they would hurt my parents if I didn't."

"That's all right. You did the right thing."

Her expression went blank for a moment, then she winked out of existence, leaving him alone, kneeling in the grass. As he began to stand, the entire plane around him seemed to shift and quake. He stumbled, landing on his back. Loki's balls, what's happening? The stars above him seemed to change and as they did, the ground beneath his back went still again. The girl in the red dress popped back into the picture.

"What happened? He asked, as he stood.

"I had to move the ship."

"How exactly are you *moving* the ship?"

She shrugged her tiny shoulders and screwed up her face, as if trying to figure out how to describe it. "I just think about where they want the ship, then it moves. That's all."

"And you must be getting instructions through this pod somehow?"

She shrugged again. "They said it was like skipping a stone. The ship is the stone, and I sort of push it with my mind. Then it skips."

"Do you want to go home with your parents?" He asked.

Her golden hair danced and she smiled.

"Alright, can you let me go back to the pod? I'm going to get you out of here. Ok? I promise."

And just like that, he was back in the engine room, standing over the girl's pod, one hand still holding hers.

Can I just disconnect her? Damn it, I have to. I need to stop this ship. He drew his sword a second time, now slicing through cables, wires, and tubes. Indicator lights began flashing, and some grating, audible alarm began barking.

Darkness fell over the room and a red light began to strobe.

"My Lord, the skip-drive is down!" An engineer said to Serkan.

"What? How? We have taken no weapons fire?"

"I know not. I'll dispatch a team immediately to assess the problem."

"Do that, damn you." What now, he fumed. Damned Ysgar technology. He knew it would not be reliable.

Hal bent over Galina and plucked the various tubes and attachments from her, then tenderly extracted her from the black liquid.

She began shivering as he set her on the floor. Damn, he supposed the pod must have provided her with all her environmental needs; heat, food, water and such. He pulled at the grey cloak hanging on his shoulders and wrapped it around the naked child. The bionan fabric was designed to regulate temperature, so at least she'd be warm.

"Better?" He asked.

She nodded jerkily, her teeth still chattering.

This Galina Cherenkov, the bald, naked creature, shivering on the floor, was a far cry from the little girl in the red dress and black ribbon. He'd make sure she could be that girl again. "You stay here, ok?"

She grabbed his arm, eye wide with terror.

"It's ok," he assured her. "I'll be back. I promise. I need to fix some things first, that way I can take you home." He gave her a fatherly smile.

"Ok?"

She nodded reluctantly.

Time for him to go forward. If he was right, there was another little person in need of help. He stepped out into the dimly lit passageway.

His stealth suit provided an extensive array of sensor data, so he wasn't hindered by the darkness. His only concern, was that they knew he was here, or at least knew something was seriously wrong with their ship. Under the pulsating red strobe-lights, he locked onto three Hrymar that had turned down the passageway toward him. They were at least thirty-meters away, so he drew his pistol and fired a bolt of orange plasma, killing the first target.

The others, seeing their comrade fall, and noticing the intruder, dashed back to the safety of the bend in the passageway.

He sprinted with a speed augmented by his RCA suit and drew his sword with his left hand while he closed on the bend. He turned the corner and fired. A second enemy was down, a smoking hole in his back. They were unarmed— probably engineers. The third Hrymar panicked when he heard the second plasma shot, and spun on Hal. Perfect.

The cledyff sword's mono-molecular blade beheaded the Hrymar with such ease, an unexperienced swordsman might think he missed; that was, until the head slid from the target's shoulders and the body slumped to the ground. No time to enjoy this, he chided himself.

Kadir stood silently, watching Serkan's reaction to the battle and events on the ship. He'd never seen his master so unnerved. The sight of the Ysgar demon twitching caught his attention. It grabbed its head and jerked, as if slapped.

"He is on the ship!" Dzakaa wailed.

Serkan spun, his concentration on the view-screen broken. "Who is here?"

"Olsen!"

"What? Are you mad?" Serkan asked.

Kadir concentrated, slowing his racing mind. With some effort he dropped his consciousness down into mind-space. He could feel waves of psychic energy wash over him. There *was* something here, *someone*. Father? Hal winced as something struck him in the head. No, not something, someone. The darkness knew he was here now. It was inevitable. He tried to focus on the shielding techniques Gwynahra had taught him. He could really use some help in this department now.

He stopped at a junction in the passageway, noting a map. He couldn't read it, but his position was marked on the map, so at least he knew where he was, in relation to where he needed to be. Still half of the ship to cover. Damn this thing was big.

Footsteps! He listened with augmented ears as well as using his mind to probe ahead—at least a dozen Hrymar. He was still stealthed, maybe he could just slip past them. He couldn't take down all twelve in a corridor armed only with a pistol and sword; four or five would come with him, but that would be little consolation if he failed his mission here. No, he had to work smarter, not harder. Inspiration filled him with elation. That was it!

The dozen Hrymar must have been baffled to find Hal standing quietly in the middle of the passageway. His plasma pistol was holstered and his sword was on his belt. He put his hands up, as if in surrender. Utter confusion. They glanced at each other, like prey coming to subdue a predator; which was exactly the case.

Hal locked each of their faces in his mind and in their brief second of confusion, he'd beaten them. Pain. Blinding, explosive, burning, freezing, boiling, pain! He gifted each of their minds with that sensation, then fed on it, and returned it amplified. The look of absolute terror that painted their faces, let him know it had worked. They all screamed, clutching their heads, dropping to their knees, and then, collapsed completely.

Breath! He was panting by the time it was done. He took a moment to catch his breath as he took in the sight before him. A dozen sentient creatures lay dead before him. Each wore a final mask of hideous agony. The Athryllith. A gift? Gods forgive him.

He battled his way past eight more Hrymar before he reached the bow of the ship. Once again he could smell and feel the person ahead. With a little concentration he knew it was another child. Another little girl. There was also a guard inside the door. He was about to repeat his killing of the first guard, when he thought better.

Instead of opening the door, Hal projected the image of a senior Hrymar knocking at the door, and calling to the guard. He heard the hatch begin to open and saw the guard, who bowed to him. Before he lost focus on this illusion, he latched onto the guard's mind, probing. *Who built this ship? How many are there? Where do they come from? What are they called?*

The guard struggled, but it was no real contest. Like a tiny child trying to break a warrior's grip, his mind attempted to resist.

Hal felt the blood leave his limbs and he shivered from the chill. Gods in Asgard! They were building hundreds of these ships. And it *was* the Ysgar.

When he had everything he needed, he killed the guard swiftly, moving to tend to the other little girl. She looked up at him and smiled. He was taken aback.

"Haldor Olsen," she thought to him. *"You've come to rescue me."*

"But how?"

"My sister, Galina, told me you were coming. She said you'd take us home."

Her sister? He nodded. *"I'm going to try."*

"Behind you!" She shouted to his mind.

Hal spun, sword drawn. Another child stood before him. A boy. "Ailan?" He felt his mouth go dry as shoe leather.

"Hello again, father."

Chapter 28

LOCATION: ABOARD MJOLNIR / STAR SYSTEM: Adhara

Mjolnir's bridge was still dark, excepting the dim glow of the organic backup lighting. Power had been off for a good while. Since his wristcom wasn't working, Maurya didn't even have the time. But he could see his breath in the glow of the bio-lights. That meant it was getting damned cold in here, and fast! His bionan suit was doing a fair job of regulating his body temperature, but it was no vacc suit. Once all the ambient heat energy bled out of the ship, they'd all be dead; and long before the oxygen ran out.

He felt selfish for worrying about himself when he was now accountable for an entire battlegroup. Accountable because his lunatic High Commander and Jarl had run off. And to think he'd idolized that man. He felt the proper fool just now. Bloody Norwegians; too much Viking blood in them, he reckoned.

A good Hindu did what was expected of him; he went to the right school, studied at the expense of his social life, and married a woman which his parents had arranged. Respectability. He was proud of that. And furious. He'd finally done something for himself; he believed in Rigsvaka, and what Jarl Haldor was doing. But what a damned mess he was in now. *I should have listened to Ama,* he thought. *First time I step out of the lines drawn for me, I* fail. Serves me right.

"Sir?" A voice dared to intrude on his self pity.

"What?" he snapped.

"You asked for a status update. On the reactor?" It was Cabrillo.

"Yes, of course I did, Mr. Cabrillo. Go ahead, if you please."

"We should have power in about five minutes—give or take."

"Give or take?"

"You know—approximately?"

"I bloody well know what give or take means, man, damnit! I want to know how much time is *give or take?*"

"They didn't say, sir."

"Of course they didn't." Lord Ganesha, why was he taking out his frustration on this poor young man. "Well done, Juan." He could see why the Commander had fled; better to go down in a hail of laser-fire than sit here and freeze to death on a dead ship.

Hal was still unsure he was really seeing his son standing before him. "What are you doing here? And why did you leave me on the planet?"

Ailan smirked arrogantly. "I should ask you the same thing. This is *my* ship. What are *you* doing here?"

He stepped toward his son, but Ailan shuffled back. Then he realized he was still holding drawn sword, point toward the boy. He shook his head and stowed his blade. "I came to stop them, son."

"Do not call me that!" Ailan said.

He could see fury boiling on Ailan's face. "Kadir? Is that how you're called now?"

Ailan shot him a curt nod.

"Kadir it is then. I'm here to try to stop the Hrymar from enslaving more innocent children."

Ailan's face grew hateful. "You mean, like me?"

He felt himself slump. "No. You're no child, Kadir. You're a man now." He pointed to the girl in the tank. "Like her. Like the one aft, controlling the engine. Do you think it's right that they take little boys and girls from their families and stick them into vats of liquid and plug them full of tubes?"

Ailan's face grew slack. He said nothing.

"I don't either," he said. "That goes far beyond slavery. Which in itself, is plain wrong. The human spirit was never meant to be confined, Kadir. We were meant to soar free, explore new places, try new things."

"What do I care of you humans?" Ailan spat beside the tank and looked down at the floor.

"You *are* human. Whether you choose to believe it or not. These bastards have tried to make you into a weapon against your own kind. Don't you see that?" He could feel his son's internal struggle now. He should keep pushing, pulling; try to bring the boy back. He focused on Ailan's mind, probing gently, seeking a crack into which he could leverage the light out of the dark.

Ailan's head snapped up. "What are you doing?"

Hal felt like he'd been slapped across the face; the door to Ailan's mind slammed shut.

"Stay out of my head, old man!" Ailan said.

Hal fell to his knees, clutching his head. Gods in Asgard! The pain! Through teary eyes, he saw a glimpse of a creature in the hatchway behind

Ailan. A scaly, dirt colored face with nubs on his head, like vestigial horns. It was the shadow which he'd felt in mind-space. It sucked in his will to live, sapped every ounce of resistance he had left. Then, like the blackness in mind-space, his own thoughts went dark.

Hal awoke on a sort of table. He tried to move, but was held fast. He tilted his head up and could see brown cords holding him down. Then they writhed under the pressure of his movement. Loki's balls, they were alive! He panicked. Breathe, Haldor, breathe. Get a grip. He tried to gently raise a leg, then flex a knee, but that too, was made impossible. There was a kind of green adhesive holding him down where the ropes were not. Like damned flypaper, he thought grimly. Only his head was free. Little bloody good that did.

So this was the end? He was destined to be an experiment on the enemy's operating table? He laughed. And his own son against him. And here he thought he had the favor of the gods? What a cosmic, fucking joke. No valkyrie would come to take him to Valhalla when he died. No, he would simply expire. His legacy would be a failed attempt, destined to crumble like all the works of men. What hubris to think he could actually make a difference.

In time, his fury subsided and his mind transitioned from a raging blood-red, to a deep blue, the hues of sadness and regret taking hold. He thought of his farm on New Midgard; how happy he and Siobhan had been there; growing things, raising Ailan. It was a beautiful life. But like all things Human, it was all too brief, all too transient. Then, there had been Gwynahra. How he loved her and wished they could have had a life together. He imagined what amazing children they would have made. But, it was not to be. He would have to say his goodbyes to her.

He closed his eyes and pictured her pale skin, and ebony hair. Like a pearl on black velvet, or the moon on a dark sky. *"I love you,"* he thought into mind-space. *"I'm so sorry. I wish … I wish for so many things. Take care of little Chloe for me, please? And Venn. Keep them together?"*

His goodbyes were interrupted by the sound of the hatch irising open. He couldn't see who entered, but heard footfalls and a strange hissy-breathing. It was the creature.

"How nice to see you, Jarl Haldor," it said. I think it is time we became acquainted better, no?"

Location: Aboard the frigate Gjallarhorn / Planet: Orbiting Rigsvaka

Haldor had assigned Gwynahra to the frigate *Gjallarhorn*, which was policing the space around Rigsvaka while the rest of the fleet was away. A dull assignment to be sure. But a safe one, as Haldor had intended, Gwynahra was certain.

She'd just finished her shift in sickbay; which had included: treating a headache, bandaging a laceration to a hand, and curing a fungal infection. High medicine, to be sure.

She missed Haldor so much, that all joy seemed to go with him. She'd never been in love before. It was an awful affliction; though one even her extensive medical schooling could not help her overcome.

As she approached the hatch to her quarters she was struck by a dizzy spell. *'I love you'* she heard in her mind. *'I'm so sorry. I wish … I wish for so many things. Take care of little Chloe for me, please? And Venn. Keep them together?'* Haldor? She thought. Her heart was thundering in her chest. "Haldor!" She screamed. He was in danger! Captured maybe. Oh gods, please, no! Then she felt a great weight press against her chest, though not physical; it was a blackness, an evil. She saw what Haldor saw—Ysgar!

She closed her eyes and took a deep breath, centering her mind, as Magister Faelar had taught her. She felt the tide of panic ebbing. She knew what to do next.

"Chloe? Can you hear me?" She projected.

"I'm here, Gwyn. Are you ok?" Chloe asked.

"I am. But Haldor needs us. I'm coming to pick you up at home. Be ready in thirty minutes."

"Ok."

Gwynahra leapt into her quarters and dropped down before her terminal. She had to compose a simple message, which took her all of ten-seconds. Then she instructed the EI to route it through the stellar-com on Rigsvaka. Done.

Now, to steal a shuttle, she thought.

Maurya's head was still pounding when the *Mjolnir's* bridge-lighting began to flicker, and finally, stayed on. He blinked and squinted as his eyes and brain adjusted to the sudden intensity. Power was back on. Thank Ganesha—and Mr. Cabrillo of course. Now, if only he had comms, which was supposed to be the priority- His thought was interrupted by his chirping wristcom. Bloody well done! He thought.

"Captain?" Cabrillo said, over the comm.

"I read you, Cabrillo. Well done! Thank engineering for me."

"Sir, internal sensors are still offline, but we're hearing noises on the outside of the hull. I think we're about to be boarded."

Maurya's elation was popped like a balloon with a pin. "Location?"

"Just ahead of the engine room sir. Bulkhead sixty-four alpha."

"Roger that. I'll order our marines there now. Maurya out." He closed the connection and was now in contact with the remaining marines. "Candella?"

"Here, sir," the marine officer replied.

"Take two squads to bulkhead sixty-four alpha and prepare to repel boarders."

"Yes, sir. ETA three minutes."

I hope that's soon enough, he thought. Now that comms were back, he remembered Aksyonova and her team of Atgeir. They'd boarded the Hrymar battleship. "Aksyonova, Maurya here. Can you read me?"

"We're here sir. We thought we'd lost you?"

Over Aksyonova's comm, he heard the sounds of energy weapons fire and shouting in the background. "We were out of commission for a while, but we've got power and comms back up. We're preparing to repel boarders. How close are you to gaining access to their virionic weapon?"

"I don't know, sir. We've lost half our team, but we're almost at the weapon. Either we'll be there in the next five minutes, or we'll all be dead."

"Understood. Godspeed, Pelagia."

"Roger that, sir. Aksyonova out."

Chapter 29

LOCATION: ABOARD LIGHT'S DOOM / STAR System: Adhara

Hal stared up at his alien captor—an Ysgar, just like Gwynahra had shown him. So this was the enigmatic and feared enemy of the mighty Alfar. They were ugly, he'd give them that.

"Do you play chess?" It asked.

"What?" The question shocked Hal.

It inclined its head on an angle. "My apologies. I should first introduce myself. My name is Dzakaa. And my question was simple. Do you play chess?"

"Yes. I've played the game."

"Excellent. Then you should have an appreciation for the game we have been playing. Though I admit you were an unwitting participant."

"What the fuck are on about? What game?" Lunatic, he thought.

"No, Jarl Haldor. I am no lunatic."

The bastard read his thoughts. That's why he felt his presence in mind-space. But why as a dark spot?

"Firstly, I am no bastard—at least as you understand the term relating to paternity. To your second thought, you feel me as a dark spot because you cannot read my mind. I absorb, but do not radiate in mind-space. My species has honed our telepathic skills over millennia. You have just picked up this instrument and are beginning to make some crude sounds with it. I have mastered its use, and can therefore play a symphony by comparison. Do you see?"

He tried not to think anything, knowing that Dzakaa could hear every thought that crossed his mind. Could he build a strong-enough wall and keep him out? He tried. One ethereal brick at a time, laid on upon another.

Dzakaa made some cackling sound. A laugh? And with the wave of the creature's hand Hal's brick wall exploded, leaving his mind burning.

"Do not try to shield yourself from me, or it will go hard for you. If you submit to my will, then you just may survive. I trust you would like to spend time with your son? Perhaps get to know him better?"

He didn't try to build the wall again, but he did try to focus on a field of black, picturing nothingness. He tried to imagine the burning cold of space, and held that image and feeling. "Yes. I would like to speak with my son," Hal said.

"Very well. First, I have questions. How many interstellar-bridge-nodes do you have access to?"

Fuck.

"Indeed." Dzakaa chuckled, again in its raspy way.

"Only a few."

"I will need a list of them. As well as the specific method for triggering the nodes," Dzakaa said.

"Do you really think I would trade my life, for the lives of billions of others? You clearly don't know humans, Dzakaa."

"Oh, I beg to differ, Jarl. I know your race all too well. I learned much from your fellow human, Benjamin Gridrmann. He was a fascinating man. It was he who taught me chess."

"A fine example of humanity," Hal said sarcastically and spat at Dzakaa's feet. "Gridrmann was a traitorous piece of shit. He'll be remembered as the man who sold out his planet. Hell, he sold out *more* than one."

"I want you to think about my offer. You may not place a great value on your own life, but what of little Chloe? Or Gwynahra? She is quite beautiful."

"You fucking maggot!" He tensed against his bonds and the green adhesive, but he couldn't move a millimeter. Every muscle in his body strained, but to no avail. Odin, hear me! Help me destroy this evil, he pleaded.

"Who is this Odin?" Dzakaa asked. "And what happened to his eye? Oh, never mind. I will send in Kadir- or rather, Ailan. You can speak with him and consider the price you place on those you love. I will be coming to collect. Soon." It cackled as it left the room.

He felt Ailan's presence in mind-space before he heard his footfalls.

"Ailan? Are you there?" He said.

"I am."

"I can't see you."

His son stepped into view.

"I'm sorry that I never came to rescue you, son. I just wanted to tell you that in case I don't get another chance to say it. I would have stormed Niflheim alone to get you and your mother back. You have to believe me."

Ailan said nothing.

"It seems that you also have the Athryllith."

Ailan's face contorted in confusion at the term.

"Telepathy—the ability to speak mind-to-mind with someone? Maybe it runs in the family. It didn't crop up in me until a few years ago, but I can feel it in you now."

"I can do more than speak," Ailan thought to him. And for the first time Hal didn't feel any hostility or hatred toward him. He simply sensed his son's personal pride in his abilities.

"Please, show me," Hal thought.

Ailan took a quick breath, then surveyed the room they were in. He took a few steps and grabbed something out of sight of Hal, then returned with a small canister in hand. He set the canister down on a table in view of Hal, then took a few steps back. Hal watched as Ailan focused on the canister and it began to rise of the table. Slowly, but surely, he was levitating it!

"Gods, that's amazing!" Hal said.

Ailan smiled, then instantly erased it from his face.

"Can you get me out of here?" He asked. "We could leave here together. I have ships here, and a place we can be safe."

Ailan shook his head.

"You won't?"

"You have no ships left. And no safe place to go, father. The Hrymar are attacking Rigsvaka while you are stuck here on this table. The attacks on the colonies were a ruse designed to draw you out and leave Rigsvaka vulnerable. My foster-sire wants to be rid of you. He is not a man to do things in half measures. You were content to peck at the Hrymar slave trade these last seven years. And while you were pecking like a chicken, Devrim built a mighty fleet and made powerful allies."

Hal felt empty now. There was no trace of rage, or fear, or sadness—nothing. He was absolutely bereft after hearing this. He was a hollow shell of a man, spending the last hours of his life on an operating room table. Likely to be tortured and experimented on while his people were slaughtered and enslaved.

So this was the end.

Location: Tyrbjorg Starport / Planet: Rigsvaka

Admittedly, trying to sneak around with a child and a two-hundred kilogram wolf in tow, was not an easy thing. But Gwynahra was in love and determined; her man needed her. She would not fail.

As a doctor and ship's officer, she had access to most areas on Rigsvaka. But access did not mean questions wouldn't be asked, or authorities not alerted, if she was discovered doing something outlandish—such as trying to steal a starship.

Her initial idea was to commandeer a hyperspace-capable shuttle, but she wasn't sure they would be equipped with a TCRP transmitter which was required to open an interstellar bridge. She knew of one ship that would be certain to have one, and, which would still be here on Rigsvaka; Hal's personal ship—the Sleipnir.

The delivery air-truck she'd borrowed from friend, seemed a reasonable cover. It was also the right size to accommodate a pony-sized wolf. Her co-conspirator, little Chloe, had swiped Hal's gene-key and codes for the Sleipnir. Normally these would be with him, but were left behind in case the ship was needed to help in an emergency; Gwynahra felt this qualified. Though she decided she'd asked for forgiveness instead of permission.

Chloe jumped out of the passenger side of the air-truck as Gwynahra ran to the rear cargo area. She pressed a button which lowered a ramp and out bounded their massive passenger. She shook herself thoroughly when she hit the runway and groaned with displeasure.

"Yes, it is stinky back there, isn't it?" Chloe thought to Venn, as she grabbed the fur on her neck, and vaulted onto her back. Some girls had ponies.

"Common," Gwynahra thought to them both. The all-telepathic party was nothing, if not quiet. They rounded the back of the 100 meter-long Sleipnir as its massive aft cargo ramp lowered to the ground. They dashed up the ramp and Gwynahra hit the button to retract it while they were still on it.

She made it to the bridge in seconds, jumped onto the pilot's seat, and plugged in Hal's bio-mechanical gene-key. It allowed the High Commander to use his own DNA scan to operate the ship's command functions, or to lend someone the gene-key to act as a proxy. They couldn't be copied and therefore helped ensure security.

A disembodied voice echoed through the bridge. *"Welcome to the Sleipnir. I am the ship's Level 6 EI, Marshall."* Marshall was the ship's new emergent intelligence, since Skallgrim had been transplanted first into the *Drekkar*, then into the *Mjolnir*. *"As you are in possession of the Captain's gene-key, I must assume that you are an authorized proxy or representative. Please state your name for the record."*

"Gwynahra Tarnallsdottir."

"Thank you Ms. Gwynahra. Do you have any instructions?"

"Yes. Prepare the ship for launch. We are headed to Najaf, in the Adhara star system."

"Very well. And who are the crew on this flight?"

"Just myself."

"I see."

"I understood you were capable of operating the ship by yourself? Was I misinformed?"

"No, I am quite capable of operating most systems. Of course if there are any hardware malfunctions I will be unable to have them repaired."

"Understood. We'll have to take our chances, Marshall.

"Indeed, Ms. Gwynahra."

Chloe skipped onto the bridge, Venn padding along beside her.

"It appears we do have some additional crew. How delightful!" Marshall said playfully.

"They programmed you with a sense of humor?" She said.

"Indeed. Commander Olsen enjoys a little repartee now and again."

For the first time in days, Gwynahra smiled. "Yes, he does." She looked down at Chloe. "Ready to save Hal?"

Chloe nodded, her mind filled with pride. Gwynahra stroked her shoulder.

"Good. Sit down and buckle up." She glanced at Venn. *"Venn, I suppose you will have to go- wherever you go during flight."*

The dire wolf promptly curled up at her feet.

Chandragupta Maurya was not a patient man; waiting didn't suit him. And he'd been forced to do far too much of it today. But his tension finally eased when a monitor at the command-chair came to life with external sensor data. Brilliant! They were no longer blind, at least to the outside world; internal sensors were still down. One brick at a time, that's how the Taj Mahal was built.

"Sir, sensors have a new ship entering the system through the bridge node," Meiriona said.

"Ours?"

"Yes, sir!" She said excitedly, then tempered her next words. "It's only the Sleipnir, sir."

"What in the world is she doing here? Kappa, who's Captaining her?"

"Hailing now, sir," Anouk Kappa said.

A raven haired Alfar appeared on the main view-screen. *"Chandra, sorry to just drop in like this, but I think Haldor is in danger."*

"Gwynahra. Of course he's in danger. That's how he bloody well likes it!"

"Where he is?"

"He took an experimental boarding pod to one of the Hrymar battleships. He hasn't contacted us since he arrived. Our sensors show his pod is successfully attached to the battleship though."

"Ok, then we need- " Her statement was interrupted as the Sleipnir rocked and bucked. *"We're taking fire, Chandra. Can you cover us?"*

"We're dead in the water. We're working on drive systems now. Try to get behind us. At least you can use us as a shield."

"Coming to you now."

He tapped his comm. "Engineering, eta on sub-light engines?"

"Sir, I'm sorry, but it could be hours yet. The virionic weapon has really messed up the drives. All the thruster ports are blocked with new growths of organic shielding. We have to cut and clear each port."

He slumped down into his seat. "Can you clear a few ports to give us crude maneuverability?"

"*That I can do, sir. We can do that in maybe fifteen minutes?*"

"You have five. Maurya out."

Chapter 30

Dzakaa had decided to move Hal, table and all, to the ship's bridge. They even stood Hal upright so he could fully appreciate the ruination of his battle group on the view-screens. *Bastards,* Hal thought.

"More comfortable?" Dzakaa asked, laconically.

"Infinitely," Hal said, looking around at the various bridge crew. He recognized one of them; the grizzled old veteran, Serkan. He'd seen him on Niflheim years ago. And Ailan was there as well, standing beside Serkan like a dutiful apprentice.

"As you can see, Jarl, your tiny fleet is all but obliterated. As I speak, our warriors are harvesting the remainder of your people. Waste not, want not. A Human axiom I believe?"

"Here's another one—go fuck yourself!"

"Such wasteful emotions. If your species harnessed all their anger, instead of projecting it out uselessly into the void, why you might even have ruled this galaxy. But you are such tempestuous creatures. That spirit is to our gain, as we harness it in our ships and weapons. Every living organism has its part to play—humanity's has only *just* started to be realized," he finished with a sickening chuckle.

"You know, Dzakaa, you're right. Chess is a great game," he said.

The Ysgar looked surprised. "I am glad to see you coming around to the proper perspective. How refreshing."

"But life is not a single chess game. Life is a tournament. *Maybe* you've won this game, but not the tournament. Not yet. And you just may find humanity and their allies are stiffer competition than you think."

The creature took on a darker expression than Hal had thought possible. "If you refer to the Alfar, then it is *you* who are overestimating their will. They are decadent creatures. They want only to tend their gardens and write poetry. They have no stomach for conflict, no killer instinct. If they had, they would have erased us from the galaxy. Their weakness in quarantining my species was the beginning of their downfall."

He felt the creature's building ecstasy in mind-space. He was elated at this triumph and his opportunity to boast.

Dzakaa continued. "They felled the oak but left the acorns. And so, we planned, and plotted, and spread quietly among the stars. Biding our time, when we could finally strike the decisive blow. The Ysgar will rule this galaxy!"

He saw Serkan and Ailan glance over at Dzakaa after his last statement. The creature shot a silencing glare at them. Hal probed Serkan's mind gently. The Hrymar had undone themselves with this alliance, Serkan was thinking. The Ysgar wanted to dominate everything, and everyone, within their reach. He could feel Serkan's hatred for this being and a new sense of horror at this lopsided partnership.

"My Lord," the sensor operator said, "we have a new contact. A small ship just passed through the gate."

"Intercept it." Serkan ordered.

"Vectoring destroyers now, my Lord."

Hal heard a voice in his mind. *"Haldor, are you there?"*

"Gwynahra?"

"Yes, we've come to help."

"We?" He thought.

"Yes, I have Chloe and Venn with me. I heard your call and we took the Sleipnir."

Oh gods, what had he done! His lament had been a goodbye, not a cry for help. *"Gwynahra, turn the ship around and go back through the bridge immediately! They're sending ships to destroy you!"*

"No! We're here to save you. Do you think you're the only one who can risk his life to save the ones he loves?"

"But why did you bring Chloe?"

"Because she is one of the strongest telepaths I've ever met. We felt the creature—the Ysgar. We know what to do."

What could he say? Maybe them dying on the Sleipnir was a more humane end. He'd rather that than see them enslaved or experimented on. And what if they *could* help?

Dzakaa spun on Hal, glaring. "Who are you communicating with?" When he didn't answer, Dzakaa punched him with a mental fist. Hal faded to black. *"Haldor, are you still there?"* Gwynahra thought to him, but got no reply. His mental footprint had disappeared from mind-space

"I can't see him anymore!" Chloe cried.

"Not to worry, we'll find him," she said.

The *Sleipnir* was still taking fire from a squadron of destroyers, but she was a tuff little ship.

"*Ms. Gwynahra, might I suggest we engage the stealth system?*" Said Marshall.

"Of course, do it."

"*Activating stealth.*"

The *Sleipnir* continued to be hit, but with far less frequency. "Is it active?" She asked.

"*The cloak is working at 85% efficiency, unfortunately the initial weapons fire has damaged some of the outer layer which conduct sand absorbs light, and other electro-magnetic wavelengths. They will still be able to target us, but with much less ease.*"

"That will have to do. Get us behind the *Mjolnir*." She could see the *Mjolnir* begin to move toward them on sensors. "Thank the Lord and Lady! They got some sub-light maneuvering back."

"That's good, right?" Chloe asked.

She smiled at the little girl. "Yes! That is very good."

Chandragupta Maurya appeared on the small view-screen in front of her. "*Gwynahra, we were able to get our docking-bay doors open. We may not be able to protect you very well by maneuvering, but you can dock inside Mjolnir. The virionic weapons have already done their damage. And as a direct effect, it's thickened our external armor. Their conventional energy weapons don't seem to be able to penetrate our newly-reinforced outer layer.*"

"Understood, Gwynahra out. Marshall, take us in."

"*Preparing to dock inside Mjolnir,*" the EI responded.

She watched as the *Mjolnir* rolled on her axis, exposing her belly and the widening maw of the docking bay. She shuddered at the sight of *Mjolnir*. It looked like some tumor-laden aberration. *Mjolnir* had been hit with two doses of the virionic weapon and was not faring well. Now she could see what Maurya mentioned; the external organic armor was markedly thicker, if not consistent.

As they sprinted to *Mjolnir's* bridge, Gwynahra navigated post-battle debris and myriad wounded. After serving on the ship, she knew the way, but found she was unable to take a direct route due to battle damage and the out-of-control armor growth.

"What a mess," Chloe noted, from atop Venn's back.

"It certainly is," she said.

The hatch to the bridge was propped open, and appeared to have been cut with a plasma torch. She had to duck under a piece of the hatch that was still hanging down. The bridge was as badly damaged as everywhere else.

Chandragupta Maurya stood as she entered. "Welcome to the bridge, such as it is."

She grimaced as she saw Maurya's battered face, instinctively reaching out to assess his wounds.

He pulled back. "Don't worry about me, I'll be fine. Tell me, why the hell are you here? And with the child?"

She understood his reproach, but she didn't want to waste time discussing the details, so instead, she showed him. Grabbing his hand, she played back the events of the last hour, complete with Haldor's mournful goodbye, and a snapshot of his situation; it hit Maurya like tsunami. She had to catch his elbow to prevent him from stumbling, as his knees buckled.

"Sorry, I didn't mean for that to be quite so intense. Do you understand now?" She asked.

Maurya was bent over at the waist, catching his breath. "Yes. I had no idea what he was doing. I thought he'd simply abandoned us so he could go down in a blaze of glory."

"Haldor would never abandon anyone, Chandra. I know him as well as I know myself."

"That's quite a gift you two share," Maurya said.

She nodded, a reluctant smile creeping onto her face. "It is. And I don't plan on relinquishing him without a fight." Her smile was replaced by a stern mask of determination.

"What do you need us to do?"

"Can you get us on the ship where Haldor's being held?"

"Both of you?"

"And Venn," she said. "We'll need her strength as well. She understands what must be done."

Maurya glanced at the wolf. "We'll try."

She put a hand on his shoulder. "Thank you, Chandra. Now, let me look at your wounds."

Pelagia Aksyonova's team had been set upon from all sides. Now she picked her way clumsily through passageways sprinkled with corpses; human and Hrymar alike.

Her ECA was suit in tatters; half the servos and mechanical-assist systems were offline. There was no way she'd made it back to the *Mjolnir* in her suit. As it was, she could barely move; worse, she'd lost forty-eight of her fifty-person team. Her and a squad leader, Colin Chapman, were all that remained; and they were certainly not fighting-fit. But, they were almost at the weapons room.

She finally decided to ditch her ECA suit. The limited protection it still offered was offset by the fact that it was slowing her down. Wriggling out of the suit was made almost impossible, due to several fused joints, but she finally managed; emerging like a wet cat from a washing machine. Even her bionan suit under the armor had been torn up badly. But she had no broken bones, at least nothing she could feel with all the adrenalin coursing through her system.

Chapman's suit seemed to have faired better, so he remained armored for the time being. "Colin, cover me while I open the hatch."

"Aye, covering you." Chapman didn't look back at her.

She had her plasma rifle raised as the hatch irised open, but the room was clear of any Hrymar. If there had been any guarding it, they'd likely joined the fray when her Atgeir got close. The room was more or less what she expected. Magister Edvit's brief had indicated there should be biological tanks and equipment, making it look more like an ER, and less like a weapons room. What he hadn't mentioned, was that she'd find a little girl connected to the machinery.

She steeled herself. The child was bald and naked, suspended in a tub of black liquid, like oil. Tubes ran in and out of ports on her body. She shuddered, ignoring the girl for the moment and looking for the tanks of viral liquid that needed to find. Turned out there were several tanks of fluid, so she decided to inoculate them all with the retrovirus. Magister Edvit said it should take only five minutes for the retrovirus to take effect. But she'd still need to find a way to fire the modified virionic beam back at infected ships. Damn it! She fumed. She'd come so far. No time for self-doubt, inject the damned tanks, and worry about the second part later.

"I can help you," she heard a little girl's voice in her mind.

She spun back to the tub holding the naked boy, her mouth agape.

"I can fire it for you," she thought to her.

She heard her inside her mind. There were no words, just meaning. Yet it was perfectly clear. "Are you in my mind?" She asked.

"Yes."

"Do you control the weapon?"

"Yes."

Merciful God, what had they done to this poor child? But if she could help … she had thousands, if not millions to save. "Ok, I'll need to inject the tanks first, but after five minutes, can you fire the weapon at a ship I tell you?"

"I can."

She wanted to cry, instead, she placed a hand on the girl's head, stroking her lightly. "Thank you."

Chapter 31

LOCATION: ABOARD LIGHT'S DOOM / STAR System: Adhara

The lame rides a horse,

the handless is herdsman,

The deaf in battle is bold;

The blind man is better than one that is burned,

No good can come of a corpse.

- Havamal

It was an alien odor that first alerted Hal to his whereabouts. Then, slowly, dim light flowed into his blinking eyes.

"Welcome back, Jarl," Dzakaa said.

He was still alive. Though he wasn't sure that was a good thing. "What's happening?"

"It appears your loved ones have come to your rescue. Not to worry, they are still fine. I promise to take good care of them. Your little troop is full of powerful telepaths. I was delighted!"

"Leave them alone," was all he could think to say, as pathetic as it sounded. He was spent. His previous fury had completely drained him; like an empty reactor, powerful, but useless.

"My noble brothers in arms, the Hrymar, have a saying—the strong rule, the weak serve. Fitting, no?"

Hal surveyed the bridge and saw Serkan and Ailan both standing silently. Devrim, that stupid fucker, he'd doomed his own people with this clever alliance. Greed was always humanity's downfall, and it looked to be the Hrymar's as well. He tried to reach out into mind-space, feel for Gwynahra, but there was nothing. His mind kept hitting a barrier, in fact it was just like physical wall. His psyche felt confined.

"There will be no more communicating with your little Alfar darling," Dzakaa thought to him.

"Please leave them alone. I'll do anything you want, just … please," Hal pleaded, mind-to-mind with Dzakaa.

"Yes, you will do anything I want. But I need not purchase that favor. I already have you."

"Wouldn't it be easier if I cooperate?"

Dzakaa seemed to be considering the idea. *"Perhaps. But would I enjoy the process as much?"* The bastard laughed.

Serkan and Ailan looked over at Dzakaa, probably wondering what the alien was laughing at. Maybe Hal couldn't communicate with Gwynahra, but maybe he could with Ailan … he was closer after all. He just had to be careful Dzakaa didn't intercept the conversation. To block another's attempt at reading his mind, he'd been taught to erect a mental wall, brick by brick. What if he built a conduit? A pipe to contain his message? So he tried. *"Ailan, can you hear me?"*

His son turned to look at him.

"Don't be obvious, look away. Just listen to me." Dzakaa didn't react, it seemed to be working.

Ailan turned back to a console beside him and began tapping buttons. *"I am listening."*

"This Ysgar is planning to destroy Niflheim and all the Hrymar with it. Or at best, enslave and experiment on all of them, just as he's done to the Human children on this ship. Do you understand? He's your enemy as well as mine."

Ailan didn't respond. Well, at least he wasn't arguing, that was some progress.

"Help me stop him. You can kill me when we're done, if that's what you, or Devrim, really wants. I don't care. But I don't want to see humanity, and my own son, doomed."

The boy still said nothing. Maybe Dzakaa was blocking him?

"Ailan?"

"I heard you."

"Then are you with me?"

Still no reply.

His attention to Ailan shifted suddenly, as voices on the bridge became raised. They were speaking in Hrymi, but between telepathy and his limited grasp on their tongue, caught the gist of it; they'd lost control of one of their battleships!

Mjolnir's bridge was still a debris-strewn wreck, though the ship had power and limited maneuverability. Their situation seemed to be improving, then it all went to shit.

"Incoming!" Meiriona said. "Four torpedoes—fired from two destroyers."

"ETA?" Maurya asked her.

"Two-minutes, sir."

"What's happening, Chandra?" Gwynahra asked Maurya.

"It seems the Hrymar are going to try to finish us off. Once they disabled us, I expected them to try to take us prisoner for their slave markets. But we repelled the first boarding party. Then you came and we got some ship's functionality back. Maybe they decided we represent too great a threat now."

"Dear Lord and Lady, is it my fault?" She felt Chandra's resignation to their fate.

"No," he said, unconvincingly.

She faced him, grabbing him by the shoulders. "Chandra, don't give up! Not now. Please?" She shared her pain and determination with him, and tried to ease some of his pain at the same time.

Maurya relaxed visibly, the tiniest of smiles creeping onto his tired face. "Thanks, Gwynahra."

She caressed his mind, as a friend might hug another in pain. "We can do this, together."

"Combatives, how are our defenses?" Maurya demanded.

That's better, she thought. He sounds more like a first officer and less like a defeated man.

Shizari didn't take his eyes of his console as he answered. "We have several batteries back up, sir. But our targeting sensors are still glitchy. The detection grid is severely compromised and that means we've got blind spots." Pelagia stared at the various tanks of fluid she'd injected with the retrovirus, hoping for some visual cue to know it worked. But there was nothing. The timer on her wristcom chirped—five minutes was up. Time to do or die.

She moved back to the tank that held the little girl, and realized she hadn't even asked her name. Here she was, maybe about to die—Pelagia had no idea how the retrovirus would affect the girl—and she didn't even know her name. She leaned toward her and placed a hand on her tiny shoulder. "What's your name?"

"Katya," she thought to Pelagia.

"You are Russian?" She said, shocked.

"Yes."

"Me too," she beamed. "My family comes from Pskov. You are from the colony? Novaya Leningrad?"

"I was born there."

"I'll get you back there, ok? My name is Pelagia Aksyonova, and an Aksyonova never breaks a promise, da? Especially to another Russian."

The barest of smiles crept onto the girl's pale face.

"Are you ready to fire the weapon now?"

"Yes."

"Ok." Despite trying to steel herself, tears were flowing as she told the girl which ship to target.

Hal smirked. His people were still fighting! Good for them.

"My Lord, First Claw Tosunbey's ship has been disabled," a crewman said.

"Get him on comms!" Serkan ordered. "And make sure the *Mjolnir* is fully disabled."

"Yes, my Lord, we have two destroyers making a torpedo run on it now," another one said.

"Ailan, can you still hear me," he thought to his son.

The boy shot him a quick glance.

"Good. Listen, my people are still fighting. If we can help them, your Hrymar friends might have a chance too." He peered into Ailan's mind, trying to figure out whether he was going to help. The boy wasn't fully convinced, at least not enough to go against Devrim's wishes. Damn it, he thought to himself. He had to try something. The boy needed to be convinced. If he could get him to help, then by the gods, he might have a chance.

While he was still connected to Ailan in mind-space, he reached out on a parallel path to Dzakaa. It felt like trying to climb a greased pole—trying to get traction was near impossible. He had to mentally squeeze, putting pressure on the slippery stream of consciousness. He held on to Ailan's, but that second stream felt just out of reach; every time he had his psychic-fingers on it, it slipped out of his grasp. Until it didn't. There. He was inside Dzakaa's head now, heading down the black hole in mind-space, and taking Ailan with him.

He felt Dzakaa's utter shock at this intrusion. The force of two streams of consciousness had acted like a wedge; once they got it in a little, they were able to pry open a crack wide enough to get into the recesses of the creature's mind.

He expected ugliness in this creature's thoughts, but he was wholly unprepared for the inhumanity and alienness. Its mind was like a cancer, filled with thoughts of reckless reproduction, and ruthless tactics to enable that singular mission. The Ysgar wanted to dominate the galaxy—the Universe.

Their kind felt that all other forms of sentient life were but tools to use in their expansion, nothing else. What he took for a sick sense of humor in Dzakaa, was pure acting. Its witty conversation was but simulation. Ysgar knew nothing of emotion—and that was terrifying. He expected this was what the mind of a sociopath might be like; capable of unspeakable acts as easily as one might take a step.

Ailan saw it now and looked at his father with a face that spoke of desperation.

"Help me," he thought to Ailan. *"Work with me. Together, we might be able to beat him."*

Dzakaa was mentally squirming now, unable to move as father and son assailed its mind. They had him!

Or did they? He felt the darkness begin to flow again; like a dark well filling back up, its water level rising.

"Sir, point defense has taken down one torpedo. Three more still inbound," Meiriona reported. "

Maurya nodded and opened a ship-wide comm channel. "This is Captain Maurya. Evacuate all decks forward of lateral bulkhead fifty-four. You have two-minutes." Maurya closed the channel. "Helm, give me all the acceleration you can muster and steer toward BB-3. We're going to ram her."

Gwynahra's guts lurched as she heard Chandra's order.

He turned to her. "You just need to get close, right?"

She nodded. "Within 1,000 kilometers should suffice."

Maurya gave her a sweeping bow. "I try never to disappoint a lady."

Mjolnir shuddered as she was struck by the first torpedo.

"Damage?" Maurya asked.

"Unknown, sir. Internal sensors are still down. The systems we just reactivated are still working, though," Meiriona said.

"It's our lucky day," he said sardonically.

She detached herself from the fate of the ship and all the activity around her, focusing instead on Hal, reaching out to him, feeling for his presence. The darkness that she'd felt before, was now diminished, a candle grown dim.

"Haldor? I'm close."

"Gwynahra, we're trying to stop him, but he's strong," Hal thought.

"We?"

"Ailan is helping me, at least for now. I showed him the real Ysgar. He knows now."

"We're almost there, hold on."

"I'll try. If I can't- "

"Yes, you can!"

"If I can't," he continued, *"I love you."*

Maurya looked over at Gwynahra with a look of surprise. "Gwynahra, are you all right?"

"Not yet."

Serkan had taken notice of the trio of oddly intense expressions. "What is going on?" Dzakaa, Kadir, and Olsen, all wore expressions of intense effort, brows furrowed, the humans both sweating. He turned to Kadir and grabbed him by the shoulders "Boy? What in Ymir's name is happening?"

Kadir looked at him with vacant eyes, head lolling. The boy looked drugged.

"My Lord, the *Mjolnir* is vectoring straight at us!" A crewman said.

Serkan released Kadir and turned to the view-screen. "Can we evade?"

"No, my Lord. The drives are still down. The human had wrought havoc on the auxiliary systems.

Serkan glared at Dzakaa. "You! You scaly bastard. What have you got to say?"

The Ysgar remained silent with his crinkled face.

"Claws, fire everything at *Mjolnir*. Weapons free!" Serkan ordered. He knew these Ysgar would be trouble, now he had confirmation of his appraisal. Devrim was a clever Over-Chieftain, but sometimes too clever for his own good; and for that of the Hrymar people. He only had himself to blame though. He'd supported Devrim's assassination of his father, Egemen, and had pledged his loyalty to the boy; present circumstances were the culmination of many poor decisions.

He motioned to a guard as he glared at the Ysgar. "Take *it* off my bridge."

An armored guard grabbed the Ysgar roughly, and was shocked at the response. Dzakaa's reptilian eyes flicked open and the guard went flying through the air, slamming hard against the bulkhead, taking another crewman with him. Dzakaa hadn't even touched him.

The creature locked eyes with Serkan. "How dare you set your dog upon me!"

Serkan felt a hammer-blow in his mind, sending him to his knees. He clutched his head in blinding agony; it was as if he'd been shot.

Kadir leapt toward the Ysgar in one bound, but like the guard, was mentally swatted, as a bothersome insect.

By Ymir he would kill this Ysgar fiend, Serkan promised himself.

Chapter 32

LOCATION: ABOARD LIGHT'S DOOM / STAR System: Adhara

The *Mjolnir* shuddered and groaned. It was like nothing Gwynahra had ever felt. Then again, she'd never rammed another starship. It was turning out to be a day of firsts.

Gwynahra and Venn wore their personal recon armor, while Chloe had to make do with a small vacc-suit. Gwynahra and the wolf, led the way from the open hatch on *Mjolnir*, through the gaping hole at the impact zone where the two ships were now joined. It was a terrible sight; large sections of organic hull and hyper-dense-alloy beams, bent and twisted at impossible angles; power conduits ruptured and sparking, smoke streaming; this might be more dangerous than open space, she mused. Her feet began to feel lose traction, and she realized it was a lack of artificial gravity. The impact had must have damaged the conductive-gravity-plating—they were now floating in zero-g.

Hand over hand—and paw over paw—they pulled themselves through the gap between the two ships. She spied a jagged tear in the bottom of a passageway. *"Follow me,"* she thought to Venn and Chloe. The three of them were tightly linked, now three minds as one. She could feel everything that Chloe and Venn felt, tripling her sensory input; it was a bit overwhelming at first, but she was starting to accept it as the new normal.

Gwynahra poked her head up through the hole, then quickly glanced left and right. It was clear. She pulled herself through, and immediately felt her full body weight return; in fact, she felt heavier. Niflheim was a 1.2G world, so it made sense their gravity setting would be higher on their ships. Thankfully, months on Rigsvaka had inured her body to the rigors of high-g. She bent down to help Venn and Chloe up.

Once they were all firmly on the Hrymar battleship, their unified psyches descended into mind-space, probing, searching. They had to find a clear path to the bridge, to Haldor. They found it, then continued moving.

As they rounded a corner, a Hrymar guard in full battle-gear trained a weapon on them; he didn't have a chance. Three joined-minds in perfect synergy, did not equal three; no, it was something far more frightening. In the micro-second it took to recognize them as a threat, the Hrymar crumpled to the deck, blood pouring from every orifice. They had *literally* melted his mind. *"Haldor, we are coming for you,"* they thought to him.

Hal hit a mental wall, as if he'd run into the side of a building face-first at speed. He was momentarily stunned. He could see Ailan and Serkan both prone and helpless. Dzakaa was a force of nature; his power utterly overshadowed Hal's ability with the Athryllith. He was like a man trying to blow away a thunderstorm by exhaling.

"Your race is pathetic," Dzakaa bellowed mentally.

Hal felt mentally downtrodden, depressed. Suddenly, he wanted to please his new master and yearned for his approval. No! The creature was twisting his mind. Fight it, Olsen! He told himself. He summoned a vision of Gwynahra to the forefront of his mind, imagining what they might do to her

—that worked. In mind-space, ripples of energy burst from him, slapping the creature; but still, it was futile. The creature shrugged off the attack. Then Dzakaa turned suddenly, distracted by something.

Ailan was back in mind-space, assailing the creature. His son had spirit! He could feel the rage and power Ailan generated. The boy was much more powerful than he was. Thank the gods. But his delight was brief. Dzakaa crushed the boy beneath a dark hand, pounding him down. Then there was only him and Dzakaa, again.

"You bastard!" He bellowed. Now he felt the Ysgar tightening its psychic grip, black fingers around his throat, squeezing, choking, crushing.

"I am done with you, Olsen. You are too much trouble to keep alive." Gwynahra winced as she felt Haldor's agony. *"He's killing Haldor!"* She screamed into mind-space. *"We don't have time to get to the bridge. Stop. We'll stand here and fight,"* she thought to Chloe and Venn.

The three moved like a storm through mind-space, roaring across the distance, seeking out the darkness. They hit the Ysgar like a comet; their resolve firm and frozen. But its mind was terrifying. They were face-to-face with their worst nightmare. This creature was the stuff of stories; the kind where something unseen came in the night, and devoured children.

Like a master harpist, the Ysgar plucked strings of doubt and fear in each of them, playing a dissonant tune. It searched for dark secrets, pulling them into the forefront of their minds. It was the epitome of evil, if not the very definition of the word. But Gwynahra fought. She too could pluck strings. Though her's were of light and joy and love. Her visions, rays of sunshine, banishing the shadows.

As she allowed a feeling of triumph to grow, he rallied. It stopped fighting their group-mind, instead, it attacked them each on their own; first Chloe. She was the weakest of them. She didn't yet have the confidence of her older comrades and crumpled in mind-space, as well as physically.

Gwynahra felt Haldor pounding on the back of the Ysgar's mind. But it was futile. This creature was a psychic titan. They were no match for his evil. Venn fell next. Finally, Gwynahra fell from mind-space and slumped to the deck.

"No!" Hal bellowed, as he felt three of his most cherished souls crushed beneath Dzakaa's heel.

The Ysgar was breathing hard. His victory had been no easy task, to be sure. But it *had* been a victory. Now the end had come, Hal thought. If so, he'd face it bravely. If this was his Wyrd, he'd feast in Valhalla tonight. Perhaps he'd see this fiend at Ragnarok and have a second chance for vengeance.

"You see, human, you are nothing!" Dzakaa cursed. "Now it is time to extinguish your annoying existence."

Hal felt the fingers tighten on his mind, and in the physical world, on his throat; the Ysgar was now face to face with him, determined to kill him twice over. Hal couldn't move, adhered and strapped to the table as he was, and was no mental match for Dzakaa. But he'd keep fighting—until he couldn't. His senses began to fade as his brain lost oxygen. Then suddenly he heard a sickening, wet crunch, and felt the full weight of Dzakaa draped on his body.

Serkan pulled his dagger out of the back of the Ysgar's skull. It was dripping with green ichor—what must pass for the creatures brain matter or blood. Dzakaa slumped down at Hal's feet, his hands still trying to tear at his throat.

Serkan spat on the Ysgar's back. "You fucking piece of shriveled dung!" Serkan proceeded kicking the Ysgar's body until he was physically spent, then slumped down on top of Dzakaa's lifeless corpse. Serkan looked up to Hal. "I hated that scaly fucker from the first time I smelled him."

He was expecting Serkan to kill him next … instead, the Hrymar began to laugh!

Hal was still dazed, but he hoped Serkan's laughter was a good sign. "What now?" He asked the Hrymar.

"I go home to Niflheim and face execution," Serkan said matter-of-factly.

"I can offer you other options," he said.

Serkan baulked. "Serve you? Or the humans? How do you think your people would take to embracing a slaver?" Serkan paused and looked at him, but he knew the old Hrymar was right. "That is exactly what I thought."

"There has to be a better way, Serkan. The Hrymar can change. Maybe they just need better leadership. Someone with a fresh perspective?"

"Me?" Serkan chuckled. "Human, I have been a warrior and a servant all my life. I am no leader or politician. In fact, I despise them." Serkan stepped over to Ailan, and helped him up. Hal's son looked battered, but not seriously injured.

"Master?" Ailan croaked.

"Yes, Kadir, we survived."

Ailan looked down at Dzakaa's corpse, and the boy spat on it. Serkan laughed as he looked back to Hal. "The boy has spirit!"

Hal had an epiphany. For the first time he was in the presence of someone who might actually know what happened to his wife. He seized the moment and plunged into mind-space, down into Serkan's memories.

There were thousands of slaves; bought, sold, born, killed ... and worse. Down years of memories, through layers of conflicting emotion ... then he found her. Two years after his wife had been captured and Ailan taken from her, and after being used like—Hal shuddered—gods, those animals. She'd finally taken her own life. His embers of fury flared to life, and he filled with burning rage. Though Serkan had not been one of her tormentors, he was Hrymar, and he was here. Hal plunged a mental knife into Serkan's brain, slashing and cutting.

Serkan screamed. Slumping to his knees, clutching his head.

Ailan dropped down to help him. "Master! What is wrong?" Ailan looked up at Hal, and knew. With reflexes honed in the combat-ring, Ailan drew his left dagger; one with a subtle purple hue to its blade, and stabbed deep into his father's stomach.

Hal gasped as he realized his own son had just killed him.

Ailan helped Serkan to his feet and led him to a chair. "Master, are you all right?"

Serkan nodded.

Hal's vision began to haze over, agony suffusing his body, spreading out like liquid fire through his veins. Poison, he thought.

A flash of something large and dark went streaking across Hal's field of vision. At first he thought he might be hallucinating. Then, suddenly, several of the crew were on their backs. He could hear snarling, biting, and Hrymar cries of terror. It was Venn! He could feel Gwynahra and Chloe behind him now. They'd just come onto the bridge, though he couldn't see them yet. They mentally assailed the rest of the crew, and in moments, the Hrymar were all dead—save for two.

He caught sight of Ailan and Serkan making their escape off the bridge; there was a second exit. He wanted to tell his rescuers, but couldn't manage to move his mouth to form the words; he was dying.

He felt Chloe hugging his legs as Gwynahra stood before him. *"Haldor, you're injured!"* she thought, looking down at his stomach. She gasped as she saw the blood oozing from his stomach. His bionan suit was doing a fair job of absorbing the blood, but it was a deep wound.

"You'll be fine, my love. Don't worry." She thought to him.

"Poison," he thought to her.

He felt her mentally wince.

Gwynahra pulled a package of hemostatic bandages from the med-pouch on her belt and began packing the wound. She might stop the bleeding, but there was no time to stop the poison.

"I love you, Gwyn," he thought. He couldn't physically smile, but he conveyed the same intent through their connection.

"Why are you smiling?" She had tears in her eyes now.

"We could have been together after all. Siobhan died years ago."

"I will not lose you!"

Little Chloe was sobbing now too.

Chapter 33

"Haldor, listen to me!" Gwynahra shouted into his mind. She could feel him slipping, and she saw the blood in his veins turning black—like he'd been injected with a liter of ink. A dark network of capillaries spread over his skin, like some plant taking root. She had to act fast. "Chloe, hold the dressing over Haldor's wound. Press hard!" Gwynahra said.

Chloe nodded, a look of determination on her face. Gwynahra could feel that Chloe wanted desperately to save the man who'd saved her.

Gwynahra pulled a small vile from the med-pouch on her belt— yggdracilin. It was a virtual panacea, standing in as an antibiotic, anti-viral, and an antidote to *most* poisons. The problem was that Haldor had the poison in his system for too long, its damage might be irreversible. No time for self-doubts. She injected his forearm with the vial.

"Chloe, I need you to help me, help Haldor, ok? Together," Gwynahra thought.

"Anything," Chloe thought.

"Just follow my lead."

"Haldor, can you hear us?" Gwynahra thought to him.

There was faint recognition, but not much.

"You need to slow down your heart rate and your metabolism. Slow down the effects of

the poison and let the yggdracilin work, ok? Do you hear us?"

She got no response. Chloe looked up at her with teary eyes.

"Damn you, Haldor! I love you. You will *not* die on me now!" Gwynahra shook him by the shoulders. "Listen to me!" His forearms, neck and face, were now covered by a cobweb of black veins.

Hal's eyes opened a crack. *"Loki's balls, woman. Are you this rough with all your patients?"* he thought to her.

She smiled through heavy tears. *"Listen to us now. Slow down your heart rate. Breath slowly, think slowly,"* she though to him

Chloe repeated what Gwynahra thought, their voices acting together, synergistically.

They could feel Haldor's heart slowing, every so gradually, but his face was still a rictus of pain, and colored like death. Together, Gwynahra and Chloe massaged his mind, helping him relax, slowing down his heart rate.

Then it stopped.

"Hal?" Gwynahra said.

Chloe was sobbing, her nose running.

"Hal!" She could feel that his heart had stopped. "No!" Gwynahra interlocked her fingers and began deep chest compressions—she thanked the Lord and Lady for her high-g training; Hal was a deep chested and well muscled man, and doing CPR on him was no easy task. She alternated thirty compression with two breaths. Each time leaving a pool of tears on his face as she held her mouth to his, but she didn't stop. Not for at least five minutes, until she could barely move her arms, but still she kept on, knowing it was hopeless—Haldor was dead.

She felt Chloe's hand stroking her arm and looked down at the girl, who's hands were covered with Haldor's blood. In one hand Chloe held the hemostatic dressing, now pulled away from his wound. Gwynahra pulled Chloe tight to her. They cried together.

When their tears had run dry, Gwynahra turned back to Haldor and stroked his cheek. Gods how she loved him. She traced a finger down his square jaw—and noticed something. The system of black capillaries which had painted his skin were receding. She could could see them visibly retreating back down his neck, leaving his complexion healthy again.

She dared not hope, but put an ear to his chest—and smiled.

"Chloe, put the dressing back on his wound. Quick! He's alive!"

Hal opened his eyes and thought he saw an angel. He did—Gwynahra. "Hey. What happened?"

"You died," Gwynahra said.

"What? I don't feel dead. Your eyes ... they're all red, are you ok?"

She leaned in and kissed him. "The yggdracilin took longer to work than I expected. I suppose the poison had been in your blood for too long. Whatever was used, it was very potent. I think you'll be ok, though."

"Well, that's a blessing." He recalled Odin's words: '*Look to the godly gifts you have been given...Make good use them, and trust the loyal retainers and friends you have. Do not discard any of them.*' He was fortunate his loyal retainers and friends hadn't discarded *him*. Next time a god tells you something, he thought, pay attention to the details. He smiled at the three most important beings in his life.

"Get me down from here, would you please?" he whispered.

Gwynahra fumbled at a control panel on the table and the bindings receded. A second button neutralized the adhesive compound. Finally, he was able to move. He tried to sit up, but was instantly checked; yep, I've been stabbed in the stomach, he noted.

He looked to Gwynahra. "Has Pelagia's team injected the virionic weapon with the retrovirus?"

"I'm not sure. *Mjolnir* was out of commission for a while. We had no comms until a few minutes ago."

"Are comms back up now?" He asked.

"They were, before we rammed this ship."

"You what?" He gasped.

Gwynahra smiled. "I'm sorry we had to dent up *Mjolnir*," she said sheepishly. "But there was no other way to get to you."

He suppressed a laugh, then took in the stillness on the bridge. There was the usual low-level thrumming, a feature of most starships, but otherwise it was graveyard-still. "Can you read Hrymi?" He asked Gwynahra

"I think so," she said. "It's an offshoot of Alfish."

"Take a look at the bridge controls. See if you can work their comm system. I need to speak with the battlegroup and see if Pelagia was successful." He looked down at the top of Chloe's head. She was still hugging his legs, steadying him. "Wanna help me over to a chair?"

Chloe gave him a nod, concern lining her little face.

How brave she was, he thought. With her help he hobbled over to what he imagined was the Captain's chair and slumped into it. He inhaled sharply as he flexed his stomach to sit.

"Does it hurt?" Chloe asked.

He smirked. He wondered why children asked the most obvious questions. "A little."

"Me and Gwyn are here to rescue you. Don't worry," Chloe said with a wink.

Hal held his breath to stop from laughing.

"Here we go," Gwynahra said. A holographic projector produced a floating, 3D image of Chandragupta Maurya on the bridge of the Mjolnir.

"Commander, are you all right?" Maurya asked.

"I will be, Chandra. How's *Mjolnir?*"

"Barely functional."

"And the impact damage?" He asked.

"Marginal. We evacuated the first third of the ship and any systems there were already damaged by the virus. We can maneuver, and we have comms. That's about it I'm afraid."

"What are the other Hrymar ships doing?"

"Two of the enemy battleships are still operational, but they just stopped firing. Maybe two-minutes ago."

"Right," he said. "Makes sense. That's when Serkan killed their Ysgar friend. Is the rest of our battlegroup still fighting?"

Maurya shook his head in disgust. *"Our ships are a bloody mess. Thankfully, our fleet auxiliary ship wasn't targeted, but otherwise only Sleipnir and two destroyers are fully operational. The bulk of the damage is from that damned virionic weapon. If Aksyonova is successful, then we have a chance of getting back in action."*

"Let me know as soon as you hear. In the meantime, send a squad of marines over. I want this ship secured."

"Aye, sir."

"Olsen out." He nodded to Gwynahra and she cut the feed.

"You look troubled," Gwynahra said.

"Serkan and Ailan ran. Why?" He asked rhetorically. "To try to escape? If so, will they sabotage the ship before they do?"

Chloe looked horrified. "Why does Ailan want to hurt you? You're his father."

"It's not his fault, sweet-pea. He's been brainwashed by some very bad people."

"What is—brain washed?" Chloe asked.

Instead of trying to tell her, he shared the concept telepathically. In one-second he conveyed what might've take five-minutes to explain properly.

Chloe scowled. "That's terrible!"

"Yes, it is," he said. Venn stood quietly beside him, on guard, alert. He reached down and stroked her fur and rubbed her ears.

As Hal waited for the marines to secure the ship called *Light's Doom*, he realized that the battle wasn't over yet. "Gwyn, I need your help."

"Anything," she said.

"There are human children—telepaths—being used to power the Hrymar engines and virionic weapons. I need your help to reach out to them on the other ships. If we can communicate with them, maybe we can persuade them to help us. We need to make sure the shooting doesn't start up again."

He reached out to take her hand, but she leaned farther in, kissing him softly on the lips. He wanted to collapse into her arms—but not yet. "Ready," he asked?"

Gwynahra took a breath and nodded.

Together they dropped into mind-space.

It was less dark than he remembered. Perhaps it was the Ysgar's absence, or maybe it was just that he was with Gwynahra. Their minds glided across the dim-grey of mind-space. They traced a figure-eight searching for the children, and in short order, found them. On each of the other Hrymar battleships, a little girl managed the weapons, and a little boy, the skip-drive; twelve children in all; including Galina and Veronika Cherenkov. Like parents herding their little ones, they gathered up the minds, pulling them close with psychic limbs.

"We need your help," he thought.

"You saved Galina," the children thought.

"Almost," he thought honestly. *"We're not safe yet. But you can help. First, we need to disable all the Hrymar ships. Can you helps us do that?"*

They could.

The first step had been to fire the immunized virionic weapon at all the Rigsvaka ships, neutralizing the viral outbreak. It wasn't an instant cure, but soon, they battle-group would be operational again.

"Good. Next, we need to know where to find more of these Ysgar. That's really important. We don't want any more kids like you stolen from your parents and homes. We must stop them. Do you know what place they call home?"

None knew.

Gwynahra had an idea. *"Have you each been in contact with the one called Dzakaa?"*

They had.

"Well then," she thought, *"let's pretend we're doing a puzzle. Share your experiences with each other. Each may have a clue. One piece alone won't give us the picture, but together, we can make it whole."*

He and Gwynahra began to see a picture coalescing in mind-space; like a jig-saw-puzzle being solved in front of them. One child had the gravity, another, the spectral class of the star, a third, the number of moons, a fourth, a count of all the planets in the star system; together their scraps of insight from Dzakaa's mind became a map. The Ysgar were on a planet 150 light years from Najaf, and only 45 light years from Rig's Vaka space—and they had a runestone portal.

Kadir and Serkan ran through *Light's Doom*, making their way to Serkan's yacht; it had a hyperdrive and should get them back to Niflheim. Suddenly, the lights in front of them began going down like dominoes—one by one. The ship was losing power. "Master, the ship must be more damaged than you thought." As he said that, a hatchway in front of them, slid closed. A loud *clack*, let them know it'd been locked remotely.

The old veteran shook his head. "Damage, no. I believe the humans are shutting down core systems. They're trying to trap us here."

"What can we do?" Kadir asked.

Serkan was breathing hard and took a moment to catch his breath. "I am getting far too old to be running, Kadir. I prefer the chase." A smiled threatened to crack his weathered face.

Kadir smiled back at his master. Serkan was the closest thing to a father he had. "Then let us fight back!"

Serkan shook his head. "No, youngling, not today. Besides, what Devrim has planted, I would rather see wither on the vine. I think we *should* fight, but not with these humans. We have both seen the fate that awaits the Hrymar with these demons as partners. They will kill us all, if not tomorrow, then next year." Serkan took Kadir by the shoulders and held his gaze for a moment. "The words you are about to hear must never echo beyond these walls. Do you so swear?"

He nodded rapidly and without hesitation. He would follow Serkan to Alfheim and back.

"Very well." And Serkan shared the plan with his student.

"We have the two Hrymar trapped, Haldor," Galina thought to him.

"Thank you!" He thought to her, then turned to Gwynahra. "The girls have Ailan and Serkan trapped in one of the passageways."

"That's a blessing," Gwynahra said. "The marines should be here any minute."

"Now, we need to finish this," he said. He took Gwynahra's hand, and together, they seeped back into the fabric of mind-space; like shadows finding a crack and leaking down into it. *"We're ready,"* he thought to the children. Together, they took control of all six ships, forcing the other five Hrymar battleships to fly to *Light's Doom*.

They docked the six behemoths nose-to-nose in a star formation, that way the enemy couldn't fire their main guns if the children lost control. They parked the destroyers in a large cube formation near the battleships. The entire Hrymar fleet was now grouped up and ready to be boarded and seized.

"Pelagia?" he comm'd.

"Yes, Commander, Aksyonova here."

"Now that the ships have been immunized, I want you to organize boarding parties for each of the Hrymar ships. You may have noticed the ship you're on just moved?"

"Indeed I did, sir. Right after the virionic weapon fired several times."

"They're all holding position now, and *Mjolnir* will be parked with her nose in the middle of the six Hrymar battleships. That should make moving your people around a little easier."

"Thank you, sir. That will be helpful."

A strange *blatting* noise ushered from the Hrymar ship's bridge. "It's the comm system, Haldor," Gwynahra said. "It's Chandra."

Chandragupta Maurya appeared on screen.

"Commander, we've got something on sensors coming toward the group of Hrymar ships," Maurya said.

"What is it? Reinforcements?" Hal asked.

"Maybe. But they were already here in-system. Whatever they are, they were powered down. So we didn't detect them until now. There's a mass that initially appeared as one object, but as it's come closer, lidar can now discriminate thousands of tiny objects, and a much larger, ship-like object behind them."

"What in Niflheim? Put it on screen." What he saw next boggled his mind. The only word that came to mind, was *swarm*.

Chapter 34

LOCATION: ABOARD LIGHT'S DOOM / STAR System: Adhara

"They are coming," Serkan said to Kadir.

With his vacc-suit helmet on, visor tinted almost opaque, Kadir nodded, then continued on the plasma torch, cutting through the bulkhead. Showers of sparks, molten metal, and a smattering of carbonized bio-matter, all erupted from the hole he was cutting. A small slab of the ship's bulkhead leaned outward, then he stood and kicked it through to the next compartment.

His vacc-suit visor went translucent again and he nodded to his master.

"Well done, youngling," Serkan said. "Now, let us make sure we meet up with our ride home."

Serkan told him that there was no way they could reach his yacht from the point they now found themselves confined. Instead, they had to get creative. It wasn't possible to cut their way through the numerous bulkheads to the yacht-bay, but they could get to the exterior of the ship, and space. There they would hitch a ride home.

Both ducked and crawled through the hole into the next compartment, which was only a safety gap between the inner-passageway and the outer hull. The long, dark compartment before them was the inside of Light's Doom's hull. He made his helmet opaque again, and fired up the plasma torch. Serkan fastened his helmet now as well. One more cut and the air would get very thin. "Chandra, which are the two destroyers still in operation?" Hal asked.

"The Clarent, under Captain Fletcher, and the Hrunting, under Captain Skellrun, sir," Maurya said.

"Patch me through."

Two grim faces met his on the view screen: the freckle-faced, Canadian, Kara Fletcher, and the fine-featured Alfar, Skellrun. "Kara, Skellrun, we have a job for you. There's a swarm of small objects and some kind of larger vessel approaching the cluster of Hrymar ships at-speed. Our other ships are still disabled. We might be able to give you some fire support, but that's it. And we've got the Hrymar ships disabled. We're helpless right now. *You* have to stop them."

"Commander," Fletcher said, "one thing before we go. You've got a hot spot showing up on our sensors. There's bits of plasma ejecting from the ship you're on. I'd guess someone's cutting their way out."

Hal focused on mind-space for a micro-second—it was Ailan and Serkan. He had two ships to stop thousands of contacts. He couldn't spare one to stop Ailan from leaving. Not that Ailan could go anywhere … or could he? Gods damn it! Sudden realization hit him like a fist—the coming ships were a rescue operation. But he couldn't split the destroyers focus. They had to concentrate on protecting the ships, not policing Ailan and Serkan.

"Thank you, we have it under control. Let's get it done."

They both nodded.

"Understood, my Lord," Fletcher said.

"Consider them stopped, Jarl," Skellrun said.

"Gods' speed, Olsen out."

He could feel Gwynahra's surprising calm. "You seem pretty much at ease," he said, matter-of-factly.

She smiled. "We're together, my love. Everything else are just details." She put an arm around his shoulder and kiss the top of his head.

"You're right." He was together with Gwynahra, Chloe, and Venn. But damn it, he wanted to live. He could see a sliver of sunshine for the second time in almost ten years. He was determined to keep it this time. "Let's see if we can help the *Clarent* and *Hrunting*." He took Gwynahra and Chloe's hands.

As a family unit, including Venn, they dropped down into mind-space and soared outward at the speed of thought. They searched for the bright spots that were other minds, but what they encountered was unexpected. There was a seething, frothy wall in front of them. Whatever they were, they were not human. There were no children controlling these ships. The thought patterns had a strange taste, a peculiar odor, something entirely alien. Mind-space was a region filled with a conglomeration of the senses. One did not see, or hear, or touch, or taste something; one felt all those things at once, and more. And the familiar feelings these minds evoked was instantly recognizable; these were Ysgar.

"It's a mother and her children," Gwynahra thought to him.

"I feel them," he thought.

"I don't like it," Chloe thought.

"Nor do I," Gwynahra thought.

"We have to stop them. Let's work together, focus on the mother-ship," he thought. At the same time, he could feel Kara and Skellrun; they were engaging the

smaller objects. As the destroyers began firing on the thousands of tiny spheres, a scream permeated mind-space.

His head jerked up and he was thrown out of mind-space. He clutched his head and tried to rub away the pain. Gods in Asgard! Gwynahra met his pained gaze, she too with a look of trauma.

"The mother," she said, "she's trying to protect her young."

"No, it's not like that. Those things are designed to be weapons. She's protecting the *mission*. These Ysgar have no feelings, why would their machines?" he said.

"She's not a machine," Chloe added, "she *is* an Ysgar."

That was extremely disturbing. "We need to keep her busy so our ships can destroy those weapons." He felt their distaste at going back into mind-space with that *thing*. For all the good the Athryllith brought, there was such evil attached as well. Was that just a comment on the state of sentience itself? Perhaps.

He grabbed their hands and nodded. Together they continued the fight. "Hold on," Kadir said, "I am about to cut through." The atmosphere began hissing out as he began the final incision through the outer hull. It was a small leak now, but once the hole was finished, there would be explosive decompression. Serkan nodded and they both clipped onto holes in a spar. Kadir put the plasma torch to the hull and the circular section exploded out into space, followed by a rush of atmosphere.

Momentarily they were yanked off their feet as the atmosphere geysered out like a mini-blizzard, the moisture in the atmosphere freezing as it left the ship. The sections of the hull were compartmentalized, so only a small part of the atmosphere would leak at any breach. The violent decompression was followed by a contrasting tranquility; there was no longer any air to conduct sound, and silence pervaded their surroundings.

Through the hole, Kadir could see Najaf, glowing orange under Adhara's light. It was beautiful, he thought, but his revery was interrupted by a violent clash of silent weapons. Flashes of red and green laser light, streaked across space, as seen through his enhanced visor. The small Ysgar mines were being shot down by the Humans. But despite their resistance, the mother-ship was growing larger in the distance.

"Our ride home, boy," Serkan said over the suit comm.

He didn't like it. This thing wasn't just a ship, it was alive. *"Are you sure we will be safe in it?"* He asked.

"Have you another ship I am not aware of?" Serkan asked. *"Then, by Ymir, be glad we have this one!"*

"Yes, Master." He could see that several of the mines had hit the destroyers, as evidenced by large green splotches over their hulls."

"See there," Serkan said, pointing. *"Those human ships should be shutting down at any moment now."*

Sure enough, the human ships stopped firing, but not before they'd disabled all the mines. The mother-ship continued to limp along. The bloated, mottled-green beast obscured his view of the beautiful Najaf. He shuddered when he saw an orifice in the creature open up, like an alien sphincter. "We have to go in *there?*"

Serkan cursed him as the mother-ship came almost skin-to-skin with *Light's Doom.* "Now, boy, push off!"

They kicked off the once beautiful battleship and floated into the monstrous vessel.

"My Lord," Captain Fletcher, said, *"We got them all except the mother ship. But the tiny ones were mines, of a sort. And they seem to have infected us with the same virus the beam-weapons used. The Clarent is shutting down, and I see, so's the Hrunting. It looks like the mother-ship has docked with the battleship you're on"*

"Good job, Kara," Hal said. "Don't worry about us, and we'll get your ships taken care of." As he said that, he felt a ripple in mind-space.

"Goodbye, father," Ailan thought to him through mind-space.

His son was no longer on the *Light's Doom.* Gods, he was on the mother-ship! *"Ailan, please, wait!"* But there was no answer. On the view-screen he saw the mother-ship accelerate away, then jump to hyperspace.

Gwynahra knelt down beside the chair he was in. "Are you all right?"

"No. Ailan is on that mother-ship." There was nothing Gwynahra could say to sooth him, but, she rubbed the back of his neck and shared the love she felt for him. For a third time he grieved the loss of his only son.

Allfather, he prayed, what should I do? Should I go after him? Is he lost to me? But Odin did not answer. Hal had to compartmentalize the loss. He had Gwynahra, Chloe, and Venn. That was a lot to be thankful for. Maybe, someday he could reach his son, but not today. Today he had to walk away with this victory and hold on to the ones he loved, and the ones who loved him.

Location: Aboard Mjolnir / Star System: Adhara

Forty-eight hours after the battle of Adhara began, Hal's ships were all operational, if not at peak efficiency, and he was once again sitting in his command-chair on the bridge of *Mjolnir*. Dr. Inglis and Gwynahra had performed a brief surgery to suture his stomach wound, and thankfully there were no major organs damaged. He had a lot of crew who weren't so lucky, many were still infected with the Ysgar virus; though they now had samples of the virus from which to create a cure; at least he hoped they could. The Alfar were millennia more advanced than humanity, with respect to medicine, and Gwynahra seemed to think it could be done.

"Commander," Maurya said to him in a low voice, "I hope you'll accept my apology for the comments I made to you when you left the ship. I- was out of line, sir. I understand if you want to have me replaced."

He smiled and shook his head. "Chandra, if I fired every officer who gave me a piece of their mind, I'd have to get rid of my best people. I don't want subservience, I want frank counsel. That's what you gave me. Maybe a bit terse," he teased, "but I didn't give you much of an explanation."

Maurya said nothing.

"Lose my shit?" Hal asked. "Where did you come up with that one, by the way?"

Maurya's face went red. "My nephew, sir. I blame it on movies. Or perhaps it's the music," Maurya shrugged, "who can say." A nascent smile, crept onto Maurya's tan face.

"That's better," Hal said. "Now, get back to work, all right? What am I paying you for?"

Maurya snapped out a crisp salute. "Sir. I shall endeavor to find something productive to do."

"As you were, Mr. Maurya." Ah, the banter of normalcy, he mused.

"Commander," Meiriona said, "the *Sleipnir* has just returned from Eplistjarna."

'Kappa, hail her," he said. He'd loaned the *Sleipnir* to Captain Shelley Garrett, given that *Svadilfari* was temporarily out of commission.

"Aye, sir. On-screen now," Kappa said. Shelley Garrett's face appeared on the view-screen, but she wore a neutral expression.

"Shelley, what did you find?"

A familiar brunette in a red bionan suit sidled into view beside Captain Garrett, who was now smiling.

"Gina! Gods, am I glad to see you!" he said, as he stood up.

"Hey, boss. Miss me?" Gina asked, a mischievous grin painting her face.

"Damn right I did! What happened over there? Where's the *Sam Houston*, and *Ascalon?*"

Gina shook her head, donning an uncharacteristically sober expression. He'd never seen Gina look this ...defeated. "They're gone, sir. All of them. We were betrayed."

Chapter 35

LOCATION: ABOARD MJOLNIR / STAR SYSTEM: Adhara

After transiting several inter-stellar-bridge-nodes and making the ten hour trip through hyperspace, *Mjolnir* was back in the Heimdall system, heading for Rigsvaka.

Hal wasn't prepared for the carnage as the view-screen was flooded with a scene that resembled an apocalyptic landscape. The view in orbit he'd last remembered, had changed from a clean, sparse tableau, to one that resembled Saturn's rings; but the debris encircling Rigsvaka was not made up of ice and rock—it was the sad wreckage of a mighty fleet.

"Commander, we're being hailed by the *Freyr*," Kappa said.

"On screen."

Standing on the bridge of the dreadnought *Freyr*, a haggard ambassador Saeran wore a red robe; that meant the Alfar had convened the Red Council—they were officially on a wartime footing. *"Lord Haldor, I'm glad to see you home."* Hal could feel the dread in her mind. *"Is my daughter with you?"*

"She's fine, Ambassador." He felt Saeran slump emotionally.

"Thank the Lord and Lady," Saeran said.

"What happened here?" He asked.

"Gwynahra sent us a message warning of the impending attack on Rigsvaka, and the

399

condition of your fleet. We got here as soon as we could. We didn't have much opportunity to prepare, but we did get here before the Hrymar and Ysgar ships arrived."

"Losses?"

"Heavy. We lost thirty-two of our ships, and 8,312 crew. Their virionic weapon decimated our fleet. We only prevailed due to our numbers. Every shot they took crippled one of our ships. Many of the damaged ships lost hull integrity, and all crew as a result. But the civilians on Rigsvaka were spared."

His relief was dampened by the heavy price the Alfar had paid to keep his people safe—a price he should have paid. "I'm sorry. I- wish I could have been here sooner- to help," he said.

"It's not your fault, Haldor. We should have taken action long ago. We Alfar were content to bottle up the Ysgar, ignoring the problem. Our benevolence cultivated an evil that has infected an entire region of space. It's a lesson we won't soon forget." She sighed. *"Earth and her colonies are mobilizing as we speak. Together, we will destroy the Ysgar colony."* She gestured to an older Alfar beside her. *"This is Hilmir Elensar, he'll be leading our combined fleet. The SID has ceded command of their ships to him for the duration, and will join us here in five days."*

The old man inclined his head. *"Lord Haldor. I had hoped to meet you under better circumstances."*

Hal bowed to the old sailor. A Hilmir was the equivalent of Earth's Chief of Naval Operations on Alfheim. His title literally meant Star King, and he had a thousand or more ships under his command. "And I you, Hilmir. I request permission to join your combined-fleet enroute to the Ysgar colony."

The Hilmir nodded. *"Granted. We'll need the support."*

"Thank you, Hilmir. Most of our ships are back up to fighting strength."

"Haldor, I would like to come to the Mjolnir. So we can catch up in person," Saeran said.

Hal felt Saeran's need to see her daughter, to touch her, to make certain she was actually alive and well. He remembered those parental imperatives. The one time he'd lost contact with Ailan at the local fairgrounds, he thought he'd lose his mind. It was the most out of control and helpless feeling he'd ever experienced. He knew how much Saeran needed to be with her daughter right now. He loved Gwynahra too, after all.

"Of course, Ambassador," he said.

"In fact, it's Councilor for the time being, Haldor. I've been called back to serve while the Red Council rules."

"I'll meet you at the airlock, Councilor. Olsen out."

As he waited before the airlock, it occurred to Hal that he'd never seen Ambassador Saeran look quite so exhausted. Each time they'd met previously, she'd been the epitome of grace, vigor, and steadfastness; today she looked worn and used up. But he had a surprise for her.

He stepped aside, revealing Gwynahra, then watched with gratitude as Saeran's face, like the slow light of dawn, began to glow, bathing them both in her love.

"Thank you," she said to him.

He nodded as mother and daughter embraced.

Saeran pulled back and locked Gwynahra in a reproving gaze. "You are a foolish girl. You know that?" Saeran said.

Gwynahra didn't answer. She just hugged her mother again.

Holding Gwynahra's hand, Saeran said, "Permission to come aboard,

High Commander?"

"Granted, Councilor."

The battered and weary crews of Rigsvaka's Fleet had three days to ensure their ships were re-stocked and repaired, then Hal decreed a two-day mandatory shore-leave so his people could replenish their bodies and souls as well. Citizens who had been evacuated, returned. Families that had been separated, were re-united. They were days of sad remembering for the dead and days of great joy, as the living lived, fully and completely. It was during these interludes between battles and wars that mankind seemed to be the most joyous and generous. Fighting the-good-fight brought out the best in people. Why did it take tragedy to bring out such beauty in people? He wondered.

Hal's spirit floated on the heavy melodies of *Lacuna Coil*, playing through the speakers in his state-room. He looked out the three-meter-wide simulated window. What he saw was the greatest inter-stellar fleet ever to be assembled, now orbiting Rigsvaka. Hundreds of warships made ready to destroy the Ysgar. To fight evil, one occasionally had to unleash a greater evil. And so, the strangest ship in the fleet, was in fact, *not* a starship; *Temenoh-Segos*—the *Dark Seed;* a nine-million-ton behemoth with no hyperdrive capability, towed by six Freyr-class dreadnoughts. Its ovoid surface, a deep brown, streaked with veins, like a dead leaf; though like all Alfar ships, the *Dark Seed* was alive. But what manner of creature was it? Hilmir Elensar had only said that they would unleash a weapon never before used, and hopefully, never would be again.

A *chiming* interrupted his contemplation. "Pause music. Enter."

He felt her before she opened the door—Gwynahra. Every time she came near him it felt like the most beautiful embrace. He chocked it up to the

Athryllith, but whatever it was, this woman was a tonic for his soul. He gathered her up in his arms as he kissed her.

She pulled her head back. "Miss me?"

"You know I did." He pulled her onto the sofa with him, her on his lap. They spent a long moment just being close. He could feel his heart slowing, his entire body relaxing. *"I thank the gods every day for you,"* he thought to her. He felt her love returned through their link.

Carefully, he slipped out from under her, and let her sink into his spot on the couch.

"Where are you going?" She asked.

He didn't go anywhere, he simply knelt before her on one knee. "Gwynahra, I don't want to lose another minute without you in my life."

"Of course you don't. Nor will you have to," she said, confused. "I'll never leave you, Haldor. I love you."

"I know ... that's not what I meant." He swallowed. He'd done this before, but it was so long ago. "When a man loves a woman ... and he gets down on one knee-"

"Lord and Lady!" She gasped, her smile creeping ear to ear. "Are you- "

"Yes."

"Oh my!"

Her hands were trembling, and he could see she was holding her breath.

"Gwynahra, will you marry me?"

In an unnamed star system the final battle began as the allied fleet dropped out of hyperspace. *Mjolnir* was in the vanguard. The allies' tactic was to use the non-organic ships as a sort of shield-wall, while the more powerful Alfar living-ships, fired on the enemy, safe from their virionic weapons.

Three hundred and twenty-one warships, clenched into a mail-fist, pummeled the enemy fleet. The Ysgar-designed ships were swept away, as the tide cleanses a beach. That left only those on the planet.

On word of the destruction of the enemy fleet, *Temenoh-Segos—the Dark Seed,* was towed into orbit around the unnamed planet, in the unnamed star system. The allied ships were ordered to hold position almost three-billion kilometers away, which Hal thought was far beyond a safe distance, but this was not his fleet.

Six dreadnought tenders pulled their weapon into position above the Ysgar outpost.

The bridge of Mjolnir was devoid of any sound now, save for the *thrumming* of the reactors, as the crew watched in morbid fascination while the headsman's sword was readied.

Gwynahra stood behind Hal's command-chair, her hand resting on his shoulder.

"What will it do to the base?" He thought to her.

She gave his shoulder a gentle squeeze. *"Wait a moment, and I'll explain,"* she thought to him.

He continued to watch as the tenders detached themselves from the *Dark Seed,* then jumped away into hyperspace.

He tapped a control on the arm of his command-chair, and zoomed in to get a closer look at the *Dark Seed.* Now the strange weapon filled the bridge.

Like a hideous flower blooming, segmented petals began opening around the entire hull. It really did look like a flower, complete with the central stamen projecting out from the base of the petals. In agonizing seconds, the *Dark Seed* began to glow. Slowly the outer hull began to grow translucent—like the abdomen of a firefly, pulsating.

"It's ready to fire now," she thought him.

The energy fluctuation seemed to peak, then conduct over to the central filaments which lit up like a bundle of bright glow-sticks. Then there was a flash as a column of toroidal-energy-rings lanced toward the Ysgar outpost. He recalled that his type of energy beam was called a spheromak, and so, it must be a plasma weapon of sorts. The beam stayed on-target for a full three-seconds before it ceased.

"And thus is the seed planted," she thought to him. And that's all she would share.

The planet's atmosphere began to catch fire, the inferno blazing in all directions for a full five-seconds. Then the entire atmosphere was consumed; the planet's surface now a smoking ruin.

"A terrible weapon," he thought to her.

"It's only just begun, Haldor."

He thought it was his imagination, but it looked like the surface of the planet flexed slightly—like a water ballon might jiggle. The sphere pulsated, swelling the tiniest fraction, then contracted violently. Twice. Three times. Four times, until it collapsed in on itself to a fraction of its original size. Then, like star going nova, it exploded.

Reflexively, Hal raised his hand to protect his eyes against the sudden intense burst of light, but of course the view-screen attenuated the radiation reaching his eyes, and he was never in any danger.

"Gods in Asgard," he whispered.

It was a scene to be repeated just once more when the Alfar destroyed the Ysgar home-world some weeks later.

Chapter 36

LOCATION: AMBASSADOR SAERAN'S RESIDENCE / PLANET: Alfheim

I discovered Billing's daughter on her bed,
more beautiful than sunlight sleeping.
A king's crown I would refuse,
if it meant living without her love.

- Havamal, (Modern, Odinsson)

For the fifth time, Hal looked to Gwynahra and asked the same question: "You're sure she won't throw me out?"

Gwynahra turned to him, and took his face in her hands. "Haldor, where is the confident Jarl I fell in love with? Is he hiding in there somewhere? Because I would really like him to show up today." Her eyebrows leapt up a foot.

"Do you know how long it's been since I've met a girl's parents?"

She threw her arms wide. "You've known my mother for years! She even knew your great-great-great-grandfather. Be lucky you'll never have to meet my father. He was hard man to please, I assure you."

"But I've never introduced myself as the man who wanted to marry her

407

daughter. Puts a different spin on things, don't you think?"

"For Freya's sake, Haldor. You'll charge onto a ship full of Hrymar and Ysgar, but I have to drag you to ask my mother for my hand? So be it." She planted a quick kiss on his cheek, and yanked his arm, dragging him over the threshold into the Ambassador's residence.

His heart was pounding as they ascended the staircase up to the living room. Hi, I'm the guy you sent your daughter to for safe-keeping, and now I want to marry her? Nope. That wouldn't work, he thought to himself. His guts tightened as he saw the always-elegant Ambassador Saeran, beaming as she greeted her daughter.

"Mother," Gwynahra said, as she squeezed Saeran. "It's good to see you."

"And you, darling." Then she looked to him. "Haldor, it's so nice of you to have brought Gwynahra back personally."

He swallowed hard.

"Mother, let's sit down. We need to talk with you."

"We?" She asked, as they sat across from her on a pair of sofas.

Gwynahra nodded innocently. "Yes, we. Haldor, and I."

"Oh? Is this about his training?" Saeran asked, insincerely.

Shit. She knew something funny was going on. But he felt nothing from her. No good vibes, nor any bad ones. But then, he wouldn't. She'd trained with the Athryllith for centuries. And damn it, if she wasn't giving anything away on her face either.

"Mother," Gwynahra began slowly, "Haldor has asked me to marry him."

She dropped the bomb, he thought, but Thor help him, Saeran didn't even flinch. And she said nothing.

"Mother? Did you hear what I said?"

"Yes. You said Haldor has asked you to marry him. I was waiting for the news. Isn't there something else? It seemed like you had some big secret to share?"

"Mother!" Gwynahra chided.

He was utterly confused. Then he saw a smile creep slowly onto Saeran's face.

"Mother, you're an evil woman! Poor Haldor has been heartsick about telling you this."

Saeran leaned toward them and placed her hands, one on knee each. "Children, I knew you were in love the first time I saw you together. The two of you were like supernovas who'd just collided. I thought you were going to tell me Gwyn was pregnant."

"Ambassador, I never!" He began to say.

"Future son-in-law, take a breath," Saeran said calmly. "That would not have been unwelcome news. A child is a blessing—love is a blessing. I couldn't be more delighted to see you two together. Haldor, I've known your family for over a hundred years. I know the good blood you bring to this union. I will be proud to call you son."

He was speechless.

"But, before you marry my daughter, there is something you must know."

He felt the other shoe drop.

"Have you ever wondered why you look so young?" Saeran asked Haldor.

He shrugged.

"You're forty-three, and by most human standards, I'd peg you at twenty-eight."

"I work out," he said. "And I watch what I eat, mostly." He shrugged. "Ok, maybe not so much lately."

Hal felt Gwynahra's curiosity seeping into mind-space. She had no clue as to what her mother was trying to tell him.

"Oh, there's a bit more to it than that, young man."

"What do you mean?" he asked.

"Do you remember the first time we met? Nine years ago, at the starport?" Saeran asked.

"Of course I do. How could I forget? I'd been told stories about you since I was knee high to a grasshopper."

"And do you remember the first thing I said to you?"

He cocked his head. "Not really. I think I was overawed by meeting you, and it was my first time on Alfheim."

"Let me refresh your memory. I said you were the spitting image of your father."

"But my father was fair-haired, and I'm dark haired. My grandfather was dark haired though. Now I remember! I thought you'd confused me with my grandfather."

"But I hadn't," Saeran said. "It was slip of the tongue, to be sure, but I meant it. You do look like your father."

"Mother, what are you saying?"

"Haldor, I've kept a secret for the Olsen family for forty-three years. Your grandfather had asked me to tell you after he died. But with the war, then you building Rigsvaka and the Tyrmundr, well, I never found the right time to tell you."

"Saeran, tell me what? Please. Just say it."

"Karin was your mother, but Birgir Olsen was *not* your father," Saeran said. She let that hang for a moment. "Your father was an Alfar, named Edreahil."

He said nothing. His face was slack, his mind in denial.

Gwynahra reached out to him, and put a hand over his. "Haldor?"

He nodded. "I'm ok." He looked up to Saeran. "Why didn't they tell me? My parents I mean- or, well, my mother?"

"Edreahil and your mother were in love. And you were the product of that union, but he was killed before you were born. I suppose, she wanted you to have a father. And I know Birgir loved you very much."

"How did he die?"

"A starship accident. Nothing nefarious, I assure you. Simply an accident He was testing a new hyperdrive."

"Wow. I don't know what to say."

"I'm sorry it took so long to tell you. Truly. And, I intended to. If you and my daughter have children, and I hope you will, they will only be one-quarter human. You are half-Alfar, Haldor. Which is why you look so young for forty-three. You are the only product of an Alfar and human pairing. There are some married couples, but your mother and Edreahil's was the only union to produce a child—at least so far. Others are trying. We weren't sure what impact half-Alfar DNA would have on your lifespan. As you know, Alfar reared on other colonies off Alfheim, don't have the long lives we do here. A couple of centuries at the outside, but nowhere near our five-century norm.

Our longevity is tied directly to the planet."

"I need a drink," he said.

Gwynahra stood. "I'll get you one." She dragged her hand lightly across his shoulder as she walked to a cupboard.

He smiled at Saeran. "Well, this is not quite the conversation I was expecting to have today."

Saeran nodded, smiling, but said nothing.

"Back to business," he said, matter-of-factly. "M'am, may I have your permission to marry your daughter?"

Saeran inclined her head. "You may."

Gwynahra ran back, squealing with delight, and threw her arms around her new fiancee.

Location: Over-Chieftain's Throne Room / Planet: Niflheim

As Kadir and Serkan strode into the throne room, Devrim rose, which was unusual. The Over-Chieftain typically sat unmoving, as he granted an audience to petitioners. Of course, Serkan was his right-hand, as he had been for his sire, Egemen; and Kadir was his fosterling.

Devrim's brow crinkled as the two approached the throne. "I had thought never to see the two of you again. I had heard that the fleet at Adhara was lost entirely?"

Kadir's senses were jarred when he saw an Ysgar seated beside his foster-sire. Gone, were his usual array of advisors, leaving only this fiend to counsel him. He heard the name in Devrim's mind — Crazal.

Serkan bowed low. "My Lord, I am sorry to report, that it the case. Except for the ship on which Kadir and I escaped on."

The brown-turd rose, a look of hateful curiosity in its eyes. A pox upon all your people, you foul thing, he thought. I curse you! Kadir kept all this to himself, though he saw the creature twitch, as if in recognition of the insults being hurled his way.

Devrim beckoned to them both to approach. With heads lowered in deference to their Lord, they ascended the black stone steps, then knelt on the dais on which Devrim's throne was perched. "Tell me everything," Devrim commanded.

Instead of speaking, Kadir connected to Devrim's mind; and he told him — everything.

His foster-sire gasped, and spun to look in fear at the Ysgar beside him. Devrim pulled back to one side of his throne, away from the beast.

"What is happening?" The Ysgar said, as it stood, looking anxious.

Shots from energy weapons echoed in cavernous throne-room. The two guards flanking the rear exits, both dropped, and two Hrymar clad in armor disarmed their corpses. Kadir looked back to the entrance, and saw that, there too, the guards had been killed, and two of his men took up positions.

"You see, my Lord," Kadir said, "this alliance you have entangled us in, has become a noose of sorts. Your ambition has set the Hrymar race on the edge of a knife blade; on one side lies victory, on the other, utter ruin. But the Ysgar hold that knife. And you can be sure they will twist, and pull, and thrust, until we *are* ruined. Your plans were but an illusion supplied by these clever task masters."

Lord Crazal hissed. "You are all tools, to be used. As you use slaves, we have used you. And will continue to do so. Bow before your true Lord and master!"

Kadir felt the mental blow, and saw Devrim and Serkan sink to their knees when he did. This creature was far more dangerous than Dzakaa had been. The three screamed, but only for a moment. Then, as he'd previously instructed, an unseen guard burned a hole through the Ysgar's brain. Crazal's face was frozen in a mad mask of hatred; Kadir knew they felt no emotion as such, just an alien compulsion to reproduce and dominate. Thankfully, such imperatives were predictable.

He stood, shaking off the assault to his psyche.

"You have saved us," Devrim said to him, as he tried to stand. " I am so prou- "

"Stay on your knees," Kadir commanded, and slapped Devrim's mind, just as if he'd struck a back-hand blow across his face. The Over-Chieftain grimaced.

"Serkan! Kill him!" Devrim commanded.

Serkan stood, as always, silently, and stoically. He was but a servant. He never wanted to lead, only to follow a worthy leader. Kadir knew his master was an honorable man.

"I read in a book, that history repeats itself," Kadir said with a wry smile. Devrim tried to move, but Kadir's grip on his mind was absolute. He could make Devrim dance like a puppet, if he wished to do so. "I am proud to be part of the Hrymar people. But I am *not* proud of what you have done, or what you have become. You are weak, Devrim, spawn of Egemen. Your sire should have had the courage to strangle you at birth, or leave you on the frozen plain of sorrow. But like you, he too was weak. I am Hrymar. And so, I will end your line today. The strong rule, and the weak serve. It is the Hrymar way, Devrim."

Devrim raised a pleading hand, his eyes begging. Kadir watched Devrim's confusion as he felt the warm sticky fluid running down his face. Devrim touched his cheeks, and brought up hands covered in blood. It oozed from his eyes, and ears, and nose. Kadir kept Devrim physically supported as he killed him, Devrim's brain-matter now, literally, seeped out of his ears. Then he let the husk drop.

Serkan nodded at him, and bowed. "My Lord."

Kadir pushed Devrim's corpse with his foot, and sent it tumbling down the stairs. Then, he took the throne.

Chapter 37

LOCATION: LLANGERNYW, THE NAW COLFEN / Planet: Alfheim

Haldor and Gwynahra prepared to exchange vows of eternal devotion in the shadow of the Naw Colfen, a grove of the Alfar's nine holiest-trees. The nine titans reached up over 150 meters, as if grasping for the stars. Arrayed in a circle they shaded the central meadow yet allowed a few golden beams to highlight the proceedings. A spicy odor of bark and the sweet scent of blossoms suffused the air.

The onlookers' focus, though, was not on the Naw Colfen, but rather, the couple holding hands before the runestone altar: a square-jawed, dark-haired man in a black military uniform with gold epaulettes. A dark-blue cloak flowing from his broad shoulders, and an empty-scabbard hung from his leather belt.

The bride-to-be stood with regal beauty in a diaphanous, green gown; the color representing growth, as their marriage and love was to grow. Her raven-black hair was braided with blossoms and flowers, and cascaded over her pale, white skin. Around her neck, an amber necklace represented Freya's tears.

Three flower-girls in yellow dresses, stood behind the couple: Chloe, and the two Cherenkov twins, Galina and Veronika. The twins' mother, Irina, and father, Maxim, were looking on with pride from the crowd. The girls' hair was still not fully grown out, but they had enough to tie up their golden strands in green-velvet bows.

Haldor and Gwynahra were the closest thing to royalty the Alfar had; the heroic half-Alfar warrior king, and the beautiful healer-princess—as they were considered by many. But he was just a man, and she, just a woman; both looking for happiness, the most basic of all desires and often the most elusive.

All of Hal and Gwynahra's friends were there to witness the special day. Gina, characteristically, wore red. But entirely out of character was the form of her attire; a delicately layered gown that rippled in the subtlest of breezes. Gina's wife Sarah stood by her side, holding her hand. Hal remembered their wedding only three years before. Drew Zelinski, Cadfael, Lythrael, and *Mjolnir's* bridge crew, were also in attendance.

Ambassador Saeran was to act as Gythya, or priestess, to marry the couple. Saeran beamed at her daughter and future son-in-law. The Gythja's white-gown looked so fragile and intricately woven, one might have mistaken it for spider-silk.

Silence descended over the crowd as Saeran raised a hand, indicating the start of the hand-fasting ceremony.

"Welcome, sons and daughters of Yggdrasil," Gythya Saeran said. "I welcome you to the hand-fasting of my daughter, Gwynahra Tarnallsdottir, and Jarl Haldor Athrylling of Rigsvaka. For those new to Alfheim, please allow me to explain the significance of this holy place. Each of the Naw Colfen, the nine trees which surround us, represents one of our classes. The nine classes are the first pillar of Alfar society, the second are the Atebol, our holy virtues," Saeran gestured to the runestone, behind which she stood. "The virtues to which all Alfar strive can be found carved here." Saeran walked around to the front of the stone, and pointed to each row of runes. "They are: accountability, interdependence, balance, truth, hospitality, justice, loyalty, industriousness, and perseverance. As the bride and groom stand before this altar I hope they are reminded of these virtues."

Saeran returned to her place behind the altar and lifted a bowl of mead to the sky, beginning her invocation.

"Hail all the gods,
Hail all the goddesses.
Hail all the holy ones,
We dwell together.

Lords of the sky,
Ladies of the sacred earth.
Spirits and the ancestors,
We dwell together.

We approach the sacred grove,
with hearts and minds and flesh and bone,
join us now in ways of old,
We, have come home."

She poured some mead on the ground, then took a sip. "Haldor and Gwynahra, step forward. Today we gather to stand witness to the wedding oaths of this couple. A marriage is one of life's great rites of passage, have the two of you prepared for this day?"

Hal and Gwynahra responded as one. "We have."

Saeran asked, "are you ready to proceed?"

"We are," the couple said.

"So be it." Saeran looked to the sky again. "Var, hand maiden of Frigga, witness of oaths between men and women, I call upon you this day and ask you to attend this rite. Tyr, shining one of honor, I ask you whisper in Haldor's and Gwynahra's ears what is right. Forseti, I ask you and Var to stand ready in case honor is forgotten." She turned back to the couple. "Gwynahra, have you brought a gift for Haldor?"

Gwynahra nodded. "I have."

"Haldor, have you brought a gift for Gwynahra?" Saeran asked.

Hal nodded. "I have."

"Haldor, present your gift to Gwynahra," Saeran asked.

Hal presented Gwynahra with the key to their residence at Tyrbjorg. "I give you the keys to my home, now our home, and yours to command."

"Gwynahra, present your gift to Haldor," Saeran said.

Gwynahra handed Hal an ornate longsword. "I give you this weapon, my father's sword, knowing you will keep me and ours, safe from harm."

Hal took the sword and sheathed it in his scabbard.

Gwynahra," Saeran said, "as it is your wish to be hand-fasted to Haldor, place the mundgjoll-ring on his finger."

That done, Saeran turned to the groom. "Haldor, as it is your wish to be hand-fasted to Gwynahra, place the mundgjoll-ring on her finger."

As Hal placed the ring on Gwynahra's finger, Saeran addressed the onlookers. "The golden rings you see them exchanging are made of mundgjoll. It's an organism that bond's to the wearer's finger for life. Each pair of living-rings are from a unique family, and they recognize each other. When not near each other for more than a full day, they tingle on the wearers' finger when they come close to each other. Thus, when lovers return to each other, their hands tingle as they meet. It's to remind us of the precious nature of marriage and love." She turned back to the couple and completed the ceremony with their hand-fasting vows, which the couple recited after her. The final act had been to bless the bride while she sat with a hammer on her lap; symbolizing Thor's hammer, Mjolnir, and ensuring the couple's fertility.

"Haldor and Gwynahra, in the eyes of the folk, in the light of the spirits, and by the law of the land, be you now married. You may now share in your first kiss as husband and wife."

It was a long, deep kiss, accompanied by much cheering and fanfare. They were in love and the rest of the world just disappeared.

Location: Tyrbjorg (Jarl's Residence) / Planet: Rigsvaka

After a satisfying dinner with *Auntie* Gina over to visit, Hal now lay stretched out on a wrinkled, brown-leather sofa. He listened to the crackling fire and soaked up the warmth of the dancing, orange flames. His right arm surrounded Chloe and Gwynahra, both curled up beside him. Venn lay in front of the sofa. Perfection, he thought, absolute perfection. He wanted this moment, this feeling, to last a thousand-million years. Gwynahra nestled in to him as she felt his contentment. Her belly was growing round—a sign their baby was coming along nicely.

"I like winter," Chloe said, smiling at Hal and Gwynahra.

He nodded. "Me too."

They both looked at Gwynahra, who shook her head with eyes closed, then sighed. "It may grow on me. We'll see."

The haunting sounds of a 21'st century composer, Ólafur Arnalds, danced like wisps of smoke through the living room. He was one of Hal's favorites, and a fellow Scandinavian from Iceland.

At this moment, his heart was full, his soul at peace. The realization caused his eyes to cloud up with a happy dampness.

His girls caressed his mind. *"We love you,"* they thought.

He never thought he'd feel this *complete* again. He gave thanks to Odin's wife, Frigga, every day, for the family he had. Life on Rigsvaka was not the uncomplicated farm he and Chloe had dreamed of all those years ago, but that was not his Wyrd. The Norns had woven a different path, and one he had to make the best of. But at this moment, with these three souls beside him, he was content.

Gwynahra's face went wide, and Hal shifted beside her. "What is it, Gwyn?" he asked.

Chloe sat upright, a look of pleasant surprise on her face.

"Did you hear that?" Gwynahra said, a smile growing now.

"Hear what?" he asked.

"I did!" Chloe exclaimed.

"Your *daughter*, Haldor," Gwynahra said. *"Listen,"* she thought to him.

He closed his eyes and let his thoughts drift into mind-space, listening, feeling. It was quiet here. He saw Gwynahra, Chloe and Venn. But wait, there was another light, just a spark, glowing in the black like a pulsing firefly. How beautiful. How had he not heard, or felt that? He'd been so wrapped up in thinking, that he forgot to listen. The spark felt happy, warm and content. She, Hal thought. A girl!

He rolled off the couch and lay his head on Gwynahra's tummy. "Our daughter …"

"*My* sister," Chloe said proudly.

Hal stroked little Chloe's hair as he looked into his Gwynahra's eyes. "I love you, both you. All of you!" He corrected, rubbing her belly.

Venn whined and lifted her head.

"And you too, of course," he ruffled Venn's ears.

Venn lay her head back down on the rug, groaning contentedly.

Location: Unknown / Planet: Unknown

Gina's neck ached from the days of shivering, as the intense cold crawled along her naked body. With arms wrapped tightly around her knees, she waited for death. She had no concept of how long she'd been there. The windowless-cell had no lighting, nor did she have any other way to mark time. It had to have been days, at least; if not weeks.

Heavy footfalls echoed down the subterranean halls. Someone was approaching. She strained to hear, and thought she could hear something said in English. Yes, she could hear her now. A woman, a new prisoner maybe? The heavy door to her cell slid sideways, letting in a gust of even more frigid air, yet no light. These Hrymar seemed to thrive in darkness. She no longer tried to rush the door, as she had the first few times it had opened. For that temerity, she'd received severe beatings, the last breaking her left-wrist, which she still couldn't use.

The newcomer was tossed into the cell in a heap, and rolled into her.

The new woman screamed. "Get away from me!" And she scrambled away.

Gina pulled back at first, but then decided that she wanted, no, needed, to know who this person was. She needed some connection to the outside world. "You're ... human?"

The woman sobbed, but said nothing.

"I'm from Earth. My name's Gina."

The woman's sobbing ceased abruptly.

"Can you tell me your name? Please?" Gina asked.

"Gina? Gina Russo?" The woman asked.

It couldn't be, Gina thought. Could it? "Captain Hutchison? Is that you Kay?"

"Oh my God, Gina? Where are we?" Captain Kay Hutchison asked.

"I have no idea.